Sign up for our newsletter to hear
about new releases, read interviews with
authors, enter giveaways,
and more.

www.ylva-publishing.com

OTHER BOOKS BY FLETCHER DELANCEY

Mac vs. PC

Chronicles of Alsea

The Caphenon (Book One)

Without A Front I
The Producer's Challenge
(Book Two)

Without A Front II
The Warrior's Challenge
(Book Three; Coming in November 2015)

CHRONICLES OF ALSEA

WITHOUT A FRONT

THE PRODUCER'S CHALLENGE

Fletcher DeLancey

For my tyree.

TABLE OF CONTENTS

PART ONE:
- Chapter 1: *Running* 9
- Chapter 2: *Political asylum* 14
- Chapter 3: *Hiding* 26
- Chapter 4: *The Lancer is lost* 30
- Chapter 5: *Ambush* 32
- Chapter 6: *Waking up* 40
- Chapter 7: *Darzen Fosta* 45
- Chapter 8: *Morning after* 48
- Chapter 9: *Procrastination* 53
- Chapter 10: *Invitation* 56
- Chapter 11: *Lancer Tal* 58
- Chapter 12: *Rumors and fact* 61
- Chapter 13: *Lying by omission* 65
- Chapter 14: *Losing her grip* 67
- Chapter 15: *The Voloth problem* 69
- Chapter 16: *Surprise visitor* 75
- Chapter 17: *Grand opening* 76
- Chapter 18: *Return to Blacksun* 84
- Chapter 19: *Investigation* 89
- Chapter 20: *Whitemoon raid* 91
- Chapter 21: *Clearing the way* 94
- Chapter 22: *Debate* 95
- Chapter 23: *Mercy* 100
- Chapter 24: *The Voloth solution* 103
- Chapter 25: *A new delegate* 109
- Chapter 26: *Quantum com call* 112
- Chapter 27: *The producer's challenge* 115
- Chapter 28: *Field of conflict* 118
- Chapter 29: *Temporary setback* 121

PART TWO:
- Chapter 30: *Hol-Opah* 125
- Chapter 31: *A new field worker* 130
- Chapter 32: *A well-kept secret* 134
- Chapter 33: *Bossy* 140
- Chapter 34: *The knife and the sword* 143
- Chapter 35: *Speedy* 149
- Chapter 36: *First lesson* 152
- Chapter 37: *Tell me a story* 158
- Chapter 38: *Tal's turn* 164
- Chapter 39: *Caprice* 172

Chapter 40: *New runner* 173
Chapter 41: *Lesson in manners* 177
Chapter 42: *Open door* 182
Chapter 43: *Fear* 184
Chapter 44: *Closed door* 185
Chapter 45: *Dreams in the field* 190
Chapter 46: *That useless little farm* 199
Chapter 47: *A different kind of bond* 203
Chapter 48: *Confession* 210
Chapter 49: *All nighter* 218
Chapter 50: *Sparring* 220
Chapter 51: *Fighting words* 226
Chapter 52: *Meadowgreen* 233
Chapter 53: *Tiles* 250
Chapter 54: *It's personal* 251
Chapter 55: *Debate points* 257
Chapter 56: *Betrayer* 264
Chapter 57: *Fallout* 267
Chapter 58: *Whitemoon Q&A* 268
Chapter 59: *Backstage* 272
Chapter 60: *Flames in the temple* 274
Chapter 61: *Prisoner request* 279
Chapter 62: *Alliance honored* 281
Chapter 63: *Not family* 284
Chapter 64: *Equal partners* 289
Chapter 65: *First rain* 295
Chapter 66: *Horten harvest* 296
Chapter 67 *Bullies* 298
Chapter 68 *The Pit* 308
Chapter 69: *Smuggler's revenge* 313
Chapter 70: *Small victories* 316
Chapter 71: *Coming home* 319
Chapter 72: *The strand vibrates* 322
Chapter 73: *Second date* 323
Chapter 74: *To find a traitor* 331
Chapter 75: *Which Opah* 333
Chapter 76: *The target* 334

Glossary 343
Other Books From Ylva Publishing 349
Coming Soon By Ylva-Publishing 353
About Fletcher DeLancey 357

ACKNOWLEDGMENTS

First and foremost, I owe buckets of gratitude to my lovely wife, Maria João, who gave me the opportunity to write without guilt. Before we met, I stole time from my life, marriage, and sleep requirements to furtively spin my fantasy worlds into real-life words. With Maria, theft has never been necessary. And so my greatest thanks must always go to her, for loving a writer and never complaining about being an occasional writing widow.

Well, almost never.

Obrigada, minha tyree; tens sempre o meu coração.

Thank you hardly seems enough for the amount of work Karyn Aho put into this manuscript, analyzing the bejeebers out of it with her psychologist's eye and delighting me by picking up on every plot thread and connection that I wove into it. Because authors are the omniscient creators of their works, we need to know whether someone without a perfect knowledge of the storyline can see the same things we do. There is little point in weaving threads so gossamer that readers cannot detect them. Karyn's work reassured me that my threads were visible and helped me to find places where I could weave in a few more.

I am also grateful to Erin Saluta, who reads with her heart in her hands and offers the viewpoint of readers looking for the emotion; and to Rick Taylor, who brushed aside my concerns about his busy life and reassured me that for him, the work of beta reading this manuscript was a pleasure he took for himself in the quiet moments of his days. Fairer words an author could not hope to hear.

Extra thanks go to Rebecca Cheek, who e-mailed me with constructive criticism of *The Caphenon* and promptly received a job offer in return—and whose "tough love" style of beta reading may have cost me some sleep, but also made a visible difference in the quality of this story. I hereby dedicate every physical description of place to her.

Glendon Haddix of Streetlight Graphics once again produced a lovely book cover from a tiny pile of words and pictures. Hol-Opah came to visual life under his hands, and every time I look at that cover, I want to dive into it.

Astrid Ohletz continues to be the publisher every author dreams of, simultaneously friend and book-shepherd. How many authors get shipments of chocolate and tea from their publishers to keep them going? (Which reminds me, Astrid—that Irish breakfast tea shipment contains enough caffeine to keep me awake and writing for a year. Was that the plan?)

Sandra Gerth's editing targeted exactly what I asked for, and our professional teamwork went so smoothly that we finished the editing a month ahead of schedule. I hereby request her on a permanent basis.

I am also permanently requesting the copy-editing services of Cheri Fuller, who is both a perfectionist and an emotionally involved reader. It is a fortunate author who finds herself laughing out loud at the sidebar comments from her copy editor.

Lisa Shaw, who staffed the last stop on the edit train, did a crack job of proofing the final layout and slaying a few escaped hyphens.

Finally, thank you to Daniela Huege and all of the folks at Ylva Publishing who make everything tick. You are a professional and polished team, and you've built a name to be proud of.

ARGOLIS

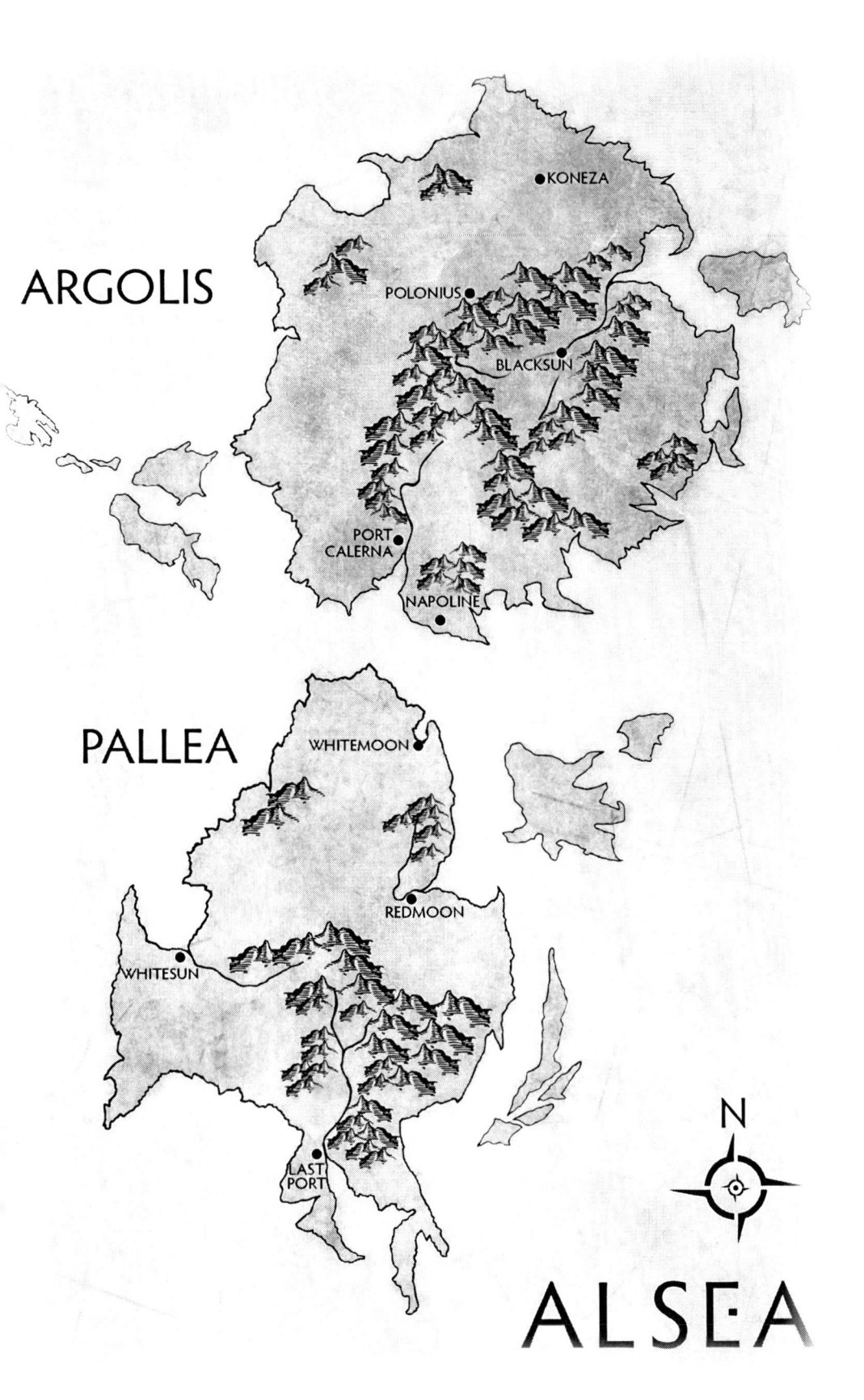

- KONEZA
- POLONIUS
- BLACKSUN
- PORT CALERNA
- NAPOLINE

PALLEA

- WHITEMOON
- REDMOON
- WHITESUN
- LAST PORT

ALSEA

N
SNOWMOUNT RANGE
HOL-OPAH
BLACKSUN
GRANELLE
SILVERRUN RIVER
FAHLINOR RIVER

PART ONE:

AFTERMATH OF WAR

CHAPTER 1
Running

"They won't take any more," said Erik Solvassen, second Protectorate Ambassador to Alsea. "I'm sorry. I did suggest sending the sane ones first."

Lancer Andira Tal leaned back in her chair and sighed. "Yes, you did. And we wanted to, but that kite flew into a tree. They've just asked for political asylum."

Ambassador Solvassen's eyes widened. "That is...unusual."

"And that is not what you were about to say. Why does this shock you? Have no Voloth asked for asylum before?"

"Yes, but never on a pre-FTL world." He shook his head. "From the beginning of my political career, I've learned to keep my reactions behind my face rather than on it. I have to keep reminding myself that won't work here."

She had to smile at his honesty. "I've heard that empathy takes some getting used to."

"It really does."

"Well, if it makes you feel better, you're already two lengths ahead of your predecessor."

"Yes, Ambassador Frank was...not the best example of what the Diplomacy Corps has to offer."

When Ambassador Frank had arrived in Blacksun, one moon after the departure of Captain Serrado and the remaining crew of the *Caphenon*, Tal had greeted him with the expectation that he would be as shining an example of Gaian ethics as Ekatya Serrado and Lhyn Rivers had been. That expectation had been disabused within the first five ticks. By the end of the first hantick, she wanted to expel him from her office and preferably off the planet. The man was unqualified, arrogant, and under the impression that he could ingratiate himself into the highest levels of Alsean government simply by virtue of his job title and patrons in the Protectorate. It was abundantly clear that his "expertise" was a synonym for wealth—he had bought his way into the job and the prestige that came with it.

Mindful of the newness of Alsea's relationship with the far more powerful Protectorate, Tal gave Ambassador Frank a moon to change her first impression. Not only did he fail, he also insulted and alienated the entire High Council in that time, along with a good number of the lower Councilors. It was Prime Merchant Parser who saw Frank's true intent. "Trust a merchant to know a merchant," he told the rest of the High Council. Frank was not a diplomat—not even a bad one. He was a businessman who had maneuvered himself into position to open up the new markets that Alsea represented. When he went one step too far and Prime Warrior Shantu threatened to kill him, Tal figured she had ample reason to do what he had wanted to that very first day.

Ambassador Solvassen was Frank's polar opposite. He was shy, unskilled at prevarication, and quite surprised to find himself in such a prestigious position. Apparently, he had been pulled from a dead-end assignment at the other end of Protectorate territory, where he expected to spend the remainder of his career. When Tal asked him why, he admitted that he wasn't good at keeping his mouth shut when he saw things that seemed wrong. Tal understood immediately: he was a scholar, not a political player.

But he certainly understood Gaian politics. As he explained, former Ambassador Frank hadn't given up on his plan to open Alsean markets. Though he was forced to retreat and regroup, he made sure no competition got in ahead of him. Solvassen was Frank's personal choice: a man with zero business prospects, a poor record of advancement, and little chance of success in the position.

Tal would dispute that last characterization. Within one hantick of meeting the portly man with his bald spot and honest smile, she had known they would work well together. Solvassen's emotions matched his words.

"I wish I could tell you that Mr. Frank is an exception to the rule," Solvassen continued, "but the truth is that the Diplomacy Corps is really two separate entities. One is made up of professional diplomats with training and experience. The other is made up of political appointees—"

"With neither," Tal finished for him. "And in one nineday you managed what Mr. Frank could not. You persuaded the Voloth to agree to Protectorate help with the prisoner lift."

The Council would not allow any Voloth shuttles on Alsea, so it had to be the Protectorate carrying the prisoners of war into orbit. But the Voloth did not want their people on Protectorate shuttles, nor Protectorate shuttles on their ships. It had been a two-moon standoff until Solvassen arrived and brokered an agreement.

"Not much of a success, though, was it?" Solvassen said. "Only two trips and they've cut us off."

"It wasn't entirely unexpected. As soon as the sedative wore off, they must have realized what they were getting."

"No, but I still hoped. These are their own people."

"Their own insane people. Those prisoners are a burden to us, and they'll be a burden to the Voloth. And now we have two hundred and forty-four to take care of instead of two hundred and seventy-four. It's an improvement." She leaned forward again and crossed her hands on her desk. "What about the sane ones? Are they asking for them?"

"Not yet. I was just about to propose that when Commander Qualon cut me off."

"Good. Then he thinks all of the prisoners are insane, and he doesn't want them. That gives us some time to decide what to do about this petition for asylum."

"You really are a planet of firsts," Solvassen said. "First to break out of the Non-Interference Act, first pre-FTL civilization to repel a Voloth invasion, and now the first that any Voloth ever asked to stay with. How many are asking for asylum?"

Tal picked up Colonel Razine's report, which she had been reading when Solvassen had knocked on her door. "All those that were turned by untrained empaths, and…" She scrolled down, scanning for the second number. "Good Fahla. All but nineteen of those that were turned and left fully intact. Why would they want to stay?"

"Well, they did kill their own people. Hard to go back after that."

She felt his revulsion. "There was only one way to win that battle, Ambassador."

"Of course. I studied it even before I got this assignment—that report blew up the Diplomacy Corps com lines. I agree with your tactics. You had every right to defend your world in whatever way possible." He shrugged. "But I still can't think about it without imagining the horror of having your free will taken away."

"And if the Voloth had won, they'd have killed most of us and enslaved the rest. How is the horror of having your free will removed via slavery any more palatable than having it removed via empathic force?"

"I hadn't thought about it that way. I suppose we're less horrified by the thought of slavery because we're used to it. The Voloth have been doing it for four generations."

"So if something unthinkable is repeated often enough, it becomes less unthinkable?"

"Seeders, when you put it that way… It doesn't reflect well on us, does it?"

"Or it's simply a way to cope." She spoke absently, having just seen her own name in Razine's report. She read the full sentence and caught her breath, then read it again. A shiver ran down her spine. "Ambassador, I'm afraid I'll have to cut this short. I'll contact you when I know more about this petition."

Somehow she got him out of her office while maintaining a calm expression, but the moment he was out she locked the door behind him, told her aide not to bother her, and picked up the report again.

The words hadn't changed. The sane Voloth prisoners had elected a spokesperson—one of the weapons officers she herself had turned.

Razine's report made it clear that the Voloth knew what they were doing. While Tal hadn't identified herself to any of the crew she turned, they had figured it out from watching Alsean broadcasts in their cells. They were leveraging their only advantage by forcing her to speak directly with one of the people she had violated.

She was still feeling sick to her stomach when an urgent report came in from Miltorin, her communications advisor. Grateful for anything to take her mind off the vision of facing that Voloth, she pulled it up on her reader card to see what new crisis he was fretting over.

The first thing that greeted her was an image of an Alsean hanging from the lowest branch of a tree, her head tilted to one side and her face slack in death.

"Oh, no," she breathed, suddenly certain why Miltorin was sending her this. His report confirmed it. The dead woman had left a note asking forgiveness from Fahla for breaking her covenant. It was the first suicide of a Battle of Alsea veteran.

Miltorin was on his way to her office. He would want to discuss how to handle this publicly, and right now Tal couldn't handle it at all. She didn't want to talk about containing the political damage. She didn't want to think about facing the Voloth she had turned.

She didn't want any of this.

A sense of urgency pushed at her as she stripped off her wristcom and tossed it in her desk drawer. Her earcuff followed. She slammed the drawer shut and exited her office at such a fast clip that the Guards in the anteroom were startled.

"Lancer Tal—"

"Leave it." She strode into the corridor, where State House staff took one look at her and edged to the sides. Without pausing, she pushed open the door to a little-used stairwell and began running down fourteen flights. At the bottom she edged open the emergency door, having deactivated its alarm a moon ago, and checked outside.

No Guards in sight.

Quickly, she slipped out and walked toward the landing pad, her heart pounding at the thought of being stopped. It was ridiculous; nobody would stop her from going wherever she wanted. Nobody except Micah, that is.

She arrived at her personal transport without any interference and wasted no time lifting off. Only when she left the State House behind and had the Snowmount Range in sight did she relax.

Fifteen ticks into her flight, the com panel beeped with an incoming message. The ID displayed a familiar code and the name Colonel Corozen Micah, and without hesitation she pressed the key to reject the call.

Ten ticks and two more rejected calls later, she landed at the entrance to a trail she knew well. It wasn't one of the scenic ones and so had few visitors, which served her purpose. She stepped between the front seats into the back, where a bag held her running gear. The space was a little cramped, but she was used to it by now. It didn't take long to change her clothes and strap on her shoes, and then she was outside, gratefully breathing in the crisp autumn air.

Dry leaves crunched beneath her feet as she walked up the trail, releasing their scent to join those of rich loam, decaying logs, and the minty smell of winterbloom. It was still too early for the winterbloom flowers to be open, but their leaves bore a fragrant oil that was used in many an Alsean recipe.

Tal didn't walk long enough for a good warmup. She simply couldn't wait, and began jogging along the trail at an ever-increasing rate until she was running at her normal speed. The trees flashed by, the scents filled her nostrils, and she heard nothing but the pounding of her feet on the trail and her own harsh breaths.

Slowly, her mind cleared until she was aware only of the rhythm of her breathing. It had evened out as her body caught up with her pace, and she ran for lengths in a perfect balance of muscle exertion and breath, effortless and unthinking.

Then she tripped over a root and stumbled, and all of her rhythm dropped away. The vision of a slack face and a rope around a neck floated into her mind, and she set off down the trail at a dead sprint. She ran as hard as she could and then she ran harder, the breath sobbing in her throat.

As if Fahla herself were in pursuit, demanding justice, Andira Tal ran.

CHAPTER 2
Political asylum

LANARIL SATRAN HAD NEVER BEEN part of a High Council meeting before. She had occasionally been invited to speak at one when her input as Blacksun's Lead Templar was required, but the High Council meetings had always been closed-door affairs, limited to the six caste Primes, the Lancer, and occasionally the Chief Counselor.

But then the *Caphenon* had landed and the changes kept coming, with no end in sight. And here she was on the fourteenth floor of the State House, sitting with the leaders of Alsea and waiting for the arrival of a Voloth soldier. A soldier who was asking to stay on the very world he had tried to take by force.

Fahla certainly did have some interesting plans.

She glanced up at the head of the table, where Andira sat with an inscrutable expression and an impenetrable front. She looked every bit the Lancer today, with her dark blue uniform and her blonde hair wound back in a formal twist. If the thought of facing one of the Voloth she had turned was bothering her, Lanaril couldn't tell.

"So the technology is identical?" Prime Merchant Parser asked.

"No, but it's close enough." Prime Scholar Yaserka tossed his thin gray hairtail over his shoulder and leaned forward. "Our healers harvested several lingual implants from dead Voloth, and Chief Kameha reverse-engineered them."

"The man is brilliant," Prime Builder Eroles added. She was resplendent today in a turquoise suit that set off her dark skin and hair to perfection. "It took him just three days to come up with a prototype. They're very similar to Protectorate implants, so he had no problem altering one of the *Caphenon*'s chip burners to produce the right chip."

"'Harvested,' what a horrible use of that word." Prime Producer Arabisar shuddered. "Could we refrain from using that for anything other than what Fahla intended? We harvest crops, not technology from the heads of dead aliens."

"My apologies," Yaserka said. "We dissected them."

Arabisar glared at him. "You did that on purpose."

"Did what? You asked—"

"Enough," Andira said in a clipped tone. "Yes, we have full communication with these Voloth. The healers said it was critical for their mental health to be able to speak with us and to understand our broadcasts. And since mental health is on all of our minds these days, I authorized both the…study of the technology and the production of new language chips."

"And look where that got you." Prime Warrior Shantu crossed his arms over his expensive tunic, his fashionably cut hair brushing his shoulders. "Watching those broadcasts is how they knew to target you."

"Excuse me," Lanaril said. Every head turned to her, and she sat a little straighter. "I understand that you're thinking like a warrior and looking for the strategic angle. But I think we should remember they're not our enemies anymore. Right now they're supplicants."

"With all due respect, Lead Templar, I killed as many Voloth as I could. I don't see them as anything but an enemy."

"And of course that's what you had to do. I stood outside my temple and rejoiced at every explosion of light I saw, because that was one less ground pounder that could attack us. But that was then. You beat them. We won. They have no power anymore. These are people who are asking us not to send them home. So I have to ask in my turn: Why? Why don't they want to go?"

"Perhaps they will be prosecuted at home for what we forced them to do here," Prime Crafter Bylwytin said in her quiet voice. "Or persecuted."

"Oh, now, you're not feeling sorry for them, are you?" Shantu snorted and shook his head. "They're invaders. They should feel exceedingly fortunate that we haven't executed the lot. Instead they've made demands and we're actually going to listen to them."

"Exactly," Andira said. "We're going to listen. We haven't agreed to anything, and we won't without a majority approval of the Council. But it costs us nothing to listen."

"Well, it's costing me a valuable hantick of my time, not to mention the strain of being in the same room with one and refraining from killing it."

"If they were 'its,' I hardly think a high empath would have killed herself from the guilt of empathically forcing one." Lanaril hadn't meant to let her own feelings show, but Shantu's attitude could only come from one who had no inkling of the suffering she had seen in her temple. "I've been counseling Blacksun high empaths for two moons, and I can assure you, their guilt comes from forcing people, not animals."

His front was as good as Andira's, but the hate burned in his eyes. "The first ground pounder bombed Duin Bridge to charred bricks and killed every adult and child in it. They would have done the same to every one of our cities if we hadn't stopped them. And those they didn't kill, they would have enslaved. Those are not the actions of *people*."

A tap on the door interrupted and Colonel Razine entered, her stern face set even harder than usual. Behind her came a Guard holding one end of a chain, then a tall Voloth with his hands shackled in front of him and attached to the chain. A second Guard brought up the rear, and the small conference room suddenly felt very crowded.

Lanaril stared at the Voloth. With his smooth, ridgeless face, he resembled the Gaians she had met and liked. How could an enemy look so similar to a friend?

The three warriors thumped their fists to their chests, a salute that was marred by the jangling of the chain still held by one.

Colonel Razine stepped forward. "Lancer Tal, members of the High Council, Lead Templar Satran, this is Rax Sestak, weapons specialist in the Voloth Third Pacification Fleet."

"Pacification?" Shantu said. "Really?"

The Voloth looked at him, then around the table. When his gaze settled on Andira, all motion in the room stopped. His unfronted emotions poured off him, buffeting Lanaril with a shock of recognition and panic, followed by the determination that wrestled his fear under control. It had never occurred to her that he might be afraid, but in hindsight it made sense. He was facing down his own personal nightmare.

Was she?

They stared at each other for what felt like five ticks before Andira finally said, "Rax Sestak. I never knew your name."

"I never knew yours, either." His voice was gravelly, as if he hadn't used it in a while. "Well met, Lancer Tal."

Great Fahla, Lanaril thought. He knew the standard greeting. Somehow she hadn't expected courtesy from an invader.

"Well met," Andira answered. The tension in the air eased, only to rise again at her next words. "Colonel Razine, this room has a long history, and I don't believe that history includes the presence of bound prisoners. Take off that chain and unbind his hands."

"Are you insane?" Shantu shoved his chair back and stood. "I know you like to prove your points, but this is going too far."

"Are you afraid of him, Prime Warrior?"

Shantu stopped with his mouth open, then snapped it shut. "I killed too many of them to be afraid of one."

"Well, I for one am not comfortable sharing the room with a bound Voloth, much less an unbound one," Eroles said. "Lancer Tal, *is* there a point to this?"

"We're here to listen to a request for political asylum. If we can't do that without keeping the petitioner in chains, then I don't see any reason for this meeting to continue. We'll have already decided on our answer."

"I agree." Prime Merchant Parser cast a sidelong glance at the still-bristling Shantu. "If the five warriors in the room can't handle one unarmed Voloth, then we have indeed come to our decision."

"Unbind him for all I care. I'd welcome the chance to kill one more. But there are others in this room whose concerns should be taken into account."

Andira turned to the Prime Builder. "I promise you, on my honor as a warrior, that this Voloth will not harm you."

"How can you make a promise like that?" Eroles asked.

Andira rose and walked over to stand in front of the Voloth. She looked slim and small in front of him, but he watched her with a resurgent fear. Without taking her eyes off his, she said, "Colonel Razine."

The colonel took out a key, unlocked the wristcuffs, and handed them to the Guard holding the chain.

"Thank you," said the Voloth as he rubbed his wrists.

"Tell me, Rax Sestak, do you intend harm to anyone in this room?"

"No, Lancer."

"And we're supposed to—"

Andira held up a hand, stopping Shantu in mid-sentence. "Would you like a chance to prove that?"

Rax looked at her in confusion. "I don't see how."

His eyes widened and his fear spiked into panic when she reached into her boot and pulled out a dagger. The entire room collectively held its breath.

Andira held the dagger for a moment, then flipped it over, caught it by the blade, and offered it to him hilt first.

He took it from her hesitantly, his panic morphing into shock and bafflement.

"I'm the one who made you do it," she said in a low voice. "I stripped you of your will and forced you to kill your fellow soldiers. I know you hate me for that."

"A little," he whispered.

"Then this is your chance. Take your revenge if you can. No one will stop you; it's a matter of honor."

He looked from her to the dagger and back again. "If I do, none of the others will get to stay."

"This is between you and me. It won't have any effect on the others."

Lanaril felt as if she were watching an entertainment vid. This couldn't be real.

Rax tightened his grip on the hilt. "Did you know that some of them were my friends?"

"No, I didn't. Did you know that I lost friends, too?"

"But you didn't kill them yourself." His voice was almost a groan. "I killed my own friends."

"Then kill me and you'll feel better about it."

"No, I shekking won't!" He threw the dagger to the ground. "It won't help! And that's not what I came here for."

One of the Guards scooped up the dagger and handed it back to Andira, who took it with a nod of thanks and slipped it into her boot. Turning to the others, she said, "Is that proof enough?"

"Great Mother!" Yaserka blurted into the shocked silence. "That was the most reckless thing I have ever seen."

"No, it wasn't. He can't harm me nor any other Alsean. He *cannot*. Do you understand?"

Lanaril finally remembered to exhale, just as Shantu let out a startled laugh.

"Oh, well done, Lancer Tal. You didn't bind him to yourself. You bound him to Alsea." Shantu sat down, still chuckling. "I must say I'm impressed."

"And I'm confused," said Arabisar. "What in Fahla's name just happened?"

"A demonstration." Andira took her seat. "Rax Sestak has free will, with one exception. He cannot harm Alsea nor any Alsean. I left that instruction when I forced him. Unless I cancel it, he'll be bound by it for the rest of his life. If we send him back to the Voloth, he'll never again be able to engage in any hostilities against Alsea. And if he stays here, he'll never be able to raise a hand against any Alsean. So as you can see, he's not a threat to you."

"Some demonstration," Erolcs said. Her dark skin was a shade lighter than usual, and Lanaril suspected her own face was still showing the shock.

"Rax Sestak, how shall we call you?" Andira asked.

"Just Rax." His desperate need to know burst its confines. "Please, tell me. Is that the only thing you did? Is that all you left inside me?"

"That's all," she assured him. "I swear."

He dropped his face into his hands, his shoulders shaking with the release, then looked up with reddened eyes. "Thank you. I know I was one of the lucky ones. If you could see the others... Seeders, they've forgotten everyone they ever loved. My friend Danek—he has a baby daughter and he doesn't even care anymore. He carried her picture everywhere and we used to tease him about how gone he was over her, and now—he doesn't care. At least you left my heart in one piece."

Lanaril didn't think anyone in the room could be unaffected by that. She glanced over. Well, anyone but Shantu.

"None of us ever wanted to do that," Andira said. "But you left us no choice."

"*We* had no choice!" he cried. "We were shekked if we did and shekked if we didn't."

"What do you mean?" Lanaril asked. "Why didn't you have a choice?"

"Because we're hangers. And the officers are all citizens."

The six caste Primes and Andira seemed to understand this, but Lanaril had no idea what he was talking about. "Hangers and citizens?"

"The Voloth Imperium has its own caste system with three castes," Andira explained. "Though they don't call them that, and there's no equality. Their people are either citizens, hangers, or slaves."

Rax rubbed his wrists again. "And being a hanger isn't much better than being a slave. You can't own property, you don't have the same legal rights as citizens, and Seeders help you if you ever get into trouble with a citizen. The police will never believe you. A citizen can do everything but murder a hanger, and nobody would turn a hair. I don't think murder is out of the question either, so long as you bribe the right person. And in the military—" He shook his head. "You don't disobey orders."

"You know what your military does," Yaserka said. "You made a choice when you joined it. Seems to me it's a little late now to say you wish you hadn't."

"But I don't—" He stopped and calmed himself with an effort. "Yes, I made a choice to join. We all did. But that's only because none of us were rich enough to buy our citizenship."

"You have to buy your way into your top caste?" Prime Merchant Parser asked.

"There are only two ways to become a citizen. You can buy it, or you can earn it through military service. I was halfway through my military service requirement. When I finished, I'd have been a citizen. And then I could have protected my parents."

"Are they also hangers?" Lanaril asked.

Rax nodded. "They couldn't afford to buy their way out. But they couldn't earn it either, because the military won't take you if you have any medical problems they can't easily fix. My dad lost his leg in a farming accident and my mom—well, she didn't have a medical problem. She just couldn't serve. She washed out of basic training because she wouldn't follow orders."

"If her orders were something like 'bomb that village and kill every innocent person in it,' then I salute her moral code," Shantu said. "But you were ready to follow any order you were given."

"You don't understand. They don't give you those orders in basic. They give you stupid orders that don't make any sense and then they beat the dokshin out of you if you dare to ask why. So you learn not to ask."

"And unlike your mother, you learned your lesson," Yaserka said.

Rax looked haunted. "I made it through. The washout rate is over seventy percent, and I made it through, and I was so proud. My dad was, too. I served for almost three of your cycles before they sent me on my first invasion. They told us that the locals were primitives, that our government had made peaceful overtures but the primitives had attacked and killed most of the landing party, including the entire squadron that had been sent to protect the diplomats. We were outraged. And we were trained not to ask questions. So when they told us to destroy the villages, we did. And it was easy and they rewarded us. And I was going to be a citizen."

The picture was coming together, and Lanaril was aghast at what she saw.

"All we had to do was follow orders," Rax continued. "They give them and we follow them and every order is a little bigger than the one before. And you keep following. And you never, ever ask why. Sometimes, somebody asks why or refuses to obey, and then you don't see them anymore. They get transferred. We always knew that really meant something else, but nobody said it out loud. We called it 'transferred to the Eighth Fleet,' because there is no Eighth Fleet."

"Are you telling us that your superiors will kill you if you don't obey orders?" Bylwytin looked faint at the thought.

"Nobody knows that for sure. Look, Colonel Razine said I had to be completely honest with you, because you'll know if I'm lying. I'm telling you the truth. I think—we all think it's either obey or die, or if it's not death, then it's something even worse, like medical experimentation. There are rumors. But I don't know. All I know is, none of us ever wanted to find out firsthand."

"And that's why you were willing to kill innocents?" Shantu crossed his arms, a look of disbelief on his patrician features. "Because it was either kill or die? You're not lying, but you're not telling us everything, either."

"I'm trying to." Rax wiped the sweat off his forehead.

"Then try harder. Tell us the rest. Tell us how proud you were to be on your way to becoming a citizen, no matter what you had to do to get there. Your superiors dropped four thousand soldiers in your *pacifiers*. Don't tell me they were all controlled by fear."

Rax shook his head. "That's the part I've only started to understand since we came here. You're all primitives—I mean, that's what they told us," he added hastily. "You don't worship the Seeders. All primitives are good for is slavery, but sometimes slaves convert. Sometimes they learn the truth, and then they're saved. If we have to kill primitives, it's not like killing real people, people who worship the Seeders. It's like..." He struggled to find the words. "Primitives get reborn when they die. They get another chance to accept the truth. We're doing them a favor."

Shantu's chair flew back with such velocity that it crashed onto the floor. "You're doing us a *favor?*" he roared. "By killing people who never lifted a finger against you? By killing *children?*"

"Great Fahla, that is disgusting," Arabisar said. Heads nodded all around the table.

Lanaril felt ill. "What a twisted theology you have. And twisted for one purpose only, so far as I can see. To justify murder, slavery, and the worst kind of theft. To justify stealing people's worlds."

Rax wiped his forehead again, his fear climbing a notch. "Please...that's not—"

"Everyone settle, please," Andira said. "I don't think Rax finished what he meant to say. Do you believe this?"

"I did," he whispered. "I did until we came here. They said you were violent primitives who had just enough technology to be dangerous, and that you'd attacked a diplomacy unit that had landed to invite you to be part of the Imperium. We offered you technological advancement and the chance to be saved by the Seeders, and you answered by killing off half the diplomats and their soldiers."

"A strangely familiar story." Shantu's voice dripped with sarcasm. "Heard that one a few times, did you?"

"Primitives are always attacking Voloth diplomats. We were taught that the diplomats are among the most courageous people in the entire Imperium because their jobs are so dangerous. Primitives have their own gods, and they get violent when you try to teach them the truth. But an attack on a diplomatic unit is an attack on the Imperium itself. It has to be answered with ruthless efficiency. So they sent us here, and we were supposed to take your cities. They said we could be live heroes or dead failures. But...the thing is, we failed but we're not dead. You took prisoners, but you didn't kill us. That cell you have me in—it's bigger than the cabin I shared with three other soldiers. You keep us fed and you don't beat us and you don't use us for labor. We killed your people and you're treating us better than we treat our slaves. And your Fahla...everyone's saying she's a Seeder. None of your temples were hit, and I don't see how that's possible when they were one of our primary hard targets."

"You were *trying* to destroy our temples?" Lanaril's spine hit the back of her chair with a thump.

"It's one of the fastest ways to pacify primitives. That's what they taught us. Take out their false gods and they'll hear the truth more easily." He looked around the table. "If your Fahla is a Seeder, then that explains everything. It explains how you could do what you did to us, and why nobody landed a hit on those temples and why you're...you're not primitives at all. And that's got us thinking about the other worlds we invaded. What if they weren't really primitives either? That would mean—" He stopped, unable to say it.

"That your government lied to you," Andira said. "And systematically trained you to murder without question."

He nodded miserably.

"I never saw a Voloth diplomat until we began negotiating to return you. Your attack—both of your attacks—were entirely unprovoked. The first Voloth to die on this planet died after they had already killed *two hundred and fifty-four* innocent Alseans who didn't even know you existed!"

Rax cringed back at her sudden rise in volume, and she did not let up. "So let me assure you that yes, your government lied to you. And you lied to yourself, because I don't believe you never asked any questions. Maybe you didn't ask them out loud, but you asked them in your head."

His guilt said she was right. "I'm a hanger, we don't—we can't—"

"Tell me something. In all your time in the military, did you ever once hear about a planet where the natives *didn't* attack the diplomats?"

He shook his head.

"What a coincidence," Yaserka said. "I guess they don't teach hangers about the laws of probability. How extraordinary that the Voloth appear to be the only peaceful race in the galaxy, and yet—how many 'pacification' fleets do you have?"

"Seven," he mumbled. Then he lifted his head and said in a stronger voice, "Five and a half now. The Protectorate destroyed half of the Fifth and you destroyed the entire Third Fleet. The ships are still there, but it will be a long time before they can restock them."

Lanaril concentrated on what she was sensing from him. He seemed strangely satisfied at the idea of the Voloth fleets being whittled down.

"Once you start asking questions, it's hard to stop, isn't it?" she asked.

He turned to her, visibly relieved by her calmer tone. "Yes, it is."

"And then you begin to feel angry at the ones who lied to you."

Andira glanced at her, one eyebrow hitching up. "Is that why you don't want to go back? The whole truth," she added when Rax hesitated.

"That's…part of it. Some of us would still go back if we could. But we committed treason. We killed our own."

"But that wasn't your fault," Bylwytin said. "You were empathically forced."

He laughed, a shocking sound given the charged emotions in the room. "You don't know our commanders. Telling them 'the primitives made us do it' won't get us very far."

"What will the penalty be? Death?" Shantu had retrieved his chair and seemed much calmer.

Rax shook his head. "No, worse. Lifetime slavery at hard labor. No chance of buying or working your way out. The only out is when they work you to death. And they will."

The room was silent as everyone digested this information.

"Then I have to wonder why nineteen of you do want to go back," Andira said.

"Some of them are officers. They're citizens; they won't get put into the grinder like we would. The others are true believers. They follow the orders because they enjoy it. They're the ones who tell the higher-ups when somebody asks a question and make people disappear. They want to go back because they have connections, and now they have inside information. They'll find a way to get rewarded for it, just like the officers will. I know some of the ones you're talking about. You don't want them here."

"Why would we want the rest of you here?" Andira asked, though her tone was not unkind. "You're asking a lot of us. What do you have to offer in return?"

His hope blossomed on Lanaril's senses. "Anything we can. We've already offered to teach you how to maintain and operate the pacifiers—"

"But for a price," Yaserka said. "You asked for access to the Alseans who turned you. That price was too high for us to pay."

"I know. We've talked about it, and it's hard for the ones whose hearts got taken. But they've agreed to offer their service without conditions."

Andira and Shantu exchanged looks.

"And we'll tell you anything we can about our military structure, invasion strategies, weaponry...whatever any of us know. You've got some good engineers in that group, too. And a few scientists. I'm not much use that way; I'm just a producer's son—but I'd gladly serve you as a soldier. So would many of us. There are some that don't ever want to see the inside of a pacifier again, but they're anxious to offer anything that might be of use." He looked around, his hope rising as the High Council members remained silent. "Can we work out a deal?"

"We can't give you an answer now," Andira said. "We'll have to discuss it and then bring it before the full Council. I can only promise to give you an answer as soon as we have one."

Lanaril actually felt sorry for him as his anticipation crashed. She didn't know why he would have expected an answer right away, but perhaps that was his experience in the Voloth military.

"Well...thank you for hearing me out. I appreciate that you even listened to me."

Andira nodded. "Thank you for your honesty. But there's one thing you need to take back to your people."

"What's that?"

"*If* we decide to grant political asylum, it will come with a non-negotiable condition. What I did to you—binding you to Alsea—will have to be done to all the others. They will all have to undergo another forced Sharing."

His jaw dropped as he stared at her. "I don't...I, um..."

"Non-negotiable," she repeated. "Talk to your people. But you can tell them that it won't hurt, and it won't cause any additional damage. All it will do is ensure their loyalty. You're already carrying that instruction; you know what it feels like. You're the best person to tell them. Colonel Razine, please escort Rax back to his cell."

The chain rattled as the Guard lifted it up and stepped toward Rax.

"Wait," Andira said. "He's to be considered a member of parley. Leave him unchained. And give him a reader card so he can record exactly who can offer what in terms of expertise or willingness to work. Rax, we may have more questions for you later."

To everyone's surprise, he snapped erect, thumped both fists to his chest, and bowed his head. "Lancer Tal."

Andira's eyes widened before she could control her expression. "Settle," she said.

He raised his head and nodded at her. "Thank you." Turning smartly on his heel, he faced Colonel Razine. "I'm ready."

When the door closed behind them, everyone at the table let out a breath.

"I'll admit that was not what I was expecting," Arabisar said.

"Nor I," said Eroles. "Was he telling the truth?"

Andira, Shantu, Yaserka, and Lanaril nodded. "That man was terrified," Lanaril said. "Though whether it was because he was facing us or because he doesn't want to face his superiors, I'm not sure."

"Both, I think." Yaserka pushed back his chair a handspan and relaxed his posture. "Imagine controlling an entire military organization through fear and lies. At some point you'd think it would have to fall apart."

"Fear, lies, and rewards," Andira said. "Don't forget the incentive to serve. It sounds like a powerful one."

"I wonder what percentage of Voloth are citizens." Parser refilled his cup of shannel. "If the hangers can't own property, can they run a business? How exactly do they fit into the Voloth economy?"

Yaserka held out a hand for the shannel pot. "I must confess I'd like to learn more about that. And that is something I never dreamed I'd say."

"I never dreamed I'd be in the same room with a Voloth and not want him chained to the wall," Eroles said. "But I can see some value in his offer."

"So can I," Yaserka agreed.

Shantu made a sound of disbelief. "A few sniffles from a prisoner of war and you're already soft? Have you forgotten what he was in the process of doing when Lancer Tal turned him? If he'd had his way, he would have blown up every building in this city." He turned to Lanaril. "And your temple would have been the first thing he'd have targeted. You heard him."

"I did hear him. I also felt him. He's a young man who has been taught to never ask any questions, and now he's asking. He's taking his first step on a spiritual journey. And that is more than I ever thought I'd see in a Voloth."

"Spiritual journey." Shantu rolled his eyes. "He's only willing to concede we might not be naked savages because he thinks Fahla is one of their Seeders."

"Maybe she is," Lanaril said quietly.

That left him flat-footed, and Andira spoke into the silence. "Lead Templar, I appreciate the time you took to be here today. There's no need for you to stay for what I'm guessing will be a protracted discussion. But I asked you to attend because you have an input that the rest of us lack."

Lanaril folded her hands in front of her. "I'll aid in any way I can."

"You've been counseling high empaths for war trauma. You know more about their fears and concerns than any of us. If we were to accept this offer, how do you think it would impact them?"

The first thing that came to mind was yesterday's suicide. Though she hadn't known the woman personally—she had lived in Whitesun—Lanaril feared it was only a matter of time before someone she did know was found hanging from a tree. In her counsels, she encouraged veterans to take advantage of the mental healing clinics set up for them, but many told her that wasn't enough. They needed more than help, they said; they needed assurance. An assurance that only a representative of Fahla could give. Every time she heard that, she remembered the first time Andira had come into her study, asking for the exact same thing.

But it wasn't really about assurance, was it? It was about forgiveness.

She thought of the dead silence when Andira and Rax first laid eyes on each other. He had been terrified of her, and she had needed time to control her speech. Yet by the end, they seemed to have come to a tentative understanding. Perhaps it was simply the relief of replacing the unknown with the known.

And perhaps understanding was the beginning of forgiveness.

"I think," Lanaril said slowly, "that if the mental healers made very careful choices and set up very controlled meetings, having these Voloth here could actually help our veterans heal."

CHAPTER 3
Hiding

THE PRISONERS AGREED TO THE terms of their asylum.

The Council made its decision in record time, probably driven by the fact that the Voloth personnel ship left orbit two days after Rax Sestak made his plea. Commander Qualon waited only a hantick after receiving the nineteen soldiers who wanted to go back before sending a message to Ambassador Solvassen and vanishing from Alsean space. The ambassador was reluctant to share Qualon's exact wording with the Council, but the media reported the gist as "They're your problem now." Speculation held that the Voloth government had lost interest in retrieving its remaining sane soldiers once it had learned that they were all hangers, and none of them would fight against Alsea again.

It was difficult to vote for rejecting asylum when returning the prisoners wasn't even an option.

Lanaril heard that the Council had tried a last-ditch attempt to divert the issue elsewhere, asking Ambassador Solvassen if the Protectorate could take them—surely they had other Voloth refugees settled somewhere? But when Rax learned of the possibility, he said they would refuse to go. The empathic force that had turned them against their own people had also tied them to Alsea.

Apparently, the Voloth commander's last message was quite accurate. They really were Alsea's problem now.

As of today, Alsea was home to one hundred and fifty-three former Voloth soldiers who were asking to join their society—in addition to the two hundred and forty-four insane soldiers still being kept under sedation.

Lanaril was watching the breaking news in her office when someone knocked at her door. She glanced at the clock and sighed; only ten ticks until her office hanticks were over. No doubt whoever it was would overstay that time by half a hantick.

She opened the door and stared. "I thought you were in the Council chamber."

Andira brushed past her. "We've tabled the discussion for now. Tempers are too hot. And I needed a break."

It was unlike the cool and controlled Lancer Tal to admit that. Lanaril flipped the switch for the sign indicating that her office was now closed and shut her door.

"Would you like a cup of shannel?" She headed for her dispenser.

"Please." Andira prowled around her office, picking up art pieces and putting them down again without really looking. She was staring out the window when Lanaril arrived with two cups of shannel and a plate of pastries.

Andira murmured her thanks and sat down. Silently, she drank her shannel while the pastry sat forgotten in her other hand.

Lanaril withstood it for three ticks before asking, "Can you tell me what's wrong?"

"Nothing's wrong."

"You're here in the middle of the day, when you must have twenty things on your to-do list and half a dozen meetings scheduled. You came during my office time, which you normally do when you have business to discuss. But this clearly isn't a business visit, so what's wrong, Andira?"

"Are you trying to counsel me? I'm not a damned battle veteran looking for absolution. I just needed a break."

Lanaril held out her hand.

Andira looked at it for a long moment before sighing, putting down her pastry, and clasping their hands together.

Everything Lanaril had deduced from her behavior was confirmed in the emotions that came through their physical touch, plus a good deal more that she hadn't expected.

"Is it Rax Sestak?" It had been a nineday since the High Council meeting, but she couldn't get it out of her mind.

Andira let go. "Him, and suicidal veterans, and people calling me a war criminal, and every caste fighting me on the matter printer technology, and two hundred and forty-four sedated Voloth that we can't get rid of, and I don't even know what else." Her light blue eyes looked through Lanaril, as if she weren't even in the room. "It's...overwhelming. I spent my whole life training to be the Lancer, and until recently I thought it was enough. Now I feel as if I'm juggling six knives and there are people holding knives all around me, waiting to throw them in. And six is all I can handle."

"Six is about four more than I can handle," Lanaril said.

"I don't believe that. You're the Lead Templar of Blacksun."

"And I got here by knowing what I'm good at. I'm not good at spreading my attention. I do best when I can focus on a few things."

"Like seeing right through a Voloth soldier? That was very well done, by the way. I didn't pick up on that. But you're right, he's angry at his government. He was glad we destroyed his fleet."

"And you think you should have seen it, don't you? Give yourself a little room to breathe. You had just met one of the soldiers you turned. No one but you has ever faced that."

Andira glanced out the window. "I wish I could have faced it in a slightly more private setting, without Shantu there looking for any weakness."

"I noticed that—I mean, that he looks for it. Not just in you, but in Parser, Yaserka, Rax of course…and himself most of all. Shantu seems to be a warrior right down to his boot soles."

A faint smile appeared. "Stereotyping, Lead Templar? We don't all spend our every waking moment thinking in terms of strength and weakness."

"Perhaps not, but he does."

"That's Shantu, not our caste. He follows a different interpretation of the Truth and the Path. Strength above all, and yes, defined rather narrowly. He's an honorable man, but he also tends to see the world in terms of right or wrong, strong or weak, love or hate."

"And he hates the Voloth. Even when it's a bound and terrified young man who is no longer a threat."

"I cannot blame him for that. And he's certainly not alone in it. I have my moments."

"So do I. So does everyone." Lanaril watched Andira sip her shannel and added, "If it helps, you didn't show any weakness in that meeting. Your front was impeccable."

"It does help, thank you." Andira set her cup down. "Rax…wasn't what I expected."

"I don't think he was what any of us expected. We expected a monster, because only monsters could do what they did."

"I didn't want a name to go with that face," she said quietly. "I didn't want to know anything about him. And now I know that his parents are producers and his father lost a leg in an accident, and his mother was too smart to be taken in by their government. I know he closed his eyes to horrors because all he wanted out of life was to be a citizen, and he was too afraid to speak. I know his superiors beat the questions out of him and I did much worse than that, but he still saluted me."

Lanaril cursed silently when her vidcom chimed and Andira's expression closed off. "Excuse me." She rose from her chair to get whoever this was off her line immediately, but even then it would probably be too late to recover this rare moment of openness.

At her desk, she read the ID and reached out to accept the call. "It's Chief Counselor Aldirk. He must be calling for you."

"Wait!"

She turned in surprise.

"I don't want to talk to him. He shouldn't even know I'm here. Dammit, Micah's having me followed even in the State Park."

Lanaril abandoned the vidcom and retook her seat. "Colonel Micah is having you followed? Why?"

"Nothing I want to talk about. Lanaril…I just need a few ticks in a quiet place where no one is throwing more knives at me. Can you give me that?"

"Of course I can." Lanaril picked up her shannel cup and took a sip. "Do you want total quiet, or can I tell you about something that made me laugh this morning?"

"People still laugh in the State Park?" Andira shook her head. "I hardly remember how."

"Then let me tell you a story, and we'll see if it comes back to you."

CHAPTER 4
The Lancer is lost

CHIEF COUNSELOR SUNSA ALDIRK SIGHED as he terminated the call. "I'm sorry," he told his guest. "She's not there either. Lead Templar Satran says she hasn't seen her since the Voloth asylum vote two ninedays ago."

"This is intolerable." Colonel Micah's stubby gray hair seemed to bristle even more than usual and his forehead ridges were red with annoyance. "It's impossible for me to protect her when the information I am given is incorrect. This is the ninth time this moon. And it was six times last moon. It's getting worse!" His chair gave an alarming groan as he abruptly stood.

Aldirk held his breath; that chair was six generations old. Like most warriors, Colonel Micah did not understand the value of such things, and Aldirk was always on edge until the man left his office. He was like a beast of the field, a little too big for any room.

Micah loomed over the desk, resting his knuckles on it. "For two moons your schedule has been remarkably inconsistent with the Lancer's activities. How am I supposed to do my duty when you're not doing yours?"

"I assure you that my schedule concurs with Lancer Tal's," Aldirk said evenly. "It has never been my intention to mislead you."

"So you're saying it's her intention to mislead me?"

"That's not for either of us to say. But I would caution you to consider your words and your emotions a little more carefully." He paused. "And perhaps consider the fact that she's not wearing her wristcom."

Micah's eyes narrowed. "I'm well aware she's not wearing her wristcom. If I could speak with her directly, do you think I'd be here asking you to call her? I do not crave your company that badly. What I do want is information. What is going on? Your schedule is incorrect, Tal drops out of contact, and I'm reduced to posting my warriors around the base and the State Park like Fahla-damned enforcement officers, trying to catch her when she leaves. And still she manages to get through!"

"Then perhaps your warriors should be better trained," Aldirk said before he could stop himself.

"My warriors are perfectly well trained. And if you would allocate another hundred or so to my detail, I'm certain I could catch the Lancer no matter where or when she crosses the border. But twenty warriors aren't enough to guard the entire perimeter, nor should they be required to do so." He pushed off the desk, his heavy ring making a scraping sound. "I am not a babysitter! And neither are my Guards."

Aldirk tried not to cringe at the scratch that he was sure had just been gouged into his desk, which was even older than the chair.

"I give you precisely what I am given," he said. "If that is insufficient for you to do your duty, then perhaps you should resign in favor of someone who can do the job."

"If anyone should resign, it's you for your pitiful performance. You're the gatekeeper to the Lancer, and you don't even know where she is."

"Neither do you!" Aldirk regretted his loss of control almost before the words were out of his mouth, but it was too late.

Micah smiled. "Ah, but I can find her," he said smugly. "Even though that is not my job."

"Fine. If you find her, perhaps you might remind her that she has an appointment with Chief Kameha at mid-two."

"Certainly, Counselor. I'm always happy to do your job for you." Colonel Micah walked out with a heavy step and banged the door behind him.

CHAPTER 5
Ambush

Tal sensed the ambush just before she rounded the curve. Veering off the trail, she leaped over a log and slowed to a walk, controlling her breathing with some effort as she silently padded over the soft ground. For two moons she had slipped his grasp, but Micah had found her at last. He must have put a tracker on her personal transport.

And now he was planning to teach her a lesson, it seemed. Well, they would see who ambushed whom. She had spent half her life under his tutelage, and he had taught her well, but sometimes he forgot that she was no longer his trainee.

She scanned the woods for signs of the ambush. Micah's greatest disadvantage was his weak front; she could pinpoint him by the emotions alone. For a moment she felt a twinge of guilt, knowing she was the reason for his anger, but it soon vanished under the sense of competition.

A broad tree made an excellent shield as she stopped to examine a spot just ahead. Micah was there, though well concealed. She couldn't see him, but she could feel his anticipation as he watched the trail, waiting for her to come through.

Keeping a rigid front on her emotions, she slipped over to another tree, then crept to a third. She was one of the strongest empaths on the planet, and her gift had required her to learn an equally strong control. Micah would have no idea she was near until it was too late.

She never saw the trip line. Focused on Micah's emotions, she had forgotten that he sometimes set an ambush within an ambush.

The immobilizer was a forceful reminder.

Her body dropped like a stone, every muscle frozen. Immobilizers employed dampening fields to counteract the electrical signals of the nervous system, rendering a victim paralyzed but still conscious. Micah had used a live model, which allowed the heart and lungs to continue operating. Had he used a terminal model, she would be dying right now. As it was, she was helpless, unable even to blink or move her eyes. But far worse than her physical helplessness was the loss of her empathic senses. She was utterly cut off and more blind than if she had merely lost her eyesight.

Footsteps crunched through the undergrowth; whoever was approaching was taking no care to hide his presence. She assumed it was Micah, but without her empathic senses it was impossible to tell. She waited, vacillating between fury and a growing alarm. If this was some sort of extremely ill-considered prank,

Micah was about to get a reminder of what could happen when she unleashed her temper. But if it wasn't…

She couldn't even consider it.

After half an eternity, the footsteps drew near enough for a shadow to fall across her field of vision. Then Micah stood there, looking down at her. She stared back, trying to discern his intentions from his body language and expression, but he was giving her no hints—until he unclipped his disruptor and slowly raised it to aim directly at her heart.

She watched in disbelief, her mind nearly as stunned as her body. Not Micah! Fahla, not him of all Alseans!

But there he stood, one twitch of a finger away from blowing her chest open.

She strained against the blanket thrown over her senses, desperate to understand whether this was real or not. Surely not; why would he use the live immobilizer if he wanted to kill her?

Unless…maybe he wanted her to see her assassin before she died. To know just how blind she had been.

Her mind raced over the possibilities as to who might have ordered her death. There were a disturbingly large number of them. Besides the usual pretenders jostling for political position, she had made enemies when she bypassed both the High Council and the main Council to break Fahla's covenant. Four moons later, the voices calling her a war criminal had not gone away. Granting amnesty to the same Voloth soldiers who had killed so many Alseans hadn't been a popular decision either. Aldirk assured her that the agitators were a small, powerless minority not worth her concern—but Aldirk cared only about political dangers, not physical ones.

And the person in charge of her physical safety was the same one who was currently threatening it.

Micah watched her, his expression giving nothing away, and Tal thought it rather incongruous that she should be so aware of the birdsong at a time like this. The forest was ringing with it as birds of several species voiced their existence, their territory, their suitability as mates. Life was in motion, all around them, and death was simply one more part of that cycle. She wished she could close her eyes and listen. A sense of calm flowed through her, and she felt ready for what came next. If she had to die, at least this was a pleasant place to do it.

Micah lowered his arm, clipped the disruptor back to his belt, and took a small control pad from his pocket.

The sudden release of her body was nearly as debilitating as the paralysis. She went limp as a sleeping newborn and blinked repeatedly, grimacing when her lids grated over dry eyes. Finally, she rolled over and pushed herself upright, getting used to movement again as she glared up at her Chief Guardian. Now that the threat had ended, so had her moment of clarity and peace, and Micah's anger made it worse as it bombarded her still-shaken senses. She couldn't get her blocks up and didn't appreciate the feeling of being so out of control.

"What the *shek* do you think you're doing?" she demanded.

"Showing you what an idiot you are!" Micah shoved the control pad back into his pocket, returning her glare in equal measure. "You think this is some kind of game, slipping your Guards, making me look like a fool? There's a damned good reason you have Guards, and you of all people should know that. What if I'd been sent by someone else, someone with an eye on your title? You're not invincible!"

"Neither am I your trainee! You presume too much on our friendship, *Colonel*. I am your Lancer, and you've just committed a level-four state crime. Are you trying to destroy yourself? Because I'm more than tempted!"

"Go ahead! Better I should be destroyed than you!"

Startled, Tal straightened up from her aggressive stance. "What does that mean?"

"It means you're choosing a poor path! You don't care about your safety, you don't care about your friends, your mind isn't on your duties. Something is weighing you down, and you're letting it distract you to the point of danger. Your enemies wait for just this—they'll strike if they think you're vulnerable. Whether it's in the Council or more physically, they *will* strike. I can't help you in the Council, but I can out here—or I could if you'd let me do my job. You're scaring me, and you won't listen to me. This was the only means I had left to get your attention. And if you want to throw me in the Pit for showing you just how bad it's gotten, then do it. But remember when you fall that at least one of your friends tried to speak the truth."

She stared at him, her own anger forgotten as she realized the extent of the feelings underlying his. Not even before the Battle of Alsea had Micah been this afraid for her.

"I know I've been…distracted lately. But is it really that bad?"

"It's really that bad," he snapped, pointing at her wrist. "Where is your wristcom? How could I warn you if I learned you were being targeted during one of these ill-advised solo runs? How could I tell you if Alsea were under attack from the Voloth?"

The last question jolted her, and in the ensuing silence she realized that he had every right to question her. She had been too caught up in her selfish need to be alone, too satisfied with her skill at escaping the confines of her title, and she had not looked beyond it to the gravest potential consequences.

Of the two of them, Micah had far more claim to anger.

"All right," she said, turning back toward the trail. "You wanted my attention, you have it. Let's talk."

He took a moment to unwind the trip wire and collect the immobilizer before following her to a fallen log, where they sat together as they had on many a training mission.

Tal crumbled a piece of decomposing wood in her hand and wondered how she had gotten so far from the simple pleasures that had once been easy for her to find. She was still happiest outside, where rocks and logs and sometimes just the ground served her better than the State Chair she occupied during Council sessions. She hated that chair. It was old and ornate and uncomfortable, built to project power. But here, on a log in the woods, she felt an ease which allowed her to say the last thing Micah expected.

"I owe you an apology, my friend."

"You do? I thought you were ready to demote me to first-cycle Guard."

"I was. But I'm not that unwise. I may have made some bad decisions lately, but exiling my most trusted advisor would border on insanity." She looked over in surprise at the reaction he couldn't front. "Micah! You haven't seriously thought that, have you?"

"Not…seriously. But you have not been behaving like the Andira Tal I know. I've never known you to be so careless of your responsibilities, and you won't tell me anything. You've been nothing but a stone wall; what was I supposed to think?"

"I'm sorry I've made your job so difficult. I can only say that it's been a difficult time for me as well."

"I already know that. What I don't know is why. I thought it might have something to do with the departure of the *Caphenon* crew, but the timing isn't right. This all started a moon after they left. Actually, it started when Ambassador Frank arrived, though I couldn't see the connection. Then he left and it got even worse. I've been over every cause I can think of, and still I come up blank. The next thing I know, you've vanished again and nobody can find you. If there were any dark hairs left on my head, they're all silver now."

She managed a faint smile. "You didn't have any left, so don't blame that on me."

"I don't want to blame you at all. And I would leave you to the little privacy you have were it not for the risks you've been taking. As your Chief Guardian and your friend, I'm asking you: What is wrong?"

There was no escaping it any longer. "Everything," she said. "Just… everything." Crumbling another bit of wood, she added, "I never imagined that beating the Voloth would be the easy part."

She had pulled out a new chunk when he gently took it from her fingers, crushed it, then opened his hand and let the remains fall to the ground. "War *is* easy," he said. "At least, that kind of war, with a clear enemy and a clear objective. You either succeed and live, or you fail and die. There's nothing in between."

"And now it's all in between and nothing is clear. Micah…I miss it. I miss that time." She looked up at him, waiting for the judgment, but he nodded.

"You had the kind of clarity we're rarely granted. You knew exactly what you had to do and be. There's no shame in missing that."

Relieved at his understanding, she broke up another piece and watched the fragments fall. "For one moment our entire world was united. I hated the reason, but great Goddess above, we were phenomenal. We couldn't be stopped. I felt like the tip of a spear with all the strength and courage of our entire race behind it, and it was *glorious*. And now—it's all politics again. Except worse, because we're dealing with things we never had to deal with before. Nothing I do is enough, and on top of all the other stupid little battles I'm fighting, they're calling me a war criminal. I saved this whole damned planet and they call me a war criminal. And then I see a high empath hanging from a tree and I have to wonder if they're right."

He put his hand on hers, stopping her from picking off more wood. "You're the Lancer. You're the one who makes the final decisions. That means you're the one people blame when they need someone to blame." He ducked his head, catching her lowered gaze. "And you know that. This wouldn't have bothered you before. Why is it bothering you now?"

Tal looked away, her attention caught by a pair of birds engaged in winter courtship. Grateful for any distraction, she watched as the female sat nonchalantly on a branch, ignoring the male, who fluttered around her. He spread his wings and tail, singing in an energetic display of his attributes, but the female seemed uninterested. He was too early.

"When the Gaians left, I lost something," she began, her eyes on the birds. "Something that mattered. And I haven't been able to move beyond it. I thought I could just keep doing what I've always done, and it worked for a while, but…it's not working anymore. Everything is piling up on me, and I'm losing control of it. All I know is that the only time I feel right is when I can get away. I come here to run because it feels like sanctuary. I can't find it anywhere else."

The female flew off the branch and the male deflated, folding his wings and tail. A moment later he launched himself in pursuit, and Tal wished him luck.

"That item you lost," Micah said slowly. "Was it by any chance your heart?"

"Warriors at my level don't give their hearts." It had been drummed into her head from childhood by a dozen different teachers. "Not unless Fahla makes them tyree. I'm not, so my heart belongs to Alsea."

"Dokshin."

She stared at him, startled that he would use such a vulgarity in reference to their code.

"Oh, don't look at me that way," he said. "Are you telling me you've never questioned that old line?"

"It's not an old line, it's the Truth and the Path!"

"The Truth and the Path have many wise and prudent teachings. That's not one of them."

"I've never heard you blaspheme the warrior's code before."

"It's not blasphemy to think. Blind belief is a poor servant to Alsea, and I never taught you that bit of idiocy. Don't tell me you've never questioned your instructors, because I know better."

Tal smiled at the reference; certainly she had challenged Micah more than once. "Of course I've questioned my instructors. They're Alseans, not Fahla herself. But that's not the same thing as questioning the Truth and the Path."

"Isn't it?" He nodded when she remained silent. "You're a faithful servant of Fahla and Alsea. You're also a discerning and extremely gifted individual. Don't confuse service to our Goddess and the warrior's code with service to interpretation of their lessons and intent. A true warrior knows more than just love of Alsea. Feeling love from and for another makes one's heart more whole, and a warrior with a whole heart is a better servant to Alsea than a warrior with only half a heart."

Her first thought was that he was contradicting his own teachings, but when she paused to consider it, she could not remember Micah ever telling her to love Alsea first. By the time she had come into his unit, that part of the code had already been instilled in her.

"Then you've given your heart?" she asked.

"We're not speaking of me; we're speaking of you. And you just answered my question."

"Has anyone ever told you that you're annoying?"

He ignored her. "I cannot imagine you bestowing your heart where it was not deserved. It must have been Captain Serrado."

"There were others on the *Caphenon* equally deserving," she said, knowing full well she had just confirmed his suspicions.

"For you? Only one that I can think of, and she wasn't the captain. You would not choose one who did not understand power and responsibility."

She gave up. "Lhyn is a treasure and a good friend. But you're right, she's not the one. Saying good-bye to Ekatya was one of the hardest things I've ever done."

"But you're still in contact, yes?"

"Yes, but it's not the same. In some ways it was actually easier when she wasn't able to call. They were in transit for half a moon and spent another half in debriefings and meetings, and I could almost convince myself it hadn't been real. Then she called on the quantum com and—" She couldn't finish, unwilling to describe what seeing Ekatya had done to her.

"So she called for the first time two moons ago. And that was when it all fell apart for you."

Fahla, it was. She hadn't even realized.

"No wonder you miss that time," he said. "Not only did you have clarity of purpose, but you had a partner in accomplishing it. Captain Serrado was your equal. And she saved us twice."

She put her face in her hands. "I didn't have a partner," she whispered. "I never did. That's the problem."

He rested his hand on her bent back, and for a moment she thought she might cry.

After a long silence, he said, "The greatest thing I could wish for you is that you might find someone worthy of your heart. I'm deeply sorry that when you did, she was not for you. There is no love more futile than the love for another's tyree. This is a heavy burden you have borne."

His sympathy made the lump in her throat harder to swallow.

"And you need a vacation," he added.

She lifted her head. "That's your solution to my problem?"

"No, that's my solution to my problem."

"Your concern is truly touching. I can't imagine why I didn't come to you earlier."

"I'm serious, Tal. You do need a vacation. If the only time you feel right is when you can get away, then we need to get you away. You need to process this emotion and purge it from your system, because until you do, you're not the leader Alsea needs. This is your first duty."

"My first duty is to my emotions? Since when?"

"Since they came between you and Alsea. *That* is what the Truth and the Path means. Not that you should never give your heart, but that you should learn when to give it priority. Sometimes thinking of yourself first is not selfish or ill-advised, but the best thing you can do."

"And why has no teacher shared this with me before?"

"Because they were all grainbirds."

Her laugh was scratchy. "Well, they did manage to teach me a few useful things. But you always were my best teacher."

"I was not," he said, reaching out to place a large hand over her heart. "This is. You have only to listen to it."

She laid her hand over his, absorbing the full strength of his emotions. The anger was gone and the fear was greatly diminished, but his worry ran deep, side by side with his love for her. Not for the first time, she wondered why a man with such a great heart called her his only family.

"Sometimes your heart makes more sense than mine," she said. "I don't believe you've never given it. Someday, you're going to tell me."

"If I ever gave my heart, it was too long ago for me to remember."

"You are full of dokshin." She knew she would get no more out of him. "Just remember that this conversation is not over."

"Our conversations never are. It's the best part of our friendship."

They smiled at each other, and Tal felt lighter than she had in a long time. She had indeed chosen a poor path, but her worst mistake was shutting Micah out. Ekatya was still gone, and her heart still ached, but with Micah at her side that burden seemed easier to bear.

"Since my run is over, I suppose we should go." She rose from the log. "Besides, I feel a sudden need to make Aldirk's life miserable."

"You're taking my advice?"

"I am." As they walked toward the trail, she added, "I do try to accept advice when it's wise and well-thought. But I must ask you to do one thing for me."

"Anything," he said quickly, and she knew he meant it.

Without warning, she dropped and spun with a leg out, sweeping his legs from beneath him. He landed heavily on his back with a startled *whuf.*

"Next time," she said as she stood over him, "find another way to make your point. That was too extreme."

He looked up at her, unrepentant. "But there won't be a next time, will there? Besides, nothing else would have gotten your attention. You weren't ready to listen, and I could no longer wait until you were."

As she narrowed her eyes, he held out a hand. Sighing, she grasped it and pulled him upright, smacking him in the abdomen for good measure. "You're beyond redemption."

"Which is exactly why I'm so good for you."

She let out a snort and resumed her path. "And to think you're my spiritual advisor. The people of Alsea should be very concerned."

"Not the people. Just Aldirk."

Tal laughed as they emerged onto the trail. "So tell me, oh spiritual advisor, where shall we go for your vacation?"

"My vacation!"

"I'm fully aware of your ulterior motives. You front like a child of six cycles. Where did you have in mind?"

He smiled wistfully. "It's been too long since I felt the sand under my feet."

"Ah." She nodded. "Then we go to the shore."

CHAPTER 6
Waking up

THIS REALLY WAS ONE OF Micah's better ideas, Tal decided.

It had taken a nineday to get her schedule cleared—Aldirk nearly had heart failure—and another nineday to get everything prepared. A Lancer did not simply trot off on vacation. No, she had to have an entire detail of Guards, and the inn chosen as her base had to be inspected and fortified and the staff frightened half to death with the presence of so many armed warriors. At least she had managed to banish the Guard detail to a separate set of cabins. They were under strict instructions to make themselves relatively invisible to her, and Lead Guard Gehrain was keeping them in line.

It was all worth it. Being free of the Council and the endless meetings, negotiations, arguments, and machinations had done wonders for her. The last few moons had been hard, even without the loss of Ekatya.

Cleaning up after the Battle of Alsea was an unending task, with every village and city convinced that their needs were more important than any others. The argument over what to do with the insane Voloth had run hot since the day of the battle. What had initially been a few radical voices suggesting merciful euthanasia was now a broad coalition that continued to grow. Both sides argued passionately, and in a matter like this, compromise was impossible. The argument over where to settle the sane soldiers was nearly as hot, with every proposal immediately inciting a firestorm of protest from local residents.

They were almost ready to test their one-fifth-scale prototype fusion reactor, and while that was good news for most, the owners of the soon-to-be-outdated fission reactors were loudly unhappy and predicting disaster. Their voices were joined by those who feared any Protectorate technology simply because it was not Alsean.

Worst of all were the matter printers. Tal had expected that such miraculous technology would need to be handled carefully, but she hadn't anticipated the heights to which the caste squabbling would rise. Some of the merchants were rubbing their hands with glee; others feared it would put them out of business. The producer caste was worried that its agricultural products would no longer be necessary. The warriors wanted to put it to use immediately, seeing unlimited potential in weaponry and defense, but thought it should be limited elsewhere. The scholar caste was triply divided, with some of the religious scholars protesting that it was not the will of Fahla, while an opposing group insisted that it was, and had very definite ideas about how it should be used. Meanwhile, the secular scholars applauded the scientific advance it represented and argued with some of the religious scholars about the potential applications. And the builder caste, or at least the engineers among them, couldn't wait to get their hands on it to see how it worked and what they could do with it. The only caste that hadn't been shouting its collective opinion was the crafters, but they always were a different sort.

Now those competing demands had been temporarily silenced. Tal was cocooned in a world far removed from her normal life, and at first she was dazed by the sudden calm. When had she last had no obligations and nowhere to be? She couldn't remember. She gloried in her solitude and reveled in her agenda, which consisted of one thing: exploring new places to run and hike.

Her desire for solo runs caused Micah no end of indigestion at first. Before arriving, they had several arguments over what he termed her "brick-headed intransigence" and finally came to a compromise. He would limit her Guard detail to two, and they would keep their distance—on the condition that she would alter her appearance in order to be less easily recognized.

Tal thought she was already unrecognizable in her running tights and favorite shirt, which had a hole in it and had scandalized Aldirk the first time he saw it. She assumed that whatever Micah planned couldn't be much different from what she already did.

It was an erroneous assumption, as she realized on the very first morning of her vacation. She had barely finished dressing for her run in the pre-dawn stillness when she felt Micah approaching. Opening her cabin door, she watched as he mounted the wooden steps to her front porch and wordlessly held up a small bottle.

"I have to change my eyes, too?" She took the bottle with a sigh.

"And your hair." He pulled a second, larger bottle out of his pocket.

She favored him with a glare before shutting the door in his face and carrying the bottles into the bathroom. Grumbling, she tipped her head back and squeezed in the eyedrops, which teemed with colorizers that absorbed nearly all wavelengths of light, giving her normally blue eyes a dark brown appearance. A spritz of colorizers combed through her hair swiftly turned it from light blonde to nearly black, and she made a face at the final result. The woman in the mirror was someone she normally saw during certain nighttime training exercises and a few stealth missions, and she was not at all happy assuming this camouflage on her own Fahla-damned vacation.

But she forgave Micah less than a hantick later when she realized the benefits of anonymity. She was delighted to receive polite nods from the other dawn runners, who saw her as just one more of their number, and by the time she returned to her cabin, she had a whole new appreciation for what had previously been nothing more than a tactical tool.

Every morning she ran on the beach, filling her lungs with the tang of the sea and thoroughly enjoying her invisibility. On his end, Micah was so pleased by the outcome that he offered to reduce the number of Guards accompanying her on her trail and shore hikes if she agreed to continue using the colorizers. She happily clasped his forearm, sealing the bargain, and proceeded to spend her days in a state as close to complete solitude as a Lancer could hope to be. The only reminder of her responsibilities came in the form of nightly reports that Aldirk sent to her reader card, some of which required answers and instructions.

Micah had done a fine job picking out this location. The village was on the northwest coast of Pallea, a world away from Blacksun in terrain, vegetation, and weather. It was early winter back home, and the mountains encircling Blacksun Basin were already dusted by the first snow. Here, so close to the Great Belt, snow was a distant fantasy and she was wearing short sleeves even at night. Her cabin was surrounded by exotic trees she couldn't name and brilliant flowers pouring their scents upon the breeze. Behind the village, steep canyons led up into the mountains, dripping with lush undergrowth that grew even on the sheer rock walls. Tal soon established an evening routine of sitting out on her front porch, enjoying the soft, scented air as she watched the waves sliding gently up the beach.

It was difficult to imagine these sedate waves rising up and crashing across the village, but the coastlines of both Argolis and Pallea were subject to severe storms and wave damage. Every cabin at her inn stood on stilts, and the high-water mark on hers was just below the top step.

Having spent most of her life in a landlocked valley, Tal didn't often see the ocean and was fascinated by its wildness. The vast reaches of open water fueled shockingly strong storms, and an entire branch of warriors existed solely to watch over and rescue those whose luck ran out. The Mariners enjoyed a mystique that even the Guards could only dream of, but Tal thought they earned every bit of it. Sometimes she wondered why the producers who fished the dangerous areas weren't warrior caste as well. They risked death with every trip, returned to safety, and went straight out to risk it again. A high number of warriors did crew those boats, but fishing was traditionally thought to be a producer caste job.

On these calm days, such dangers seemed far away. Tal loved running at the edge of the water, racing the waves up and down the sand and sometimes simply splashing straight ahead, grinning like a pre-Rite child at the sensation.

It was a magical time. She walked and hiked and climbed and sometimes just sat, watching the waves on the beach or listening to the wind in the canyons. Alone and undisturbed, she gave herself permission to remember Ekatya and work through her heartache. It was time to let this one go. And somehow, what had been impossible in Blacksun was happening naturally here. She didn't know whether it was the beauty of her surroundings, the constant physical activity, the privacy, or the fact that she no longer had that desperate need to get away, but the clouds were lifting out of her head. She felt as if she were waking up.

After five days of blissful privacy, Tal decided she was ready for company again. Micah's expression when he found her on his cabin porch, sword grip in hand, was worth the walk over.

"You want to spar?" he asked in disbelief. "I thought you'd forgotten how by now."

"You hoped I'd forgotten, you mean." Her high spirits were manifesting themselves in a cockiness that she couldn't rein in. "Are you coming out, or do I go to the Guard cabin to find someone younger?"

He narrowed his eyes. "You'd be wise to remember that age has advantages. I know every trick in the teachings."

"Not every trick. Don't forget that you weren't my only instructor." She thumbed the control and smiled at the familiar *shinng* as the blade instantly expanded from the grip, the individual sections merging into a solid whole. Making a show of inspecting her blade, she angled it so that it reflected the bright morning sunlight into Micah's eyes.

"Oh, my apologies," she said sweetly when he winced and brought his hand up. "I assumed you'd know that old trick."

He growled at her and vanished into his cabin while she laughed quietly to herself. A moment later he reappeared, grip in hand.

"Let's see if you can back up that attitude with actual skill."

She gave him a wide grin. "It will be my pleasure."

They faced off in the sandy clearing just below his porch. It had been more than a moon since Tal had last sparred, but the feeling of excitement was always the same. As the child of both a scholar and a warrior, she had the choice to enter either caste, but in moments like these, balanced on the balls of her feet and facing the blade of an opponent, she knew she would never have survived as a scholar. She loved physical activity and the thrill of competition far too much to choose a caste where such activity was not a daily requirement. As it was, the demands of her title already took her too far from the level of action she preferred. Sometimes it was nice not to think or feel, and when she was fighting, she tapped into a part of her mind that was too narrowly focused for such distractions. When she was deep enough into it, even her empathic senses were dulled. In physical activity—and especially in fighting—she found a mental clarity that was unattainable in any other part of her life.

Micah moved in first, testing her defenses in a flurry of thrusts and slashes that soon drove all thoughts from her head save the most basic: defend, attack, and win. There was no Lancer here and no Colonel of the Guard, only two fighters and two swords. A lifetime of training enabled her to dissociate mind from body, letting her muscles react instinctively while her mind worked several steps ahead, strategizing and seeking to create an opening that she could use against her opponent.

In the end, she didn't need to create it. Micah gave it to her with a lapse of judgment that she gleefully exploited, using the hard end of her grip to strike his wrist at a pressure point guaranteed to numb his fingers. His sword dropped to the ground, and she held the edge of hers at his throat.

They stared at each other, chests heaving from the effort, and for just a moment she saw not her friend but a vanquished opponent. Then her head cleared and she stepped back, retracting her blade.

"It seems I need no tricks after all. You were kind enough to leave yourself wide open."

Micah bent over to retrieve his sword and took his time brushing off the sand before thumbing the grip control. "You mistake my kindness for inferior skills. I left myself open in order to build your confidence."

She snorted. "Yes, you're famed for your kindness."

"You're out of practice, and it would have been detrimental to your confidence had I thoroughly beaten you on your first attempt. Obviously, my duty is not to destroy your mental preparedness, but to increase it."

"Ah. So you allowed your hand to be numbed out of a sense of duty?"

"Quite so."

"If you're going to tell such outrageous lies, you must learn to front better. I can see right through you."

"You see what I want you to."

Tal laughed and clapped him on the back. "Come, my good and very deluded friend. I'll buy you a drink to make up for your loss."

CHAPTER 7
Darzen Fosta

Every morning after her run Tal now enjoyed a sparring session, sometimes with Micah, sometimes with one of her Guards. The resentment she had felt for her Guards shifted into appreciation for their skills and even their companionship, and one night she invited Micah, Gehrain, and several of the senior Guards to her cabin for a game of tiles. She matched them drink for drink, laughing and remembering a time when she had done this far more often. Perhaps she needed to get back to that younger version of herself.

The next morning she remembered why that was a bad idea and decided that today's run was going to be at a later time. Much later.

Her second awakening was kinder than the first, and with a sense of happy anticipation she rose and pulled on her running clothes. The colorizers took mere pipticks to apply; by now the routine was second nature. She left her porch looking like one more runner on the beach, pleased when two Guards magically appeared behind her before she had gone ten steps. Even though her schedule was off this morning, they were prompt and professional. Then again, neither Micah nor Gehrain would allow anything else.

The air had less of the tang than she was used to from her dawn runs, but the extra warmth of the sun made up for it. In fact, she mused, it was rather pleasant to run this late in the morning. Maybe she would change her schedule.

The dawn runners had finished their exercise long ago, and she found herself among an entirely different group. They all nodded at her, emanating curiosity and interest at the new person in their midst. As she overtook and passed one runner, she sensed more than the usual interest. If she wasn't mistaken, the redheaded woman behind her was having distinctly sexual thoughts.

Tal smiled; she hadn't felt that in a while. At least not this kind of interest, which was purely physical and not mixed with desire for the power and prestige that came with her title. This woman, whoever she was, had no idea that she was ogling the Lancer of Alsea. And Tal intended to keep it that way.

She slowed her pace enough for the other runner to catch up and flashed her a smile when they drew even. "Good morning."

"Morning." The woman's long, red hair was pulled back in a tail, bringing her gray eyes and unusually narrow facial ridges into sharp focus. Tal hadn't seen cheekbone ridges like that in some time and found herself staring at the graceful curves.

"I haven't seen you here before." The pleasant voice jolted Tal out of her rather rude assessment. "Did you just arrive?"

"No, I've been here a nineday. But I usually run earlier than this."

"Whatever for?"

Tal laughed. "I see you dislike mornings. It's the best time of day, truly. The air is crisp, and there's such a sense of possibility."

"And you think there's less possibility later in the day?"

"In my life, there usually is."

They came to a stop, and the woman held up her palm. "I'm Darzen Fosta. May I have the pleasure of knowing you?"

"Well met, Darzen. I'm Dira Shaldone." It wasn't imaginative—her childhood nickname and her mother's family name—but it was the best she could do on a moment's notice. Judging by Darzen's front, she was a mid empath and would never detect the pretense.

They touched palms and smiled at each other as the physical connection bridged their emotions. For Darzen it was probably a significant glimpse, impossible without the touch, but Tal had already skimmed her emotions before their hands met. Darzen was genuinely happy to meet her, quite attracted, and a little nervous. There was also an underlying sorrow and loneliness whose source Tal could not discern without deeper probing.

They resumed their run, with Tal matching her pace to the slower one of her companion. Darzen might be taller, but her height wasn't in her legs.

"You're warrior caste," Darzen said. "I think I'd have known that even without our touch."

"And you're scholar caste. What do you study?"

"Economics."

"Ugh." Tal made a face; economics haunted her life. "And you chose that?"

Darzen laughed. "I did. It's really quite fascinating, like assembling a puzzle from a slightly different set of pieces every day. I'm never bored."

"I don't even know the meaning of the word."

"I sensed that about you." Darzen glanced over. "I heard the Lancer was staying in the village for her vacation. Are you entailed to her Guard?"

Tal barely paused. "Yes."

"Truly? How fascinating. What's it like to serve with her?"

"I serve under Colonel Micah." It was a lie only in timing; for much of her life he had indeed been her superior. "He's demanding, but fair and honorable. I'm proud to be one of his students."

"I've always found that interesting. Warriors spend much of their lives studying, and yet we're called the scholar caste."

"You study far more than we do. It's a matter of percentages. And how is it that you know so much about the life of a warrior?"

"I was bondmate to one."

They ran in silence for a few ticks, but it wasn't awkward. Tal knew that Darzen was simply trying to decide how much to say, and in the end it was quite a bit. She learned that Darzen lived in Whitesun, the largest city in Pallea, where she worked as an advisor to the city council. She had loved a Mariner, and for six cycles they had enjoyed a happy bond. But then her bondmate was lost in a storm.

"The remains of their ship washed up here," she said. "So I come here every cycle to be with him on the anniversary of his Return. This is my third trip."

"You loved him very much."

"Too much, I think. He was my first love, but his first love was the Mariners."

Tal stopped running. When Darzen turned to her in question, she said, "I'm truly sorry for your loss. I'm also sorry that you still feel such resentment for the Mariners. It complicates your recovery."

"Is it that obvious?" Darzen gave a short laugh. "I didn't realize it was so close to the surface."

It wasn't, but Tal had no intention of admitting that she had skimmed her companion's emotions. She wasn't ready to disclose her empathic rating just yet, not when she was trying to appear a very ordinary warrior.

Darzen turned to the sea. "I should resent *that*. It's what killed him. It was hard, always knowing that I counted for less than his precious Mariners. He said his heart belonged to Alsea, as if I should somehow accept that. As if I shouldn't feel hurt, because Alsea is bigger than I am. But I never understood how he could put such a value on a love that can't be returned. Alsea didn't love him. Neither did the Mariners. I did, but my love had less value." She faced Tal again, her expression sharp. "Do all warriors think that way, or is it just the Mariners?"

Here was a consequence of the warrior's code that Tal had never considered. She wondered how many Alseans had paid a price for the strict interpretation she had been taught.

"Many of us think that way," she said. "We're taught that lesson from a very early age. I suspect it's necessary for hearts prone to quick changes of allegiance, as ours are when we're young. But I've recently come to understand that loving another does not mean we must love Alsea any less. And loving Alsea does not mean we must love another less."

Darzen blinked rapidly and turned her head. "I wish Helus had put as much thought into it as you have."

"He might have, had Fahla given him more time. A true heart has a way of overcoming old lessons."

They stood side by side, watching the waves in silence until Darzen asked, "Will you join me for midmeal?"

"It would be my pleasure, if you allow me to buy."

"Warriors." Darzen moved into a smooth jog and led them back down the beach. "No wonder they're always poor. They can never let a non-warrior buy."

"That's part of the code. Poverty and chastity above all."

"That is not part of the code."

"Just determining how much you knew."

"I see. Then you should know I'm interested in neither poverty nor chastity."

Tal kept her eyes straight ahead, but she didn't need her vision to understand.

CHAPTER 8
Morning after

THE COURTSHIP OF LANCER TAL and Darzen Fosta was the number one topic in the Guard cabin. Micah heard it and occasionally pulled a Guard aside for speaking with too little respect, but most of the gossip reflected his own thoughts. Darzen was smart and had a strong sense of self, making her a good match for Tal's intelligence and intense personality. Once her background check came back clean, Micah ordered the watch details to stay out of sight as much as possible. Tal had a rare opportunity to court as just herself, and it was his great pleasure to give her this gift of anonymity. Who knew when she would have another chance?

One sunny morning just before midmeal, he answered a knock on his cabin door and found a very relaxed Andira Tal on his porch. She was in a good mood, and it didn't take a high empath to sense her news.

"Good morning." He stepped aside to invite her in. "No run today? It's late for you."

She walked past him and dropped into a chair with a thump. "It's a very good morning. And I've already had my exercise, thank you."

"An exercise conducted entirely indoors, I see." He sat across from her and added, "You've set no speed records, but at least you got there eventually."

Her grin lit up the room. "Speed is not the point, Micah. Have you learned nothing from me in all these cycles?"

"Yes, I've learned that I'm glad I have no need to make something simple into something unnecessarily complicated. I'd have managed this a nineday ago. She wanted you the day you met."

"What you call complicated, I call sublime." She laid her head on the back of the chair and sighed. "She's wonderful."

"One joining and already you're in a swoon? I'm afraid you're beyond my aid."

"Why would you assume it was just one? We had the whole night. And in these matters, I was beyond your aid long ago. I'm not sure when the student surpassed the teacher, but it's been many cycles."

"Oh, the dokshin is deep this morning!" He laughed, delighted to see her so happy. "I see your joining has made you completely insufferable, as if you weren't already well on your way."

Crossing one leg over the other, she exuded satisfaction and contentment. "I speak mere truth and you call me insufferable. This says much about your own self-doubts, Micah. I can help you with those."

"No thanks. With your kind of help it would be another three cycles before I touched the skin of a woman."

"Well, there's something to be said for quality versus quantity. But I forget, you have no time for complicated issues such as true joining."

"I'm glad it was so perfect and true. Will there be a Sharing, then?"

Her easy contentment vanished. "We've only just joined! Give me a little time."

A Sharing was normally more intimate than a mere physical joining. Sexual pleasure was simple and transitory, but to open one's full emotions to another, with no front at all, required a level of trust that most Alseans did not give so early in an acquaintance. Especially someone like Tal. And especially when that Sharing meant revealing a rather large secret.

"I wish I could," he said, "but your time is limited."

"Believe me, I know. I want to tell her. I've already let too many opportunities pass, but…it's been too long since a woman wanted me for myself. I'd forgotten what it felt like."

"It has not been that long. Captain Serrado knew who you were."

Tal looked pained. "Darzen is not Ekatya."

"Ah. She's a vacation tryst, then?"

"No, she's more than that." She shook her head. "You knew that. You're baiting me."

"I want to understand. Tell me." Micah leaned forward, watching her fidget in her chair.

"She's good for me in so many ways. Smart and funny and thoughtful and easy to be with. And she challenges me and keeps me thinking. I doubt I would grow bored with her. But…" She hesitated.

"But?"

"She's not my tyree."

"Oh, Tal." He sat back, his heart aching for her. "We're not all destined to be tyrees. You cannot turn your back on someone who is good for you and may love you, simply because you hope for more. That 'more' might never come. You know how rare it is."

"I know, I know. But I've *felt* it." She looked up at him, a deep longing in her expression. "Ekatya and Lhyn couldn't feel it on their own, so I linked them. Every night for a nineday and a half, I was part of a tyree bond."

He sucked in a breath, and she gave him a wry smile.

"That's why I didn't tell you."

"I'm not judging," he said. "I'm just…"

"Shocked."

He nodded. "You're not usually so…imprudent. You linked a pair of sonsales tyrees. There's no precedent for that. You had no idea what it would do." But it didn't take much thought to come up with the most likely scenario. "They couldn't control it. It all came back on you, didn't it? Why would you do that to yourself?"

"Because they didn't understand. Fahla gave them one of her greatest gifts, but not the ability to truly feel it or understand it. I couldn't stand by and let them flounder when it was so easy to show them the truth. It was an in-the-moment decision the first time, and an addiction after that. Yes, it was impulsive and unwise, but it was the most spectacular thing I've ever felt. Ever. And then they left, and it was gone. I thought I'd come to peace with that. I thought I could make Alsea my bondmate. But then Ekatya called, and there went that little bit of philosophy."

He couldn't imagine what she had been going through. This explained everything.

"I am so sorry, my friend. In a way, you've lost your tyree. That was never supposed to be your bond, but you made it yours, and then you lost it."

"It's my own Fahla-damned fault. I have no claim to sympathy."

"Yes, you do," he said gently.

Her expression tightened and she looked away, fixing her gaze on the window behind him. "That's why I cannot make myself give up hoping. How can I accept that I'm not one of the special ones when for those precious few days, I was?"

He had no answer to that, nor did she seem to expect one. The morning sun streaming through the window gave her light eyes an almost surreal glow, and he thought uncomfortably that Darzen had never seen these eyes. She didn't know about Captain Serrado and Lhyn Rivers or what was in Tal's heart. She didn't know the critical role Tal had played in beating back the Voloth or anything about her normal life.

For the first time, he questioned his own wisdom in facilitating this charade. It had been good for Tal in the short term, but had they done the right thing? They had kept the Lancer off the stage, but in truth, the Lancer was part of Tal's identity.

"I suppose I should put my fantasies behind me and think about this from a more realistic point of view." Tal met his eyes again. "It's ironic, though. I spent so much of my vacation thinking about what you told me, accepting the idea of loving another without compromising my service to Alsea, and now the opportunity is knocking at my door—but I'm hesitating. I'm not certain if Darzen is the one I should be with."

Micah shook off his unease. "A Sharing is not immutable. It doesn't mean you're bonded."

"No, but it means giving all of myself. It may only be momentary, but that doesn't change the fact that a Sharing is a big step."

"True, but exactly how big it is depends on the two of you."

"I think it depends more on Darzen than on me. She's the one who will be learning more than she ever imagined."

"If the truth changes how she treats you, then she was not for you."

"You think I haven't told myself that, every day? Every hantick? Yet the risk is still there, and…this time has been magical. I'm not ready for the magic to end. I've already been through that once; I don't want to do it again."

"It doesn't have to end. But the longer you delay, the worse it might be. Especially now that you've joined."

"I know." She sat up straight and gave him a cocky grin. "And what a joining it was."

"Oh, of course." He understood that she'd had enough; their serious conversation was at an end. "With you, every joining is spectacular."

"Micah, you finally noticed! I'm so pleased." She stood and walked to his door, pausing with her hand on the lever. "I'd be happy to give you some training tips. With a little practice, you might even convince a woman to join with you twice consecutively."

"Why, you—" He launched himself from the chair in a mock attack, and she was out the door in an instant.

Laughing, she jumped down the steps and ran a few paces before stopping. "Don't forget," she called, "I'm right down the path if you change your mind."

He held up two fingers in a very rude gesture, and she waved as she turned toward her own cabin. He watched her go, his smile falling away when she rounded a corner.

The morning breeze tugged at his shirt as he walked to the other side of the porch. From there he could watch the waves crashing onto the beach, a sight he hadn't tired of even after half a moon.

Tal had been hurting more than he knew, and he castigated himself for not trying harder to find out what was wrong. When she began skipping meetings and vanishing on those damned solo runs, he had allowed his anger at her poor choices to overwhelm his sense. He should have known better. Only something big could push her so far off her path.

Now it all fit. A tyree who lost a bondmate was normally supported by the community. No one would expect the survivor to function beyond the most basic levels for quite some time, since the effects of severing that bond included mental, emotional, and physical debilitation.

Tal's bond had not been a full one, but its loss had still damaged her. The recklessness, the inability to cope, the way she had drawn into herself—they were classic symptoms. And not only had she been given zero support through her trauma, but she was also shouldering vast responsibilities and ridiculous levels of stress at the time.

And he had been furious with her.

He remembered the sharp lesson he had taught her, when she lay paralyzed on the forest floor, and cringed in hindsight. If there had been a worse way to go about it, he couldn't think of one.

Now here she was, taking her first steps of real recovery, and he might have sabotaged it before it even began. Everything depended on Darzen's reaction to finding out the truth. And yet…even if she reacted well, she wasn't Tal's tyree. Would Tal ever be truly happy with anything else? When she had glimpsed the divine, how could she settle for the mundane?

A bit of floating driftwood caught his eye, and he focused on it while clearing his mind of wayward thoughts. When he felt centered, he offered up a prayer with all the emotional strength he could muster.

"Fahla, if you're still listening to the prayers of an old warrior, please hear me now. I ask this not for myself, but for one I love. Please…let her have her dream."

CHAPTER 9
Procrastination

Despite Micah's advice and the urgings of her own conscience, Tal let another nineday slip by without revealing herself to Darzen. She hated herself for being a liar and a coward, but every time she thought about a Sharing, she would see a certain smile on Darzen's face or a hand gesture she had come to love, and her courage would fail her. What if the truth meant she never saw any of those things again? If that was to be the result, then shouldn't she enjoy as much of this time as possible before it came to the inevitable end? Her heart had been too recently broken for her to invite a repetition so soon.

In the meantime, she guiltily enjoyed these precious days. What a refreshing change it was to run with her lover instead of a unit of Guards! To sit on rocks and talk, walk up into the canyons, or enjoy a meal together—all simple pleasures that Tal found exotic. She even enjoyed watching Darzen pick a restaurant, just for the novelty of having someone make a decision based on the menu rather than security concerns. Darzen was choosy about her food, and the odds of them staying at a restaurant once they had seen the menu were about one in three. The benefit was that Tal became acquainted with a number of excellent restaurants in the village. While sitting to midmeal in one of them, she was delighted to discover horten soup on the menu and was preparing to order it when Darzen wrinkled her nose.

"You don't like horten soup?" Tal asked incredulously.

"No. How can you eat it? It's just…unbearable."

"You've never had it made properly if you can say that."

Darzen shook her head. "I tried it at the most expensive restaurant in Whitesun. I couldn't get past the smell of it."

"That's part of the experience! Fahla, I could just breathe in the fumes and be happy." Tal had never met anyone who didn't like horten soup. It was a delicacy available only during limited times each cycle and could send one to the stars if properly prepared. She would walk ten lengths for a good bowl of it.

"I've heard other people say that, too. But I have no idea what any of you are talking about. It smells like urine."

Tal laughed. "It does not! You must have a few wires crossed in your nose. But if that's your perception, I can certainly see why you wouldn't want to eat it. I hope you won't mind if I do."

"Actually…" Darzen hesitated. "I would. If you could keep the smell on your side of the table, that would be fine. But it doesn't stay there."

"Then I'll order something else."

"Thank you. Their dokker stew is supposed to be excellent, according to the owner of my inn."

"Dokker stew it is," Tal said, secretly mourning her horten soup. Oh, well. She could come back this evening and get some to take back to her cabin.

True to the word of Darzen's innkeeper, the dokker stew was very good, as was the rest of the meal. They got into a discussion about the most popular authors of the day, discovering that they had similar tastes and had enjoyed several of the same books. Darzen had more reading time, however, and kept coming up with titles that Tal had heard of but hadn't yet read.

"I can't believe you haven't read that one," Darzen said. "Galness is one of my favorite authors! She makes history come alive."

"Maybe so, but she's not terribly accurate while breathing all that life into her histories."

"How can you judge if you haven't read it?"

"I read one of her earlier books about the founding of Whitemoon. She glossed over the abuse of the builder caste during that era and glorified the scholar caste to no end."

"The scholar caste was solely responsible for the planning and architecture of Whitemoon. I don't think she glorified its role at all."

"Do I detect a bit of caste centrism here?" Tal teased. "Certainly the scholars planned the layout and designed the buildings, but they had builder input in the process. Galness skipped right over that part."

"But input isn't the same thing as design. That's like saying I should get credit because you captured a criminal after I told you where he was hiding. You're the one with the skills; you're the one who completed the job. I just gave you input that helped you do what you're trained to."

"In that instance, I would certainly give you credit for enabling the successful capture, because it might not have happened without you. And in the Whitemoon example, I think a better analogy would be if you saw a beautifully engineered boat that someone had forgotten to tie down. You picked up the mooring rope, which was just about to fall in the water, and tied the boat to the dock. You didn't design that boat, but if you hadn't tied it down it would have drifted off and been of no use to anyone. The builder caste had a similar input into the layout and building design of Whitemoon. They were the practical ones who said, 'Certainly that *looks* nice, but it won't actually work.' Not only did Galness write them out of her history, she also omitted any mention of the abuse they suffered while turning those designs into reality."

Darzen gave her a knowing smile. "From your spirited defense of the builders, I'm guessing your family reaches into that caste."

"What would you like to bet on that?"

"Nothing, based on that answer. I admit I'm surprised."

"That I would defend against an injustice when I see it? I'm a warrior. That's part of my caste responsibility."

"Even when reading a book?"

Tal had to laugh at the innocent expression on her face. "All right, perhaps I take my responsibility a little further than most. But if Galness were a true representative of her caste, she'd make a little more effort to round up all of the facts before writing the first word."

"You realize you're insulting one of my favorite authors."

"But not your caste. Besides, is it an insult if it's accurate?" Tal picked up her glass of spirits. "If you can prove me wrong, I'll retract my so-called insult immediately. Can you?" She took a sip of the excellent drink—Darzen had a knack for picking the good ones—and tilted her head as if listening. "Hm. I didn't hear anything. Do you need more time?"

Darzen shook her head, her lips compressed as she tried not to smile. "My birth mother would call you impudent."

"Ah, the dreaded mother weapon, only to be dragged out when all others fail. Which means you must be conceding my point."

"I'll concede your point only after I've looked into the history myself. Now I'm curious."

"Fair enough. You do your research and report back when you're done."

"In the meantime," Darzen said, "you should read another of her books and tell me if you still hold her in such a low opinion. I'd recommend *When the Mountain Fell*. It's about the conquest of Blacksun."

Tal grinned. "You realize that I know every detail of that battle."

"Of course. You're a warrior." Darzen matched her grin with one of her own. "If Galness gets that right, you'll have to concede her skill as a historian."

"Only for that book."

"Are you trying to be argumentative?"

"No," said Tal. "I never have to try very hard."

CHAPTER 10
Invitation

It was a bright, clear morning when reality finally intruded on Tal's vacation. She and Darzen were running their now-familiar route on the beach, saying little but enjoying each other's emotional presence. Tal watched a flock of sandbirds drilling down for a meal and wondered how they managed to locate their prey. What did they see at the surface of the sand that looked any different from the rest of the beach? She had never thought about it before and was enjoying the mental distraction enough that it took a moment for Darzen's words to penetrate.

"I'm leaving in three days."

Tal stopped so quickly that she left deep gouges in the sand. She bent over with her hands on her knees, not so much to recover her breath as to give herself a moment to prepare. When her front was in place, she straightened, meeting Darzen's gaze with outward calm. "You never spoke of a departure time before."

"I didn't want to think about it. This time with you has been too…"

"Perfect," Tal suggested.

Smiling, Darzen said, "Yes. Perfect. I have loved every tick that I've spent with you. But my time is running out, and there's still so much I don't know about you."

"I know. I do want to Share with you, truly. It's just…" She paused, searching for the right words, but Darzen saved her the effort.

"Whatever it is, it can't be that terrible. Can it?"

"It's not to me. But I don't know if it will be to you. And I'm afraid of finding out."

"You're a warrior. You're not afraid of anything."

"No warrior worth her training would ever say that. It's usually a prelude to death." Or at least disaster.

"This is hardly a life-or-death situation."

"It's *my* life."

Darzen tilted her head to one side, watching her. "I can feel it," she said softly. "Please, Dira. Share it with me. Otherwise, this is as far as we'll ever go."

"I know." Tal turned to watch the waves, hoping for inspiration. A warm hand burrowed into hers, and she relaxed as they stood side by side, holding hands and looking out to sea. It should have been an awkward moment, but Darzen somehow made it comfortable. Rarely had Tal felt so at peace with another person, and in the end it was that peace that made her decision for her. She turned back to Darzen, releasing her hand and reaching out to cup her face instead. Gently rubbing her thumbs over the narrow cheekbone ridges that had fascinated her from their first meeting, she asked, "Will you Share with me tonight?"

Darzen's smile was dazzling. "Nothing would give me greater pleasure."

Their kiss was as comfortable as everything else about the relationship, and Tal felt a sudden surge of hope. Tonight would undoubtedly be a shock for Darzen, and Tal would have a lot of explaining to do. But after their Sharing, Darzen would understand her need for this brief interlude of anonymity. She understood so much already, even without an empathic connection.

This Sharing would be the gate to their future. Suffused with certainty, Tal wondered why she had waited so long.

CHAPTER 11
Lancer Tal

Darzen brought an expensive bottle of spirits to Tal's cabin that night. "I thought this might help relax you," she said as she took off her jacket. "Besides, we have to enjoy things like this while we still can."

"What do you mean?" Tal busied herself opening the bottle.

"The matter printer technology. I know you're loyal to the Lancer, but I must say that in this instance she's been very unwise. Not to mention stubborn. I hear the Council has a thousand concerns about it, but she's overriding them all. This technology will be an economic disaster."

With the ease of long practice, Tal strengthened her emotional front as she poured two glasses. "Why do you say that?" she asked, offering a glass.

Darzen took it and held it up. "Because it will turn items like this into luxury products that only the wealthy can afford. Lancer Tal speaks of that technology as a great equalizer, but in reality it will polarize our culture. The vast majority of us will use matter printer products because they'll be so cheap, costing only the energy required to produce them. That means fewer buyers of real products, which means the price of real products will increase exponentially, until only the elite can afford them. If the producers and the merchants don't die out altogether, that is."

"I think you're underestimating the Lancer." Normally, Tal enjoyed their intellectual debates, but tonight of all nights she did not want to participate. "I also think we should leave politics out of the evening, don't you?"

"This isn't politics. It's economics, and that's my life."

"I know that, and you're very good at it. I just hoped we could move to a different topic."

"Why?"

"Because it's our Sharing! I didn't expect to be discussing matter printer economics tonight."

"We have plenty of time. I hadn't planned to begin our Sharing as soon as I walked in the door, did you? I was expecting a glass of spirits, a few snacks, some time to talk… It's been a few cycles since I've done this."

A sudden realization led Tal to skim her emotions, confirming what she suspected. Darzen was nervous and had no idea why matter printer economics might be a touchy issue, and whose fault was that?

She projected calm, watching as it took visible effect. "You're right. It doesn't matter what we talk about. What matters is that you're here, and you've brought some very good spirits."

Darzen smiled and raised her glass. "To good spirits, then. May we enjoy them while they last." She took a sip and added, "I've been stockpiling my favorite spirits at home. It's a pity that I can't do the same for all of the other products that won't be available by this time next cycle."

"Surely you're just a little on the pessimistic side. There will be changes, yes, but they'll hardly be as drastic as that."

"What you call pessimism, I call realism. This technology is putting the very fabric of our culture at risk. Have you never thought of this?"

"I have," Tal said. "And I believe the risk can be minimized with the proper preparation before the matter printer technology is released."

"Well, if I'm realistic, you're optimistic." Darzen gave her an appraising look. "I'd be tempted to say foolishly so, but I know you too well. You have specific ideas. You got them from the Lancer, didn't you?"

"Yes."

Darzen wanted details, probing after them until Tal gave up, motioned her to one of the dining chairs, and settled herself on the opposite side of the table with the bottle of spirits between them. This wasn't what she'd had in mind, but clearly her original vision of their evening was not working out.

The level of spirits steadily decreased as Tal outlined her plan for the release of the technology and answered any number of discerning questions. By the time the last drop was poured, Darzen was smiling and shaking her head.

"You're wasted as a warrior. You'd be far better used as an economist. Perhaps the Lancer gave you these ideas, but you've obviously expanded on them yourself. I can feel your involvement with this issue."

"I *am* involved. That's what I wanted to tell you, before we—"

A sharp knock startled her. She had been so focused on Darzen that she hadn't sensed an approach. Extending her senses, she was dismayed to feel one of her Guards outside, and in an agitated mood.

"Excuse me," she said as she rose.

Senshalon was standing stiffly at attention on her porch. "Forgive me, Lancer Tal," he said breathlessly. "I know you asked not to be disturbed, but Lead Guard Gehrain ordered me to alert you. There's been a containment failure at the Redmoon fusion test facility."

Great Mother, she had actually forgotten. They were testing the prototype today. It was only a one-fifth scale reactor, but it if had been up to full pressure when it failed…

"When did it happen?" she asked.

"Half a hantick ago."

"Fatalities?"

"Yes, but I don't know any details."

"Tell Gehrain to get everyone ready to go. Is Colonel Micah on the grounds?"

"He was in town, but he's on his way back now."

"Then we'll leave when he gets here. Thank you, Senshalon."

He brought his fists together against his chest, bowed briefly, and ran off the porch.

She closed the door and took a moment to gather herself before turning back to her guest. Darzen's gray eyes were as wide open as her emotions, and Tal winced at her mingled hurt and shock.

"I'm sorry," she said. "This is not how I wanted you to find out."

Darzen stared wordlessly for several pipticks, searching Tal's face. "Lancer Tal?" she whispered. "You're Lancer Tal? Oh, Fahla—" A sudden understanding colored her emotions. "Lancer *Andira* Tal."

"Dira was my childhood nickname, and Shaldone is my mother's family name. I took my father's name when I chose his caste." Tal pulled a small neutralizer out of her kit and deactivated the colorizers. In a moment she was stripped of her anonymity, looking into Darzen's eyes and hoping for understanding. "You would have known tonight. I had to tell you before we could Share. There's so much I wanted to tell you, to show you, but—"

Darzen held up one hand, her lips tightening as her emotions hardened. "This was your secret. Not some sad past history or an act you thought I might disapprove of. You were hiding your very identity from me."

"No, I wasn't. I mean—you've seen more of my real identity than most people. I hid my hair and eye color, not myself. You *have* seen me."

"That is not true." Darzen's voice rose. "You showed me only the tiniest part of yourself. What was this, some sort of game? Was I the prize? I was falling for you, Dira." She stopped and shook her head. "Andira. Goddess above, I didn't even know your name. You let me fall for a shadow."

"Wait, please—"

But Darzen was already pulling on her jacket. She zipped it up and pinned Tal with a glare, her anger fueled by the hurt and betrayal right at the surface of her emotions.

"You're not the woman I knew. Dira wouldn't deceive me this way. She wouldn't stand by while I made a fool of myself!" Her frown intensified. "No wonder you had such a grasp of matter printer economics."

"I deceived you because I was afraid of exactly this! And you have been anything but a fool. Will you please just take one tick and think about what we've had together? Everything has been true and real. Everything except my title."

Darzen yanked open the door. "There's just one problem with that, Lancer Tal. Your title *is* everything." With a rustle of fabric she was gone, leaving the door open behind her.

"Shek!" Tal took a step toward the door and stopped. She couldn't chase after Darzen; there was no time. Her responsibilities had reappeared, and there was nothing she could do now. She had barely enough time to throw a few clothes into her bag as it was.

Quietly, she closed the door and began to pack. Darzen would have to wait.

CHAPTER 12
Rumors and fact

THERE WERE FOUR FATALITIES. A small number considering what might have been, but still four too many.

The initial tests had gone perfectly. Based on the results and a system analysis, Chief Kameha had authorized a sustained test of two hanticks. This, too, had gone well—until the reaction powered past its established safe limit. No one knew how it happened. One moment the sensor readings were normal, the next they indicated a runaway reaction. Kameha initiated the shutdown procedure, and all of the personnel evacuated to wait in a safe zone.

When the readouts indicated that the reactor was sufficiently cool, a team of four RadCon technicians suited up in radiation containment gear and entered the facility. Their job was to assess the damage and determine what would be needed for a full recovery before the next test. When they reached the control room, they found that the shutdown had not been completed and the reaction was approaching critical overload. They reported their findings as they raced for the doors, but the containment chamber failed twelve pipticks after their com call, releasing the extreme high pressures and heat of the fusion reaction.

The resulting explosion flattened half of the facility.

Public response was immediate and loud. Some commentators declared that since the very first attempt at using Gaian technology had failed so badly, the matter printers were surely going to be a disaster. Others accused the Gaians of sending bad blueprints and went from there to questioning the treaty and the Council's culpability in accepting it. Tal's name was frequently brought up as the one who had rammed the treaty through and was now ramming through the changes to Alsean society. The accusation of war criminality, which had died down while she was on vacation, surged back to the front. Still others said it had nothing to do with the Gaians and hinted darkly at sabotage by fission reactor owners who had a vested interest in making sure the fusion technology failed.

When an investigative team led by Chief Kameha found the actual cause, it was both simpler and more infuriating than the rumors: old-fashioned merchant corruption. The failure was due to substandard sensors supplied by a merchant who had listed the highest-grade sensors in his bid. The cheaper sensors had worked perfectly during the first, limited tests, but failed when subjected to the prolonged heat and pressure of the scaled-up test. Their faulty readouts had prevented the shutdown and led Kameha to believe the reactor had cooled, when in fact it was still out of control.

While a few on the fringe insisted that the corruption charge was just a cover-up of Gaian sabotage, the vast majority of the furor that had swirled around differing camps of belief now coalesced into a planet-wide rage against the merchant caste. The corrupt merchant was detained and brought into Blacksun Base, and a team of investigators began tracking the route the sensors had taken from production to final use.

Tal was furious when Kameha's report came in. She hadn't fought for the advancement of her people only to see them cut off their own feet, and vowed that every individual involved in this flagrant disregard for the sanctity of Alsean life would be punished to the full extent of the law. The High Tribunal would decide the fate of the merchant and any collaborators, but as Lancer she had the right to petition for lesser or more grave punishments. Though she did not often choose to exercise that right, in this case she would ask for the maximum penalty.

Six days after the destruction of the Redmoon facility, Tal walked through her private entry onto the dais at one end of the Council chamber and stood next to the ornate, uncomfortable State Chair. The session was fully attended: all thirty Councilors from each caste plus the six caste Primes were in tiered seating lining the room's two long sides. Stacked above them were the guest gallery and the visitor's gallery, and at the other end two enormous and beautifully carved wooden doors gave the Council members entry onto the chamber floor.

While her dais had a clear view of the entire chamber, the Councilors' best views were of the members sitting across from them. Over the generations, this arrangement had resulted in a seating pattern dictated largely by caste affiliation, with warriors, scholars, and crafters on one side and merchants, builders, and producers on the other. A seat's location in the tiers was a status symbol, with the lowest seats going to those with the greatest power and strongest connections. Only the elite could walk straight into the chamber and sit, rather than climbing up into the tiers.

Tal picked up the staff that leaned against her chair and struck the large bell hanging from the ceiling, opening the Council meeting. The arguing started before she could even sit down.

"This disaster only clarifies the need to put the matter printer technology to instant use. Why are we still waiting? What is the Council afraid of?"

"You're insane. If we release that technology now it will make the merchant caste's corruption worse than it already is!"

"I resent your insinuation. You can't lay the criminal actions of one person on an entire caste—"

"My colleague wasn't making an insinuation. That was a statement of fact. The merchants are well known for—"

"Do the warriors have evidence of widespread corruption, or are they just waving their swords around as usual?"

"Yes, of course the merchants are more worried about their tattered reputations than the four warriors who died in the line of duty. If you wanted to badly enough, you could rehabilitate your bad reputation, but we can't bring back our dead—"

Tal listened in silence, casting frequent glances at the timer built into her chair's armrest. She was required to allow at least two hanticks of discussion on any matter of general security and was prepared to endure this shouting match for exactly as long as the law mandated. The effort needed to shut out the intense emotions generated by one hundred and eighty-six agitated Alseans was taxing enough; the noise itself was worse. She watched the timer count down the pipticks, and the moment the blessed zero appeared she stood up, signaling that the debate was at an end. When the arguing failed to die down, she struck the bell a bit harder than necessary.

"That is quite sufficient," she said. "I am appalled at your behavior. We all have reason for anger, but the purpose of this Council is to find solutions to problems, not shout about them. In two hanticks, not one of you has managed to say anything of use." She turned to the warrior tier. "Prime Warrior Shantu, I am deeply sorry for the loss of four noble warriors, but proud that they gave their lives in service to others. They reflect the best of the warrior caste, and their names will be honored to the highest ability of a grateful people."

Shantu bowed his head, casting a sidelong look at the Prime Merchant across the chamber.

"However," Tal continued, "I do not share your opinion that the merchants are more concerned with their reputations than these deaths. Nor do I believe you truly feel that way, though I understand that tempers are high today."

Put on the spot, Shantu straightened. "I do not believe that all of the merchants feel that way," he said carefully.

Tal shifted her gaze to the merchant tier. "Prime Merchant Parser, do you not think it possible that there are other members of your caste involved in the type of corruption that led to these deaths?"

Parser looked every bit as uncomfortable as Shantu had. "I know of no—"

"I did not ask if you knew," she interrupted. "I asked if you thought it possible."

He hesitated, and her senses vibrated with the intense curiosity of the other Councilors. They couldn't wait to see what came out of his mouth.

"Yes," he muttered. "It is possible that some extremely tiny faction of our caste is involved in this type of corruption."

"But those individuals do not represent your caste as a whole, do they?"

"No," he said in a firmer voice. "They do not. Our caste takes pride in providing the best in products and services."

Tal thought that was a debatable generalization, but this was not the time to pursue it.

"No one here questions the pride or honor of the merchant caste," she said. "I believe the warrior caste was speaking only of those few you mention. Am I correct, Prime Warrior Shantu?"

"Yes, Lancer Tal," Shantu answered crisply, and she knew he saw her intention. "We respect the merchant caste—"

Parser snorted.

"—but we cannot stand by while members of any caste pose a danger to our own," Shantu finished with a glare at Parser.

"No caste could stand idly by while members of its own were in danger. Which is why the merchant and warrior castes will make perfect allies in their pursuit of this corruption." Tal turned back to Parser. "For as long as such corruption persists, your own caste is in danger, Prime Merchant. I do not think the merchant caste will enjoy the results if the Council is forced to legislate means of preventing it."

The threat was clear, and there wasn't a soul in the room who missed it.

"You and Counselor Shantu will come to an agreement on a strategy to root out this corruption. It has persisted too long, and though I don't expect it can ever be eradicated, I can expect a comprehensive plan for its reduction and control. If that plan is not on my desk within the next nineday, I will bring the issue before the Council, complete with my own recommendations."

She swept her gaze from one end of the room to the other. "The matter printer technology is not a panacea for the ills of our society. We bear the responsibility of guiding Alsea along a path that safeguards the honor, prosperity, and safety of all its citizens. The new technology is but one tool at our disposal and cannot substitute for our own wisdom. *I* acquired this technology for our people, and *I* will release it when it is in the best interests of Alsea to do so. And that is not now."

A few mutters were heard, which she silenced with another strike of the bell. "This Council meeting is ended," she said, and walked out.

CHAPTER 13

Lying by omission

"Your name is on the lips of every Councilor today," Micah said, stretching his legs out in front of him. "And many of those lips are twisted in anger."

Tal had invited him to her quarters for a drink, which he thought she sorely needed. She had stalked out of the Council chamber like a vallcat on the prowl and was still bristling even now.

It was unlike her to be so high-handed. Normally, she employed backroom tactics and artful manipulation, quietly arranging things and letting others think it had been their idea. While he understood her ire, such a blatant flexing of her power was bound to have repercussions.

"Let them be angry," she said. "They mewl and posture while four good warriors lie dead. They concern themselves with their own advancement at the expense of the very people they're sworn to guide and protect. I swear, Micah, some days I'm tempted to wipe away the entire Council and start anew."

"Please notify me in advance if you do. I'll sell tickets."

"And even you are concerned with profit."

"Not at all." Micah reached for his spirits and took a sip. "I'm concerned with making sure that all interested Alseans have an equal opportunity to see something so wildly entertaining."

Her mouth twitched just before she gave up and laughed. "You always know how to make me feel better." She took a healthy gulp of her own spirits and stared at the blue liquid.

"This is not the only issue making you unhappy," he said.

"When did you become a high empath?"

"Don't I wish. But I do have the eyes of a friend." And the knowledge that in the six days since their precipitous return to Blacksun, Darzen had not answered any of Tal's calls.

When she didn't respond, he added, "I could find her and speak with her."

"Micah..." She sighed. "If she won't return my calls, I don't think she's any more likely to speak with you. Not to mention the fact that your presence will emphasize the title I kept from her."

"Then she is a fool."

"You are sitting with the fool."

He sat up, ready to argue, but stopped when she held up a hand.

"I appreciate your support, truly. But the fact is, I based a relationship on a lie. I have very much earned her disdain."

"Did you lie, or did you simply not share all the facts?"

"When it comes to matters of the heart, is there a difference?"

They sat in silence, sipping idly, until she put her glass down and said, "Ekatya once told me that I was a master of lying by omission."

"When was that?"

"Right after we fought our honor challenge."

"Ah. You mean when you failed to tell her that a projection Sharing might put you in the healing center?"

"No, when I hid the fact that she cracked my rib."

That made no sense. "She expected you to admit she'd hurt you? They must teach a whole different fighting philosophy in Fleet."

She chuckled. "I didn't understand at first either. But that was when she let go of her anger. I've thought about it a lot since then, and I think it all came down to power. We're both used to having it, but she lost most of hers that day. When she realized she'd hurt me, it gave her back some of that power. That was what she needed."

"And you think you took away Darzen's power by not telling her who you were?"

"I can see you're not taking that idea seriously."

"She's an economist, Tal. Not a warrior."

"She's a person who thought we both had the same number of tiles on the board and then found out we weren't even playing the same game."

He sat back. "Well, when you put it that way...I do have to admit that I felt bad for her. But then she walked out on you and I haven't had much sympathy since."

She gave him a wry smile. "Always in my corner, even when I don't deserve it."

"Not true," he said, remembering a disruptor aimed at her heart.

"The truth is, you and I both forgot how to let go of strategy. We've been living and breathing military tactics and politics, where withholding information is a useful strategy. But for two people contemplating a Sharing? I knew it was wrong, but I was enjoying our affair too much to risk it. So I strategized to keep it going as long as I could. I made a mistake, and this is the price."

"But I'm paying that price, too," he said. "I enjoyed your happiness, and I miss it."

She reached out to touch his hand, giving him the gift of her emotions. "So do I. But I don't think it will ever come from Darzen."

CHAPTER 14
Losing her grip

"So we're in agreement, then. Lancer Tal is losing her grip and needs to be removed."

"We're agreed."

Of course they weren't. He didn't want to remove her; he just wanted to control her. But this was going to be a long-term and carefully planned strategy, and he would need allies. Especially this one. If his ally wanted to think their end game was actual removal, that was fine with him. There would be only one winner, after all.

And it wouldn't be the taller man sitting opposite him.

"It's a pity," his ally said. "I actually respected her after the Battle of Alsea. If she hadn't discovered how to take down those shields, our losses would have been far, far higher. But she's lost sight of her priorities. Of all the technology the *Caphenon* brought with it, the matter printers are by far the most transformative. We need them and we need them now. She's sitting on that tech like a bird sits on its eggs."

Now that, he could agree with. "She's sitting on it because she's too caught up in the details. Really, meeting with non-ranking delegates from every caste to discuss their concerns? What do they know about it?" The whole point to fighting one's way to the top was to benefit from the power that only those at the top wielded. Lancer Tal should have been consulting him and the others at his level. Instead she was talking to every half-witted tree grower, musician, and carpenter, while telling him and the rest of the Council that they had no say in her decisions.

His ally snorted. "Nothing. They know nothing. They think the space elevator and FTL engines are the most impressive tech the Protectorate gave us."

"People are always impressed by the big things. But it's the small things that change the world."

"True words. And the matter printers really will change our world. Those who control them will control everything."

"She knows that." He prided himself on never underestimating an opponent. "That's the other reason she's sitting on it. She wants all of the castes to have equal control over the matter printers. She's always been too idealistic."

"Yes, and that's the problem."

"It won't be hard to stir up resistance to them. People are easily swayed by fear."

"And then easily convinced to support the person who will protect them from what they fear," his ally said.

"Exactly." It was so simple to lead this man where he wanted him to go. "We're going to need new names while we play this particular game of tiles. We can't be known to be communicating with each other. What would you like me to call you?"

His ally tilted his head, then smiled. "Challenger."

He barely kept himself from rolling his eyes. Of course. How predictable. "And I will be Spinner."

He could see that his ally wasn't impressed with the name. But Spinner suited him perfectly. It would take him many moons to spin his web and probably several more for Lancer Tal to fall into it. But when she did, she would be well and truly stuck. Then he would control her—and everything else.

CHAPTER 15
The Voloth problem

Lanaril straightened her tunic and followed the aide through a beautifully furnished antechamber to a wooden door inlaid with the design of a molwyn tree. She admired the craftwork while the aide tapped on the door, cracked it open, and said, "Lancer Tal? Your mid-four is here."

"Thank you."

He opened the door the rest of the way, giving Lanaril a respectful nod as she stepped into the inner office.

Andira's eyes lit up, and she pushed her chair back from the desk. "Lanaril! I forgot you were my mid-four appointment."

"That doesn't speak well for me." Lanaril touched her palm.

"It doesn't speak of you at all; it speaks of my ridiculous schedule. Come, sit with me. Would you like some shannel?"

"Yes, please." Lanaril chose one of the comfortable chairs by the windows. "How is your schedule ridiculous already? Didn't you just get back from vacation?"

"Vacation? Did I have one of those? It's been so long I can't recall," Andira said from the other side of the room. The shannel dispenser made a quiet splashing sound as it filled a cup.

"It's only been half a moon. If you've forgotten already, it didn't do you much good."

"In some ways it did me a world of good. In others…not so much." Andira came back with two cups, handing one to her before she sat in the other chair.

"Thank you." Lanaril hummed with happiness when she took her first sip. "Your office has the best shannel."

"Some days it's the only way they can keep me in here."

"They keep me in my office far too long as well, but nobody's offering me a shannel dispenser like that."

"Perhaps you should get Fahla to put in a good word for you."

Lanaril chuckled. "Not even the Lead Templar of Blacksun gets personal favors from Fahla. Though I could certainly wish for it. Your vacation sounds like it might be an interesting story," she added, throwing out the bait.

"Is that what you came here for?"

"No. But I'd enjoy hearing it if it's something you can talk about."

Andira sipped her shannel thoughtfully. Her front was impenetrable as always; Lanaril rarely knew what was going on inside her head. But over the last half cycle they had struck up a friendship, and she decided to err on the side of presumption.

"The short version is that I met someone," Andira said. "Someone I thought might mean something in my life. But I was in disguise, because that was the only way I could have any privacy, so the person I met didn't know who I was."

Lanaril could see the end of this story from two lengths away. "How long did you wait before you told her?"

Andira winced. "Too long. I was enjoying my anonymity too much, and, well—she didn't learn it from me."

"Oh, no."

"She found out the same night I was planning to tell her, but I don't get any points for that. Aldirk is always saying that intent counts for nothing in politics. Apparently, it counts for nothing in romance as well."

"Is there any hope for resolving it?"

"Not if half a moon of silence is any indication. I've stopped trying to call. My pride can only take so much."

"Then it seems she hasn't yet learned the value of forgiveness. It's a hard lesson for many of us to learn, but I don't think a suitable mate for you would be so spiritually young."

Andira stared at her. "Thank you. That is…really quite comforting. I hadn't thought of it that way."

"Because you're too busy blaming yourself."

"I'm beginning to question your empathic rating. I suspect you might be a higher empath than you let on."

"Don't worry, your front is still a brick wall. I can't see through it."

"That's a relief."

"But a templar cannot rely solely on empathic abilities. Not all of us are high empaths, and not all of what we need to know can be determined from a surface skim. So we learn other ways."

"You must have gone to the same classes Micah did. He's better at reading people than anyone I know."

"It's a useful skill," Lanaril acknowledged.

"Indeed it is. Let me see if I can do as well as you." Andira set her cup down and leaned forward. "You're here to ask me for something, but you don't know how to approach it, so you're trying to find a side entrance to the conversation. Which tells me that whatever it is you want, it's big."

She had to smile. "I'd say you did very well. If you'd like to change castes, there might be a position in my temple for you."

"Thank you, but my days of taking orders are well behind me. The door is open now, so tell me about this big thing."

Lanaril put her cup down as well. They had moved from friendly chat to business more quickly than she had anticipated, and she was a little unsettled by it. For a moment she wondered if that had been intentional.

"It's about the Voloth," she said. "The ones with shattered minds."

Andira nodded, waiting.

"I've put a great deal of thought and prayer into this, and I now believe that we're taking the wrong path. Keeping them permanently sedated is not a solution. They're not living."

"They're not living if we let them wake, either."

"No. Letting them be conscious is nothing short of torture. But keeping them asleep until they die is just the lesser of two evils. That doesn't make it the right choice."

"Since the Voloth won't accept them and the Protectorate doesn't want them, there's only one other option," Andira said. "The option you spoke out against two moons ago."

"Two moons ago I believed that mercy killing was still murder. But I've counseled a number of healers who are caring for the Voloth in Blacksun, and what I've learned has made me reconsider. Our healers are suffering. Even when the Voloth are unconscious, the horror they're trapped in comes out. They broadcast it like children, and not every healer has the ability to block it. In fact, very few of them do. I've been counseling people who show every sign of war trauma even though they weren't in the battle. It became common enough that I checked with several templars in Whitemoon, Whitesun, and Redmoon. They're all seeing the same thing."

Andira frowned. "Why haven't I heard of this before now?"

"Because healers will speak to a templar long before they'll speak to a politician."

"Granted, but why aren't they telling their superiors? I should have heard about this from the Prime Scholar, not Blacksun's Lead Templar."

"I can't answer that, but my guess is that templars are also higher than supervisors on the list of people who are deemed safe to speak with. The supervisors tend to be high empaths who don't feel the impact. It's difficult for mid empaths to admit that they're incapable of doing a job when their supervisors not only don't feel the same impact, but can't understand what it's like to not be able to block it."

"If the effects are as bad as you say, then sooner or later those mid empaths will have to admit it."

"Yes, they will, at which point the job of caring for these Voloth will be open only to high empaths. But it's really an assistant healer position. There's not much expertise required to care for a patient in an enforced unconscious state."

Andira sighed. "So we're going to be shunting our high empath healers into jobs they're overqualified for and taking them away from jobs where they're needed."

"After burning out a significant percentage of our assistant healers, yes. And then we'll have the added burden of treating their trauma. On top of that, the fact that they're being harmed by even the unconscious broadcasts means that those Voloth are still suffering. Sedating them isn't the mercy we thought it was." Lanaril took a sip of her shannel, needing a bit of courage. Even though she believed this was the right choice, it was still hard.

"We can't let the Voloth wake because it's torture for them," she said. "We can't keep them asleep because it's torture for them *and* our healers. There's only one viable choice. We have to release them from their pain."

"I agree."

"That's why I hoped—what?"

"I agree. I've thought that from the beginning."

"But...why didn't you ever say so?" Even privately, Andira had never given any indication that she supported mercy killing.

"Because this isn't a matter of politics or law, it's a matter of morality. That's not my sphere of power. I had to wait until the templars spoke up. They need to demand that the Council do the right thing."

"Some of them are ready to do that."

"But not all of them?"

"No, and that's where I need your help. If you come out in support, I'll have a much stronger position from which to swing the others over to our side."

Andira shook her head. "I'm sorry. I can't do that."

That was not what Lanaril had expected, not after hearing that Andira was on her side. "Why not? You said you were waiting for the templars to speak. I'm right here, speaking to you now."

"*You* are, yes. But you're not representing the templars as a group."

"So you're saying you support my position, but you won't come out publicly with that support until I don't need it anymore?"

"I want to, believe me. But I'm sitting on top of a volcano right now. Since the fusion reactor failed, I'm having Fahla's own nightmares trying to deal with the release of the matter printer technology. Half of the population wants it yesterday, and the other half thinks the prototypes and blueprints should all be shot directly into the sun. All of them think I'm going about it the wrong way. And you must have heard the calls for my prosecution as a war criminal."

"That's just the fringe radicals. No one with any intelligence or common sense listens to them."

Andira gave her a half-smile. "Wouldn't it be a perfect world if all of our citizens had those traits?"

"I stood up there with you and supported your call to break Fahla's covenant. It certainly didn't win me many fans in the higher echelon of the templars, but no one is calling me a war criminal."

"Of course they aren't. You spoke in support of a decision. That's not the same thing as being the person who not only made that decision, but also bypassed both the Council and the High Council to implement a policy that some believe was the worst act ever committed in modern Alsean history."

"It's an overreaction and it will never hold water. Why would you let that affect your decisions?"

"If it were the only thing I had to worry about, I wouldn't. But it's one more thing on top of all the others."

"And that's why you won't support me? Because you don't want to give fuel to a very tiny fire?"

"Giving fuel to very tiny fires is precisely how they grow into very big fires. And it might not help your cause much if the Lancer who broke Fahla's covenant stands up and says she's advocating mass murder."

"You're oversimplifying it to make a point. This is not mass—"

"Lanaril," Andira said sharply. "I'm telling you that I have to pick my battles. And as much as I would like to, I cannot pick this one. I'm sorry."

Lanaril could not believe it. She couldn't be this close to what she needed and then have it taken away through soulless political calculations. This wasn't the Andira she knew as a friend; this was the Lancer.

"You owe me a favor," she said.

It hung in the air between them. Andira's expression did not change, but the warmth vanished from her eyes.

"Is that really how you want to do this?" she asked.

Their friendship was balanced on the tip of a knife. Lanaril knew it as clearly as if Fahla herself were in the room, showing her the divergent paths in their future.

"No," she said. "I don't want to lose your friendship over this. But it's so important, and that was the only tile I had left to play."

Andira exhaled. "You have no idea how glad I am that you said that. I don't want to lose yours, either."

"So where does that leave us?"

"It leaves us looking for some different tiles to play."

"There are none. Don't you think I exhausted my options before I came here? You were the big weapon I was leaving for the last resort."

Andira smiled. "That might be the first time anyone called me a big weapon. I rather like it, thank you."

"Warriors and their egos," Lanaril said, and their chuckles broke the remaining tension between them.

"Of course there are other tiles." Andira picked up her shannel and leaned back in her chair. "Did you go to Yaserka?"

Lanaril shook her head. "Yaserka has been a capable Prime Scholar, but he's a secular scholar. He prefers not to dabble in templar affairs. Normally we think that's a positive trait, but in this instance it means he would give me the same answer you did: he won't throw his support behind me until I already have the rest of the templars in line. And that's never going to happen. The moral schism is too deep."

"Ah, but Yaserka doesn't have the same reasoning. There are no volcanoes under his seat. His caution stems from not wanting to get involved in an issue where he wouldn't be able to look like a strong leader."

"I understand that, but the result is the same. He's not a tile I can play."

"Because you're thinking like a templar. Sit back and let the warrior work a little tactical strategy for you."

CHAPTER 16
Surprise visitor

Not four days after Lanaril's meeting with Andira, she received a surprise visitor in her office.

"I hope you don't mind my dropping in unannounced." Prime Scholar Yaserka settled into one of her guest chairs, his long, thin body looking somewhat lost in its wide cushions. "I came to burn an offering and thought I'd check on a rumor while I was here."

"It's always a pleasure to see you, though I'm not certain how much help I can be with rumors," Lanaril said. "I'm not well-connected with the political rumor circuit."

"Of course not. But this one was about you."

"Really? I can't think how. My life is not that interesting."

"No, no, not a personal rumor. I'm sorry if I gave that impression. No, I was informed that you were in the Lancer's office earlier this nineday, asking for her support on something. And that you left looking, er, less than pleased with the result."

"Ah, that. I'm afraid that's fact, not a rumor." She smiled inwardly. Yaserka had poked his nose in her business even earlier than Andira had predicted.

"May I ask why you went to the Lancer rather than coming to me? You know my door is open to you."

"I do know that, and thank you. I would have gone to you with this, but it's such a critical and volatile issue that I thought it needed the power of the Lancer's office to handle it. But she refused."

"She refused to help you?" His eyes glinted. "For what reason?"

"She said she had too much on her agenda to bother with something that was an internal scholar caste issue. It wasn't important enough to her. But she's wrong; her office *should* be handling it. It may only be affecting the scholars, but we can't do anything about it without full Council approval. And without the Lancer's support, I don't see how we'll ever get that."

He settled back and rested his hands on one bony knee. "Tell me about this caste issue that our Lancer thinks is beneath her office."

CHAPTER 17
Grand opening

"We have beaten all the projections and done what many said we could not do," Prime Builder Eroles said in a clear voice. The crowd below them cheered, as they had for almost every other sentence she uttered.

Standing next to her, Tal couldn't help smiling at such enthusiasm. She had never attended a grand opening like this one.

"Of course only Fahla can perform miracles," Eroles continued, "but I think the builders have come pretty close, don't you?"

This time the cheers could probably be heard all the way to Redmoon, and Eroles shot Tal a grin before turning back to the crowd.

"Just seven moons ago, this building was a pile of rubble. Eight hundred cycles of history gone in one morning. Gone in less than a hantick, because of an enemy that cared nothing for what they destroyed. But we have rebuilt, and we have done so with the very same stones that our ancestors shaped. Hundreds, thousands of hands helped us gather the stones. Six castes came together in the effort, a perfect illustration of why the Voloth could not break us. Because we are too strong together!"

More cheers, accompanied by whistles and shouts, and Tal had to admire the speaking skills of their Prime Builder. She held this crowd in her hand.

"In the last two days, as we have toured the reconstruction efforts here in Whitesun, Lancer Tal and I have been impressed over and over again by your determination, your industry, your resourcefulness. We have been humbled by the courage of a people who paid the highest price during the Battle of Alsea. We have rejoiced in the energy you are bringing to your recovery. And we are proud of your unbroken spirit. This house may belong to the builders, but it could not exist today without the help of all the castes and all of you. From the bottom of my heart, I thank you. And it is with great joy that I invite you in, because…" She took a breath and threw out her arms. "The Whitesun Builder Caste House is now open!"

The crowd roared, and the night sky exploded in light and color as the fireworks began. It was a rare moment of unadulterated triumph in a hard cycle, and Tal happily craned her neck to watch.

"Lancer Tal, will you be my guest?" Eroles held out a bent arm.

"I would be delighted." Tal hooked their elbows together, and they walked side by side into the newly rebuilt caste house.

The high-ceilinged lobby was impressive with its intricate carvings and hand-painted floor tiles. A group of musicians played quietly to one side, while at least twenty servers at the long bar braced themselves for the onslaught.

"We'd better get our drinks now, or we'll never see that bar again," Eroles said.

"I like your priorities."

Drinks in hand, they retreated to a quiet corner, taking a moment to themselves before a long night of political performance. Eroles looked even more brilliant than usual in a suit patterned with vivid blues, purples, and oranges, which contrasted sharply with her dark skin and black hair. Every time she moved her hands, musical sounds emanated from the many shining bracelets she wore. She was color and vivacious movement, and Tal felt a bit drab by comparison. Not even her dress uniform with its high-necked crimson jacket could stand up to the eyeful that Eroles presented, but that was just as well. She was only a guest tonight. The real star of the evening was the Prime Builder, who had presided over a reconstruction program that Tal had once thought overly optimistic.

"I have to agree with your speech," she said. "The builders really did accomplish a miracle. I had chills walking through these doors just now. It seems like only last nineday that I was here after the battle and found nothing but debris. I almost wept."

"I *did* weep."

Tal nodded. The news footage showing the Prime Builder openly crying over the destruction of her caste's second-greatest house had been replayed many times on the broadcasts. Eroles had always enjoyed a fair amount of popularity in her caste, but after that hit the news, she had become more than just their Prime. Now she embodied their visceral pain and their fierce drive to rebuild.

"I'm glad the builders decided to reconstruct the caste house as it was," Tal said. "It seems…more appropriate, somehow. Like a great gesture of defiance to the Voloth. A statement that they couldn't change us."

"Oh, you have no idea what a debate that inspired. All over Alsea our caste houses spoke of nothing else. I was getting unsolicited architectural plans every day, and some of them would have put the State House to shame."

Tal chuckled. "Imagine the jealousy."

"I know. The Council would have had no peace until we'd authorized funds to 'improve' the other five Whitesun caste houses so they could catch up. And then all of the Blacksun caste houses would have been agitated because nothing in Blacksun is supposed to be smaller. I've got enough to do with rebuilding what we lost; Fahla knows I don't need to be worrying about improving anything that isn't broken."

"Not to mention rebuilding what we blew up," Tal said, thinking of Redmoon.

"That too." Eroles shook her head. "I still can't believe that after all we went through with the Voloth, some merchants are still thinking only of how they can profit."

"It's not limited to the merchants."

"I know, but that dokker almost cost us Chief Kameha. He's possibly the most valuable person on Alsea right now, and we could have lost him because some stupendously greedy fantenshekken wanted an extra twelve percent on his sale."

They had restarted the Redmoon fusion test facility just two days ago, a moon and a half after the containment failure. Having already constructed the facility once, the builders were able to reconstruct it at a dizzying speed. Kameha and his team double- and triple-checked everything and ran at least thirty tests and simulations—fifty on the sensors. Even so, Tal had held her breath when they started the reactor. But it was performing perfectly.

"At least we derived some benefit from that disaster," she said. "The merchant caste was sufficiently embarrassed to actually get behind Parser and Shantu's plan for the task force. I think we have a better chance of addressing that corruption now than we've had in a long time."

"I hope you're right." Eroles looked over the crowd that was streaming in. "We've got about two ticks before our show begins. I wanted to say something first." She fixed Tal with her nearly black eyes. "One of the reasons the builders have been able to perform miracles is because we've got the *Caphenon*'s cargo matter printers behind us. I know you've been under a lot of pressure to open up those printers to the other castes, but I'm deeply grateful that you've reserved them for reconstruction. We have to rebuild first and *then* move forward. And I think your strategy with the caste delegates is brilliant." She gave Tal a knowing smile. "It isn't just about listening to the concerns of the people. It's also about delaying implementation until we're done running around like yardbirds with twenty chicks."

Tal tapped their glasses together in acknowledgment. "Very astute, Prime Builder. But that's not a winning argument in the Council, so I didn't offer it."

"Half of the Councilors are idiots anyway," Eroles said in a matter-of-fact tone, and Tal had to laugh.

"I'm afraid I can't respond to that assessment," she said.

Eroles chuckled and then turned as her name was called. "Show time," she said, and moved away.

Tal was in no hurry to dive into that crowd. She sipped her drink, watching the finely dressed people drifting through the grand lobby, and enjoyed the few ticks she could get before her own performance began.

Eroles was right about the matter printers. Even discounting the enormous amount of work still to be done in laying the legal, social, and physical infrastructure for them, they were far too disruptive a technology to be released now. Not when so many of their resources were devoted to reconstruction after the Battle of Alsea, and especially not when the Alsean people were still so nervous about new technology. The Redmoon fusion disaster loomed large, and two days of flawless operation hadn't magically erased everyone's fears. It didn't matter that the explosion had been caused by substandard parts and not the actual technology—after all, Alsea would still be depending on its merchants to provide parts for the other new technologies, such as the matter printers and space elevator. Current polls showed that the majority of Alseans wouldn't be comfortable using the space elevator until it had already been in operation for at least a cycle.

It was crucial to regain the people's trust before doing anything so drastic as releasing those matter printers. The Anti-Corruption Task Force spearheaded by Prime Merchant Parser and Prime Warrior Shantu was their best chance of accomplishing that—along with a steady, ongoing demonstration that Tal's government had things in hand and was taking the people's concerns into account.

With that in mind, she had been meeting regularly with delegations from the six castes, both to listen to their concerns and to explain her strategies and expectations. By her decree, the delegations excluded Council members, instead involving individuals selected by a lottery system. Those who wished to have a voice put their names in the system, and the randomly selected individuals were transported to Blacksun at the government's expense. Tal wanted true representation and found herself enjoying these delegate meetings far more than any Council session. Some of the delegates were every bit as politically astute as their Council leaders, but most were simply concerned with their livelihoods and families, often bringing up considerations that neither Tal nor her advisors had thought of. Her policy drafts shifted with the input she took away from these meetings, and she was confident that if the matter printer technology had any unforeseen ill effects, it would not be for lack of effort on her part.

A knot of Whitesun city officials approached, and Tal put on her politician's mantle. For the next two hanticks she mingled, chatted, and smiled, keeping a half-full glass of spirits in her hand to ward off the offers of additional drinks. At times like these, it was best to stay alert. Her Guards lined the walls and had empathically screened everyone entering, but the sheer number of people around her meant anything could happen.

If she were honest with herself, she would admit to another reason for staying sharp. Darzen lived in Whitesun and advised the city council. She had certainly been invited to this grand opening, but just to be sure, Tal had sent her a message confirming her own attendance along with an invitation for her to drop by. Perhaps a public venue would make Darzen more comfortable about speaking with her.

But as the night wore on with no sign of her, Tal mentally closed the door on that relationship. Yes, it would have been nice to patch things up, but it wasn't going to happen. And she had too much on her agenda to waste any more time wishing otherwise.

She had just said good night to a departing group of crafters when a soft voice sounded from behind her.

"Lancer Tal?"

"Yes?" Tal turned to find a woman with graying hair piled atop her head in an elegant twist. She wore a dark blue evening dress and had a white-knuckled grip on her drink.

The woman held up her palm. "I'm Kylinn Tousander. Head librarian at West Quarter Academy in Whitemoon."

"Well met, Deme Tousander." Tal addressed her by the honorific for a secular scholar and touched their palms together. She paused for a moment, startled by the fear coming through their touch and the whisper of deep pain that ran beneath it.

"Please, call me Kylinn. The children call me Deme Tousander." Her smile was brief and did not reach her eyes. "I wonder if I might speak with you about… ah…about…"

Her front was almost impervious to Tal's senses, which meant she was a very highly rated empath. Tal added up the signs and said, "About the Voloth?"

Kylinn sagged, nearly dropping her glass. "How did you know that?"

"I recognize that particular flavor of pain. It's a new one to our people." Tal rescued the glass from Kylinn's hand and escorted her over to the nearest wall. In the relative quiet, she asked, "You fought in Whitemoon?"

Kylinn nodded. "I'm here visiting a friend, the head librarian at Whitesun University. She had an invitation to this opening and asked if I wanted to come along. I hoped I could speak with you."

"And here you are," Tal said gently. "What can I do for you, Kylinn?"

It took the scholar a few moments to find her words. "I've been watching the news…I mean, about the resettlement. When Whitemoon was mentioned as a possible site, it felt as if we were being invaded all over again. I couldn't believe anyone would consider it."

Tal handed her drink back, projecting understanding as their fingers brushed.

The Council had run into local resistance with every proposed settlement site for exactly that reason. No veterans could stomach the idea of Voloth soldiers living anywhere near them, and those who hadn't fought protested simply on principle. Having run out of options, the Council finally voted to set aside some land near Blacksun Base. It kept the Voloth away from Alsean populations and under the eye of the warriors, which satisfied popular opinion. It also kept them from any real opportunity of integration, which was not at all what Tal had hoped for. For now they seemed content, since they were occupied in building their own community from the ground up, but she wondered what would happen when that was done and they began to realize their isolation. Rax Sestak had remained their spokesperson and told Tal that isolation was exactly what most of them wanted, but she couldn't help thinking that this was a skin-sealer solution to a much deeper wound.

"When I heard they were going to be settled by Blacksun Base, I thought that was it," Kylinn said. "They were far away and I'd never have to see or think of them again. But then my counselor mentioned the new program—the one that sets up meetings between us and the Voloth we turned."

"It's had some good results," Tal said. "Though it's not yet running at full speed. The mental healers are being cautious and everyone is still learning what to expect. But overall, it has helped both sides."

"I don't know anyone who's done it. Actually, I hardly know any other veterans, except Rafalon. He was in my unit."

There would have been two others in her unit as well. The fact that Kylinn didn't mention them meant her unit had suffered a fifty percent fatality rate.

Tal's heart went out to this soft-spoken scholar who had seen too much. "You do know someone who has done it."

"That's why I wanted to see you. You were the very first one to face a soldier you turned. I'm not a warrior; I don't have the courage you—"

"Stop," Tal said. "Don't speak to me of not having courage. You volunteered to fight an enemy you'd never seen before. You fought the worst battle our people have ever lived through, and you did it with no training other than four days of frantic instruction. I honor your courage."

Kylinn leaned against the wall, her eyes tearing up. "Thank you," she whispered. "But I don't feel like that. I feel...afraid. Like I got away with something, but I know that somewhere, sometime, there has to be a reckoning."

"Like you committed a crime and should be punished?"

The tears slipped down Kylinn's cheeks. "You understand."

"I do. So do thousands of other veterans. Surely your counselor has told you you're not alone in this."

"Yes, he does that at practically every session. But that doesn't help when I go home and look at my bondmate and son. They're so...*innocent*, and so are all of the children at my school and most of the other instructors. I don't feel like I belong. And before you ask, yes, we have a veterans group and my counselor says I should join it. But I'm not interested in being part of a group where the only thing we have in common is the way we're all—"

She stopped abruptly, wiped her cheeks dry, and looked at Tal as if she had all the answers. "Should I do it? Did it help you?"

Tal wished she had refilled her drink after all. Stalling for time, she drained her glass and waited a few pipticks for the nearest catering staff to wander by. After setting the glass on his tray, she turned back to Kylinn, who by now had straightened and regained her outward control.

"Our situations aren't the same," Tal said carefully. "I didn't have to turn mine the way you did yours."

"But you still turned them. You still made them kill their own people."

"Yes. And Rax will probably never forgive me. But we did at least come to an understanding, I suppose. I understand better how he could do what he did, and he's realized that we had the right to fight back any way we could. And just having that bit of understanding does help." She smiled wryly. "Though I didn't think so at first. After I met him the first time I...slid back a bit. It took another meeting or two for it to really sink in."

"For what to sink in?"

"That neither one of us are monsters."

Kylinn put a hand over her mouth, and Tal silently touched her other wrist, projecting her sympathy.

"Oh, Fahla," Kylinn managed at last. "If I could have that..."

"I can't guarantee you'll feel the same way. But if you do...it would be worth it."

"Great Mother, yes. But—I never really thought they were monsters."

"Then you're already ahead of most of us. Are you sure you're not a templar?"

This time the fleeting smile actually touched her eyes. "No, I'm not a templar. It just seemed so obvious to me. We broke them with love. How can you do that to a monster? Monsters don't love."

Tal stared. In all of the many debates she had heard on the topic, no one had ever brought up such a simple—and obvious—piece of logic. Not even Lanaril. "I'm going to remember that," she said. "You're absolutely right."

"But it makes it that much harder. It wouldn't be so bad if I could tell myself that I only broke monsters."

"What you did...what *we* did had to be done. A good friend of mine once told me that sometimes it's not a question of right and wrong. It's a question of wrong and more wrong. There was only one way to save ourselves. It feels wrong because it *was* wrong, but there was no right way. And the alternative was to lose our whole world. You helped save us from that. I only wish the price weren't so high."

"Well." Kylinn drew herself up. "It can't be any worse, can it? So perhaps I should try to make it better and join the program."

"There have been a few meetings that didn't go well," Tal said. "Make your decision with all the facts. But I don't think your counselor would have mentioned it to you if he didn't believe you were a good candidate."

"He said I was. But I was so terrified by the mere suggestion that I hardly heard him."

"And yet you came here to talk to me about it." Tal smiled at her. "Sounds to me as if you're halfway to a decision already."

"I might have been halfway before I walked in here. Now it's about three-quarters." Kylinn looked past her. "I think I've had more of your time than most, and some very nicely dressed people are waiting to speak to you."

"They can wait if you have any other questions."

"You've answered the most important ones. Thank you, Lancer Tal. I really appreciate that you took the time to speak with me."

"You're welcome. I'm glad you found me." Tal held up her hand, and though the fear was still in Kylinn's touch, she thought it might be a little less strong.

The waiting group didn't take long to dispatch, and right behind them was Eroles.

"That looked like an intense conversation," Eroles said as she joined her. "With the woman in the blue dress."

"She's a veteran."

"Ah. Is she all right?"

"I hope she will be."

Eroles met her eyes. "Are you?"

Tal liked Eroles, and these last two days had shown that they could work well together. But they were never going to have this conversation.

"I am, thank you," she said. "And this has been the best grand opening I've ever attended."

Eroles nodded. "We're in agreement there. But I think we've put in our time as the obligatory dignitaries. If you're ready to call it a night, I am as well."

"Then let's call it."

CHAPTER 18
Return to Blacksun

"L*ancer* T*al,* we are now *on the Blacksun beacon.*"

Tal was startled by the voice on the com; she had been deep into a status report on manufacturing the space elevator seed cable.

"Thank you, Thornlan. I appreciate the smooth flight." She slipped her reader card into its case.

"She's a good addition to the unit, isn't she?"

Tal glanced at Micah, who gave every appearance of being asleep in his nearly horizontal seat.

He cocked one eye open and grinned. "Go ahead, you can say it."

"I have no idea why you're making such a point of this. I never said she wasn't qualified." After Continal's death in the Battle of Alsea, Tal had been subjected to more pilot tryouts than she could count. First Pilot Thornlan was Micah's final pick.

"You never said she was, either. And you nearly froze the poor woman when you boarded at the beginning of this trip." Micah opened his other eye, stretched luxuriously, and pushed the control to transform his bed back into a seat.

"You're exaggerating as usual. I was merely preoccupied, and since when do Guards require coddling and personal attention?"

"I think you were just a tiny bit disappointed that I didn't give the seat to Brinkove."

"I liked Brinkove. He had the top score on the flight challenge, and he didn't go stiff as a staff when I spoke to him. I found it rather refreshing."

"What you call refreshing, I call a lack of respect. And getting the top score doesn't mean he was the best. That boy needs a little time to season properly before I'll even consider putting your life in his hands. Thornlan was the better choice."

Tal rolled her eyes. Micah's overprotectiveness was endearing at times and more than a little frustrating at others. "Then by your own definition you treat me with an appalling lack of respect."

"I've more than earned it."

"So *you* say."

Micah chuckled as he stood. "I'm getting a snack. Do you want something?"

"Not for me, but let me ask Eroles." Tal stood as well, stretched the kinks out of her back, and walked over to the conference table. "Would you like something to eat before we land?"

Eroles looked up from the blueprints that were spread all over the table. "I'm not sure where I'd put it."

"Given that we're on approach to Blacksun, perhaps you should give up working and relax for a few ticks. Besides, I can't have my Prime Builder working herself into exhaustion."

She could practically feel Micah's eyes roll from across the cabin. It was true that she hadn't been setting much of an example lately, but was that her fault? She couldn't even get through a vacation without being interrupted by a crisis, and things hadn't slowed down since.

Eroles began rolling up her blueprints. "You're right. I've done what I can. And I love this part of the flight."

"So do I. Even if I didn't have to fly all over for work, I'd do it just for the joy of flying back into Blacksun Basin."

A few ticks later the three of them were settled into the cushy seats by the windows, watching the snow-covered mountains pass beneath them. The approach to Blacksun was one of the loveliest on the planet, though that was not why the Wandering King chose it for the site of his city. Alsean society had been violent and volatile then, and defensibility was the most important consideration in establishing a holding. Blacksun's location was perfect in that respect. It sat in an enormous bowl, surrounded on all sides by mountains with only a few narrow and easily defended passes. Any army that managed to get past the mountain defenses would then be exposed on the open valley floor before getting to Blacksun itself, allowing the city defenders plenty of time to cause damage with long-distance artillery. In the time before aerial transports, an invading army could not move heavy artillery through the mountains and was therefore unable to bombard the city from a safe distance. Blacksun had fought off many attempted invasions over the cycles; only one had succeeded. Every Alsean child learned of that battle in school, and Tal loved to imagine it when she flew over the site.

"There's the Fall of Tears," Micah said.

Tal nodded, absorbed in the view of the magnificent waterfall, plummeting nearly two thousand paces down a sheer cliff. "I'm so glad we're coming from this direction. Oh, look at the winden!"

"Blessed Fahla, I've never seen them before!" Eroles exclaimed.

The herd of winden dashed down the mountainside as the transport flew overhead, their six-toed feet clinging to every point of rock and giving them a stability and speed unmatched by any other large animal. Between their speed and their subtle coloration, winden weren't often seen except from the air, and Tal was as thrilled as Eroles at this rare glimpse. She watched them for as long as she could, and when they vanished from sight, she looked ahead just in time to see the last mountain peak float beneath them, opening up the view she loved so well.

The mountains tumbled down to the plains, which no longer housed a single city as in the old days. Blacksun Basin had been farmed for hundreds of generations, and a network of towns both small and large had sprung up in the vast bowl. Most of them clustered along the two rivers that carved through the valley.

Sunlight flashed off the bright thread of the Fahlinor River as their transport followed it north. This was the great river of Blacksun Basin, its enormous volume of water cutting a nearly straight line from the southeast corner of the valley to the northern exit, where it emptied into the largest bay on the continent. Over to the west, the smaller Silverrun River wound its way southeast, then turned northeast, picked up speed, and rushed to join the Fahlinor at Blacksun.

From this side of the transport, they were unable to see the Silverrun as it approached. Tal craned her head, waiting, and smiled when she caught her first glimpse. This was a sight she never tired of: the two rivers coming together, swelling into an unstoppable power that roared to the sea. And right at their junction, in a perfect location for defensibility, transportation of goods, and irrigation of precious crops, was the most magnificent city of them all.

It was possible that she was biased—this was her home, after all. She had grown up here and knew every corner of it. But she had also been all over Alsea, both as a young warrior following a career path and later as Lancer. Whitesun was a vast and bustling port, Redmoon had much to boast of, and Whitemoon was undoubtedly their most beautiful city. But Blacksun was the jewel in the crown.

They flew over the outermost buildings, their bright white domes standing out against the lush green surroundings, and began following one of the main boulevards into the city. Their altitude was low enough now that Tal could see the hive of activity in the streets. Pedestrians jostled for space with rollers, while an occasional privately owned skimmer darted past the larger, slower delivery vehicles. A string of dark cylinders whizzed through the transparent tube which seemed to float above the boulevard, carrying its passengers at a ground speed matching that of Tal's transport. As she watched, the magtran slowed on approach to a station. Its rearmost cylinder popped off, gliding smoothly into a branching tube that led to the station, while a second cylinder left the station in another access tube and accelerated to match the magtran's speed. Merging into the main tube, it quickly latched on to the magtran's front end, the entire exchange having taken perhaps seven pipticks. The magtran resumed speed, gradually outpacing the transport as Thornlan slowed their approach. They were nearing the State Park.

Every population center on the planet, from the great cities down to the smallest village, was built on the same plan: a wheel-and-spoke design with the spokes converging on a central park. No matter how small the village, its park always housed a temple and sometimes a caste house or two.

Blacksun's State Park was unrivaled. Situated on the west bank of the Fahlinor River, it was a village-sized sweep of forest, manicured lawns, and landscaping so glorious that producers the world over made pilgrimages to Blacksun just to see the park.

All six caste houses ringed the park, each capped with the color of its caste flag. For the warriors, it was crimson red. The scholar house had a dark blue cap; for the builders it was sky blue. The merchant house bore a purple cap, the producers a dark green one, and the crafters, who always had to be different, decorated their flag and caste house with a distinctive three-striped pattern of blue, gold, and green. According to legend, the original crafters choosing their design were unable to agree on just one color. Based on the crafters she knew, Tal believed it.

Near the center of the park stood Blacksun Temple, a spectacular, soaring edifice, dwarfing every building in the city but one. Like all temples, it was black due to the unique rock used in its construction—and disallowed for any other Alsean buildings. The rock naturally glowed with a soft blue-white light at night, and with the aid of any light from Alsea's two moons, its glow became a beacon visible for many lengths. Full moons were, of course, the best of all. In times past, the temples were used as navigation aids; today this characteristic was simply appreciated for its beauty. And while Tal was not ordinarily one to visit a temple—she preferred to make her connection with Fahla outdoors—she still loved to see the building glowing on a full moon night.

Sharing the center with the temple, but still half a length away, was the State House of Alsea. The largest building in Blacksun, its great main dome reached fifteen stories high, while four smaller domes surrounded it. Each was encircled with two bands of color, one crimson and one a deep blue, representing the two castes capable of producing a Lancer. When Tal was a child, her father took her there for a tour, pointing out the color bands and telling her that she bore both of those castes in her heart. He had her future planned from the very beginning. Now she watched the sunlight flash off a familiar set of windows at the top and thought that her father would have enjoyed her personal quarters more than she did. The view from those windows was second to none, but she had to wade through far too many people to get there, and every one of them wanted something.

As they flew over the wall encircling the State House grounds, the view out the window shifted down, up, and down again before leveling out—Thornlan had just performed the wing salute signifying that the Lancer had returned to Blacksun. A tick later they were hovering above the landing pad, and a slight jar beneath Tal's feet told her that the ground thrusters were firing. Slowly, the transport sank downward and settled on the pad with hardly a vibration. An experienced pilot herself, Tal knew that the skill required in landing such a large transport so quietly was impressive indeed. Unfortunately, her smile of appreciation was witnessed by the worst possible audience.

"Told you," Micah said.

Eroles looked over. "Am I missing something?"

"Colonel Micah was just commenting on our new pilot," Tal said.

"Ah. Thornlan, wasn't it? Very smooth, I have to say. Give her my compliments." Micah's smugness was almost audible.

Once Eroles had disembarked, they lifted off and flew another twenty ticks to Blacksun Base. The long-distance transport was housed there due to its size, and Tal planned to spend a few days catching up on caste duties.

Thornlan's second landing was just as smooth as the first. As Tal rose and shouldered her bag, Micah asked, "Are you going to pass on those compliments?"

She bumped him with her hip. "Out of my way. I have a hot shower calling my name, and you're keeping me from it."

Micah chuckled, picking up his own bag and walking ahead of her toward the cabin door. Instead of following him, she turned right, walked the few steps down the short corridor, and poked her head into the pilot's cabin. Genra Thornlan sat in the pilot's seat, checking a reader card in her hand.

"First Pilot Thornlan," said Tal sternly.

"Lancer Tal!" Thornlan leaped out of her chair, a maneuver cut short by the safety harness she hadn't yet unhooked. She quickly unlatched it and stood up, looking straight ahead while a deep blush suffused her face.

"Settle." Tal smiled as the younger woman eased her posture by the tiniest hair. Yes, Micah was proud of this one. She rested a hand on Thornlan's shoulder, startling her into meeting her eyes.

"That was an excellent landing. You're a good addition to the unit," she said, and felt an enormous swell of surprise and pride which the pilot was incapable of fronting.

"Thank you, Lancer." Thornlan couldn't maintain her gaze, shifting back into the rigid stance that had been trained into her from the moment she had chosen her caste.

Tal squeezed her shoulder once before letting go. "No need to thank me for stating the truth." She turned and saw Micah's grinning face in the doorway. With a steely glare, she pushed him in front of her and whispered, "Shut up."

Micah laughed as they stepped through the door into the sunshine. Wisely, he said nothing more.

CHAPTER 19

Investigation

Two days after the grand opening in Whitesun, the High Council came together for its regular meeting. They spent nearly two hanticks working through the agenda, and Tal was more than ready to call it a day when she opened the floor to the other members.

"Is there any other issue that we need to consider?" she asked, as she did every moon.

"Yes, there is," said Prime Scholar Yaserka. "Over the past moon I've been investigating an extremely serious issue, and I'm now convinced that it requires the full support of the High Council."

"You've been investigating?" Prime Warrior Shantu asked. "Why wouldn't you involve the warriors in something like that?"

"Not that kind of investigation. Perhaps I should have said 'gathering information.' About the shattered Voloth." He shot a triumphant glance at Tal, who schooled her expression into one of polite interest.

"What about them?" she asked.

As it turned out, Yaserka surpassed her expectations. He had actually gone to Blacksun Base, where one of the barracks had been converted into a holding facility for sedated Voloth prisoners. There he spoke with a number of healer assistants, who were first shocked and then relieved to the point of tears to know that someone at his level was aware of their situation. More than that, he lowered his blocks and subjected himself to the broadcast horrors that were traumatizing the healers. Tal's respect for him climbed several notches as he described his experience.

"This cannot be allowed to continue," he finished. "I know that some of us think this is an impossibly thorny moral issue, but my personal experience proves that it is not. There *is* a right answer."

"Great Fahla." Prime Producer Arabisar's horror was as clear on her face as it was in her emotions. "You think we should kill them."

"Oh, no," said Bylwytin, the Prime Crafter. "I can't support that. You can't ask us to play Fahla. We already broke her covenant and look where that got us: traumatized high empaths and hundreds of prisoners so shattered that even you can't handle their emotions."

Voices rose as the High Council members talked over each other, apparently believing that the louder their opinions were expressed, the more correct they had to be. Tal let it go on for several ticks before calling the meeting to order. When they had settled down, she looked at Yaserka. "I admit that when this situation first came to my attention, I discounted its seriousness. But your investigation puts it in a different light."

He nodded, a pleased smile crossing his face, and she glanced around the table. "It seems to me that we cannot make a decision when we don't all hold the same information. Rather than debating it here on the fourteenth floor of the State House, I propose that we follow our Prime Scholar's example. The High Council should visit Blacksun Base and see—no, *feel* the situation for ourselves."

In the furor that her suggestion inspired, she caught Yaserka's eye and found him offering her a genuine smile of respect. She smiled back, enjoying the moment. Her strategy had paid off, Lanaril was getting exactly what she wanted, and Yaserka might even be an ally.

At least for the moment.

CHAPTER 20
Whitemoon raid

First Pilot Thornlan's skills were put to frequent use over the next two moons as Tal ranged all over Alsea, dealing with various matters that hadn't received enough attention while she had been tied up with Gaian, Voloth, and technology-related crises. One of those matters came to Tal's attention through the new Anti-Corruption Task Force, which had created a network of merchant informers and a unit of warriors who investigated and responded to the merchants' tips.

In the short time since Tal had ordered Prime Merchant Parser to deal with the corruption in his caste, the task force had already shut down several merchants operating illegally and had even uncovered a ring of smugglers based in Port Calerna. But it wasn't until a second smuggling ring was found in Whitemoon that Tal became personally involved.

Besides being one of the biggest ports in Pallea, Whitemoon was home to the Sensoral Institute, Alsea's premier training facility for gifted empaths. A well-organized smuggling ring and a population of young, partially trained high empaths were a bad combination: the Institute had become a fertile recruiting ground. The smugglers somehow procured the names of students who had been reprimanded for behavioral violations and were actively targeting them for induction into the ring. For young students confident in their abilities and chafing at the discipline imposed by the Institute, a promise of freedom from that discipline—along with easy income—was too tempting.

But they were breaking Fahla's covenant.

The Battle of Alsea had been a one-time exemption. Empathic violation was a level-five state crime carrying a harsh mandatory sentence. Once an Alsean crossed the line into illegal emotional probes and behavioral manipulation, the only means of ensuring that society would be safe from such predation was by isolating the criminal from all potential contact.

The High Security Detention Facility had been built for this reason. It was the worst place on Alsea, a wholly underground prison, and a terrible fate for young high empaths who had simply been too greedy, too arrogant, or too stupid. But time and experience had proven that aboveground facilities were insecure, allowing prisoners to make contact with susceptible Alseans. Now empathic violators were literally buried. The idea of such a fate was so abhorrent that no one called the High Security Detention Facility by its full name. They called it the Pit.

The smugglers might have operated indefinitely had they kept to their illegal port activities and left the students alone, but targeting the cream of Alsean empaths brought them to the attention of the task force. When Tal read the report, it took her half a hantick to calm herself. She insisted on being there when the smugglers were shut down.

Once the investigative work had been completed and a raid planned, Tal flew to Whitemoon to take part. Of course, Micah insisted that she go in disguise. She had to laugh when he handed her the colorizer eyedrops and spray.

It was a short and effective operation, made possible by an anonymous tip that the group would be gathered in a waterfront warehouse for a midmeal meeting that day. Half of the task force warriors covered the exits, while Tal and the other half entered the warehouse from three different directions. Tal was delighted when one of the smugglers targeted her as the easiest person to run over on his way out the door—she did so love it when people underestimated her because of her height. She waited until he was nearly on top of her and then used his own speed and size to launch him straight into the wall behind her. He bounced off in a rage, but when she broke his nose, he crumpled. She was sorry he folded so easily.

But her righteous anger evaporated when she realized just what they had rounded up. Yes, they had wiped out the ring, apprehending six of the high-level smugglers as well a number of low-level workers. But they had also captured five Institute students—and two Battle of Alsea veterans.

She watched as the high empaths were led to the detention transport, so terrified that none of them could keep up their fronts. They seemed unable to believe this had happened to them; the students because they were young and thought themselves invincible, and the veterans because their battle experience had given them an inflated belief in their power.

On the transport home, Micah sat in the opposite seat and looked at her in sympathy. "Your front does you no good today. Your feelings are written on your face."

"We just sent five young people to the Pit. And the veterans…" Tal sighed. "They fought for Alsea, and now they'll be put underground."

"They earned their incarceration."

"The students are hardly past their Rite of Ascension. How can anyone earn a lifetime sentence when they're barely done with childhood stupidities?"

"Why would you think they'll get a lifetime sentence? Their empathic offenses were relatively light."

"Because they were stupid enough to commit those offenses after I broke Fahla's covenant. And would the older two have done this if they hadn't fought in the battle? If they hadn't learned firsthand just how easy it is to manipulate those who are weaker?"

"Ah," he said, the realization coloring his emotions. "You're right. The court will make an example out of them."

"They'll have to. And the media will cover every piptick of it."

"You could petition for leniency," he said carefully.

"Certainly, and give the war criminal fringe a gigantic platform while I'm at it. That might be all it would take to push the fringe into the mainstream. Do you want to see Shantu or Yaserka in the State Chair?"

He propped his chin on his fist, looking out the window. "What a mess."

"True words. They dug their own way into the Pit, and I can't help them out of it. So I'm trying to remind myself that my focus shouldn't be on them. I have an obligation to all of the less gifted Alseans who have no protection from them. It had to be done. It was the right thing. And I hate it."

"If doing the right thing was always fun, there'd be no need for our caste. Alsea will always need us to protect those who cannot protect themselves."

Tal thought about that while watching the coastline of Pallea pass beneath them. "Father said that a Lancer was not the greatest warrior in the land, but rather the greatest protector."

"Your father was a wise man and a good friend."

"At times like this I really wish he were here."

"He is." Micah touched her shoulder. "He lives in your heart, along with your mother. You know that."

She covered his hand with her own. "I know. Sometimes it's just not enough."

He squeezed her shoulder, and she opened her senses to the reassuring warmth of his friendship. The familiar, almost physical comfort was a sensation she had known from her earliest memories. Micah had always been there. He and her father had been the best of friends, and now he watched over her with more love and loyalty than she could possibly have earned. Sometimes she wondered if her father had extracted a promise from Micah to look after her, but she never asked. The answer would change nothing, but the asking would. It was enough that he was there.

CHAPTER 21
Clearing the way

When the coded message appeared on his reader card, Spinner excused himself from the meeting and went into the corridor to read it. He input the decryption key and watched the letters resolve themselves into the news he was waiting for.

Whitemoon is yours. The task force rounded up every person except Hallwell. He's already back in place and ready. You can send in your own people now.

Best part: Lancer Tal showed up personally.

He laughed out loud. Of course she did. When she had left Blacksun that morning, he was fairly certain he knew where she was going. She couldn't resist where high empaths were involved.

Someday, when he could tell her exactly how this game had been played, he would enjoy seeing the look on her face when she realized what she had done: removed his competition and left the field open for him.

The funding from Whitemoon's black market would enable him to set a few more tiles in place. The end game was a little closer today than it had been yesterday. And somewhere, sometime soon, Lancer Tal would make a mistake and give him the last tiles he needed.

This was the best part of the game, he thought—the part that Challenger would never understand nor appreciate. The end game was important, yes, but the game itself was half the joy of it.

And Lancer Tal didn't even know she was playing.

CHAPTER 22
Debate

"...AND WITH US TODAY WE have Lanaril Satran, Blacksun's Lead Templar, and the Lead Templar of Whitesun, Khasar Circassinor." The host of the government broadcast station turned to Lanaril and Khasar, sitting on opposite sides of the table. "Lead Templar Circassinor, as the leading voice of the opposition, what are your thoughts regarding the High Council's decision today?"

Khasar crossed his hands on the table and leaned forward. "First of all, I think we're framing this discussion badly. It is *not* euthanasia. It's murder, plain and simple. Premeditated, state-sanctioned murder. And that is not something I ever envisioned my people taking part in."

"Did you ever envision your people fighting off an alien invasion?" Lanaril asked mildly.

Khasar shot her an exasperated look. "That is beside the point."

"I think it's very much the point. We are in deep waters we've never navigated before. There are no precedents. We can't rely on past law or texts. We can only rely on what our hearts tell us is right. My heart tells me we cannot let the Voloth suffer, nor can we ask our healers to suffer with them."

"You have a good heart, Lanaril, but I don't believe we should be murdering two hundred and forty-four sentient beings based on what it says. In the interest of ending one form of suffering, you would introduce another—and one that goes against Fahla's teachings."

First-name usage in a public debate? He was going for the kindly minister approach.

"I can't think which teachings you're referring to," she said. "Fahla never addressed the situation we're facing."

"Well, we could start with the principle that life is sacred—"

"*Quality* of life is sacred. The Book of Stewardship tells us that if we come upon an injured animal and that animal is too badly hurt to be saved, it is better to end its life than to let it suffer."

"The Book of Stewardship is a set of instructions for producers! It's about animal husbandry, not the souls of sentients."

"It is about *life*. Who are we to say we accept responsibility for this kind of life but not for that one? Fahla gave us the responsibility to care for Alsea and all the life upon it. In that sense, we are all stewards."

"We should not be arguing semantics over the issue of murder when there are other alternatives we haven't explored."

"What alternatives are those?" asked the host.

"The Protectorate is at the top of the list," Khasar said. "Why are we even being held responsible for these prisoners? They brought the Voloth to us; they should take them off our hands."

Lanaril stifled a sigh. This debate had been raging amongst the templars for almost nine moons; she had already heard everything Khasar was going to say. The difference today was that they were revisiting these arguments in front of a worldwide audience—and the High Council had voted in favor of euthanasia. Now it had become a matter for the full Council to decide, and suddenly the stakes were far higher than a discussion of moral philosophy.

"I agree with you," she said. "And our government has asked for exactly that. But the answer has consistently been no. Ambassador Solvassen reiterated that just today: the Protectorate will not take our prisoners. To continue stomping our feet and whining 'but you should' is not only counterproductive but also makes us look like a junior partner in this treaty. We need to accept that answer, as unsatisfying as it is, and move on from there."

"Ambassador Solvassen did convey the Protectorate's regrets," the host interjected.

"Well, that makes it better." Khasar gave a practiced snort of disgust.

Lanaril privately agreed with that, too, but she wasn't about to do so on a live broadcast. "Regardless, we are faced with a situation that must be remedied somehow. Our healers are suffering, and the Voloth are suffering. We cannot allow this to continue."

"The healers needn't suffer," Khasar said. "The technical expertise required to maintain sedation is not significant. We could train low empaths to be caretakers. For that matter, why not train the Voloth themselves? The ones we are allowing to stay here? Let them contribute to their new society by dealing with this problem they brought with them."

"In both situations, more highly trained healers would still need to be on site, managing the caretakers. We cannot train unskilled people in one medical task and then leave them to it and hope nothing goes wrong. Though your strategy would reduce the numbers of healers being affected, it would not remove them altogether."

"The few necessary healers could be high empaths. They're capable of blocking the Voloth broadcasts."

"Then we are asking extensively trained high empath healers to waste their talents on a low-skill job that has no possibility of advancement and no end. We already have a shortage of those healers. I don't believe it serves Alsea to direct any of them to this duty. And," she continued when he would have interrupted, "none of those solutions solve the other half of the issue. The Voloth are suffering."

"That is a matter of subjective interpretation," he said.

"I know it makes you feel better to think so. But it is not at all. Ask any healer currently serving—"

"I've spoken with the manager of the Whitemoon clinic—"

"Who is a high empath!"

"But that does not—"

"Excuse me," the host said, raising his hands.

They stopped arguing and faced him.

"Thank you," he said. "I have another guest who may be able to illuminate this side of the discussion. May I introduce Rax Sestak, spokesperson for New Haven, the Voloth community near Blacksun Base."

A chill ran down Lanaril's spine as Rax walked out from the side of the broadcast set, three hovering vidcams recording his movements from all angles. As he leaned over the table to offer palm touches, the vidcams joined the others already airing the debate.

"Lead Templar Satran," he said as their hands touched. "Well met."

"Well met, Rax." At least her voice didn't reflect her disquiet, and fortunately, he couldn't sense it. "This is…unexpected."

"It turns out that being a spokesperson isn't a job you get to quit," he said wryly.

Khasar's shock was written all over his face when Rax turned to him. He had never seen a walking, talking Voloth in person until this moment, and Lanaril suspected their host was quite enjoying the moment he had engineered. Certainly this would be all over the news tomorrow.

When greetings had been exchanged and Rax was seated, the host wasted no time getting to the big question.

"As you may have heard before coming on, there is some debate as to whether your compatriots are suffering even though they're sedated. Rax, what is your opinion?"

"I believe they're suffering," Rax said. "Look, we're all soldiers. We always knew we could end up dead or disabled. But this…" He hesitated. "I saw some of them, you know. That day. We were all being brought to the same place before getting sorted out, and I saw people I knew, but they weren't who I knew anymore. None of them recognized us. They didn't even know where they were. They were just…in torment."

"Which is why we sedated them," Khasar said. "They're no longer aware of the memories. They just sleep."

Rax met his eyes. "Ever had nightmares?"

Khasar was visibly taken aback. "I do not think this is the same thing. Their level of sleep is too deep—"

"Dokshin," Rax said, and Lanaril nearly cracked a highly inappropriate smile. "If their level of sleep is as deep as you say, they wouldn't be putting out such horrible emotions that your healers can't handle it. They would just be...blank. Wouldn't they?"

"Yes, they would," Lanaril said. "That was what we believed would happen. But we've never dealt with this precise medical situation before, and the actual results did not match the healers' expectations."

The host cut in. "If your compatriots are indeed in torment, what do you think they would want for themselves? If they were here to speak, what would they say?"

"They'd say 'let us go.'" Rax spoke without hesitation. "They'd say 'put us out of this misery.' You sedated them as an act of mercy, but that was before you knew it wasn't. Now that you know, you can't just keep them there. Or at least, we don't think you should."

"We?" the host repeated. "Are you speaking in your official role?"

Rax nodded. "We voted. The majority of us believe that your mercy, as well-intentioned as it was, is really torture."

"What would your compatriots say if there was a chance they could recover?" Khasar asked.

Rax went still. "Is there? Nobody mentioned that."

"Because it's highly unlikely," Lanaril began, but Khasar spoke over her.

"Our medicine is more advanced than yours. And now we have a treaty with the Protectorate, which means we have access to any advances they make. Who knows what will happen one, two, three cycles from now? Fahla gives us life, and only Fahla can decide when that life is over. She has decided that your compatriots have not yet finished their journeys. How would you feel if we murdered them all now, and two cycles from now we learn how we could have saved them?"

"But is that a real possibility?" Rax asked. His tentative hope was so bright and clear that Lanaril winced.

"Yes," said Khasar.

"No," said Lanaril at the same time.

Rax looked back and forth between them. "Which of you are we supposed to believe?"

"It is an extremely remote possibility—"

"But it *is* a possibility!" Khasar interrupted. "Who are we to play the role of the Goddess when we do not have her knowledge?"

This was always the sticking point. Lanaril had lost count of the number of times a templar discussion on the topic ended right here, because there was no definitive answer and each camp was firmly entrenched.

When she received the invitation to take part in this broadcast, she had thought long and hard about how she could change that dynamic and had come up with something she thought might be powerful enough. But she hadn't known she would be doing it in front of Rax.

She reached into the satchel sitting on the floor by her feet and took out a large, overripe panfruit. "Rax, I apologize in advance for what you're about to see. But you have asked the same question many, many Alseans have asked. You want to know if it's a real possibility that your fellow soldiers might be healed. It is not. Those who say it is are speaking in terms of faith, not in terms of medical science."

"Faith is all we—"

"If I might finish," Lanaril said firmly.

Khasar subsided, a suspicious look on his face as he glanced from her to the panfruit.

"Thank you." She set the panfruit in the middle of the table. "The medical facts are these: The Voloth have had their entire neural capacity burned out. They are no longer capable of coherent thought. They cannot function at even the most basic level, and they are irretrievably broken. Everything that made them who they were is gone. Forever."

She reached into the satchel again, stood up, and smashed a heavy mallet onto the panfruit.

It exploded, splattering bright red pulp and seeds in all directions. Half the table was covered, and a few seeds stuck to her jacket. In her peripheral vision she saw two of the vidcams zoom directly overhead to get a top-down image of the red, glistening mess.

"That is what has happened to the Voloth," she said. "Now tell me, Khasar: Do you believe that in one, two, or three cycles, we will be able to put that panfruit back the way it was?"

CHAPTER 23
Mercy

Talinn opened the sealed package and looked inside at the five identical skinsprays. The four other healers on his team crowded around.

"I expected them to look different," said one.

"Me too," Talinn said. "Like…solid black, maybe."

"Or red."

After several pipticks of uncomfortable silence, Talinn reached in and selected one at random. "Come on, choose. It's time."

One by one, each of them chose a skinspray.

"I'm required to explain the process once more before we begin," Talinn said. "One of these holds the fatal dose. The others are biologically neutral. Each of us will inject the patient, with no more than ten pipticks between injections. The sedative won't take effect for three to four ticks, so there's no way of knowing which of us gave the fatal dose. We have sixty-three patients but only three injection teams. That means each of us will be giving twenty-one injections."

"Yes, I noticed how many declined," one healer said bitterly. "We were only supposed to be injecting a maximum of ten."

"I know. We expected more volunteers. But I don't blame the conscientious objectors, and I hope you won't either. This is a very difficult duty."

They murmured their fervent agreement.

"The hope was that we could reasonably say you might not give a fatal dose. Statistically, there is still a chance, but…it's not a good one. This is your final opportunity to withdraw. If you don't believe you can live with this, tell me now."

He looked each of them in the eye. All four stood straight and silent, skinsprays in their hands.

"All right. Then I just want to say…" He hesitated, then continued, "I'm proud to be part of this team. We're doing the right thing. Some people won't see it that way, but none of those people have felt what we've felt."

"Words for Fahla," muttered one.

"Let's just get started," another said. "I've been wanting this and dreading it for what feels like five cycles already. I need it to be over."

Talinn turned and led his team out into the corridor. As they neared the barracks, the horror reached out for him, just as it had every day.

He had never thought much about his mid empath rating before this job. He was on the high end of the midrange and that was fine; he didn't pine for more. What he had was what Fahla gave him.

But he didn't think Fahla meant for them to deal with what lay behind those doors. If she had, she would have made them all high empaths, with blocks strong enough to wall off their minds completely.

The horror grew blacker and thicker, and when he opened the door, his stomach rebelled at the stench of fear. In ten moons he had never gotten used to it. By his third moon here he was getting sick even before leaving his house for work, the mere thought of walking into that room enough to make him nauseous. That he had survived for seven more moons of it was something of a miracle. Today's nausea had been the worst of all, and the thought that this would be his last day was all that kept him going.

Curtained cubicles stretched the length of the barracks, housing beds on both sides of the central aisle. The first cubicle was open, and a healer stood at the head of the bed. She looked pale when they came through the door.

"Right on time," she said in a misplaced attempt to sound cheerful.

Talinn had no patience for that. "Do you have the monitor set?"

"Yes. The patient is ready."

He looked down at the Voloth, whose smooth, slack facial features belied the activity of his subconscious. Like all of the insane Voloth, this man's mind had been shattered by a blast of pure terror, and terror was all that remained. It leaked out even under sedation, because as long as there was any brain activity at all, there was terror.

The only cure was in his hand. Without any fanfare, he lifted his skinspray, rested it against the patient's wrist, and pressed the button. The medication hissed into the Voloth's bloodstream.

He stepped back and motioned his team forward. One took his place while another went to the opposite side of the bed and injected the Voloth's other wrist. Bare pipticks later, the last two healers had injected their skinsprays. All six of them stood back and watched the status displays.

They wouldn't do this for each of the Voloth. There wasn't time to stand and watch every one of them die, not when they had so many to get through. Or rather, there *was* time, but none of them could tolerate it. It was one thing to deliver what might be the fatal dose, and something else to watch it take effect twenty-one times.

But this first one—this they had to see through to the end.

The displays didn't change, their blue and red graphs showing normal readouts for what seemed like half a hantick. When the heartbeat finally dropped by a single digit, his own heart nearly stopped. He glanced at the other readouts, seeing similar minuscule drops in all of them.

It was very slow at first, hardly even noticeable and certainly not obvious without the readouts. But after the agonizingly gradual start, the overdose seemed to slam into the patient's systems. The heartbeat dropped so rapidly that the numbers were scrolling, and the vertical graphs looked as if someone had unplugged them, draining all the color out.

Less than two ticks later, all readouts had zeroed. Their patient was dead.

Talinn looked at the Voloth's face again. It appeared exactly the same as before. But the horror was gone. It still filled the air all around them, accompanied by that awful stench, but the leakage from this Voloth had ended at last.

He frowned when the Voloth's face shifted, not understanding how it could be moving after death. Then he realized that it was his own vision creating the illusion. As the tears dropped down his cheeks, he dashed them away with his free hand and glanced at his team to see if they had noticed.

Every one of them was weeping.

And they had twenty more to go.

CHAPTER 24
The Voloth solution

Upon hearing that the full Council had voted in favor of euthanasia, Lanaril poured herself a celebratory glass of spirits and lifted it in the direction of the State House. Its main dome loomed over the trees, and she focused on its top floor as she called upon Fahla to bless the Lancer and keep her in office for a very long time.

In the past, there had been many a time when she had scowled at that view and wished she could visit a few old-fashioned plagues on its inhabitant. Lancer Tordax had been an arrogant ass and an embarrassment to the scholar caste. When his seat was won by the relatively young warrior she had voted against, she was sure they were in for more of the same.

But Lancer Tal had surprised her. While Lanaril didn't agree with all of her decisions, she supported more of them than she would have expected. As the cycles passed, she even found herself supporting some she had initially opposed, once the long-term consequences manifested themselves. She came to realize that their new Lancer played a long game, foregoing the quick, easy positions in favor of the harder, less popular ones that looked toward the future.

And then one day the Lancer appeared in her study, looking for assurances while she made one of the hardest decisions of all. From there they had begun a friendship, which Lanaril had come close to exploding in one ill-advised moment.

She should have known that Andira would play the long game in this as well. The debate had been intense, but with the Prime Scholar spearheading the yes vote, supported by the Lancer and the Lead Templars of Blacksun and Redmoon, opinions had begun to shift. Lanaril's visceral demonstration on the broadcast debate had been replayed over and over again, along with the now-famous quote from Rax Sestak: *They'd say "let us go." They'd say "put us out of this misery."*

The Council vote was decisive, with a two-thirds majority voting yes.

When Andira made the official announcement, she had Rax at her side. He thanked the Council and the people of Alsea for showing true mercy.

Three days later, the shattered Voloth were finally being released from their suffering. Every news channel had wall-to-wall coverage of the event, most with a readout on the screen counting the number of Voloth reported dead. Lanaril spent the morning and afternoon in her temple, helping those who sought guidance or reassurance on this terrible day and praying when she had a moment to herself. Now and again she would slip into her study for a breather and to check the ongoing count.

It was almost evenmeal when the readout reached its final count of two hundred and forty-four.

Lanaril turned off her vidcom and called her aide. "It's time," she told him.

She was pouring her first drink when the great bell of her temple rang out a single, sonorous note. One tick later, it tolled again.

It would take nearly two and a half hanticks for the bell to toll once for every Voloth death. She had consoled and prayed all she was going to; now she just wanted to be alone in her study. Perhaps she could drink enough to forget the part she had played in this event. Releasing the Voloth was the right thing to do; she had never questioned that once her decision was made. But it was done and there was no going back. She had helped—no, she had actively strategized and fought—to kill two hundred and forty-four living beings.

The knock on her door startled her as she was picking up her glass, and she swore softly when a few drops spilled. "Just a moment," she called, wiping up the liquid.

A second knock sounded before she could reach the door, and she opened it impatiently. "What is your—oh."

Andira held up a bottle. "Have you started drinking yet?"

"Only just." She stepped aside and watched her walk in, tension in every line of her body.

"Oh, no. Not that," Andira said, setting her bottle next to Lanaril's. "That's much too light. We'd have to drink at least a bottle each to stop feeling. I've brought something much more efficient."

Indeed she had. "I don't normally drink grain spirits."

"This is not a normal day." Andira fetched new glasses from the sideboard, uncapped the bottle, and poured their drinks. Handing one to Lanaril, she held up the other in a salute and then tipped its entire contents down her throat.

Lanaril watched in amazement. "I can't do that."

"Yes, you can. Go on, the first is the hardest. It will get easier after that."

She had never seen her friend in a mood like this. Hesitantly, she lifted the glass and took a sniff. "Great Mother! Did you get this from the small-engine repair shop? I think they use it as a degreaser."

Andira chuckled, the tension in her body easing slightly. "That probably would have been quite a bit cheaper. Come on, Lanaril. I brought you the expensive stuff. The least you can do is try it."

Taking a breath, Lanaril drank off half the contents of the glass, which was as much as she could force down before her lips closed of their own accord. She swallowed hard and gasped for air. "Holy shekking—"

"Ah, it seems to be working."

"Whew! I can feel it all the way down to my stomach." Lanaril licked her lips and examined her glass. "And now it's up in my nose. This is potent."

"That's the point." Andira was already topping off the glass. She refilled her own, set the bottle on the side table, and flopped into the armchair next to it.

Lanaril took the other chair. "Are you all right?"

"Are you? We just killed two hundred and forty-four Voloth in their beds. Your bell is tolling for them right now. Should we be all right?"

Lanaril sipped her drink, which didn't taste quite so harsh now. "I thought it might be easier for you," she said. "You never gave any indication that you had a moral issue with this."

"You mean you thought it might be easier for me because I'm a warrior."

Lanaril reached for her hand. The emotions that came through their touch were stronger than she would have guessed, and she sucked in a breath. "I'm sorry. I should know you well enough by now to know better."

Andira squeezed her hand once and let go. "I'm trying to tell myself that this is just an extension of the battle. The logical end. They either died back then, or they died today, but either way they had to die."

"And I'm trying to tell myself that this was an act of mercy," Lanaril said. "Which it was, but there isn't anything in my training or a single one of my interpretive texts that applies to it. And I looked, believe me. I wanted to find some precedent to guide me or at least help me feel better about it, but it doesn't exist. So I'm left with knowing it's right, yet being unable to point to any trusted source to explain *how* I know it's right."

"I know what you mean. I stopped looking at the Truth and the Path for precedents while I was on vacation. That's when I realized that Alsea has outgrown its past. We can't keep looking backward for guidance. We have to look forward and inward instead."

"Exactly. But it's hard to convince other templars in a moral debate when my main source is…me."

"Perhaps you should write the next text, then."

"Well, someone has to do it, yes?"

They shared a chuckle before Lanaril continued, "I just wish my inner voice was a little louder right now. It was perfectly confident while you and I were strategizing. It was confident when I smashed that panfruit on a global broadcast, and it's been confident while I waited for the Council to decide. But now…"

She trailed off, and in the silence, the next toll of the bell sounded twice as loud.

"I don't know how many Voloth I killed in the battle. I didn't keep track. It was a lot, but it certainly wasn't two hundred and forty-four." Andira tossed down half her drink and didn't seem to notice. "One of them I shot at point-blank range after I empathically forced her out of her ground pounder. She was climbing down the leg and I shot her without a second thought. Then I ran past her almost before her body hit the ground."

Lanaril watched her silently and wondered if she had ever spoken of this before now.

"When I climbed inside that ground pounder and saw the results of our projection—you don't want to know what it looked like. Gehrain came up behind me and said…" She paused, a wry smile crossing her face. "He said we overdid it. And just for a moment, it was funny, because Fahla, we really did. There were brains—" She looked up in sudden realization. "Sorry."

"It's all right. I've heard quite a few stories about what our people saw."

"I guess you have."

"But I haven't heard yours."

Andira's expression said it all. She heard the encouragement to unburden herself, and part of her wanted to reject it. The other part, the part that was finally stronger tonight, couldn't stop speaking.

"If I hadn't been so focused on battle strategy, I would have laughed. I'd have stood there with blood running past my boots and laughed, because I'd spent so much time worrying about how we could beat this invincible foe and it was so *easy*. All we had to do was break the bond that holds us to civilization."

"Temporarily," Lanaril said.

"Yes, but it's not something you can ever put back again, is it? Not entirely. None of us who did that will ever forget it."

"I would worry if you *could* forget it."

"Hm." Andira tilted her head as the bell tolled again. "Hard to forget any of it tonight."

Lanaril made a noise of agreement and sipped her drink.

"The problem is that we're remembering in different ways," Andira said. "I remember and want to do everything I can to make sure this never happens to us again. Most of the scholars remember and wish they didn't have to. And a few have made sure they never remember again."

"May Fahla grant them what they seek," Lanaril murmured. They hadn't had many suicides, but every one of them broke her heart.

"The veterans who joined those Whitemoon smugglers remembered and decided that mental manipulation was far too easy to give up. They'd been in trouble before, but it was all minor until now. They broke the covenant because we asked them to, and then they couldn't find the boundary again."

Lanaril sighed. "There were bound to be some. A battle doesn't end with the defeat of the enemy."

"You know it's only a matter of time before we end up with a veteran who turns to empathic rape or murder."

"Yes, but I also know that in most cases, they would have done it on their own anyway. The kind of mind that enjoys inflicting harm doesn't suddenly discover the attraction. It's built in. We dug the Pit a long time ago. Empathic criminals aren't new."

Andira nodded, staring at her drink as she swirled the liquid in the glass. "I met a veteran at the grand opening of the Whitesun Builder Caste House. She was so...not a warrior. Soft voice and gentle manners and a librarian at a children's school, for Fahla's sake. And we threw her into a soul-destroying battle because we had no other choice. She asked if I thought she should join the program and meet the Voloth she turned."

"What did you tell her?"

"I said it helped me realize that neither of us were monsters. She said she already knew the Voloth weren't monsters, because monsters don't love."

Lanaril paused. "Great Mother. She's right. I should have thought of that argument back when we were debating the amnesty."

"I asked if she was sure she wasn't a templar."

"She should be."

"I know. And that's the kind of heart I worry about. She knows the Voloth soldiers aren't monsters, but she still thinks she is. I'm not worried about the few that can't find the boundary again. I'm worried about the majority. All those high empath scholars and the untrained warriors...all the people I asked to do the unthinkable. I once thought I'd have to pay the highest price for Alsea, but in the end I paid the lowest. I'm one of the least affected. And I don't understand why I feel guilty about killing for mercy when I don't feel guilty for anything I did in that battle. Not one single thing. Not the empathic force, not using the Voloth to kill their own people, not even the fatal covert projection. It was war and it was easy. Live or die. Save Alsea or die trying. There wasn't any mercy involved."

"Of course there was."

Andira looked up. "What?"

"Why didn't you destroy your Voloth the same way the untrained high empaths did? Wouldn't it have been easier just to break them, rather than leave them intact? I've met Rax twice now; he seems entirely whole."

"Because I take pride in my skill."

Lanaril picked up her drink and waited.

After a long moment of silence, Andira sighed. "Because I didn't have to. It wasn't necessary. And...I didn't want to live with that."

Leaning forward, Lanaril said, "Let me see if I understand. You were in a pitched battle the likes of which Alsea has never seen, with an enemy that we already knew was bent on our utter destruction and enslavement. If there was ever a time when I could understand hatred and revenge, that would be it. You could have destroyed them—taken away everything that made them who they are. But you didn't. Do you know what that sounds like to me? It sounds like mercy."

Andira stared at her.

"Or maybe it was just pride." Lanaril saluted her with her glass and sipped it.

"I'm beginning to understand how you made Lead Templar," Andira said.

"And I'm relieved you made Lancer. Because you did save Alsea."

"We all did. You were ready to do your part as well. You would have been the very first to break Fahla's covenant. Did I ever tell you how shekking impressed I was with that? With your courage?"

Lanaril shook her head, startled by the compliment.

"I was. It's part of the reason we're friends. So I was hoping we could listen to that bell together, without any fronts, because tonight I want to relax and be with someone who understands what it is we've just done. And maybe you can explain to me why it so often feels wrong to do the right thing."

Instead of answering with words, Lanaril dropped her front.

A smile spread across Andira's face, and a moment later Lanaril received the gift of full access to her emotions. There was no greater proof of friendship.

"I'm honored," Lanaril said. "Both by your trust and by the fact that you chose to come here this evening. Besides, I wasn't looking forward to spending two hanticks alone, listening to that bell and thinking far too much." She lifted her glass. "So this will help us not think, right?"

"Eventually. If we drink enough of it."

"Did you bring enough?"

"If I didn't, there are Guards right outside your door who would be delighted to bring us a fresh bottle."

"There are definite advantages to your position," Lanaril said, and tossed down the rest of her drink. This time it didn't burn.

CHAPTER 25
A new delegate

After the Voloth euthanasia, Tal was swept up into a whirlwind of meetings and appearances. The demand for her time was unending, most of it still centered around matter printer issues. There were days when she wondered what in Fahla's name she had been thinking when she negotiated that particular part of the Gaian treaty. Today was one of those days.

She hurried through the State House, already late for a meeting with the producer delegation. She did not tolerate tardiness in others, and knowing that she was guilty of it put her in a poor temper.

So it was with considerable embarrassment and displeasure that she entered the meeting room to hear a delegate saying, "How can we trust the Lancer to control the effects of this technology when she can't even track her calendar?"

"I assure you I am perfectly capable of tracking my calendar," Tal said, taking her seat at the head of the long table. The delegation went silent and every member sat down in unison. Tal glared down the length of the table at the speaker, a tall, dark-haired woman who stared back at her with a distinct lack of respect. "You're not an original delegate. Why are you here?"

The woman answered immediately and in a clear voice. "Delegate Norsen is ill today and asked me to attend in his stead."

"I see." Tal hadn't been notified of the substitution, but then she hadn't had time to read Aldirk's morning report either. She hated being caught off stride, and her mood deteriorated further. "What is your name?"

"Salomen Opah. My family has owned a holding near Granelle for twelve generations."

"Well, Raiz Opah," Tal said, using the formal address for a producer, "as a substitute, you may be unaware of delegation protocol. I will not waste the time of your fellows explaining it, but one aspect you should know is that you will be expected to limit your opinions to the issue at hand. Speculation on my leadership, or even my calendar-tracking capability, is not considered to be the purview of this delegation."

The mood of the room shifted into one of sharp-edged caution as the delegates registered Tal's ire. She felt it easily; these people were untrained and did not front their emotions well. It had made the meetings rather interesting in the past, but today it just annoyed her. What annoyed her most, however, was that the one person who should have been most cautious remained stubbornly immune.

She called the meeting to order and moved to the agenda, wanting nothing more than to get this over with and retreat to her quarters for a little quiet time.

Discussion was subdued at first, but Opah quickly established herself as the most active member, speaking with great conviction whenever an agenda item was opened to comment. As the hantick wore on, Tal found herself grudgingly admiring her obvious intelligence and ability to articulate concerns and issues. Indeed, Opah was a far better contributor to discussion than Norsen had ever been. By the end of the meeting, Tal's earlier ire had evaporated and she found herself looking forward to what was sure to be an interesting interaction.

With considerable though well-fronted relief, she dismissed the group at the end of the hantick, thanking them for their attendance and contributions. As the room filled with the sounds of scraping chairs and rustling fabric, Tal raised her voice to add, "Raiz Opah, please stay a moment."

There was a slight pause before the bustle resumed, and Opah sat down as the delegates finished collecting their belongings and filed out. Tal could easily feel their concern, along with a few gleeful thoughts. Apparently, Opah was not universally loved among her peers.

The last delegate closed the door behind him. Still Tal waited, feeling Opah's nervousness increase. She certainly had presence; by her face and posture no one would know she felt anything but complete self-assurance. Nevertheless, she did not like being alone in the room with the Lancer.

At last Tal said quietly, "Please inform Delegate Norsen that if he does not wish to attend these meetings, there are other and far more advisable methods for resolving that issue than sending in a substitute to lie for him."

Opah's eyes widened as her nervousness turned sharp. "Lancer Tal, I assure you that he was truly unable to attend today. He—"

"Do not compound one lie with another," Tal interrupted. "The first I can excuse, because you lied not for yourself but for a friend. The second I will not, because I don't appreciate being taken for a fool."

There was a heavy silence as they stared at each other, but Opah's trepidation was swiftly overtaken by curiosity.

"I don't think anyone could take you for a fool," she said. "How did you know?"

"You don't front your emotions well."

"I front my emotions very well," Opah said indignantly, then paused. "Oh…I'd heard you were a powerful empath."

Tal nodded. "It takes empathic strength to fill this role. Without it I'd be easily hoodwinked by well-meaning delegates."

Opah smiled, but it soon slipped from her face. "Is Norsen in trouble?"

"Yes."

She leaned forward in alarm. "Please, Lancer Tal, can't you possibly just… overlook it? He means well, and he did his best, but he's just not comfortable with these proceedings. His bondmate put his name in the system without his knowledge, and when he was selected, he felt he should do his duty. But he told me he's not making a contribution and wished my name had been drawn instead. So I told him I'd go in his place."

Tal wanted to laugh but kept a straight face and a rigid emotional front. "I see," she said calmly. "That does change things. Instead of one lawbreaker I must deal with two."

Opah sat back, stunned. But before she could become truly afraid, Tal continued, "Then the punishment is this: Raiz Norsen is hereby removed from the delegation permanently, and you will take his place. You're about to become very familiar with the State House, Delegate Opah."

She opened her mouth, then shut it again. "You're making me a delegate?"

Never one to repeat herself, Tal simply waited.

"But…I had the distinct impression that you didn't appreciate my input today. You argued me down at least four times. I would have expected you to prefer someone who was…easier to work with."

A chuckle escaped. "You've never attended a Council session, have you?"

Opah shook her head.

"Come to the public gallery some time, and you'll see that relative to what I'm forced to deal with in that chamber, you're easy to work with. But you don't have that reputation among your peers, do you?"

Mutely, she shook her head again, and Tal felt a tiny bit of sympathy for her.

"I don't favor sycophants," she said. "I prefer intelligent, thoughtful individuals who have something to say, are not afraid to say it, and are motivated by what's best for Alsea rather than themselves. You qualify." She rose, and as Opah followed suit, she added, "However, I'd advise against lying to me again. I appreciate forthrightness, even if it's not necessarily something I want to hear. But I don't appreciate deception in any form."

"I understand. It won't happen."

Tal nodded and opened the door. "Until next time, then."

Opah hesitated, plainly uncertain about preceding the Lancer. When Tal waved her through, she stopped on the other side and turned. "Thank you," she said. "For looking past my, er, excuse—and for that backhanded compliment. I'll do my best to be a good delegate."

"I have a feeling you'd do your best regardless of the situation. You don't strike me as the kind of person who does anything with less than a full heart."

"Can you tell that from skimming me?"

"No. I could tell that from arguing with you."

Opah raised an eyebrow. "Change your policies and you'll hear a lot less of that from me."

"Well, there's a novel form of political blackmail. But not an effective one, I'm afraid."

"It was worth a try. Until next time, Lancer Tal."

Tal watched her walk down the corridor, noting that her confident stride matched her attitude.

The producer delegate meetings had just gotten more interesting.

CHAPTER 26
Quantum com call

Tal nearly jumped out of her chair when the pad chimed, announcing a quantum com call being routed in from the *Caphenon*. She was expecting it, but a thrill of anticipation still charged down her spine as she set her book on the side table. She crossed the room to the waist-high bookcase beneath the wall of windows and picked up the pad from its stand next to her Filessian orchid. It was active, showing the Protectorate Fleet symbol and the name *Captain Ekatya Serrado*.

Tal tapped the symbol and watched it give way to the smiling face of Ekatya.

"Well met, stranger," Ekatya said.

"Well met." Tal's own smile was out of proportion to the banality of their greeting. "I haven't seen you in a moon. Where are you?"

"At the Quinton Shipyards. I'm overseeing the final preparations, and Lhyn's joining me in three days for the ceremony. Shippers, I wish you could be here for this."

"I wish I could, too."

"She's beautiful, Andira." Ekatya's dark blue eyes were glowing with happiness. "Absolutely beautiful, and I still can't quite believe she's mine. Have I thanked you for that lately?"

"At least six times."

"Make it seven. I took photos during my tour today. Want to see?"

"Of course I want to see. Let me get set up." Tal carried the pad back to her chair, set it on the side table, and tapped it to bring up the larger virtual screen. She oriented it to face her and sat back with her glass of spirits in hand. "I'm ready."

"Okay. This is from the observation deck."

Ekatya vanished, and in her place was a sleek silver ship crouched inside the protective arms of a space dock. It looked like the *Caphenon* in every way, except it had no crash damage and its hullskin was perfect, reflecting the lights that shone from the dock. Tiny craft could be seen buzzing around it—though, of course, tiny was relative. Those craft were probably half the size of Tal's state transport.

"I never saw the *Caphenon* look like that," Tal said. "It really is gorgeous."

"I know." Ekatya's voice was light. "And she's not an it. She's a she. Get your terminology right."

"Yes, Captain."

Ekatya laughed. "I'll make a Fleeter out of you yet. We just have to work on the obeying orders part."

"You'll be working on that for a long time."

The image shifted again, and now she was looking at a closer view.

"This is from the dock ferry. I was being taken out to the shuttle bay."

"Ferry? You mean you can't just walk aboard from the space dock?"

"I could if I wanted to spend half a hantick walking. One of the privileges of being a captain is that I can request a dock ferry to take me on the scenic route." Now the gigantic engine cradle filled the screen, emblazoned with the name of Ekatya's new Pulsar-class ship.

Tal translated the Common letters and sounded it out. "Pho…nix?"

"Phoenix. Just pretend the o isn't there."

"That isn't what you told me it would be called."

"She."

"She," Tal repeated.

"I won't give up on you. Yes, Fleet changed the name. It's unusual, but not unheard of. And in this case, it's perfect. A phoenix is an old Gaian legend, a bird that was associated with the sun. It lived a thousand cycles or more, and when it died, it died like a star shedding its outer layers: kaboom. Then it was resurrected from the ashes of its old body to start life anew."

Tal sucked in a breath. "She's the resurrection of the *Caphenon*."

Ekatya reappeared on the screen, her face alight with pleasure. "You *are* trainable!"

For a moment Tal's heart ached to see such joy in her friend. In the short time they had together on Alsea, there wasn't much occasion for joy. She wished she could have been the one putting that expression on Ekatya's face.

Then again…wasn't she? Ekatya had command of that ship because Tal had pulled every negotiating trick she knew to get it.

They chatted about the ship, the upcoming launch ceremony, and Lhyn's latest activities, and when they had exhausted Ekatya's life, they turned to Alsea.

"I'm about to pull out my hair with the matter printers," Tal said.

"I thought the delegate meetings were going well?"

"They are—to a point. Remember that producer I told you about, the one who replaced an original delegate and lied about it?"

"You mean the one you said was opinionated, outspoken, argumentative, and generally a thorn in your side?"

"Did I say all that?" Tal was a little embarrassed now, hearing such a description quoted back to her. Not that it wasn't true.

"Mm-hm. I had the impression of a woman twice as tall as you and four times as wide, red in the face from shouting, and her hair standing on end."

Tal laughed. "Wrong, wrong, and wrong. But entertaining to be sure. Actually, she's quite attractive when she's not driving me insane. And extremely intelligent—she makes every other delegate in that meeting look as if they have the brains of a dokker. Half the time I want to throw her out, but I can't because she's the smartest person in the room…besides me." She ignored Ekatya's knowing grin. "And hardworking, too. She's made it a policy to meet with her community of producers before and after every delegate meeting, so she can share what she learned in the State House. Then she records all of their questions and input and brings it back to our next meeting. It's been so useful that I asked the other delegates to do the same thing."

"The other producer delegates?"

"No, all of them. In all the caste meetings."

Ekatya whistled. "Bet they hate her now."

"Probably, but she wouldn't care. At any rate, it's very effective. We're getting closer and closer to consensus, and last moon the warriors and the crafters said they were done. I think the builders will probably say the same next nineday."

"So you have half the castes signed on? That sounds like good news to me. Why are you pulling out your hair?"

"Because the other half are digging in their heels, and out of all of them, the producers are the worst. And it's because of Delegate Opah!"

"The opinionated one?"

"Yes! The producers are still afraid of the matter printers. I think I could have talked them around by now, but that woman is obdurate. She's resistant to every line of logic." Tal hesitated. "No, that's not fair. She does listen to logic. If I can make a good enough argument, she'll generally concede, but there are two or three obstacles I simply cannot talk my way around. I've tried and tried, for four moons now. I'm at my wits' end. And she's not just a delegate; she's also a major landholder in Blacksun Basin. Her opinion carries far too much weight in her caste. I don't think I'll ever convince them until I can convince her, and I just don't know how to do it."

"Hm." Ekatya looked thoughtful. "Well, if nothing you've tried has worked so far, then it's time to think outside the box."

"I can tell this is one of those visual Gaian sayings, but I have no idea what it means."

"It means, stop thinking like a Lancer asserting her power over a producer. Think outside your normal methods. If you were a Lead Guard again, having this discussion with a landholder, would you approach it a different way?"

"Yes, I'd throw up my hands and walk away."

Ekatya snorted. "This from the woman who figured out how to breach a ground pounder's shielding. *That* was thinking outside the box. Nobody even considered that possibility, but you did."

Tal paused. "You mean think about it tactically."

"Well…yes, if that's what works. Since diplomacy is off the list and so is logical debate."

"Hm."

"I recognize that look," Ekatya said. "Delegate Opah is probably in trouble now. When is your next meeting?"

"Tomorrow."

"Oh, yes. She's in trouble."

CHAPTER 27
The producer's challenge

IN THE PRODUCER DELEGATE MEETING the next day, it took less than twenty ticks before Tal and Delegate Opah were once again arguing the issue of sustainability. To Tal this was no issue at all, but she could not convince the producers, especially Opah, no matter how reasoned her argument. And on this late summer day, the heat coming through the large windows pushed already-tenuous tempers to the fraying point.

"You cannot do that; it would destroy our profitability!" Opah's face was flushed and her voice was louder than necessary. "There must be limitations to the output of the matter printers. Why can't you see that?"

"What I see is a bigger picture." Tal was so irritated that it took conscious effort to keep her front intact. "You look at this from a circumscribed perspective; I'm looking from a broader viewpoint. You're all too focused on your caste's interests—you're not seeing the flock for the birds."

"Oh, I think we're seeing the flock quite well!" Opah was almost shouting now. "What we're seeing is that you're willing to sacrifice our caste to the interest of the others. The merchants will certainly benefit if the producers have no pricing leverage!"

"You could not be more wrong!" Tal's own voice rose. "Why do you think I've spent a cycle meeting with every single caste? So I can decide which ones to throw away?"

"It would certainly be the effective way of doing it!"

The other delegates watched in nervous silence. Their emotional state finally got through to Tal, who forced herself to relax in her chair. "Then I open the floor to you," she said calmly. "Tell us how you would resolve this issue."

"I don't have a solution; that's the problem!" Opah slapped her palm on the table. "If I did, we wouldn't be arguing over this. I just know that what you're proposing will be the death of us. And you can't seem to see that, because you sit here in your magical dome with your privileged lifestyle and you have no idea what we working Alseans face in our daily lives. If you ever worked a holding, you wouldn't be trying to shove this ridiculous policy down our throats. You'd see for yourself why we need protection."

Her magical dome?

Tal was seething now. Opah always pushed her, but this was too much. She was just about to say something she would regret when she remembered Ekatya's advice. *Stop thinking like a Lancer. Think outside your normal methods.*

The idea came out of nowhere. It was too outrageous to consider—which was exactly why it might work.

In a voice that nearly purred, Tal said, "Delegate Opah, your disrespect has crossed the line."

The room electrified as every delegate sat up straight. Opah stared, her anger rapidly dissipating into apprehension.

"I make you a formal challenge," Tal continued. "You say I know nothing about your daily life, and I know for a fact that you have not the slightest conception of mine. So we will trade. I'll work with you on your holding for a nineday, and you'll accompany me in my workday for the same period of time. Do you accept?"

Everyone held their breath.

"No," Opah said.

The collective expulsion of air was audible, but the delegates tensed up when Opah spoke again.

"A nineday won't teach you anything about the life of a producer. You'd need to work with us for a cycle. But since it would be impossible for you to leave your position for that long, I propose a moon. That will see us through the harvest, and you'll at least get a glimpse of what it means to work for every cintek that we earn."

Tal considered it. She knew Opah expected her to back down; after all, a moon was a long time. But it had been almost ten moons since her vacation, and every one of them had been nonstop work punctuated by crises. The idea of getting out of Blacksun, even if it was just to work on a holding nearby, was very appealing.

Plus, Aldirk and Micah would both have coronary seizures.

The last thought made her smile, and she saw Opah's brows draw together.

"I accept."

Opah's mouth dropped open. "You do?"

"I do. When shall I arrive at your holding?"

"Ah..." Her emotional front, never a challenge to Tal in the best of times, slipped entirely. Opah was shocked and dismayed; she had bluffed and lost. "Well, I...I will need time to notify my family, and make a room ready for you—"

"And for my Guards," Tal added.

"Your Guards? How many?" The dismay grew.

Tal pretended to think. "Since your holding is so close to Blacksun, I shouldn't need more than twenty." That was double the number she actually planned to take, but she was enjoying herself.

"Twenty? I haven't room for twenty guests!"

"Twenty-one; surely you haven't forgotten me?"

"You did not mention twenty Guards when you proposed this!"

"Then you withdraw from the challenge?"

The question galvanized Opah; in a moment her emotions coalesced into a solid determination.

"No, I do not. I will find housing for your twenty Guards. You may plan your arrival for the first day of next moon." Her smile was not friendly. "You might also wish to bring your personal masseuse, Lancer Tal. On a holding, we work for our livings."

"I would expect nothing less. And you may wish to borrow my personal masseuse when your turn arrives. That magical dome existence you expect will also involve a training mission, and there will be no accommodation made for one who finds her legs unused to walking twenty lengths or her back unused to sleeping on the ground afterward."

"You cannot frighten me with such stories. I walk several lengths every day on my holding, and I've slept under the stars many a night. I suspect you don't lead nearly as active an existence as you portray."

"Then it will be my very great pleasure to show you the truth."

The air sizzled between them, and for the first time in many moons, Tal had something to look forward to. No matter what happened, it was going to be entertaining. At best, she would win over the producers. At worst, she would be exactly where she was right now, having lost nothing—but Salomen Opah would have to publicly admit that she was wrong about the magical dome existence. That alone would be worth the price of entrance.

CHAPTER 28
Field of conflict

"Are you trying to kill me?" Micah could not believe his ears. How could she be so reckless? He thought they were past this; she hadn't done anything this idiotic since before her vacation.

"Micah—"

"Could you at least have *considered* the ramifications before agreeing to such folly? I cannot believe this. What were you thinking? How am I supposed to protect you while you run around a holding with a woman who believes you're out to destroy her caste? You will be sleeping in the house of your enemy, for Fahla's sake!"

Tal watched calmly as he paced her office. "She's not an enemy. Her voice is simply louder than her thought."

"Voices can cause a great deal of damage. They can incite action."

"Then don't you think it would be more dangerous not to do this? What better way to silence that voice, and all others who might take up the cry, than by actively proving it wrong? I'm truly at an impasse with the producers. Almost a full cycle of meetings and they still don't trust my intentions. Something has to change, and my instinct tells me this could be it."

He stopped pacing and stood in front of her desk, hands on his hips. "Is that all it is? Or are you running again?"

For a moment there was fire in her eyes, but then she shook her head. "I suppose it's going to take a few more moons before you stop worrying about that. I'm fine, Micah. Yes, I spoke with Ekatya last night, and no, that's not why I'm doing this. Although she did give me the idea, in a way. It's been an entire cycle since she left—I'm past that. But I need a break, and I need to get out of Blacksun. So maybe I can hit two targets with one throw."

He sighed. "You realize that every gray hair on my head is thanks to you."

"You say that every time I put a foot off the line. And I can still recall my first days in your unit; you had gray hair then."

"Yes, and I acquired every strand of it the moment I learned that Andira Shaldone Tal had been assigned to me." He collapsed into the chair and looked at her beseechingly. "If I cannot inspire sense in you, can I at least inspire caution? Please take this situation seriously. Your security will be difficult to safeguard in that environment. You must allow me to do my job."

"I promise. I think you're overstating the danger, but I'll do as you ask."

"Thank you." Relieved to have an actual promise, Micah relaxed. Then he began to chuckle. "You told her you were bringing twenty Guards?"

Tal grinned. "I did."

"Poor woman."

Micah was in Tal's office the next day when she finally told Opah that she would in fact require only ten Guards. The producer's relief was obvious even over the vidcom.

It wasn't until Tal ended the call that her composure broke and she laughed. "Did you see her face? Fahla, but that was worth the wait."

"This looks more like the kind of stunt you'd pull on me. Why are you tormenting her?"

"Because she tormented me first. I've spent four moons fighting her in those delegate meetings, and believe me, this is the first time I've ever had the upper hand. She set up the field of conflict; now she must let the battle play out."

Micah had already run a thorough background check on Opah and was no longer concerned about any danger she might pose. But the check hadn't satisfied his curiosity about how a producer had managed to get so far under Tal's skin when many others had tried and failed. Never would he have imagined Tal issuing a challenge like this, much less accepting a counterchallenge that increased the difficulty by a factor of four.

Now he listened to her humming contentedly as she pulled up a file for him and wondered about her word choices. A conflict, a battle—and she seemed delighted at the prospect.

Ever since the invasion, Tal had been enmeshed in difficult decisions, negotiations, and compromises where her options tended to range from bad to worse. Nothing could be checked off and forgotten; everything had long-lasting ramifications. But this challenge would have a beginning and an end. It would have a winner and a loser.

He nodded to himself. Tal was looking for a quick win and a sense of closure. He could work with that.

Unless, of course, she lost—in which case he would hear her moan about it for the rest of the cycle.

Two days later, he returned from inspecting the holding and reported that Opah had managed to create a makeshift bunkhouse in the building normally reserved for storing heavy equipment.

"It's better than a field tent by an order of magnitude," he said. "And she and her family will be preparing our meals. No field rations—the Guards will be ecstatic. Other than the headache of protecting you in such an exposed location, this will be a plush assignment."

"She's making the meals?" Tal asked incredulously. "For ten Guards?"

"She seemed to believe it was required."

Tal chuckled. "No doubt she's wondering if she hasn't poured more than she can drink."

"I'd say she has things well in hand. In fact, I'm beginning to wonder if it's not you who poured more than you thought. Don't underestimate your opponent."

"Ha. She's the one underestimating me. She thinks I'll fold the first day, but I'm looking forward to it. One moon of peaceful field work sounds like a vacation to me. I can't wait to get out of here." Sobering, she added, "Feeding ten Guards for a moon is much too expensive. Tell Aldirk to allocate appropriate funding if he hasn't already. And add a cook to our Guard complement."

"So now I must go back and tell her we are eleven, not ten? In addition to you and me?"

"I see you've already run afoul of her sharp tongue. Your fear is palpable."

"The day a producer strikes fear into my heart is the day you set my pyre alight." He raised his eyebrows. "However, I will readily admit that Raiz Opah has the most…direct communication style I've encountered in many cycles. She would make an excellent unit trainer."

"If she trained units, we'd have an entire Alsean Defense Force cowering at the sight of a producer."

He smiled at the image. "I'm certain she'd consider that a positive development."

CHAPTER 29
Temporary setback

"Can you believe this? She's spending an entire moon playing at being a producer! If we didn't already know she can't hold the State Chair, this would certainly prove it." Challenger sat down with a huff. "This is it. We need to start rounding up our support. She'll never be more vulnerable to a caste coup than she is right now."

Spinner held back a sigh. As usual, his ally saw only what he wanted to. "She's not vulnerable. Not by a long throw. Don't you realize what she's done? The producers were her greatest weakness; they're too afraid of the matter printers. And in one stroke she's brought half the caste over to her side. By the end of this challenge moon, she might even bring over the other half."

He had to admit, it was a brilliant move. While it was not unknown for a Lancer to issue or accept a challenge, it was usually limited to the warrior and scholar castes. No Lancer in memory had done something like this. The producers were thrilled—their caste had just been catapulted into the spotlight. It gave them a welcome boost of power, and before the challenge had even begun, Lancer Tal was enjoying a swelling of support. It was a setback, but he was certain it would be a temporary one.

"Who cares what the producers think? They're not the ones we need for a caste coup. We need the warriors and scholars."

"Do try to think at least one step ahead. No, we don't need the producers to take power. But we do need them if we want to keep it."

"Let me guess: your counsel is to wait. Again. I'm beginning to question your commitment to this cause."

Sometimes Spinner didn't know who he hated more, Lancer Tal or Challenger. "If I were not committed to this cause, I wouldn't have spent the last eight moons investing in it."

"To what end? I fail to see any real progress. You talk a great game of tiles, but if talking is all you do…"

The threat was clear, and Spinner did not appreciate it. Someday, he would put Challenger in his place. But for now he still needed him, so he swallowed his anger and spoke calmly. "Not all progress happens out in the open. And with something like this, very little of it does. Let's just say I've been cooking up a surprise. It should be ready in another nineday or two, and I guarantee that Lancer Tal won't be expecting it. That's when you'll see the vulnerability you're waiting for."

"What is it?"

"A report."

"A report? That's your great plan? What is it about, our Lancer's nonexistent sex life? Please tell me you've got something explosive."

Spinner smiled at the idea of a report on Lancer Tal's sex life. That would be a short one indeed. "We don't need explosive," he said. "We just need fear."

PART TWO:

SANCTUARY

CHAPTER 30
Hol-Opah

"Welcome to Hol-Opah, Lancer Tal."

Salomen Opah and her family stood on the front porch of their large home, dressed in what must have been their finest clothing. At the end of the greeting line, a small boy of nine or ten cycles fidgeted with his collar.

"Thank you," Tal said. "I'm honored to receive your hospitality."

"Please allow me to introduce you to my family," Opah continued in a formal voice that Tal had never heard from her. "My father, Shikal Arrin."

Tal held up her hand. "Well met, Raiz Arrin."

"Well met, Lancer Tal." Shikal beamed at her as they touched palms; it seemed he did not share his daughter's political opinions. "You do great honor to our house. I never thought to receive the Lancer herself! My only regret is that Nashta isn't here to see it."

"Your loss is recent and deep," Tal said. Salomen and her family were all on the lower end of mid-empathic ability; their fronts were barely there. Shikal's grief for his bondmate was like a second suit of clothing. "Please accept my condolences. She must have been a true heart."

He nodded. "She was. But her heart lives on in all of us, especially my daughter."

Opah clearly wanted to end this line of conversation. "These are my brothers, Nikin, Herot, and Jaros."

Tal touched palms with each brother in turn, thanking them for hosting her and her Guards. They all had the same nearly black hair and deep brown eyes as their sister, and the two eldest shared her height. The Opahs were a tall family.

Nikin was the oldest sibling, his hair already brushed with silver. His smile was open and easy, and Tal liked him on sight. Lurking under his gentle formality was a quick sense of humor.

Herot was younger than Salomen but held himself with a familiar self-confidence. In looks he resembled Salomen more than Nikin, but his squared jaw and thicker facial ridges lent his appearance a masculine charm. He seemed all too aware of his good looks and gave Tal an appraising gaze that made her want to laugh. Obviously, he considered himself irresistible and was enjoying fantasies that she would be glad to disabuse him of.

At the end of the line, she crouched down to look into Jaros's eyes, smiling to see the same dimple in his chin that Salomen had in hers. "Are those clothes as uncomfortable as they look?" she whispered as she held her palm to his.

His eyes lit up. "Yes! The collar itches. But Salomen insisted. She said we must look our best to honor you."

"Did she?" Tal asked in a louder voice. "I'm delighted to know that your sister finds honor in my visit."

"Oh yes, she's been talking of nothing else. Lancer Tal this, Lancer Tal that. We must be on our best behavior and speak properly and never—"

"That's enough, Jaros." Opah's embarrassment was crystalline, and Tal held back a smile.

"Raiz Opah," she said without looking up, "I am quite interested in what Jaros has to say. Please do him the honor of allowing him to speak as freely as your other siblings."

Jaros visibly swelled with pride, and Tal knew she had made a devout ally. "Thank you, Lancer Tal," he said in his best formal voice. Then it broke down as he leaned in excitedly. "Nobody ever speaks to Salomen that way! Is that because you're the Lancer?"

"It's one of the few benefits, yes. May I ask you a question?"

His formal mien returned. "You may," he said grandly.

"What do your friends at school say about my visit here?" She knew she would get a more accurate picture of the local political climate from this boy than from anyone else on the porch.

"The older ones say they don't care, but my friends are so envious they can barely walk straight! They want to know all about you. When I tell them you touched palms with me, they'll turn red with envy."

"We'll do more than touch palms, won't we? Do you not plan to work with me on the holding?"

"I will today and tomorrow, because they're free days. But after that I have to go to school. Besides, I'm not allowed to work the field equipment."

Which told her at least part of what Opah had planned for her. "Then I'll see you at meals, yes?" He nodded, and she gave him a smile before standing.

"Lancer Tal," Opah said, "while on my holding I will ask you to call me Salomen. I'm not accustomed to formal address in my home."

"Thank you, Salomen. I'm honored." Tal did not make a reciprocal offer. She allowed very few people such an informality; surely this producer did not expect it.

It seemed she did, judging by her annoyance. Well, if Salomen Opah chose to be irritated because she was not being given a familiarity that only Tal's closest friends enjoyed, that was a problem of her own making.

"Please come in. I'll show you your room."

Tal followed her through the door arch into a spacious entry that glowed with the richness of old and oft-rubbed wood. This was a style she appreciated: simple, but of high quality and well-cared for. The ornate décor of the State House had never appealed to her, and not for the first time she wished that she might redesign the entire building. But it was untouchable, part of their global tradition, and she was only a temporary inhabitant.

"This way." Salomen led her up a flight of stairs, down a curving hallway, and through a door into a spacious, comfortable room. It was lit by a pair of very old lamps that were surely heirlooms. A wide, cushioned window seat was flanked on each side by built-in bookcases crammed with books of every size and color. Through the large window, a magnificent vista of fields and trees stretched toward the Snowmount Range, and Tal knew right away that seat was going to be her favorite part of the room. The bed was neatly made with a hand-sewn quilt featuring the Opah family crest, and on the wall above it was a portrait of a woman who bore a strong resemblance to Salomen.

Tal dropped her bag on the floor. "This is your mother?"

"Yes."

The answer was short and unemotional, but Tal felt a different story altogether. She examined the portrait carefully. "She was beautiful."

The pain from behind her was so sharp that she had to close her eyes. Salomen Opah had not recovered from her mother's Return. Tal felt a sudden surge of sympathy; she knew too well what that was like.

"Yes, she was," Salomen said quietly.

"I see her in you."

There was no response, and she turned to catch an expression of surprise on Salomen's face.

"Thank you." Salomen turned toward the door. "Colonel Micah will be in the next room."

"Yes, he was most pleased about his accommodations." Tal followed her out and looked through the next doorway with approval. Micah had already settled in and was currently in the kitchen, speaking with the cook regarding the food preparation for the rest of the Guards. "This is far more pleasant than the tent he expected."

"Lancer Tal," Salomen said stiffly, "please do me the courtesy of treating me as a landholder, not a mere field worker. I would never house the Chief Guardian of our Lancer in a tent."

Tal's sympathy vanished as quickly as it had come. "I'll be happy to honor your request, provided you return the favor. You've treated me from the very beginning with a palpable prejudice. I'd appreciate being treated with more respect and perhaps, if it's not too much of a reach for you, an open mind. My words regarding Colonel Micah were not meant as an insult, yet you insist in taking it as such. Are you that unsure of your own position that you feel such a need to defend it?"

Now we're on familiar ground, she thought as Salomen glared at her.

"As long as you're a guest in my home, I will treat you with courtesy. But my respect is earned, not given. And accusing me of prejudice and narrow-mindedness is not the way to earn it."

"It wasn't an accusation. Merely an observation." Before Salomen could give her no doubt sizzling response, Tal continued, "Your home is lovely and well-loved. May I see the rest?"

Salomen stood still, her warring emotions clear to Tal's senses.

"Or if you prefer, I could ask Jaros for a tour," Tal offered.

That galvanized Salomen into action, and Tal passed a pleasant half-hantick viewing the old house and surrounding grounds. That her hostess was fuming beside her bothered her not at all; she had learned at an early age how to tune out the emotions of others. It was an essential self-defense mechanism for a gifted empath and served her well in her role as Lancer.

The main house was a traditional dome design, with six bedrooms arranged around the outside of the top floor so that each would have a view. A circular hallway divided the outside rooms from the inner core, which consisted of three bathrooms, all naturally lit by a glass opening in the roof. Salomen and Nikin each had their own, while Herot and Jaros shared the third. For this moon, however, Salomen would use Nikin's bathroom, leaving hers for Tal and Micah. It had originally been shared by Shikal and Nashta, but when Nashta became ill and could no longer negotiate stairs, Shikal had moved them both to a room on the ground floor. He had never moved back up again, and their original bedroom was now the guest room where Tal was staying.

Two beautiful wooden staircases led up to the top floor, one from the front entry and the other from the large dining area on the opposite side of the dome. The kitchen was located in a smaller, attached dome accessed through the dining area, and the rest of the ground floor was divided into a spacious parlor, an office, a storage room, Shikal's bedroom, and another bathroom.

The entire dome was flanked by a wraparound wooden porch, interrupted only by the kitchen dome. Three steps led up to the porch at the front entry, while the back porch required six due to the sloping land. Tal loved the scenery, which was serene, wide open, and utterly different from the city landscape she was used to. Hol-Opah had a commanding view from its hilltop perch, a fact Micah had approved of when he had done his security check.

Looking west from the back porch, Tal was treated to a spectacular panorama of the Snowmount Range, which loomed far closer here than in Blacksun. Only the very tops of the mountains still held snow this late in the summer, but she could imagine how glorious this scene would be in a few moons.

Off to the south, sunlight glinted off the Silverrun River. It curved sharply around the southeast corner of Hol-Opah and then flowed mostly north, making up both the southern and eastern boundaries of the holding. The river gave Hol-Opah much of its value, providing a natural fence for the herdstock, an endless supply of water, and a regular replenishment of nutrients when it flooded the lower fields. As required by caste law, the Opahs had left a broad buffer of untouched land next to the river, which was marked by a nearly unbroken band of ancient trees. Many of them bore the distinctive black trunk of the molwyn, Fahla's sacred tree.

Tal couldn't wait to go running there.

The outbuildings were all rectangular and clustered in a group north of the main house. Tal was impressed to note that even the harvest storage building was clean and well-kept, and let out a low whistle of appreciation when she stepped into the converted equipment building that now housed her Guards. Each Guard had a cot and a small table serving as a nightstand, complete with water pitcher and lamp. The row of high windows on each wall made the building light and airy; by field standards it was palatial. Five Guards were currently in residence, having rotated off duty just a short while ago, and three of them were fast asleep in their cots, wearing eye masks against the light pouring in the windows. Lead Guard Gehrain moved to wake his staff at Tal's entrance, but she stopped him with a raised hand. "They've earned their sleep," she said quietly. "Tell them I came by to see how they were doing, and that next time I want to see flowers on those nightstands."

Gehrain grinned. "It's no field tent." The grin dropped from his face as Salomen entered behind Tal, and he gave her a short bow. "Raiz Opah, please accept my grateful thanks on behalf of myself and ten very happy Guards. We never expected such comfortable lodgings."

Tal waited for Salomen to snap at him, since this was nearly the same thing she had said earlier, but the producer gave him a kind smile instead. "You're very welcome, Lead Guard Gehrain. It was the least I could do for the service you perform. If you or your staff need anything else, please let me know."

Tal barely kept her jaw shut as Gehrain assured Salomen that he couldn't imagine lacking for anything, and when they left the building, she shot a sidelong glance at her hostess. Did Salomen have a twin sister who had switched places with her while Tal's back was turned?

The tour ended at the main house, with Salomen leading Tal up the back stairs and to the guest room. Standing just outside the doorway, she said, "Please make yourself at home. We sit to midmeal in half a hantick."

"Thank you for your hospitality," Tal said. "You've gone out of your way to make my staff comfortable, and I appreciate it."

"You're welcome." The words were courteous, but the warmth she had shown Gehrain was nowhere to be seen.

Tal gave a mental shrug. "I'll see you downstairs, then," she said, and began to unpack.

CHAPTER 31
A new field worker

MIDMEAL WAS A PLEASANT AFFAIR. Tal liked the gracious but comfortable atmosphere of the dining room, and Salomen's family had enough questions to keep the conversation easy and light. Beside her, Micah rumbled with laughter at many of the questions coming from Jaros, who was overwhelmed at having two high-ranking warriors at his table and determined to make the most of his opportunity.

Eventually, it came to light that this was an unusual meal: during the busy harvest season, the family normally ate in the fields to save time. Tal caught Salomen's eye and saw a telltale glint in them. *Don't expect such coddling after this,* it said, and Tal gave her an acknowledging smile. She would bet half a moon's salary that Salomen was planning to run her into the ground this afternoon.

When Shikal joined them in the six-seat skimmer for their journey to the fields, she had second thoughts. Shikal was older than Micah. If he was involved in today's activities, then the labor couldn't be very physical.

Nor was it. After presenting Tal to her field workers—who politely welcomed her but otherwise kept their distance—Salomen set her up in a row of panfruit vines and showed her how to determine which were ready for harvest. It was simple enough, and for the first hantick Tal quite enjoyed it, though she had to be careful of the thorns on the vines. The sun was warm, the air was laden with the sweet scent of crushed panfruits that had fallen too early, and she was cocooned in a world all her own with the vines towering on either side of her. The only sounds she could hear were bird calls, the conversation of field workers, and the occasional clack of crates being stacked together at the ends of the rows. The work was simple enough to lull her into a state of serenity, and she thought this challenge might have been the best idea she'd ever had. As she expected, this was practically a vacation.

By the end of the second hantick, the repetitive motion of picking panfruits was beginning to make itself felt. The vines were taller than she was and the fruits grew all along their lengths, so she was both reaching over her head and squatting down to pick at ground level. Up, down, up and down, and the sun was warmer than it had been earlier.

After the third hantick, she had been scratched several times by thorns and was dripping with sweat. Her arms, legs, and back ached. Salomen had started in the row right next to hers, but was now two rows away. Tal couldn't believe how fast that woman moved. In fact, everyone was picking at least twice as fast as she was, including Jaros, and he couldn't even reach that high.

A field worker appeared at the other end of Tal's row and began picking. She scowled; he had no doubt been sent by Salomen to help her finish so she could move ahead with the others. She was not used to needing help to keep up and resented this unknown man with his damned efficiency.

He progressed rapidly toward her, and she did her best to speed up, but it was taking a great deal more effort to move from a squat to a stand. She'd had training missions that were easier than this.

They met two-thirds of the way down the row, and he smiled at her. "Never thought I'd see the Lancer in the fields of Hol-Opah. But you're doing fine."

"I am? I thought I was slower than a zalren after a big meal."

He laughed. Zalrens might be the most venomous of their serpents, but they tended to swallow prey three times their size and not move for days afterward.

"Nah, you're doing well for a beginner. Salomen didn't think you'd finish the last row."

She bristled. "Then I'm happy to have surprised her."

"Aye, you did that. And me as well; I thought you'd be soft."

He had even less of a front than Salomen, and his lack of judgment made it possible for her to drop her irritation. She wiped the sweat off her forehead and offered him a genuine smile. "Warriors aren't supposed to be soft, Raiz...?"

"Just Jeshen. Can't be bothered with titles except in town."

She held up a palm. "Well met, Jeshen."

"Well met. Shall we take a break and then start a new row?"

"A break?"

"Aye, every hantick and a half. Didn't Salomen tell you?"

That little—

"It must have slipped her mind," Tal said.

"Well, she's had a lot on it lately, what with making Hol-Opah ready for you. Come on, let's cool down."

He led her out of the row and over to a mobile refreshment unit, where Tal washed her hands and face in the cold water and thought it was paradise. A selection of small pastries had already been well picked over, but there were enough left to quiet the rumbling in her stomach. She had so many other aches and pains that she hadn't even noticed her hunger until now.

She peppered Jeshen with questions about the holding, and in twenty ticks learned more about Salomen than in five moons of delegate meetings. Nashta had trained her daughter to take her role as both landholder and family head, so none of the field workers were surprised when Salomen took over after Nashta's death. Shikal had never been family head; Jeshen called him the "family heart" instead. And while Nikin might have been expected to inherit one or both roles as the eldest sibling, he always deferred to Salomen. Tal thought about the gentle man she had met earlier that day and understood why Nashta chose to pass the responsibilities to her more fiery daughter.

Jeshen's respect for Salomen was obvious, and he spoke warmly of the way she cared for her field workers. Landholders had a traditional duty to their workers, but not all of them upheld that duty with the same care. Salomen was well known in this district for being tough but very fair, and kind to those who needed help.

Tal definitely believed the tough part. The kindness she would believe when she saw it.

Going back to work was harder than she expected. The twenty-tick break had been just long enough for her muscles to stiffen, and asking her legs to squat, stand, and squat again was torture. She was glad Jeshen was at the other end of the row; at least she could grumble about her aches and pains without being overheard. Her arms felt like dead weight, and she was getting scratched by the thorns more and more often.

A quarter of the way down the row, she reached deep into the vine for a particularly well-buried panfruit and let her tired arm drop too soon. A thorn ripped into her skin, tearing open a bleeding wound that burned.

"Ouch! Spawn of a fantenshekken!" She gripped her arm to stop the bleeding, but thought better of it when she remembered how filthy her hand was. The blood dripped off her elbow and the burning increased. Were those damned thorns tipped in some sort of toxin? Why hadn't Salomen warned her?

She rolled her eyes. Of course Salomen hadn't warned her; what was she thinking? That woman had probably been waiting for this.

She walked back up the row, intending to wash off her arm at the refreshment station, but stopped when she saw a familiar figure coming toward her at a fast trot.

"Are you all right?" Salomen reached for her arm. "Let me see." Her hands felt cool on Tal's aching arm as she examined the wound.

"It's just a scratch," Tal said. Why did it have to be Salomen who found her bleeding?

"No, scratches are what's covering the rest of your arms. I can't believe you're picking with your sleeves rolled up. You look like you lost a fight with a vallcat."

Only then did Tal notice that Salomen's long sleeves were still fastened at the wrist. Come to think of it, Jeshen's had been, too.

"It's hot," she said lamely.

"Of course it's hot. That doesn't mean you should be tempting fate and Fahla. All right, let's get this taken care of."

Tal followed her out of the row, feeling like a new trainee being called out for a stupid mistake. The embarrassment intensified when Salomen took over, washing her arm and pressing a clean cloth against the wound.

"I can take care of it myself."

"The way you've taken care of yourself so far? You'll excuse me if I prefer to be sure." Salomen lifted the cloth and checked for bleeding.

"I do not need—yeow!" Tal sucked in a breath, staring at the white foam on her arm. Salomen had sprayed it with something that felt like icicles shooting under her skin.

"Sorry," Salomen said, but her amusement belied the apology. "Perhaps I should have warned you about that. It'll feel better in a moment."

Tal wanted to suggest that she could have warned her about the thorns, too, but clamped her mouth shut and watched the foam on her arm melt away. By the time it was absorbed, both the initial burning sensation and the icicles had vanished.

"Ah," she said in relief. "Whatever that was, it worked."

"Panfruit thorns can be nasty. Keep your sleeves rolled down."

"Thanks for the timely advice."

Salomen glanced up, then returned her attention to the skin sealer she was applying to the cut. "I didn't think the Lancer of Alsea needed anyone's advice."

Tal bit back three different rude answers before saying, "If that's true, the government is wasting its cinteks on my advisors."

"Do you listen to them?"

"That depends on whether their advice is worth taking."

"Of course." Salomen rolled down the sleeve and fastened it at the wrist. Without pausing, she rolled down the other as well, making Tal feel like a child being dressed by an adult. "Best get back to it before Jeshen finishes your row."

She walked away, leaving Tal shaking her head.

"Kind to those who need help?" she muttered. "Sure, Jeshen. I believe that."

CHAPTER 32
A well-kept secret

TAL SLEPT LIKE THE DEAD that first night, so tired that she failed to wake at her usual hantick and missed her morning run. Micah's knock on her door finally woke her, and she barely made it to mornmeal in time. It was just as well, since she couldn't have run more than four steps this morning. As it was, she could barely lift her fork to her mouth.

If she had thought yesterday afternoon was hard, today was worse. Her muscles were already aching, and now she was asking them to do exactly the same thing for twice as long. Midmeal couldn't come soon enough, and by the end of the day she would happily have slept on the ground in her row. The idea of walking as far as the skimmer was almost more than she could handle.

Her steps dragged as she hauled herself to the end of her row, but when she saw Salomen standing near the skimmer, her spine stiffened of its own accord. Micah would light her funeral pyre before she'd let that woman see her aches and pains.

She nearly fell asleep in the shower. Dressing took more time than usual, and she cast longing glances at the bed, which was exerting an almost physical pull. This was ridiculous; at this rate she might actually plant her face in her plate at evenmeal. It was time for drastic measures. She dug out her healing kit and injected herself with a stimulant, closing her eyes until she felt the familiar rush. The last time she had needed stims was after the *Caphenon* crashed. Of course, she had been preparing for war then.

In some ways, it felt as if she was doing the same now.

She was just tucking away her kit when she felt a presence outside her door and was immediately annoyed that she could already recognize Salomen's emotional signature. The woman was distinctive; she had to admit that much. Thank Fahla she had already injected herself. Five ticks earlier and she would not have been able to conceal her exhaustion.

She opened the door before Salomen could knock and took some satisfaction in her surprise. "Yes?"

"I just wanted to tell you that there are fresh towels in your bathroom. I meant to bring them up earlier, but you beat me into the shower." Salomen held out a small tube. "And this will help your muscles."

Tal looked at the tube as if it were poisonous. "What about my muscles?"

"Lancer Tal, while you're under my roof, you're under my care. If you think I can't see what you're trying to hide, then either you're blind or you think I am. I assure you I am not."

Tal glared at her but had no way to refute her statement without an outright lie. She took the tube with little grace. "Thank you."

"You're welcome."

It should have ended there, but Salomen kept looking at her, and Tal couldn't close the door in her face. "Was there something else?"

"Why are you here?" Salomen asked.

"You accepted my challenge." Something was off; her empathic senses were tingling.

Salomen shook her head. "That's the political answer. You could have refused my counterchallenge without losing face—surely a Lancer can't easily leave the capital for an entire moon. That's why I made it, so we'd both have a way out. But you came anyway, and I've been watching you killing yourself for two days trying to prove something you have no need to prove. I just can't figure out why."

Tal went still, shocked by what she had just felt. It was impossible. There was no way a mid empath could be doing that.

But she was.

"Great Goddess, you're probing me," she breathed.

Salomen's eyes went wide, her instant fear slicing into Tal's mind. "No, I—"

"You are. Don't lie to me."

"I...I didn't mean to. It was an accident. I'm sorry."

Tal stared into dark brown eyes, focusing all of her empathic powers directly on Salomen's mind. It would have been a violation at any other time, but Salomen's own transgression had changed the rules.

There was no sound but that of panicked breathing. Tal made her probe as gentle as she could under the circumstances, but Salomen still felt it and was terrified by the invasion of her mind. Instinctively, Tal expanded her own front, protecting Salomen from being read by anyone else. Even the least empathic Alseans were usually sensitive to their own kin, and terror like this was bound to be picked up. Jaros in particular would be upset; he was closely bonded to his sister.

At last she withdrew from her probe and took a step back, letting physical distance reduce the perceived threat. "How is it possible that you're this strong and yet untrained?"

Salomen sagged against the doorframe, her distress transmitted as clearly as if she were a child.

Feeling awkward at the shift in their dynamic, Tal took her hand, drew her into the room and shut the door behind them. Gently pushing Salomen onto the foot of the bed, she crouched on her heels in front of her. "It's all right. I'm not going to report you."

"But I probed you." Her voice was so small that Tal had to lean in to hear. "I probed the Lancer. Fahla, I didn't even realize… I'm so sorry. It was an accident, I swear. Please forgive me."

"I already have. But you haven't answered my question. This is important."

Salomen said nothing, but Tal could feel her fighting a resurgent panic.

"Look at me." Wide eyes stared into hers, and she gave a reassuring nod. "Take a deep breath, and let it out slowly. Good. Now another."

The fear receded, and Salomen shook her head. "You're being kinder than I have a right to expect."

"I would not prosecute an innocent probe. You have no control, but you need to learn it. Probe the wrong person and you could be in serious trouble. Do it more than once and you could find yourself in the Pit."

"I know," she whispered.

"Why aren't you scholar or warrior caste? With your powers you should have been marked by your tenth cycle."

She shook her head.

"Tell me."

Clearly, Salomen wished to be anywhere else, but under Tal's steady gaze she finally gained control of both her emotions and her voice. "Because I didn't want to go."

"Most children are afraid of the separation, but it's necessary. How did you manage to stay out of the system?"

"Please get up. You're making me uncomfortable there."

Tal sat on the bed next to her. "And you're stalling."

Salomen rested her elbows on her knees and her head in her hands. "I never spoke of my powers," she said to the floor. "No one in my family has them, nor did any of my friends. They marked me as something…different. I didn't want that. I never asked for it."

Tal came from a family of strong empaths; her own talent had been celebrated and nurtured. But she could easily imagine how confusing such powers might be to a young child who did not understand them.

"Then the testers came and spoke of changing castes and all that a high empath could look forward to. I was ten cycles and from a producer community. All I knew of warriors was what I read in books. They always seemed to be sleeping outside in the rain, or getting in fights and having friends die, and they never stayed at home. I couldn't imagine it. The only scholars I knew were my teachers, and I didn't care for any of them either. The idea of leaving my family was frightening enough; doing it to become like my teachers or like those warriors in the stories was unthinkable. I would not let them take me."

"Determined and stubborn even at ten cycles."

Salomen raised her head and looked at her.

"Merely an observation," Tal added.

"Not an accusation?" There was a hint of humor in the question.

"No. Now tell me how you avoided being marked."

"I don't know. I went to my test knowing that I could not allow them to see what no one else had. And they didn't."

"You beat the testers?" She had expected Salomen to say that she skipped her testing and somehow the omission was lost in the records. This story was barely credible.

Salomen shrugged. "I did what I had to."

"What you did was beyond belief. Testers are high empaths and extensively trained in the detection of empathic gifts, including all the ways of keeping them hidden. You weren't the first child to try to fool them, but you're the first one I ever heard of who actually succeeded."

"I never heard of it either. If I'd known then what I know now, I probably wouldn't have had the courage to try. I'd have assumed it was impossible."

"Isn't it amazing what you can do if you just believe it?"

Salomen studied her. "Why are you being so nice?"

"Because I just scared you halfway to your Return and I really didn't mean to. But this cannot continue. An untrained empath of your strength is a danger." Tal held up her hand at the surge of dread. "No, don't worry. I said I wouldn't report you and I won't. But there is a price."

Instant wariness. Salomen might be a strong empath, but she had no ability to front her emotions from Tal's senses. "And what is that?"

"You will accept an instructor immediately. I know several who would be honored to train one of your strength. The Whitemoon Sensoral Institute could—"

"No. I won't go."

Tal could not believe her ears. "You'd rather be reported?"

"Lancer Tal, please—I cannot leave my family. Not for that length of time. Don't you see the role I play here? I'm the head of our house. If I spent the next five cycles in Whitemoon, what would happen to my father? And Jaros? Nikin and Herot can run the holding, but they don't have the capacity to hold our family together."

Tal considered her thoughtfully. Taking a child of ten from her family was one thing; removing the head of the house was another. Salomen had a point. Full training, and the change of caste it would entail, would devastate her family. The law did not exist merely to protect less gifted Alseans. It was also meant to make sure that gifted empaths were detected and given the means of developing their powers. Allowing Salomen's tremendous potential to go undeveloped would be a tragic waste, but it was her loss and affected no one else. If Tal could guarantee that she had sufficient skills to protect other Alseans from the potential misuse of her powers, then the main concern of the law would be satisfied.

"Then there's only one alternative," she said. "I'll instruct you."

"Ah. Right. The Lancer of Alsea just happens to have sufficient spare time to spend five cycles training a single person—I think not."

"No, I don't have five cycles. But I have two moons, and in that time I can teach you the basics. You only need to know enough to protect yourself."

Salomen's laugh had no humor in it. "And you believe I would allow you into my mind?"

"Stop me if you can." Tal dove in, penetrating without effort and projecting her intent.

"I agree to your terms. Please train me."

She withdrew and watched the shock register.

"I didn't mean that!" Salomen said in horror.

"Of course not. But you have the power to do what I just did. You have the strength for covert projection and empathic force. You could make someone transfer their fortune to you, or influence a Council member's vote. You could even use another Alsean to commit murder. You *are* a danger."

"I would never do any of those things! For Fahla's sake, even if I wanted to, I wouldn't know how."

"I believe you, but in this instance I'm afraid your word is not sufficient. There's another danger as well. Though you're not a criminal, you could easily be used by one. I had no trouble entering your mind, even with you on your guard. Another strong empath could do the same thing, with more sinister intent. You could be forced to use your powers under someone else's control."

"But I—"

"Salomen, listen to me. You've avoided discovery so far, but your luck won't hold out forever. You're using your empathic strength every day without thinking about it, aren't you? How did you know I tore open my arm yesterday? And don't tell me you just happened to be walking by and heard me."

Salomen couldn't hold her gaze. "I felt it."

"I thought it was an unfortunate coincidence that you were the one to find me. Someday there will be one too many coincidences, and now is not a good time for a high empath to be caught breaking Fahla's covenant. It's been a cycle and I still have people calling me a war criminal. Did you see what happened to the high empaths working with the smugglers in Whitemoon?"

"A lifetime sentence in the Pit," she whispered. "I couldn't believe it. All they did was make a few people look the other way."

"Right now, that's all it takes to destroy a life."

Salomen dropped her head back into her hands.

"I'm sorry," Tal said, "but I cannot allow this situation to continue. Either accept me as your instructor, or leave your family for a full training and change of caste."

"Shek!" Salomen looked at her in despair. "Such an attractive set of options. Abandon my caste or allow the most proud, unfeeling, arrogant woman I have ever met full access to my mind."

The words hit with surprising force. Certainly Tal felt the same about Salomen—at least regarding the pride and arrogance—so why would it bother her to hear that Salomen viewed her that way?

"What you lack in tact or consideration you certainly make up in honesty," she said. "But you needn't have made the effort; I already know what you think of me. You have a choice. Consider it, and give me an answer by tomorrow night." She stood up. "Now if you don't mind, I have a few things to do before coming down to evenmeal."

Slowly, Salomen made her way to the door. She looked back once, then shook her head and walked through.

The moment the door shut behind her, Tal dropped back onto the bed. "What a mess," she whispered.

CHAPTER 33
Bossy

Micah knew something was off the moment Salomen Opah came into the dining room. In all of his interactions with her, she had been supremely confident and outspoken, but this evening it was as if the light inside her had dimmed.

Fortunately, Jaros had not yet run out of questions even after three meals of asking, so there was no lack of conversation. Tal had to reassure his siblings that no, she wasn't tired of answering.

"So you get to tell everyone what to do?" Jaros wanted to know. "And they have to do it, right?"

"If only it were that simple. There are laws far older than you or I which bind all of us, including me. I can order some people around, but not everyone, and I'm limited in what I can ask for."

Jaros frowned as he reached for a biscuit. "Then why be Lancer if you can't tell everyone what to do?"

Good question, Micah thought. That would certainly make both of their jobs easier.

"If someone wanted to harm your holding or your family, would you allow it?" Tal asked.

He bristled. "I would make them sorry they ever had the thought!"

"I feel exactly the same way about Alsea. Your holding is Hol-Opah; mine is Alsea. Your family sits here in this room; mine is the population of our world. I love Alsea, and it's my duty to keep her whole and safe and productive. That's why I'm Lancer." A smile crossed her face as she added, "But it *is* nice to be able to tell people what to do. Sometimes they have to do it."

Jaros smiled back as he chewed. "So you—"

"Jaros," interrupted Salomen, "do *not* speak until you have swallowed."

He instantly swallowed an enormous amount of food, and Micah winced.

"So you're like Salomen," he said as soon as he could get his mouth open. "She's the head of our family. You're like her, but head of Alsea."

"That's exactly right."

"But you're not as bossy as she is."

Micah snorted, and Tal shot him a glare.

"She certainly is," Salomen said. "You just haven't seen it yet, Jaros."

Tal leaned toward the boy. "I am not," she whispered, and he grinned.

The rest of the meal went by relatively quickly, though there was a difficult moment when Jaros announced that he wanted to be a warrior and Salomen informed him that he most certainly would not. Tal answered many more questions about her role as Lancer, eventually turning the conversation toward the holding itself. Micah learned more than he could have wished about its crops, operations, and market transport, though most of the information came from Shikal and his sons. Salomen was still quiet, and he knew her family noticed. They were curious and concerned, but would not speak of the matter in front of the Lancer and her Chief Guardian.

Tal didn't linger at the table, excusing them as soon as she could politely do so. Micah rose with her and was pushing in his chair when Salomen spoke up.

"Just a moment, Lancer Tal. Today's mornmeal was later than normal since it was a free day. Tomorrow we're back to our regular work routine, and Jaros has to go to school, so we'll be having mornmeal a hantick after sunrise, at morn-two." She gave Tal a look of pure challenge and added, "I apologize if that's too early for you."

"No apology necessary," Tal said. "I'll have finished my daily run by then and will be more than ready for a good mornmeal. Thank you."

Micah exchanged his goodnights with the family and followed Tal up the stairs, mulling over that look on Salomen's face. The woman had been quiet all through the meal, and she lit up only when she could challenge Tal?

"I'm revising my opinion," he said as they approached Tal's room. "I thought this assignment would be an enormous headache, but instead it shows much promise. I'll enjoy watching the battle."

"It's a challenge, not a battle." Tal opened her door and stepped through.

That wasn't what she had said last moon, but he knew better than to mention it. Leaning in the doorway, he said, "Why does she dislike you so intensely? You must have done something special to earn it."

"I've done nothing but my duty. She apparently has a different definition of my duty and will not forgive me for not performing to her expectations."

"Then you *have* earned her ire. And I suspect it will only get worse." Chuckling, he added, "I'm fortunate to have the best tickets in the house."

"Don't be too satisfied with your seats. You might find yourself injured by an ill-aimed weapon, namely Salomen's tongue."

"Oh, I think not. Raiz Opah has extremely good aim, and she seems to have found a particular target. I'm feeling quite safe."

Tal smiled as she picked up her reader card. "Ever hear of friendly fire?" She unrolled the reader card and tapped it once, her smile falling instantly.

"That must be from Aldirk," Micah said. His own reaction to this ridiculous challenge had been a baby's fart compared to Aldirk's eruption. The only way Tal had calmed him down was by agreeing to regular meetings during the next moon, and the first was in two days. Aldirk was not about to let her stop being Lancer just because she had decided to be a field worker.

She looked up at him in despair. "Twelve reports, Micah. Twelve!"

He made a show of looking at his wristcom. "That gives you just enough time to finish them before your next attempt to impress Raiz Opah. Really, a run tomorrow? When I could barely get you out of bed today?"

She groaned. "I don't know what I was thinking. She just gets to me."

"There are probably a hundred and eighty councilors who would pay her for her secret. I've never seen you fall into a trap so easily." He paused. "Come to think of it, I might pay her for it, too."

He laughed as the door shut in his face.

CHAPTER 34
The knife and the sword

The Guards who greeted Tal for her morning run looked somewhat worse for wear. As they set off along the route that had already been scouted, she glanced at Gehrain. "Tiles last night?"

He grimaced, then nodded. "It won't affect our performance."

"Of course not." She was feeling quite a bit better this morning, thanks to another night of sleeping like the dead. Too bad her Guards hadn't been smart enough to have their party a day earlier.

"I had hoped to extend my usual run this morning," she began. The total dismay of every Guard taxed her ability to keep a straight face. "…but I must be at mornmeal on time or risk verbal annihilation. So I'll be content with the route we planned."

A collective relief flooded her empathic senses.

"The next best thing is to run the route at a faster pace, don't you agree?" she finished.

"Yes, Lancer," Gehrain groaned.

She smiled and put on a burst of speed.

Tal felt a great sense of satisfaction at Salomen's surprise when she strolled into the dining room, alert and freshly bathed. She sniffed the air with appreciation.

"Good morning. Is that fanten?"

"Yes, we raise them for ourselves. You won't find a fresher cut anywhere."

"Excellent! I adore fanten." Tal poured herself a cup of shannel and sat across from Salomen, savoring the refreshing scent wafting off the hot drink. After her run, she could use its energy-giving properties. "Your holding is beautiful and very well cared for. I ran the south border this morning."

"Which part?"

For a moment Tal didn't understand the question. Then she smiled. "All of it. It was a little short for my normal run, but I wanted to be sure I'd be at mornmeal on time."

"You ran the entire south border," Salomen repeated blankly. "That's eight lengths."

"Mm-hm." Tal sipped her shannel and closed her eyes as the flavor burst through her mouth. The first sip of shannel was always a bit of a jolt. "Those molwyn trees are gorgeous, and I saw a spearfisher in the river, teaching its young how to fish. What a way to start the day."

Any reply Salomen might have made was preempted by the noisy arrival of Jaros.

"Lancer Tal!" He bounded into the room and happily pulled out the chair next to hers. "I saw you from my window, coming up our road. She runs with five Guards," he informed Salomen.

"Yes, I know." Salomen was far less impressed, but she smiled as her brother gazed up at Tal with worshipful eyes.

"Are those Guards the fastest in all Alsea? Is that why they run with you?"

"No, they run with me for my protection."

He frowned. "You don't need protection. You're the most powerful warrior on Alsea."

"But I'm not immune to physical harm. Not all Alseans agree with my policies, and some of them feel Alsea would be better served with another in my place. So they seek to remove me."

"They cannot," Jaros said stoutly. "We learned in school that the Lancer's term ends in one of three ways: resignation, a caste coup, or a…" He thought for a moment. "A vote of no something."

"A vote of no confidence," Tal said, hiding her amusement.

"That's what I meant. But my teacher says the warrior caste supports you, so there can't be a caste coup. And he says that if there wasn't a vote of no confidence after you broke Fahla's covenant, it won't happen now. So you can't be removed." He sat back, proud of his grasp of civics.

Tal felt a burst of affection for this boy who was so happy to have her in his house. "You've obviously paid attention in class."

A secondary pride filtered through as Salomen said, "He always does. Jaros leads his class."

Jaros straightened his shoulders and attempted to look modest, but his emotions had all the unfronted strength of most children his age.

"You have the right to be proud," Tal said. "Knowledge is what separates those who do from those who don't. But there is one more means of removal than the three you learned about. It's called assassination."

"Assassi…assassination?"

Salomen's concern was sharp, and Tal met her eyes.

"He hosts the Lancer in his home. He should know."

"Know what?" Jaros's attention bounced between them.

After a pause, Salomen gave a reluctant nod.

"Assassination means murder," Tal explained. "Usually for political reasons. The Guards run with me to prevent that from happening."

"But why would anyone want to kill you?" he asked with wide eyes. "Salomen says Alsea has never been so prosperous as it has been under your rule. She says you're the best leader Alsea has had in generations, and that no one else could have saved us from the Voloth."

Salomen shook her head. "Jaros, saying anything to you is like alerting the media."

"It is not!"

"I appreciate his honesty." Tal smiled at her hostess, whose cheeks were slightly pink. "It's refreshing to hear the full truth."

Salomen ignored the emphasis on *full* and addressed her brother. "Lancer Tal is a good leader, it's true. But no matter how good any leader is, there will always be some who disagree with the government. And of those who disagree, there will always be a few who are willing to kill for their beliefs. So Lancer Tal can never just run on the public road like you and me. She has to have Guards."

"That doesn't make sense."

"No, it doesn't," said Tal. "But it's life, and we must simply accept it and find ways to work around it."

"And Lancer Tal is very good at that." Micah had just arrived. "She simplifies my professional life with her easy acceptance of this less enjoyable aspect of her title."

Now it was Tal's turn to look discomfited while Salomen smiled broadly. Jaros plowed ahead with more questions from his seemingly inexhaustible supply.

"So you always have Guards? No matter what you do or where you are? Do you have Guards in your bedroom?"

"No!" Tal said quickly. She shot an evil look at Micah, who had not quite managed to suppress his chuckle, and continued, "I can move freely in my home and here in yours. But only because I have Guards outside who make sure no unauthorized person can enter. That's why you had to tell your friends that they couldn't drop by this moon. They have to go through the Guards first."

"Oh." Jaros poured a glass of juice and drank it with a pensive air.

"Jaros," said Salomen as she rose, "why don't you pour juices for the Lancer and Colonel Micah, and I'll bring breakfast to the table."

Micah rose with her. "May I assist?"

"Thank you, Colonel, but it's plain that your duties leave you very little time for relaxation. While you're my guest, you should relax at least within the confines of my house."

The words were gracious and well-spoken, but Salomen had clearly understood every nuance of Micah's comment regarding his professional life. She swept from the room, and Micah sat with a twinkle in his eye.

"At last, a little sympathy," he said.

"Drink your juice, Micah." Tal pushed the glass over to him. "At least I have an ally in Jaros."

Jaros looked up. "What's an ally?"

"A friend who will support me when I need assistance."

"Oh!" He nodded enthusiastically. "Yes, I will." He finished pouring the second glass and handed it to her. She thanked him and took a taste, swallowing hastily when the next question came. "Does that mean you're my ally too?"

"Yes, I am." Never in her political life had Tal been so certain of the sincerity of an ally. "If you ever need help, call me or Colonel Micah."

"Thank you, Lancer Tal. And if you ever need help, you must call me as well."

Tal put on a properly serious expression. "Thank you, my friend. I will."

Footsteps sounded on the stairs, and Tal sensed Herot's arrival. She gave Micah a knowing look just before the young man walked into the room. His hair was still damp from the shower, and he was wearing nicer clothes than Tal would have expected for someone who would be working in the fields after mornmeal.

"Good morning." Herot graced her with an easy grin as he sat next to Jaros. After pouring himself a juice, he reached over and pulled the plate of biscuits from beneath Jaros's hand just as the boy was reaching for one.

"Hey!"

"Wait your turn." Herot took his time selecting a biscuit before handing the plate back, and Tal did a slow burn.

"Herot, why in Fahla's name are you wearing that shirt?" Salomen reentered the room, followed closely by Nikin. As the two eldest children, they held the responsibility of bringing the food to the table. It was an ancient tradition that had fallen into disuse in many city families, but it felt right at Hol-Opah.

"The others were dirty," Herot said.

Tal glanced at Salomen to see if she could sense the obvious lie.

"You will not impress the Lancer by ruining a dress shirt in the field. Go upstairs and change." Salomen didn't even look at him as she set two aromatic platters on the table and pulled out her chair. Nikin put two bowls down and took his own seat with a tiny smile on his face.

That answered that question, Tal thought. Trust Salomen to show no tact whatsoever. She almost felt sorry for Herot, who pushed his chair back with a baleful glare at his sister and went stomping up the stairs.

"Please excuse Herot's...enthusiasm, Lancer Tal." A warm smile wreathed Salomen's face just before she turned her head. "Good morning, Father."

"Good morning." Shikal dropped a kiss onto her upturned cheek before taking his seat at the head of the table. "Good morning, Lancer Tal...Colonel Micah." He smiled at Tal. "I saw you returning from your run this morning. You move like one who knows the winden."

"Thank you. I've always loved to run, even as a child. It helps me order my thoughts."

Shikal nodded. "For that, I go fishing."

"You would fish no matter what order your thoughts were in," Salomen said, but the affection in her tone negated any sharpness in her words.

Tal studied her in fascination. Salomen had gradually relaxed at their meals, last night's evenmeal notwithstanding, and Tal was beginning to see a whole new side of her. In their delegate meetings, she had freely acknowledged Salomen's obvious intelligence and strength of mind, but the woman's unyielding stubbornness, abrasive personality, and ill-concealed distaste for Tal's decisions had led to an instinctive antagonism that she hadn't worked very hard to overcome.

In her home, surrounded by family, Salomen was a different person. Her face was transformed by a loving smile as she teased her father, and Tal opened her senses to fully appreciate the warmth that poured out of this unlikely source. Unfortunately, being so open meant that she was also treated to the full extent of Herot's sulking, self-pitying mood as he reentered the room, now in a worn work shirt. Even with that, she enjoyed the exposure to a family situation so different from her own and was sorry when the meal ended.

The two younger children cleared the table, and Tal noted that Herot managed to carry less than Jaros. She met Micah's eyes and saw his recognition as well.

Micah leaned closer. "Give me one nineday for proper training, and I would make him a different man."

"By 'different,' do you mean dead?"

"You have such little faith in me. I managed to train you, didn't I?"

"I came pre-trained. Your role was largely that of an observer."

Micah's laugh drew the attention of everyone in the room, and he waved a hand at Tal. "Pardon me. The Lancer was testing the limits of my credulity."

Tal grinned at him and felt a prickle of surprise from someone in the room. She turned her head just in time to catch Salomen watching her with a thoughtful expression. Then her hostess spoke to Jaros, who was getting ready to leave for school, and the feeling faded.

There was quite a bit of bustle getting Jaros out the door and the rest of the family to work, reminding Tal of a unit breaking camp and moving. Salomen informed her that today they would be harvesting grain and intimated that the change in routine would give her muscles a break. Tal ignored the gibe.

She soon found herself in a two-person skimmer, with Salomen driving them to the field currently under harvest. It was a quiet ride down the hill and toward the eastern border, and Tal made no effort to initiate conversation. After the morning's controlled chaos, she was enjoying a few moments of peace before the day's labor began.

When they arrived at the field, her Guards were already there, looking out of place in their uniforms as they patrolled the perimeter. The previous two days she had been buried in tall vines and hadn't seen them, but today their presence was all too obvious. She called Micah on her wristcom and asked him to provide the Guards with something a bit less conspicuous, and at midmeal they suddenly took on the appearance of field workers. Tal nodded in satisfaction at Micah's efficiency.

Through the course of the day, Tal learned a new respect for her hostess. Salomen was physically strong, never flagging as she worked side by side with Tal. She didn't ask Tal to do anything she wasn't doing herself, and at midmeal she made sure that all of the field workers were taking the necessary time to relax and eat, even though a few protested that they could finish their tasks if given another quarter-hantick. Tal watched in interest, knowing that not all landholders treated their field workers with such care. But the Opah field workers seemed to be more than just hired laborers. They laughed and joked with Salomen, asking her questions and making observations that demonstrated a personal knowledge of her and her family. Salomen showed the same warmth and affection with them that she had at her own table, and their affection for her was plain to sense.

After midmeal they resumed the hard physical labor of loading newly cut grain into the bulk transport, and by the end of the workday, Tal was more than happy to throw her tools in the back of the skimmer and take a seat. It wasn't as bad as her first two days, but she was still relieved to be done.

Salomen settled in beside her and started the engine. As they sailed over the fields, she glanced at Tal and said, "You're doing well—for a soft politician."

"Thank you so much. I look forward to the day you learn the difference between a soft politician and a trained warrior."

Salomen smiled and turned her attention back to the controls. The rest of the drive passed in a silence that was oddly comfortable.

When they had skimmed back up the hill and pulled in beside the house, Tal gathered their tools and walked toward the equipment outbuilding.

"What are you doing?"

She stopped and turned. "Don't they need to be cleaned?"

"Eventually, yes, but we'll be using them again tomorrow and the day after. Leave them in the skimmer and we'll clean them when we're done."

"And in the meantime, the grime and debris build up and they grow less and less effective. The first rule a warrior learns is that your weapons are only as good as the care you give them."

"They're not weapons," Salomen said. "They're tools."

"Weapons *are* my tools. Along with knowledge, power, psychology, and any number of other items at my disposal. I try to keep all of them sharp."

"You must take extremely good care of your tongue, then." Salomen walked up the porch steps and vanished inside.

Tal stared after her, hardly believing that a producer had just called her sharp-tongued to her face. Did the woman have no respect at all?

Resuming her trek toward the equipment outbuilding, she chuckled. Rarely had she heard such a perfect example of the knife calling the sword a blade.

CHAPTER 35
Speedy

Evenmeal was more comfortable than the previous night's had been, but the ease Salomen had shown at mornmeal was absent. Though she presented a sufficient front to avoid any questions from her family, Tal could sense her turmoil.

Fortunately, Jaros distracted everyone with his happy chatter about the day's lessons. Apparently, the Lancer's presence in their community had inspired his instructors to speak in more detail about the history, responsibilities, and legal issues associated with the title, and he was eager to demonstrate his new knowledge. He rattled off several rather bloody historical tales, his eyes shining with enthusiasm.

"And, Lancer Tal," he continued after quickly swallowing some food, "we also learned that there is a *fifth* way your term could end. You didn't tell me about the ritual challenge of combat this morning!"

"I didn't even consider it. That hasn't been invoked for several hundred cycles."

"Tell us about it, Jaros," said Shikal. He glanced at Tal and smiled, his pride in his son clear to her senses.

Jaros put his fork down, concentrating on his recitation. "It can only be used by a member of the warrior caste. If a warrior wants to take the title of Lancer, but he doesn't have enough caste support, he can challenge the Lancer to single combat. To the death." Plainly, this was an extremely exciting thought. "The winner takes the title legally. Nobody can argue, even if they don't like the person who won."

"Which is precisely why it's no longer in use," Tal said. "It's a relic from the days when Alsean leadership passed from one military leader to another, by right of strength in battle. But good leadership requires more than strength in arms. It requires education, strategic thinking, understanding of Alsean nature and motivations, an ability to plan far beyond the current generation…in fact, a scholar often made a much better Lancer than a typical warrior, and ritual challenge of combat passed out of use shortly after the scholar caste became eligible for the title. Few scholars could have won such a challenge."

"But they could choose a champion," Jaros said.

"They could, yes. But Alsean culture has changed too much for those old ways. We no longer tolerate rulers who take their title violently. Any warrior who wants to challenge the sitting Lancer today would need the support of the warrior caste or risk being immediately unseated. And if a challenger has the support of the warriors, then the title would be taken by a caste coup, not a single challenge."

"Oh."

Tal wanted to laugh at his disappointment. "However, there's one aspect of the ritual challenge that still continues to this day."

He perked up. "There is?"

"All warriors are trained in the art of sword fighting, even though swords haven't been part of Alsean warfare for generations. But they were the only weapon allowed in a ritual challenge."

"Really? So you know how to use a sword?"

Tal nodded. "I'm not a master by any means, but yes, I've trained with a sword since I was your age."

"Speedy! Do you have your sword here?"

Tal turned to Salomen. "Speedy?"

Salomen smiled. "The newest slang term. It means Jaros is impressed."

"It means I want to see it! Fahla, don't you know what speedy means?"

"Jaros!" Three adult voices spoke at once, and Jaros sat back in his seat. Even Tal felt a little intimidated.

"You will not use the name of our Goddess so lightly," Shikal scolded.

"But you do." Jaros's tone was indignant, and Tal pressed her lips together to prevent the smile from escaping.

"That's because Father is an adult," said Salomen. "When you pass your Rite of Ascension, you can do it too. But not before then."

"That's not fair. If I can say it as an adult, why can't I say it now?"

"Because adults carry burdens that children do not," Nikin said. "So one of our rewards is that we get to use words you don't."

"What burdens? You don't even have to go to school!"

"We've already been to school. And now we have to work. And worry about things you don't have to worry about."

Jaros grumbled under his breath, not buying a word of it.

Tal touched his shoulder. "I don't have my sword here, but I could have it brought later."

He looked up, all disgruntlement vanishing under renewed enthusiasm. "Really?"

She nodded. "Perhaps I could even challenge Colonel Micah to a little sparring. It's been more than a nineday since I last slapped him with the flat of my sword."

"Time has obviously clouded your memory," Micah said. "The last time we sparred, it was you who found yourself disarmed. My own sword was firmly in my hand."

"My memory is perfectly clear. I'm afraid age has affected yours, though. Don't worry, Micah, there are many ways an aged warrior can make himself useful."

"I never worry. As long as your youthful exuberance continues to overpower your wisdom, I'll always have a job."

"How old are you, Colonel Micah?"

"Jaros," said Salomen, "that is not an appropriate question to ask an adult."

"I've no objection to answering," Micah assured her, then turned to Jaros. "Sixty-two cycles."

Jaros's eyes widened. "You're almost as old as Father!"

Amid the laughter, Micah said, "And aging faster than he, I'm sure. Serving the Lancer has made me old before my time."

"I thought you appreciated the challenges of your job. Be sure to notify me if they become more than you can handle. I'll replace you with someone younger and more exuberant." Tal looked at the boy next to her. "Perhaps Jaros would accept the position."

"Yes!" Jaros lit up, then just as quickly deflated. "But I'm the wrong caste."

"A boy of your intelligence and talents could challenge his caste."

No sooner were the words out of her mouth than she was pierced by a blast of disapproval. Across the table, Salomen frowned at her.

"Really?" Jaros asked excitedly.

"It's very rare, Jaros." Salomen turned a more kindly expression on her brother. "And being in the warrior caste is not all glory and adventure, despite what you hear at school."

Tal took the hint. "No indeed. Micah could tell many a tale of privation and hardship, and that was before he came to serve me."

The laughter shifted the momentary darkness of Salomen's mood, and for the remainder of evenmeal Tal was careful to steer away from topics that might excite Jaros's imagination regarding his caste. It was clear that his desire to be a warrior did not sit well with his sister.

When the meal ended, Tal thanked her hosts and excused herself from the table, allowing Salomen as much peace and space as she could under the circumstances. She expected that the producer might need the rest of the evening to make her decision. After all, whichever way she chose would irrevocably alter her life.

CHAPTER 36
First lesson

TAL WAS A BIG FAN of the window seat in her room. The cushion was luxuriously comfortable, and if she sat sideways with her back to one wall, she had a lovely view of the Snowmount Range to soothe her eyes whenever she looked up from her reader card. If she had to spend her evenings reading reports and dispatches, the window seat was a fair consolation.

She settled down to work, but her concentration was interrupted after just four dispatches when she felt Salomen approaching her door. She glanced at her wristcom, startled by the time. Salomen clearly did not put off distasteful tasks.

"Enter," she said without waiting for the knock.

The door opened and Salomen walked in. Her bearing exuded self-confidence as she closed the door behind her, but her emotions told a different story.

"I accept you as my instructor," she said stiffly. "I think you know this is not my desire. But it's the only choice I can make. You will not mention this training to my family. They're not aware of my...talent. I've told them that we'll be working on delegate matters in the evenings."

Tal nodded. "Then I accept you as my student, and your family will hear nothing of it from me. Please sit." She indicated the chair she had placed facing the window seat.

Salomen sat, her back rigid.

Tal looked at her in silence, then raised her eyes to the portrait of Nashta Opah.

"Tell me about your mother," she said.

"What?" Salomen frowned. "My mother has nothing to do with this."

"Everything that makes you who you are has something to do with this." Tal rolled up her reader card, put it in its case, and sat up straight. "Your emotions cannot be unlinked from your past or your present. To be effective as your instructor, I need to know you. I already know the present. But I need you to tell me about the past."

"And this is what any other instructor would say?"

Tal let that question hang in the air before asking, "Are you accusing me of something?"

"I don't... No. I'm not." Salomen took a deep breath. "This frightens me."

Tal already knew that. She just hadn't expected her to admit it.

"It takes true courage to admit fear," she said. "I respect courage. It will be my honor to teach you."

Salomen's expression shifted. "Thank you. From you, that means something."

"You're welcome. Thank you for accepting me. Now, will you tell me about your mother? I'd like to know more about the woman whose presence still breathes in this house."

Salomen leaned back in her chair, brushing an invisible bit of lint from her pant leg as she thought. "My mother was my best friend. We were the only women in a house full of men, so we naturally gravitated toward each other." She looked toward the window at Tal's back, not quite meeting her eyes. "But it was more than just that. I shared everything with her, far beyond the age at which most young women begin keeping secrets from their parents. I just never felt the need to assert my independence…maybe because Mother treated me with so much respect. From the moment of my Rite of Ascension, she treated me almost as an equal, asking my advice on things and telling me some of her hopes and dreams."

At last she met Tal's gaze. "I was there when Jaros was born. As you might have guessed, he was a surprise."

Tal nodded; the age difference between Jaros and Herot made that fairly obvious.

"I've never been able to prevent myself from feeling the emotions of others," Salomen said with a half-smile. "Even at the best of times. But when the healer put Jaros in Mother's arms, I had to sit down. Her love for him was—" She searched for the words. "Overwhelming. It was so strong that it hit me physically. To this day I think it must have lodged in my heart. I don't love him like a brother; I love him like my own child. I always have. And when Mother fell ill…"

There was a long pause while she struggled. Tal said nothing, respecting her grief.

"She asked me to finish what she could not," Salomen said at last. "It was never a burden to me. I accepted without a second thought. But it's been very hard without her. I miss her. I miss my best friend." She folded her hands in her lap and stared at them, unwilling to say anything more.

Tal was surprised at the depth of her own sympathy. Salomen Opah had been an unremitting pain in her backside since their very first meeting, but this kind of grief was something she would not wish on even an enemy. And after seeing Salomen in her own home, surrounded by her family, Tal's opinion of her had changed. Fahla only knew why, but she wanted to help.

"My mother was my friend too," she said.

Salomen lifted her head, a startled look in her eyes.

"But my father was my best friend. I was a little too…active for Mother's tastes. She was scholar caste and had hopes for me that didn't include wielding a blade or a molecular disruptor. But I wanted to be like my father. He was my hero."

"So you chose his caste and his name." Salomen had been drawn in despite herself.

"Mother was very good at fronting her emotions, but I always knew it hurt her when I chose not to be Shaldone. She told me that as a scholar I had the potential to be Lancer. She never had faith in my abilities as a warrior, or maybe she just tried to steer me to a safer place. But Father believed enough for both of them. The moment my warrior training began, my Lancer training began as well. I think it never occurred to my father that I would *not* be Lancer someday."

"Well, he was right."

"He was." Tal hesitated before saying the rest. "But his dreams cost both him and my mother their lives."

Salomen's brows drew together. "But your parents died in a transport accident."

"You've done your research, I see."

"I didn't—"

"I've worked with you for nearly five moons now," Tal interrupted. "Your thoroughness doesn't surprise me. But in this case you didn't find the whole truth. That transport crash wasn't an accident."

This was not something she told casual acquaintances. In fact, the circumstances of her parents' deaths had been kept from public knowledge. But she needed Salomen to trust her in order for the training to be effective, and the best means of earning trust was giving it.

Salomen was staring at her. "Are you…they were murdered?"

"They were assassinated," Tal said flatly. "My father had made alliances and deals for my benefit, preparing as much of my way as he could with the connections he had. But others saw his actions and misinterpreted them. They thought he sought the title of Lancer for himself. So they removed him, and my mother along with him. I don't think she was actually targeted, but it didn't matter."

"Lancer Tal…" Salomen's voice was pained. "I'm so sorry."

"I know you are. Thank you for that."

"But…why did they leave you alive? I mean, sooner or later it must have become obvious that you were seeking the title."

Tal watched her for a moment, considering her answer. "When you researched me, did you learn about the Truth and the Path?"

"The warrior's code. I know of it, but no, I didn't spend much time on the details."

"There are a few overriding principles. Loyalty and honor govern our lives and bind us to certain paths. For instance, we're bound to avenge any mortal harm to our oath holder. The tie to family is, of course, the strongest and most sacred of all. When I learned the truth about my parents' accident, I was bound by the code to avenge them." She paused. "It was not a hardship."

"When you say avenge," Salomen said slowly, "I have a feeling you're not referring to capturing the assassin and turning him over to the Alsean Investigative Force."

"In certain cases, the wronged party can apply to the AIF for special dispensation. I applied."

They stared at each other in silence.

"So you...killed him?" It was a hesitant question, spoken by one who wasn't certain she wanted to know the answer.

"There were three. And yes, I fulfilled my obligation."

"Good Fahla. Suddenly I'm understanding who I have under my roof. You are a terrible enemy."

"I'm a good friend and ally, and a loyal warrior. And as your instructor I will also be *your* friend and ally."

"Well, I would certainly prefer that to making you an enemy!" Salomen ran her hand through her hair. "Shek! This is..." She dropped her hand and shook her head. "I'm not comfortable with this."

"There's nothing comfortable about this kind of instruction. That's not what I seek. I seek your trust."

"I'm supposed to trust a woman capable of what you've just admitted to?"

"If someone hurt Jaros, and I mean really hurt him, on purpose, what would you be capable of?"

Clearly, Salomen had never considered this, not in a conscious, honest manner. At last she said, "I would kill them with my bare hands."

"Then perhaps you understand me more than you thought."

Tal waited, undisturbed by the long silence, and knew when the decision was made. The sense of resolution that descended on Salomen's mind was critical to their relationship as instructor and student.

"I'm not sure why you've told me this. But it does give me a different view of you. You make me nervous, Lancer Tal. You're not a safe woman."

"I'm not in a safe line of work."

"I don't think I fully realized that until tonight. But I believe I can trust you. We're here right now because you chose not to follow the letter of the law and report me." She fixed Tal with a penetrating look. "I don't understand the code you follow. But if you're offering your friendship and alliance, I accept it."

Tal noticed that she didn't offer her own friendship in return. This woman did not give of herself lightly. Neither did Tal, but she had a better understanding of the nature of the relationship they were about to enter.

"Then we can begin," she said.

Salomen nodded, visibly preparing herself.

"This won't resemble traditional instruction in any way. We don't have time for that. My priorities are to teach you blocking and fronting techniques, and the discipline to prevent yourself from probing others. You're very strong, but you have neither control nor consistency. I hope I can help you with both of those, but if I cannot, control is the most important."

"Am I really that strong?"

It was an odd question from a high empath, but Salomen had never been properly assessed.

"You fooled the testers when you were ten. And you fooled me until last night. I'm embarrassed that I thought you were a mid empath." Tal caught the sense of pleased pride and added, "Why am I not surprised that the happiest you've been all evening is when I admit you made me look like a grainbird?"

One side of Salomen's mouth quirked up. "I suppose it's just nice to know I could hold my own against the all-seeing Lancer Tal."

Tal swallowed her instinctive retort and reminded herself why they were there. "We'll start with the first step in both blocking and fronting," she said. "Close your eyes."

Salomen looked at her for a long moment, and when she finally obeyed, Tal felt as if a major victory had been achieved. This was not going to be a traditional student-teacher relationship at all.

In a lower voice, she said, "Now think of a time when you were utterly serene. Calm, content, quiet…at peace. Perhaps somewhere special, a place that you love, where you smile just from the pleasure of being there. Tell me when you have that in your mind."

She remembered needing several attempts to find the right thought in her own training. Salomen spoke in less than one tick.

"I have it."

"Good. Focus on that. Close down every other thought, every other concern. There is nothing right now but that single thought. This is your place of serenity. It's a place only you know about, a place where you can go and no one else can follow. Just stay there and enjoy it. Hold that place close."

She extended her own senses, feeling Salomen gradually centering herself. When no more progress had been made for several ticks, she judged that Salomen had gone as far as she was capable—which was surprisingly far for a beginning student.

Sharpening her senses to a focused point, she reached out with a light probe.

"Oh!" Salomen's eyes flew open. "What was that?"

Tal couldn't stop her smile. She felt oddly proud.

"That was something you shouldn't be detecting at this point in your training. It was me probing you, and the fact that you felt it puts you several steps ahead of where I thought we'd be starting. Your powers are very impressive."

"Thank you. But why didn't I feel it last night, when you made me say what you wanted?"

"Because last night your mind was spread thinly, which is normal for an untrained person. A scattered thought pattern is easy to penetrate. But when you focused yourself as you just did, your emotions and mental powers coalesced into something far more dense. My probe impacted your thoughts, and that's why you sensed it."

"Remarkable," Salomen breathed. "Can we do it again?"

Tal almost laughed; in that moment she had sounded just like Jaros. "We can, and we will," she said. "So many times that you'll grow tired of it."

"I do not think I will ever grow tired of this."

"We'll see." But Tal remembered the joy of learning control. "Ready for another try?"

Salomen closed her eyes, a small smile playing about her mouth. "I'm ready."

"Then concentrate, and take yourself back to your place of serenity."

CHAPTER 37
Tell me a story

Life at Hol-Opah settled into a pattern. Tal began each day with her run, using the exercise as a means of exploring every corner of the Opah holding. After mornmeal, she worked in the fields with the Opah family and their workers. She listened to the spare conversation of people who had known each other for a lifetime, and found herself wondering about the richness of detail that was absent from their words but plainly present in their memories.

At one time or another, each member of the Opah family contrived to work next to her. She enjoyed her conversations with all of them except Herot, who reminded her of a first-cycle warrior who hadn't yet had his ego deflated to the proper size. Salomen's arrogance at least had a reasonable source: she was intelligent, determined, and accomplished. Herot just thought he was.

Upon ending her daily fieldwork, Tal became the Lancer again, reading dispatches and reports, consulting with her advisors, and making the thousand decisions that rested in her hands. Sometimes it truly felt as if the weight of the world was on her shoulders as she took responsibility for allocation of resources, health issues, social issues, environmental concerns, and—new since the crash of the *Caphenon*—planetary defense, interplanetary diplomacy, and breathtaking technological advances.

With decisions in hand, she would send instructions to Aldirk, who never missed an opportunity to inform her of how difficult this arrangement made his life. When he arrived at the holding for their first meeting, she left the field at midmeal to spend the afternoon sorting out the kind of minutiae that made her question her own sanity for giving so much of her life and soul to this position. Making the big decisions was one thing; dealing with the innumerable political calculations that made actual progress possible was something entirely different.

At the end of the day, when she had completed both her fieldwork and her Lancer's duties, she became an instructor. Every night after evenmeal, Salomen came to her room for a lesson. Tal found herself looking forward to these sessions, which were a unique mixture of study, practice, and subtle battle, demanding a mental flexibility very different from what was normally required of her.

Salomen was a worthy opponent. She would walk in, stiff and reserved, and Tal would smile from the window seat and disarm her with questions she knew Salomen did not expect: what kind of toys she played with as a child, how her parents met, why she chose the various crops she planted. When she asked why the Opah fanten tasted so much better than anyone else's, she had the rare enjoyment of watching Salomen's reserve melt away in her earnest response on the advantages of the feed she used for the animals, as well as the unique quality of the grass they grazed on in the south pasture. When Salomen discussed her holding, she seemed to forget her distrust and speak almost as to a friend. Perhaps, Tal mused, it was because she was speaking *of* a friend, for that seemed to be how she viewed her holding—as an old, dear, and well-loved friend, worth every bit of the love and labor she poured into it.

One night, she asked why the holding used so many field workers instead of investing in labor-saving equipment. Her query inspired a startled look and then a lecture on the economics of the Opah holding, as she learned that most of the profits of each cycle's harvest went to pay off last cycle's debts and the laborer's wages.

"But if you took out a second loan to buy the equipment, you would be using the profits to pay that instead of worker's wages," Tal said. "And within a few cycles you'll have paid off the equipment and can begin investing the profit in other improvements."

"And just how 'improved' do you think my workers' lives would be?" Salomen asked. "I don't employ them simply to work my fields. I employ them because they've always worked this holding, as their parents did before them and their grandparents before them. I have a responsibility to them, handed down to me through the same generations. We depend on each other, and I will not be the first to end that."

Suddenly, Tal understood a great deal more about the woman facing her and found her respect rising. She and Salomen had more in common than she had first thought.

"That's why I'm so afraid of your policies," Salomen continued. "By destroying our profitability, your matter printers will end the livelihoods of these people more surely, and more quickly, than any equipment I could buy."

"I can understand why you would think that," Tal said carefully. "But think about this as well: It's not just the need for workers that will be reduced. The workers' need for income will also be reduced. If they can acquire the same goods and services without spending six or eight hanticks in the field every day, is that not an improvement for them? Is it not an improvement for you to work less hard, produce the same output, sell it for less so that more can benefit from it, and have more time to enjoy your life? Because the same lower prices for goods and services will apply to you, too. Or, if you wish, you could reinvest that income into growing more varieties and improving the holding. You have so many options! That's what I've been trying to tell you in our meetings. Yes, the matter printer technology will reduce your profitability. But it will also reduce your expenses, and that's the key."

"Do you really believe that will happen?"

"Yes! I would never release that technology otherwise."

She held her breath as Salomen considered it. This was what they had fought over so furiously during their last few delegate meetings, and the fact that they were now speaking in normal tones of voice was already a big step forward.

"I want to believe your vision," Salomen said at last. "It sounds wonderful. But I'm afraid it's just fanciful economics, and we'll pay the price for it."

"Do you honestly think I would risk the very fabric of our culture on fanciful economics? Remember what I told Jaros: Alsea is my holding. I'm responsible for the lives of *all* Alseans. I'm not making choices based on what's best for certain castes; I'm making them based on what's best for all of us."

She was close to a breakthrough. It was right at the surface of Salomen's emotions.

"Don't take my word for it," she said. "Feel for yourself."

That earned her a wide-eyed stare, and the rest of the evening was spent on a lesson in controlling emotional skimming. Once again, Salomen was an excellent student. Not only that, but by the end of the evening Tal thought she might even have converted Salomen to her policies.

Of course, the infuriating woman wouldn't give her the satisfaction of saying so.

As the days passed, Tal became comfortable at Hol-Opah. She was working her legs off, but her body had adapted and she enjoyed the physicality of it. More than that, she relished the peace. Sometimes she stopped what she was doing and simply looked around, soaking up the beauty of her surroundings, the delicious scents of sun-heated soil and growing things, and the absence of city noise. It felt like sanctuary—a refuge not just from Blacksun, but from what Alsea had become. Nowhere in her field of view could she see any sign of the Voloth invasion or the changes it had wrought. Conversation here centered on the holding, its products, the harvest, and the people, just as it had for generations. This was the Alsea of old, and she loved it.

Strangely enough, she had even become comfortable with Salomen. Though their lessons continued to be a form of genteel combat, something had shifted between them. It was less edgy. Of course, that didn't prevent her from occasionally baiting her student. She couldn't help herself; it was too much fun.

One night, half a moon into their challenge, she asked Salomen to tell her an amusing story.

"A story about what?" Salomen asked in dismay.

"Anything you find amusing."

"But…I can't think up something on demand. It has to be more spontaneous."

"All right, I'll make it simpler. Tell me about a time when you were so embarrassed you wanted to crawl under a rock. I'm sure that will be amusing."

The sizzling glare made her laugh.

After a pause, Salomen began to speak, but her story was not what Tal had expected. She told of an evening when she was a young woman of nineteen cycles, just before her Rite of Ascension. A local boy had invited her to join him at a dance, and since it was the first time anyone had asked her, she had been full of excitement—until she arrived at the tavern where the party was to take place and learned that there was no dance after all. It was just another night at the tavern, and she stood out like a Council member at a fanten farm in her fine clothes. A shout of laughter drew her attention to a table near the fire, where the boy who had invited her held out his hand. "Pay up!" he called, loud enough for everyone to hear. "I told you I could do it!"

To her complete mortification, half the people in the room shuffled over to slap coins on the table. Amid a general roar of laughter, she turned and left, her cheeks burning with rage and humiliation.

Tal's cheeks were warm as well. Had she been there, that little fantenshekken wouldn't have laughed at Salomen for long.

"That was not amusing at all," she said stiffly. "Does he still live around here?"

"You've met him. It was Norsen."

Norsen. The producer who had said nothing of value in their delegate meetings and asked Salomen to not only take his place, but also to lie for him.

"Norsen was a waste of space," she growled. "You're worth ten of him."

After a startled pause, Salomen said, "It was a long time ago. But thank you."

It wasn't long ago to Tal, who wanted to find Norsen right now and teach him a lesson. But Salomen was puzzled by her anger, and with some effort she reined it in. "Why did he do it? What made you the target?"

"I think it was because I didn't take part in the school social life. I had too many responsibilities on the holding. By then I was doing our accounting and worrying about whether this cycle's harvest would pay last cycle's debt and still leave us enough to repair the west fence line and the oldest outbuilding. But the others in my class were worrying about wearing last cycle's fashions or buying the fastest skimmer. Their concerns seemed so trivial, and I don't think I hid my impressions very well."

"So you snubbed them and they made you pay?"

"They must have thought I was snubbing them. But I wasn't. I liked most of them; I just couldn't understand why they attached so much importance to such minor issues."

"Ah. You grew up before they did."

Salomen shrugged. "I suppose that's what happened. And they could not forgive me for it."

A half-moon of practice had vastly improved her ability to front, but her expressive face often reflected the emotions she was working so hard to conceal. Watching her, Tal couldn't help feeling sympathetic for that young pre-Rite girl who had taken on so many responsibilities and paid such a high price.

And was still doing it, she realized. Salomen had antagonized her from day one, but it had always been in defense of her caste—and by extension, her field workers, her family, and her holding, which Tal now knew was the driving force behind everything Salomen did. She would risk anything for them, including the personal enmity of the Lancer.

She looked at Salomen with new eyes, understanding then that she had chosen her story to make a point. For two ninedays, their lessons had been more than just instruction. They had also been a subtle war of words and power. Salomen would not fully accept the subordinate role of student, and Tal could not prevent herself from repeatedly asserting her authority. In truth, it had never been a healthy student-teacher relationship.

"You've changed the rules of our engagement, haven't you?" she asked.

"I don't understand."

"Yes, you do. We've sparred since the day we met. But you just dropped your sword, and I think you did it intentionally."

"You asked for an embarrassing story. To amuse you."

Now it was Tal who was embarrassed. Hearing her own request repeated back to her made it seem so…callous.

"I'm not like you," Salomen added. "I don't always have the stomach for sparring. But sometimes it seems as if it's all we ever do, and I don't know how to make it stop."

Tal's shoulders hit the window as she slumped back. Salomen was so good at their verbal battles that it had never occurred to her they weren't equally enjoying it. She had been battling an unwilling opponent? But that was impossible; she would have sensed it if—oh, no.

She hadn't sensed it because Salomen had *fronted* it, with the same selectively impervious front she used against the testers all those cycles ago. Her skills may have been patchy, but the one thing she had always known how to do was protect herself. And Tal had forced her into the position of protecting herself here, where she should have been safe.

A wave of hot shame washed over her as she thought of all the instances where she had used her position to needle, poke, and bait her student—and been pleased with herself, as if she was winning some sort of shekking competition. And she called Salomen the arrogant one?

"You just made it stop," she said. "Salomen, I—Goddess above, I swear I didn't realize— Why didn't you…?" She shook her head. No. No excuses. Clearing her throat, she spoke more formally. "I apologize. I've abused my position and shamed myself."

Salomen stared in open astonishment.

"You're right, there's no reason you should be forced to spar with me in this room." Tal waved her hand toward the window. "Out there, or in the State House, we've been in a civilized form of battle from the moment I walked into that delegate meeting and heard you questioning my competence. You made no secret of your disdain for my policies or for me personally, and I enjoyed having someone of your caliber to spar with. But we shouldn't be sparring here. Not while I'm teaching you. I carried that in from outside and didn't even recognize it until now, and for that I am truly sorry. It was—inappropriate."

Still Salomen said nothing, and Tal found herself speaking into the silence.

"I gave you very few options when we began. You deserved more than that. If you'd prefer a different instructor, I can find someone who will train you here on Hol-Opah. You wouldn't have to leave. It's the least I can do to make up for my behavior."

Of course Salomen would leap at the opportunity to learn from someone else. She had never trusted Tal in the first place—and for good reason, as it turned out. Tal closed down her senses, not wanting to feel Salomen's relief at being released. Nor did she wish to examine her own inexplicable regret at having to relinquish her role as instructor. Hadn't this been a thorn in her side since the first day? Why wouldn't she want someone else to take over? Fahla knew she could use the extra time.

At last Salomen rose from her chair, stepped to the window seat, and held out a hand.

It was the last thing Tal had expected. Cautiously, she reached out, and Salomen took her hand in a firm hold.

"On our first night, I said that accepting you as my instructor was not a free choice. But that was because you were more an opponent than anything else. Judging from your words and from what I'm feeling—" she gripped Tal's hand more tightly—"I think you are not my opponent now."

"No," Tal said ruefully. "You just knocked me flat in the dirt, without even a sword in your hand. I believe I've lost the desire to spar—I'm completely overmatched."

Salomen chuckled. "Somehow I don't think that's likely. And I'm not interested in another instructor. You've taught me so much in the last half moon, and I don't want to start over with someone else. You *are* my choice."

Rarely had Tal been so humbled. "Thank you," she managed. "I'm honored to teach you."

Salomen stepped back and sat down, settling herself comfortably in her chair. "In that case, what is tonight's lesson?"

"You must be joking. Tonight's lesson has already been taught. I'm still recovering from it."

The full smile that earned her made all the rest worthwhile.

CHAPTER 38
Tal's turn

IF SALOMEN CHANGED THE RULES of engagement that night, on the next night she changed the battlefield completely. She arrived at the usual time, sat in her chair, and spoke before Tal could say a word.

"How did you feel when you killed the ones who murdered your parents?"

"What? No. I know what you're doing, and it's not appropriate."

"Why not? Are you the only one who can ask questions? You said that you needed to know my past and present to teach me. I think I need to know your past and present to learn."

"Salomen..." Tal rubbed her forehead. "That is not part of a student-teacher relationship."

"Do we have a normal student-teacher relationship?"

"I think that very little about us could be considered normal."

"I agree. Then you'll answer my question?"

Two days ago Tal would have met that with a stinging parry, but after last night's lesson she found herself unable to refuse.

"Yes, I will, but you should take care in your choice of questions. You may not enjoy the answers."

"It's not about enjoyment. It's about learning."

Tal heard the message beneath the words. She leaned her head against the window and closed her eyes, allowing her thoughts to revisit a room she had not opened in some time.

"The first one was the worst," she said at last. "I tracked him down and waited until he was alone in his home, except for the private guard that he was never without. The guard was good. I was better." She paused, remembering that fight. It had been silent, quick, and vicious. Both combatants had their honor at stake, and it made them brutal. She had not wanted—

"Did you kill him?" Salomen's voice interrupted her thoughts. "The guard, I mean."

"I knew what you meant. And no, I didn't. I just made sure she couldn't stop me." By ending her fighting days forever, it turned out. That had been the worst part of the whole thing, because she had no quarrel with the guard. The woman was just doing her duty, and Tal had been too young and inexperienced to know how to defeat her without causing permanent damage. She would do it so differently now.

"The guard was right outside the study. I had to take her out silently and block her emotions as well, because I couldn't give Norshank any warning. If he'd heard or felt anything, he would have been gone before I could get into the room. But I surprised him."

You know why I'm here, she had said.

Yes, he answered, facing her with an insufferable lack of fear. *Because I made the mistake of not killing you as well.*

Now is your chance to rectify that error, she said, and he tried.

"He had a disruptor in his desk drawer, and when I opened the door, he already had his hand in the drawer. Either he heard something, or he simply lived in that much paranoia. But it didn't matter; I was ready for him. When he lifted his arm, I put a knife through his shoulder."

"You stabbed him?"

"No." Tal's eyes were still closed; she was watching the scene play out in her memory. "I threw it from across the room."

"Fahla," Salomen whispered.

"He dropped the disruptor, and I walked up to him with a dagger in my hand. I wanted to savor his death. That's why I didn't shoot him; it would have been too quick. I'd planned this for a long time, and I had so much hatred. Nothing but a slow death could satisfy me. I needed him to die slowly enough to *know* he was dying, and to know that he had no control and that I was watching every moment of it. Because he had taken both of my parents from me."

There was no sound from Salomen, but Tal could feel her horror. She opened her eyes. "You wanted to know."

"Yes." Salomen met her gaze steadily. "I still do."

Tal nodded, but she no longer saw Salomen in front of her. It was Norshank's face, full of fear. Finally.

"He tried to run. I hadn't expected that kind of cowardice. I thought he would die like a warrior, but he was a warrior in name only. But I would not have it said that I stabbed a man in the back, so I brought him down and smashed his face into the floor until he stopped struggling. Then I turned him over so that he could look into the face of his death."

Her eyes refocused; Salomen's expression had not changed. "And that was when I lost the taste for a slow kill."

"Why?"

"Because of the damage I had already done. He was broken and bleeding, and his lips were a pulp, and I thought it would make me feel...right. Because I had honor and justice on my side. But it didn't feel right; it just felt unnecessary. I had the right to kill him. But I didn't have the right to make him suffer.

"I planned to stab him through the heart. A cleanly punctured heart won't bleed out right away—the muscle still works and the blood pressure will often keep the puncture sealed. But that only lasts until something disturbs the equilibrium.

I'd thought about this so often, fantasized the whole scene. I was going to stab him and he'd know that he was a dead man, that it was just a matter of time. And then I would tell him all of the things I'd wanted to, for so long. I had the whole conversation planned out. And when I was done, I'd stand up, bring my boot heel down on his chest as hard as I could, and watch him die like the blindworm he was."

"But you didn't."

Tal shook her head. "When it came to it, I didn't have a thing to say to him. I just stabbed him and moved the blade in his heart. Up and down, back and forth. It was probably a more painful death, but it was also far quicker." And messier. She should have just slit his throat from behind, keeping his body between her and all that blood.

"How did you feel when it was done?" Salomen asked gently.

"Tired. And filthy. Fahla, it was such a mess. And…disappointed. I had been living for that moment—it was supposed to free me. But it didn't. And I still had two more to go."

"Were they any easier?"

"Yes. Because I no longer expected the kill to make me feel better."

"So when it didn't…"

"I wasn't disappointed. Killing them didn't bring my parents back."

Salomen's brows contracted. "But you knew it would not."

"No, I had to learn it. I had to learn the difference between avenging my parents and revenging myself. One is a duty. The other is an emotion that a true warrior rejects. And since then, I have."

"You've never killed in revenge?"

"No. Not since that first time."

Salomen nodded silently.

Tal reached out with her senses, relieved to see that her horror had faded into acceptance. Not understanding, but acceptance. She didn't think she could hope for more than that. The warrior's code was learned over a lifetime; it was too much to ask that one not raised in it could easily comprehend the loyalties and duties that made some actions not simply justifiable, but necessary.

"Thank you," Salomen said at last.

"You're welcome. Why did you ask?"

"Because I wanted to understand you."

"Do you?"

"No. But I'm one step closer."

Tal looked into dark eyes that seemed so much warmer than they ever had, and spoke the truth in her heart. "I think…that I want you to understand me."

The smile that appeared on Salomen's face was truly beautiful. Tal was too lost in contemplation of it to be prepared for what came next.

"I owe you an apology, Lancer Tal."

Tal shook herself out of her daze. "No, you don't."

The smile turned self-deprecating. "The night after you arrived, I sat here beneath my mother's portrait and called a guest in my home proud, arrogant, and unfeeling. She would have been ashamed of me."

There was nothing Tal could say to that, so she waited.

"Last night you apologized to me. The Lancer of Alsea, apologizing to a landholder. I thought you proud, and you humbled me. I thought you arrogant, and you showed up my own arrogance. I thought you unfeeling, but now…" Salomen paused. "I confused depth of emotion with lack of it. And I of all people should know better. Will you accept my apology?"

"Without hesitation. I misjudged you as well, with very little excuse. I'm a fully trained high empath, yet I still mistook your integrity and strength of will for arrogance. You fight for what you believe is right. You may be a producer, but you have the heart of a warrior." Tal looked up at the portrait. "I didn't have the pleasure of knowing your mother, but I think she would have had much to be proud of."

Salomen's eyes grew suspiciously shiny and she dropped her head, but hiding her face could not conceal her emotions.

Tal watched in alarm, praying that she wasn't actually going to cry.

The prayer was to no avail, and when she heard the quiet sniff, Tal found herself slipping off the window seat to kneel by Salomen's chair. "Please don't," she said. "Warriors have no idea what to do with tears."

Salomen laughed and wiped her eyes, but the tears continued to flow. "Neither do stubborn producers who carry the weight of a family and a holding on their back. Fahla, I miss her."

She looked up and opened herself, and Tal was taken aback at the sudden onslaught of grief and longing. Salomen Opah had been keeping a great deal of pain inside.

A memory surfaced in her mind, perhaps released by Salomen's deep need for comfort. She remembered Ekatya saying *Please accept this as the gift I mean it to be* and the compact body molding itself to hers. For a nineday and a half, she had experienced the precious physical comfort which Alseans denied themselves and which Gaians took for granted.

Perhaps warriors did know what to do with tears.

"Come," she said, standing up and pulling Salomen with her. "I think you might require a hug."

"A what?"

"A warmron, but between unbonded adults."

"But—"

"I know, it's not done. And that is our loss." At Salomen's questioning look, she added, "I learned something from the Gaians during their stay. Captain Serrado taught me that in their culture, warmrons aren't limited to bondmates or lovers, or parents and children. And they don't end when the child reaches the

Rite of Ascension. They're given freely, among family, friends, and lovers, from birth to death. If you'll allow me, I would like to give one to you. I can tell you from experience that it's a wonderful thing."

"Experience? You allowed one of them to give you a warmron?"

Tal didn't need her emotional sense to know how shocked Salomen was at that bit of news.

"Look into me." She dropped her own blocks and let her mind replay the precious memories, unable to stop the smile as she did so. She had never envisioned herself sharing this with anyone, but felt certain that Salomen would keep it safe. Even so, she was careful to exclude her deepest emotion from the remembrance, guarding it out of long habit. None but Micah knew of it, and he would be both first and last.

"And I called you proud and unfeeling." Salomen's tone was self-castigating.

"We both made mistakes. But we've also taught each other a great deal in these last two days. Will you let me teach you this?"

Salomen searched her face for long moments, then nodded.

Tal felt a sudden sense of responsibility; Salomen had placed an enormous amount of trust in her. Such close physical contact would render not just their surface emotions but also some deeper emotions instantly clear. In a way, it was like dropping a front. But Salomen needed more than just words. She needed to know that someone understood what she felt, and Tal knew from experience that such understanding combined with physical closeness was the most comforting thing in the world.

Carefully, she wrapped the other woman in her arms, not surprised at the initial rigidity. But then Salomen melted into her and held on, absorbing the comfort with something approaching anxiety, as if she were afraid it would end before she could get her fill. Tal tightened her own hold in response.

"Why do we ever give this up?" Salomen asked, her voice thick with tears.

"Because it's too close to a Sharing, I suppose. But this is one thing the Gaians do far better than we."

"Oh, Fahla..." Salomen burrowed deeper into the warmron, clinging desperately, and her pain poured out.

Tal held her close, projecting her sympathy and understanding. Salomen's emotion was all too familiar to her. It had been many cycles since her parents' Return, but that kind of pain could never be forgotten.

"I think we've allowed fear to keep us from comfort," she said quietly.

Salomen made a small sound, then loosened her hold and pushed herself back. But she did not release her arms from around Tal's waist, and Tal did not correct a presumption which would have been inconceivable at any other time.

"You mean we withhold warmrons after the Rite of Ascension because of the emotional connection?"

Tal nodded, looking into the dark brown eyes so close to hers. Until last night she had never seen Salomen this close, and then she had been too consumed by her own shame to really observe her. Now she noticed the marks that cycles in the fields had left on Salomen's face: the lines radiating outward from the corners of her eyes, the slight creases around her mouth. They complemented her cheekbone ridges and set off her dark eyes, which held a depth and seriousness that belied their owner's age. Salomen's life and character had marked her with beauty, but Tal could only observe it in silence. Speaking her thoughts would end this moment and raise all the walls that had just been dropped between them.

"For a culture built around emotions, we seem to have a surprising number of defenses against them," she said. "We deny ourselves the comfort of physical touch for fear of revealing too much, and in the process forget how necessary that touch is. We accept it as normal and desirable from birth until the Rite of Ascension, and then we're expected to relinquish it, instantly and without regret. And we do, because we're taught to revere the loss as a mark of adulthood. Loss disguised as gain. It took an alien culture to show me that no matter the disguise, it's still a loss."

"It is," Salomen said in wonder. "And we are fools."

"We are the result of generations of tradition. We're only fools if we continue to follow it blindly, even after our eyes are opened."

"My eyes feel wide open." Salomen's expression grew distant as she added, "I held my mother this way, just before her Return. I could feel her leaving. She was so fragile in my arms, and she smiled up at me with such joy. I thought then that she must be reliving her childhood, as they say we sometimes do when our minds leave our bodies. I couldn't understand any other reason for the way she accepted the warmron, and I couldn't stop myself from giving it to her. It felt selfish, and I was ashamed, but…she was so happy."

"It's not selfish to give a gift." Tal reached up to brush away a tear that Salomen seemed not to have noticed. "Your mother felt that for what it was. You made her last moments joyous, and none of us could ask for more than that."

"Do you really believe that?"

"What have we been doing in this room if not to make such a question unnecessary? Look for yourself."

Tal watched as Salomen centered herself and extended her senses. Her powers and discipline were remarkable; after just two ninedays of training, there was a pronounced change in her abilities. It took less than ten pipticks before Tal felt the brush of another mind against hers, and she willingly opened her emotions to the skim.

Salomen smiled sadly. "Thank you. You have no idea what your belief means to me." She shook her head, releasing her hold and stepping back. "Of course you do. Sometimes I forget how powerful you are. You have such control that I'm almost never aware of it when you skim me."

"I didn't need to skim you. Your emotions are stronger than you realize. To my mind, they're very clear."

"Have I not gained any strength in my fronting, then?"

"Of course you have. But—" Tal stopped, and Salomen looked at her curiously.

"But what?"

There was no option but to speak a truth which Tal herself was just realizing.

"I'm paying closer attention."

"Because I'm your student."

Tal shook her head. "Because I care."

Salomen frowned slightly in concentration, and Tal knew when she had sensed what she was reaching for. The tiny frown changed to a lovely smile, transforming her face.

"You're not what I took you to be. But perhaps I'm the one who hasn't been paying attention. The Lancer I thought I knew would never have said something so kind, nor would she have apologized to a mere landholder."

"The Lancer did not apologize to a landholder. Andira Shaldone Tal apologized to Salomen Opah."

"Salomen Arrin Opah," Salomen corrected.

"Of course. I've just never heard you use your father's name."

"Only on formal occasions. We producers seldom have need for all of our names, you know. Not like fancy warriors."

Though the bait was temptingly dangled, Tal didn't take it. "I think I have little need of all my names in this room. When we're here, alone, will you call me Andira?"

"I'm honored." Salomen narrowed her eyes. "Is this what any other instructor would say?"

Tal smiled as she recognized the words from their first night. "Not a single one I can think of. Are you accusing me of something?"

"Yes. I'm accusing you of being a friend."

"Then I have no defense, and can only await the judgment."

"No judgment," Salomen said softly. "Just my thanks, and the offer of my friendship, whatever it's worth."

"It's worth a great deal." Tal knew this for a certainty. "I suspect you don't offer it easily, and I'm honored by it."

Salomen looked away, her arms held tightly over her chest. When she looked back again, her expression was nearly as open as her emotions. "Do you think…I mean, could we…?"

"Yes." Tal opened her arms, and Salomen lost no time moving into her embrace.

"Thank you," she whispered.

When they finally released each other, neither of them knew where to look. They had crossed a line, and everything after this was new territory.

Tal took refuge behind her teaching responsibilities. "You've done an admirable job of distracting me. But we're still having a lesson."

"And what did you have planned for tonight?" Salomen played along, and Tal could sense her relief at having something familiar to fall back on.

"Broadsensing."

"What?"

"Opening your senses to the point where you can feel the surface emotions of everyone around you."

Salomen frowned. "I already do that. I don't like it. Can you teach me how to turn it off instead?"

"To learn one, you must fully understand the other."

"I knew you'd say something like that. Remind me again why I chose you?"

CHAPTER 39
Caprice

Micah punched the feed button for his reader card and divested himself of his belt and weapons as it loaded the day's news, dispatches, and reports. He was thoroughly enjoying being out of Blacksun, which sometimes felt like a pit of venomous zalrens. Point him toward an enemy or a clearly defined project, and he was a happy man. But Blacksun was full of shadows and half-truths and actions with multiple motives, and nothing was as clear-cut as he would have liked. He had never wanted to be involved in government, but he waded through those zalrens and more for Andira Tal. Besides being the daughter of his closest friends, she was a friend in her own right and had earned his loyalty ten times over.

He was grateful to her for bringing him on what he was increasingly considering a vacation. For once in her life, Tal was making things easy for him. Other than the morning runs, she didn't move around much, and in the last nineday had never left the Opah holding. It made guarding her no more challenging than guarding a dokker. He chuckled at the thought, knowing that she would be outraged at the comparison.

The chuckle died in his throat as he scanned the first story on his card. He went back to the beginning and read the whole article carefully, then dropped his head back to glare at the ceiling. Fahla was a capricious goddess, damn her.

"Couldn't you have let just *one* thing go right?" he demanded. "Why did it have to be her?"

CHAPTER 40
New runner

When Tal walked out the back door just before dawn, she found an unwelcome addition to her running group. Herot dawdled near her Guards, conspicuous both in his lack of uniform and his bearing. The Guards stood straight, watching him with bemusement. As the brother of their hostess, he had certain rights, but no one had the right to run with the Lancer unless she had specifically stated it. And she certainly had given them no such statement.

Rolling her eyes, Tal trotted down the porch stairs. She was only surprised that Herot had waited this long.

"Good morning," she said.

The Guards saluted, while Herot flashed her a smile.

"Good morning, Lancer Tal." His tone hinted at a friendship to which he had no claim, and she resisted the urge to dump him on his backside.

"I have little time," she said. "Did you wish to speak with me about something?"

"Nothing in particular." He glanced at the Guards, then at her with what was probably supposed to be a charming grin. "I don't see you in the fields as often as I'd like, so I was hoping I might join you on your run."

"Ah, then you're a runner." She knew he wasn't.

"No, but I used to be. I've been meaning to start again, and I thought now would be a good time. You set such a good example."

The contempt rolling off her Guards was palpable. They would love nothing more than for her to put this presumptuous young man in his place.

Guards, she thought, *this is my gift to you this morning.*

"Then by all means, join us." With no further words she set off, running easily at half speed. She had already stretched in her room, preferring to do it in privacy. Her Guards knew this and had completed their stretches as well. Tal was reasonably certain that Herot had not, and the pace she was setting would render him very sore if he tried to keep up with cold muscles.

He did try. He even made an attempt at conversation, but she put an end to that by announcing that she was nicely warmed up now and it was time to begin the run.

"Begin?" Herot gasped, and that was the last word he said for quite some time. Tal was now running at full speed, and the effort of keeping up rendered him incapable of speaking, which Tal—and all the Guards, she knew—considered a vast improvement.

She showed no mercy, her speed unchanging even as Herot's distress became obvious. A part of her grudgingly respected him for pressing on. If he actually made it through their entire ten-length run, she might even revise her opinion of him.

Less than two lengths in, he stopped, tumbling onto his back in the grass and gasping for air.

Tal didn't slow down. "Make sure he gets back to the house," she said, and Gehrain motioned to Varsi, the newest member of the squad. Tal felt Varsi's disgust at being left behind on what she no doubt considered garbage detail. There was also a sense of resignation, as if she had expected the assignment.

"Why Varsi?" she asked as they swept around a curve in the path.

Gehrain grunted. "Shekker beat me out of a quarter-moon's salary at tiles."

"Oh, she's a young one. She'll learn." It was dangerous to play tiles with a superior officer for just that reason: the warrior code of honor had never excluded revenge for a gambling loss. While she didn't engage in those behaviors—which made her a popular tile player—she also didn't discourage it in her Guards. In a culture as rigid as theirs, a little sublimation went a long way toward relieving pressure.

The rest of the run was blessedly peaceful, and she arrived back at the house in a relaxed frame of mind. She might even have stayed that way, but Micah intercepted her as she walked down the hall toward the shower.

"Tal. You need to see this." He held out his reader card, and a comment on his poor timing died on her lips when she felt him. Micah was deeply upset about something.

She took the card from his hand and perused the text. It was an open letter to all major Alsean news agencies from a coalition of economists, declaring their opposition to the use of matter printers and their belief that such use would result in a global economic collapse.

"Shek."

"Keep reading."

Below the letter was a report containing a statistical assessment and projection, which had been undertaken over the course of six moons. The coalition had put a considerable amount of work into their report. This was no mere political opinion. It was serious, documented scholarly research, and it was going to have an enormous impact on both the Council and Alsean public opinion.

"Perfect," she said. "That's just what I need right now."

"Keep reading." Micah folded his arms across his chest.

She scanned past the source list for the data, and came upon the list of signatures. There were more than fifty of them.

"Who in Fahla's name got fifty economists to agree on something?"

His expression gave her the sinking feeling that she knew the answer. With a sense of foreboding she scrolled down to the final line, which acknowledged the lead authors of the report. After staring at it for a moment, she returned the card to Micah. "Well," she said with false cheer, "now I know why Darzen wouldn't return my calls. She was busy with her research."

"I never thought she would do something like this. My instincts failed me. I believed she would be good for you."

"I believed the same thing. At least our instincts are consistent."

"Consistently wrong," he said in disgust.

"I disagree. If circumstances had been different, Darzen could have been good for me. But I hurt her and damaged her pride, and we both know that few wounds go deeper than those. Besides—" she tapped the reader card—"everything here reflects what she told me on our last night, before she knew who I was. This is her truth."

"Well, her truth is more wrong than my instincts."

Despite the seriousness of the situation, Tal laughed. "I think you're more angry about this than I am."

"Why aren't you? This is bad, Tal. You've spent the last cycle working and strategizing and educating and holding the hands of every Alsean who cannot envision a greater future, and now this. You know it will set off a firestorm."

"I know." The brief humor of the moment vanished. "I'm sure there's a message from Aldirk waiting for me, and I'm sure the next few ninedays are going to be a Fahla-damned battle, but we'll just have to fight it intelligently." She looked longingly toward the shower. "And if the global economy is going to collapse, can I at least bathe first?"

Micah stepped aside. "I'll prepare the Guards for our departure," he said as she walked past him.

She stopped and turned. "I'm not leaving."

"You cannot stay."

"Yes, I can. I agreed to a challenge. I'll leave when it's finished."

"That was a ridiculous power play, and I never did understand the point of it, though I've certainly enjoyed my time here. But this is serious, Tal!"

"So is this!"

As he stared at her, she sighed and walked back. "Something is happening between Salomen and me," she said in a low voice. "I don't know—"

"*What?*" Micah burst out. "You and—"

She clapped a hand over his mouth, horrified at his volume. "A little discretion, please," she whispered furiously. He nodded, wide-eyed, and she dropped her hand.

"You and Salomen? When did that start? And why didn't you tell me? Fahla, you keep your tiles close to your chest!"

He was hurt, she marveled. "I didn't keep anything from you. This has taken me completely by surprise. It's been creeping up on me so slowly that I noticed nothing until just last night."

"Well, what happened last night?"

She opened her mouth, then closed it again as she was swamped by a memory of Salomen in her arms. Micah's astonishment was as warm to her senses as the blood was in her face.

"Andira Shaldone Tal, you are *blushing*." All concern for Alsea's economic future vanished from Micah's emotions, replaced by a sincere delight. "To think I should have lived to see this day! You and a producer? And not only that, but the most obstinate, argumentative, unyielding woman I have ever met besides…" He paused for theatrical effect. "Come to think of it, you're perfect for each other."

"Funny, Micah. Enjoy it while you can."

"Oh, I will." He chuckled. "Are you going to tell Aldirk we're staying, or shall I?"

"Since you already seem to be in such a fine mood, why don't you? Then I can take a Fahla-damned shower, and we'll deal with the Darzens of the world."

He nodded. "For what my opinion is worth, she's a fine woman."

"I know." She gave him a wry smile. "What I don't know is whether she holds the same opinion of me."

He clapped her on the back. "If she doesn't now, she will soon. Go shower. You stink."

CHAPTER 41
Lesson in manners

Herot was late for mornmeal, and when he finally shambled in, Tal swore she could see a black cloud over his head. She blocked her senses rather than be subjected to his anger and self-pity at such close range, and knew by the faintly distracted look on Salomen's face that she was doing the same.

"Salomen," she said, "there's a situation forming that will require a great deal of my time in the next few days. I'm afraid I'll have to cut back on my field work. And would you mind a more frequent use of your parlor? And perhaps a few more guests?"

"Are you sure this isn't an attempt to wriggle out of pipe repair? I know how much you enjoyed it yesterday."

"You *like* digging pipe?" Jaros asked incredulously.

"About as much as you like homework."

"Oh." Plainly, this made far more sense. "Maybe we could trade."

"You'd rather dig pipe than do homework?" He nodded so enthusiastically that she couldn't restrain herself from ruffling his hair. "Well then, perhaps we can work something out."

"Don't get your hopes up, Jaros. I have prior claim to the Lancer's time, or at least as much of it as she's able to give." Salomen reached for the juice pitcher. "Can you tell us anything about the situation?"

Tal explained the coalition's report and the loss of civic confidence that was sure to follow unless she could head it off. She and her advisors would be meeting that very afternoon to determine a strategy, and a Council session had been scheduled in Blacksun for the next day.

"But surely you and your advisors took these considerations into account when you devised the original strategy," Shikal said.

"We did."

"And have these economists been privy to the development of that strategy?"

"No one on my team signed that letter. These people weren't involved in the original planning meetings. But I made the documents public as soon as they were complete."

"So you made a decision and informed everyone else of it after the fact, and now you're surprised that some people disagree with it?" Herot asked.

Everyone stared at him.

"Herot…" Salomen began, but Tal cut in.

"I'm not surprised at all. I just wish the coalition had chosen a less damaging method to air its disagreements than a worldwide press release guaranteed to frighten the entire population."

Jaros had been listening with a look of confusion. "I don't understand. You wouldn't do anything to hurt Alsea."

"No, I would not."

"Then why are these people saying you would?"

"Because they don't think she knows quite as much as she thinks she does," Herot answered.

"Herot!" Salomen glared daggers across the table. "Where does this come from? You will not insult a guest of our home. Apologize, now."

Herot glared right back. "You're not my mother!"

"Well, I'm your father," Shikal said angrily, "and you *will* apologize."

"Not to me." Tal was watching Salomen's white face with concern, and when she lowered her blocks for a quick skim, her suspicions were confirmed. She turned to Herot. "You can't hurt me with words. But you certainly know how to hurt your sister, don't you? I believe you owe *her* an apology."

Herot threw his napkin on the table and walked out, leaving a heavy silence behind him.

"Lancer Tal," said Shikal, "Please accept my apologies in place of my son's. His behavior is inexcusable."

"His behavior to me is...understandable. He learned a hard lesson this morning and hasn't worked past it. What I won't excuse is him diverting his anger from me to Salomen. I have no right to interfere in family issues, and there's more going on here than I'm aware of. But I'm here as a guest of Salomen, and her welfare is my concern."

"Enough." Salomen had found her voice. "Father, we don't need to involve the Lancer in this. Can we simply agree to move on with our day? We have much to do."

Shikal agreed, but the rest of mornmeal was subdued until Tal told a story about a training mission that had ended with Micah falling face-first into a mud pit. Micah's outraged response to the story had most of the family laughing, and Jaros was wide-eyed with fascination. He was extremely reluctant to leave for school afterward, and only an affectionate swat on the rump from Salomen was sufficient to get him moving.

Soon after, Tal and Salomen were settling into the skimmer, which was bristling with the tools they were using on the irrigation project.

"Wait!" Tal said just as Salomen started the engine.

"What?"

"I forgot my gloves. Don't leave without me."

"You only wish I would."

Tal jumped out of the skimmer and jogged to the equipment outbuilding, where she had left her gloves drying the night before. Preoccupied with thoughts of how to defuse the economist situation, she didn't sense anything outside her own mind until two distinct sources of white-hot anger singed her. It was Herot and Jaros, and they were both behind the outbuilding.

She ran to the corner of the building and stopped abruptly, debating her course of action. Her instinct had been to step in, but this was between two brothers. Who was she to interfere?

Then she heard the dull thud of a body hitting wood and Jaros's cry, and that was all it took to send her around the corner wanting Herot's blood.

Jaros was picking himself up off the ground and rubbing his shoulder, while Herot stood over him threateningly.

"Leave my things alone, you little fantenshekken," Herot snarled.

"I didn't take it! You probably lost it!"

Herot reached out to shove his brother again, but stopped when Tal moved into his field of view.

"You *are* having a bad day, aren't you?" She turned her attention to Jaros. "Are you hurt?"

"No," he said sullenly.

She crouched in front of him, her senses alert for any movement behind her. "Are you sure?" she whispered.

He nodded, his expression growing more open. "I'm fine."

"In that case, you're late." She winked at him. "But before you go, I need to know one thing. Are we still allies?"

She felt understanding dawn. "Yes," he said, casting a sidelong look at his brother.

"Then, my ally, you go to school, and I'll take care of this."

Without warning he wrapped his arms around her, gave her a quick warmron, picked up his bag, and sped off. She took a moment to savor his spontaneous affection before turning to face the far less affectionate brother behind her.

"I see you're unaccustomed to rejection," she said.

He glared at her. "I'm unaccustomed to being treated like dirt."

"Really? How interesting. You certainly know how to treat others that way. I've seen you do it twice in half a hantick."

"You have no right to speak to me of my family!"

"I have a right based on my alliance with Jaros. I always honor my alliances, which means any threat to Jaros is a threat to me. Would you care to push me into the wall now?"

He scowled at her and turned to walk away. In two steps she closed the gap, caught his arm, and swung him around. He threw his own momentum into the swing, raising his fist as he turned, but she caught it, tripped him up, and in a moment was sitting on his back as he struggled beneath her. His efforts were hampered considerably by the hold she still had on his arm, which was twisted up behind him.

"Let's consider your morning so far," she said conversationally. "You've had a sexual interest in me from the moment we met—no, don't worry, I doubt anyone else knows except Colonel Micah...and Salomen...and the rest of your family except Jaros...oh, and all of my Guards. But after half a moon of receiving zero encouragement, you decided to push your interest on me by simply appearing for my morning run. It did not occur to you to ask permission beforehand, nor did you think your actions through to their possible conclusions. A serious flaw in your strategy, by the way."

He growled and tried to buck her off, but stilled when she twisted his arm a little higher up.

Settling herself more comfortably, she continued. "You also did no research on your target. If you had, you would have known that I run ten lengths each morning, that my Guards are chosen in part for their ability to keep up, and that I don't tolerate interference in my morning exercise. Did you actually think I would slow my pace or even end my run because you couldn't keep up? Is that why you feel you were treated like dirt? You interfere with my activities and then feel mistreated because I didn't drop everything in order to adjust for your lack of consideration, your misplaced arrogance, and your appalling presumption?"

She paused, aware that Salomen was nearby. Turning her head, she saw her hostess leaning against the corner of the building, arms crossed over her chest. Their eyes met, and the message was clear: Salomen would not interfere.

"You earned this morning's lesson," she said. "Actions lead to consequences. And just so you're aware, I reduced my Guard in order to assure your safety and health. I do not jeopardize my personal safety for dirt. But I did it for you."

"You did it for your guilt," he snapped.

"No, I did it because you're a member of my host family. That's all. You personally have earned no consideration from me, nor have your actions been worthy of any respect. But I really didn't think you'd be so obtuse as to earn two lessons in one day. Taking your anger out on your family is the mark of a very small man. Is that what you want to be?"

He was silent, but she had skimmed his emotions and knew the truth, even if he didn't recognize it in himself. She loosened her hold on his arm and leaned forward, speaking quietly and in a kinder voice. "It doesn't matter what others think of you. Be your own man. Prove them wrong. Prove *me* wrong."

She released him and stood back, balanced on the balls of her feet as she watched him scramble up. He turned to her with fury etched in his face, and she closed her senses against it.

"I have nothing to prove to you!"

"But you do have something to prove to yourself. And what you're doing now isn't working, is it?"

He raised his eyes, seeing Salomen for the first time, then turned with an oath and stalked away. Tal watched him go for a few moments before walking back to her hostess.

"That was quite a show," Salomen remarked.

"I'm surprised you allowed it."

Salomen pushed off the wall, and Tal fell in step next to her as they made their way back to the skimmer.

"I allowed it because I knew you wouldn't hurt him. And I'm afraid that someday, somebody will if he doesn't pull himself together. He's made enemies in town. But I'm more worried about his choice of friends."

"This is about losing Nashta, isn't it?"

Salomen gave her a startled glance, then shook her head. "After our training sessions, I should know better than to be surprised by anything you say. Yes, I think so. Herot adored her. They had a special bond."

"I'm sorry this has been so difficult for you."

Salomen stopped and looked toward the south border. "It has been, but I realized something back there, watching you do what none of us could. It's less difficult with you here." She strode off again. "Come on, we're late already."

Tal jogged to catch up, and they walked the rest of the way to the skimmer in silence. Salomen had just started the engine when Tal said, "Wait!"

"What now?"

"I never got my gloves."

Salomen dropped her head to the steering yoke. "And you lead our world?"

CHAPTER 42
Open door

Tal returned to the house after midmeal for a hastily arranged meeting with Tophalamon and Ponsard, her top economic advisors, and Miltorin, her communications advisor. For the rest of the afternoon they worked on a plan to deal with the expected fallout from the economist coalition's report, and by the end Tal was satisfied that they had a firm grip on the situation. She just wished it didn't involve quite so much of her time, but there was no way to avoid the public appearances. And tomorrow she had to go to Blacksun for the Council session, which was sure to be full of posturing. Some of the Councilors would seize on this publicity to further their own maneuverings for power within their regions and castes, and she wasn't looking forward to an entire afternoon of useless bickering. In fact she wasn't looking forward to leaving Hol-Opah at all, but the real world had intruded on her sanctuary.

After the meeting she recorded a message for the citizenry of Alsea, calmly countering the coalition's forecasts, reiterating her implementation plan, and assuring her people that if she had any doubt as to the benefit of the matter printer technology, she would never use it. She also reminded them that she had pursued a carefully thought-out and timed implementation precisely to avoid such catastrophes as those predicted in the statement, and that the opinion of the coalition did not reflect the opinions of her top advisors. A reference to the qualifications of her advisors left the distinct impression that the coalition was comprised of those who hadn't been good enough to be selected for the Lancer's team—a tidy bit of phrasing for which she could thank Miltorin. The man was a master manipulator, and Tal had originally brought him on her team not because she wanted him working for her, but because she wanted to avoid having him work against her. It had been a wise choice.

Though she sat in the parlor for the recording, viewers would not see Salomen's furniture in the background. To ensure the Opah family's privacy and to imbue the message with the authority of her office, the vid would be reproduced to appear as if she were speaking from her office in the State House, with the Alsean flag and the Seal of the Lancer behind her. Technology had its benefits, she thought as the vid crew packed up and trooped out.

Then again, so did generations of tradition. She had come to love this house, with its well-rubbed furniture and lived-in appearance. Salomen's home breathed history and life, and Tal could sense the energy its previous inhabitants had left behind.

She moved to the window and leaned against the sill, watching the nearby trees swaying in a gentle afternoon breeze. It was a beautiful day, and she would far rather have spent it in the fields than in a strategy meeting. On the other hand, if she had been in the fields she wouldn't have had her revelation.

It happened during a break from the meeting, when they were getting drinks and stretching their bodies. She had gone to this same window, letting her mind wander away from the task at hand, and had suddenly tuned into Salomen's emotions. For a moment she thought her hostess must be returning to the house. Tal held the highest empathic rating they could measure, but even her senses did not extend more than a few lengths. Yet when she examined the emotions and their source more clearly, she knew Salomen was still in the field, working on the irrigation project.

She could sense Salomen at *nine* lengths?

The meeting had resumed then, and she had to focus on politics and economics. But now the inevitable conclusion was knocking at her brain. Long-distance sensing was rare among Alseans, occurring only in those who were bonded tyrees.

But they weren't bonded. And they certainly weren't tyrees.

A shocking thought occurred to her: perhaps they weren't tyrees *yet*.

She thumped her forehead against the glass, welcoming the cool smoothness on her hot skin.

"This is not possible," she murmured. "I know something is happening, but it cannot be that."

She reached out with her senses, attempting to reproduce the connection. Nothing. Just the emotions of the Guards at the doors, and the vid crew and advisors who were still loading up their transports. Salomen was beyond her range. It was as if a door had opened in her mind, given her a brief glimpse of what lay on the other side, and then closed again.

Did she want that door to be open?

She honestly couldn't say. Because if it did open, permanently—if this really was a symptom of a future tyree bond—then it would provide more than an unprecedented, almost unthinkable view into Salomen.

It would give Salomen the same view into her.

CHAPTER 43
Fear

Spinner set his reader card down and smiled. The news was full of nothing but the economic report, and opinions were flying. A few defended Lancer Tal's policies, but new and sensational always beat old and established. She had lost a significant amount of support, particularly in the producer caste. He couldn't help feeling smug that it had taken him just one day to tear down what she had spent so much time building up. She was too idealistic, thinking she could reach the people through education and dialogue. But fear was always the most powerful tile on the board.

The challenge had been too quiet. If Lancer Tal had any sense, she'd have made regular statements from Hol-Opah, speaking about her "learning experience" or some such garbage. She should have released vids showing her working in the fields, side by side with the other workers—playing up her image as the people's Lancer. But for some inexplicable reason, she had let all of the publicity possibilities slip through her fingers. He couldn't understand it, given the brilliance of her initial acceptance of the producer's challenge.

He tapped his fingers on the desk, thinking about the most intriguing report of the day. According to his spy in Granelle, all was not well at Hol-Opah. The middle son—who until now had been throwing around references to his special relationship with the Lancer—had apparently suffered a setback and been taught a stinging lesson. Of course, he hadn't put it quite that way while complaining at his favorite tavern, but it was obvious to anyone who could read between the lines. For Lancer Tal to interfere in family matters was very interesting indeed. And she told Herot that she was stepping in due to an alliance with the youngest son.

Was it possible that she wasn't taking advantage of the public image possibilities because she was actually becoming invested in that family?

He drummed his fingers again, staring out the window. How ironic it would be if the final tiles he needed were on Hol-Opah. Because if they were, then Lancer Tal herself would hand them to him.

CHAPTER 44
Closed door

"Your message was very well done," Salomen said as she settled in for their evening session. "You made me believe."

"Good. One believer on my side, five hundred million to convert. No, wait, make that three believers. I think Micah and Jaros are with me as well." Tal pushed her reader card to the other edge of the window seat. She had already received the preliminary assessments from her strategic team, who felt the message had been as successful as they could hope. But that hadn't assuaged the general poor temper that left her feeling unsettled all evening.

"I don't even have to skim you to feel your anger." Salomen spoke carefully. "What happened between midmeal and now?"

Tal rested her head against the window with a sigh. "Everything and nothing."

"That's a politician's answer. And you are not a politician."

"Yes, I am," Tal snapped. "If I were not, I'd simply exercise my power as Lancer and inform everyone that the matter printers are being implemented in three moons whether they agree with me or not. Instead I'm playing a game of approval, and it galls me that I should have to do so after an entire cycle of being so Fahla-damned careful with the concerns of every shekking caste!"

She closed her eyes, ashamed of her outburst and vividly aware of Salomen's surprise. In the long silence that followed, she listened to Salomen's shifting emotions and waited for the battle of words to begin. After all, it was what they did best—what they had done through their entire relationship. The last two nights had been different, but she wasn't convinced that it signified a true shift in their interactions.

And that, she realized, was what had been bothering her all day. She didn't know if their truce would hold, and her strange connection during the strategy meeting had left her feeling much too exposed.

"I think," Salomen said at last, "that I believed the lie just like every other Alsean. And now I see the truth."

Here we go, Tal thought.

"And what is the truth?" she asked. It was almost like a ritual bow before the fight.

"You're Alsean."

"I think that particular truth might be self-evident."

"No, it's not. You work very hard to convince all of us that you're omnipotent. The all-knowing, all-seeing, all-powerful Lancer Tal. Someone above and beyond a simple Alsean. But you're not. You're one of us. And yet you carry a burden far above and beyond what any Alsean should carry, don't you? And so the lie is necessary. Because without it, we wouldn't believe that you could carry that burden. It's our very belief in your omnipotence that makes your office possible."

While Tal was recovering her tongue, Salomen continued. "I'm thinking out loud, because I've never thought about it in these terms before. But your predecessor was removed by a caste coup because he couldn't sustain the lie. Not because he was incapable as a leader—he certainly was an idiot, but that alone wouldn't have unseated him. The critical issue was the lie. Wasn't it?"

The smile came despite Tal's best efforts. "Have you any interest in becoming an advisor? I have need of one who sees as clearly as you."

Salomen smiled back. "Then I'm right."

"You are. Tordax was an idiot, but we've had idiots in power before. His true failure was in losing the faith of the warriors. When we ceased to believe in his effectiveness, we removed him."

"And the warrior and scholar castes chose you to replace him." Salomen's curiosity regarding this secretive process was easily readable. "Why you?"

"Do you mean why me as opposed to another, more qualified candidate?"

"No, I do not. I mean, why you? How were you elected?"

Belatedly, Tal realized that she had slipped into sparring mode. She was dreading a battle, yet she swung the sword first.

"Partly because of my connections," she said. "I had the support of some powerful families in both castes. I think I owed that to their sense of justice. My parents were assassinated for a misinterpretation of Father's intentions, and though that truth isn't commonly known, those who do know it wield a great deal of power. And partly it was a backlash against Tordax. He was scholar caste and had failed. That swung the favor to the warrior caste. But because I come from both castes, the scholars could also support me. It was ironic, really—my mother believed I would never rise to Lancer as a warrior, and in fact if I were only a warrior, I probably wouldn't have. It was her influence in raising me as both scholar and warrior that made the difference."

"Hm." Salomen stretched out her legs and leaned back in her chair. "You say nothing about strategy. Did you not strategize for much of your life to be in the right position when the time came?"

Tal had been distracted by her graceful movements and those legs, which she didn't remember being quite so long. When she looked up again, she found Salomen watching her with a steady gaze.

"I strategized to be as prepared as I could if the time came," she said. "But I never wanted to fight that kind of battle, removing competitors and putting myself where I thought I should be. I've seen those fights and defended myself against them. They're dirty and I wanted no part in them."

"Perhaps that's another reason you were chosen."

"Sometimes I think it might be. Other times, when I'm in a cynical frame of mind, I think it might actually have worked against me."

"Are you in a cynical frame of mind now?"

Tal hesitated, wondering about the motives behind that question. But Salomen's expression was open, showing no signs of the wariness which had so marked their interactions until two nights ago.

Perhaps it was time to take a chance.

"Yes, I'm feeling cynical," she admitted. "But more than that, I'm tired. I've spent a cycle trying to bring six squabbling castes into a united vision of the future, and just when I thought my efforts were coming to fruition, that coalition released a warhead. So now I begin a new battle, trying to make up ground I thought I'd already won, and I'm just…" She raised a hand and let it drop into her lap. "Tired."

"I'm sorry. Is there anything I can do to help?"

"No. Thank you, but there's nothing you can do. Unless you'd be willing to offer a public testimonial as to how you once opposed my policies but now believe in them wholeheartedly."

"I could do that. Actually, I've already made plans. The Granelle Producer Caste House has called an emergency meeting in three days to discuss this new situation, and I'll be speaking on your behalf. I know," she added at Tal's obvious surprise, "I've not been your greatest supporter."

"You have a gift for understatement."

A faint embarrassment surfaced. "I can be…stubborn. But I like to think that I'm also willing to admit my error when facts prove me wrong. Which occurs very rarely." A full smile creased her face, crinkling the corners of her eyes and deepening the dimple in her chin.

Tal chuckled. "Once per cycle, I'm thinking."

"No, no, more like once every five cycles."

"Then I'm privileged to witness such a rare event."

"Yes, you are."

She had to know. "So you really believe in me? When did that change?"

"I said I will be testifying to a belief in your *policies*." Salomen raised her eyebrows.

"Oh. I suppose that was too much to hope for. Perhaps in another five cycles, then."

"Would it really matter whether I believed in you personally?"

With a single question Tal was disarmed. She could lie, but…

"Yes," she said. "It would."

"Why?"

"I told you last night. I care."

"Good, because I care, too. And I don't like to see you cynical and tired." Salomen stood up, stepped to the window seat, and held out a hand. "Come. I have a potential aid for you."

As Tal slid out of her seat, Salomen reached for her other hand and said, "Sometimes, when I was a girl and my responsibilities seemed too heavy to bear, I would tell my mother that I was too tired. Too tired to go into the fields, too tired to make yet another flight to the distribution center, too tired for school. And she'd tell me that she understood. Then she would say, 'You need a little more strength. Here, take some of mine.' And she would give me a warmron." A sense of warmth and safety rose in her emotions, the by-product of her memories. She tugged gently on Tal's hands. "You need a little more strength, Andira. Here, take some of mine."

Tal allowed herself to be pulled into the warmron, marveling at the improbability of it even as she sank into the freely offered comfort. Gradually she relaxed—until a flash of Salomen's emotions nearly burned out her empathic senses.

She jerked her head back, her eyes squeezed shut in an instinctive effort to shut out the intrusion. It was the emotional equivalent of staring into the sun, an overdose of sensory input that left the viewer temporarily blind. Not even in her Sharings with Ekatya and Lhyn had she experienced a power like that.

She stumbled backward, bumping into the window seat. When her head cleared, she looked up to see Salomen staring at her with wide eyes.

"What was that?" Salomen whispered.

"You felt it too?" But she already knew the answer. Oh, no. This wasn't possible.

"Fahla, I felt *you*. As if I were inside you." Salomen was unsteady on her feet, fumbling her way into her chair. "And…I felt…" She met Tal's eyes briefly before looking away. "Something I cannot put a name to."

Tal buried her face in her hands. "Shek. Nor can I. But now we have to." She pushed herself up onto the window seat and leaned against the cool glass. "Did you sense anything unusual this afternoon? Sometime around mid-three?"

"No," Salomen said thoughtfully, and Tal breathed a sigh of relief. "Wait. Yes. I remember now. Just for a moment, I thought you were there in the field with me. I actually looked around for you, but of course you were here in the house. I didn't think much of it, but… Why do you ask?"

"Because at mid-three I was taking a break from my strategy meeting, and I connected with you."

"What? You were nine lengths away!"

"I know. Don't look so shocked; I'm not the only one in this room who sensed another mind from nine lengths."

"I didn't…" Salomen's eyes widened. "That was really you?"

Tal nodded.

"But…" The rapidly moving kaleidoscope of emotions settled into pure denial. "No. This is not possible."

Tal had to laugh. "Precisely what I was thinking."

But Salomen wasn't laughing, and when she stood up, her emotions vanished behind a front that was suddenly impenetrable.

"I require a break from our lessons. Please excuse me." She walked out and shut the door behind her with a decisive click.

Tal stared at the closed door, then up at the ceiling. "You do have a sense of humor, don't you?"

She jumped off the window seat and began to pace, too wound up to stay still.

This was really happening. But how could it be? They had done nothing but battle each other from the moment they met. Weren't tyrees supposed to sense it from the beginning? For Fahla's sake, she was one of the strongest empaths on the planet and Salomen might be in the same category—how could they not have known?

And Salomen clearly didn't want her. She couldn't even stay in the same room with her.

A strangled laugh escaped. In any other situation, Tal would have dropped to her knees to thank Fahla for making her tyree. It was the dream of her life. And when it finally happened…

Pacing wasn't enough. She needed to run.

She stripped off her shirt and yanked her running clothes out of the drawer. Micah was about to become an unhappy man. Guarding her at night was a whole different prospect than guarding her in daylight, but she would not wait. Besides, she was on Opah land.

Though after this, she might not be welcome on Opah land much longer.

CHAPTER 45
Dreams in the field

It was a subdued Tal who made her way to mornmeal the next day. She had skipped her morning run, having thoroughly exhausted both herself and her Guards the night before, and enjoyed a rare opportunity to lounge in bed. Had she been given the choice, she would have stayed there rather than face Salomen across the table.

Salomen was equally reluctant to appear. Her front no longer had the strength it had briefly developed the night before, and Tal could not prevent herself from skimming the emotions of the woman who had occupied her thoughts all night long. The head of Hol-Opah was hiding in the kitchen, delaying her entrance until the last possible moment. When it could no longer be avoided, Tal sensed her consciously gathering her courage before walking through the doorway.

When their eyes met, an electric charge ran down her spine. She offered a cautious smile and was ridiculously gratified when Salomen responded in kind. Part of her was lost in contemplation of those lovely lines at the sides of Salomen's mouth, and part of her was disgusted with the whole situation. This was not the behavior of Alsea's highest-ranked warrior; it was the behavior of a trainee barely past her Rite of Ascension.

But then Salomen sat across from her, giving Tal her first close-up view since the previous night, and she forgot everything else in her appreciation of a pair of dark brown eyes.

Until Micah kicked her under the table.

"I'm sorry, Jaros," she said, realizing what she had missed. "I didn't hear the last part of your question."

"I said, did you know that our continents used to be squished together?"

Thank Fahla, it was something easy. "I did. You're learning about continental drift in school?"

He nodded. "They keep going back and forth. They crash together on one side of the globe and then bounce off and crash together on the other side. My teacher said that right now they're bouncing off." Frowning, he added, "But he didn't say when they'd crash again."

"Not before you finish school," Nikin said. Salomen gave him a playful push on the shoulder.

"Your brother is displaying just how much he has forgotten since his own days in school," she told Jaros, and received a push in her turn.

"If I am, then I've forgotten more than you ever knew." Nikin looked at Jaros. "It won't happen for a long, long time. Millions of cycles."

"Oh," Jaros said in disappointed tones. "I wanted to see it."

The rest of mornmeal was spent on discussions of travel and how alike or different Alseans were in other cities and holdings. Even Herot took part, with no signs of the sullen behavior that had so marked the meal yesterday. Tal was grateful for the distraction. But the reprieve lasted only until the meal ended and Jaros left for school; his departure was always the cue for the rest of the family to scatter to their various tasks for the day.

She walked to the skimmer and leaned against it, wishing her heart would calm itself. It was embarrassing to have so little control over her body.

With her gaze fixed on the landscape and her back toward the house, she gave herself every possible moment of delay as she sensed Salomen's approach. Only when the skimmer door opened did she turn, catching Salomen looking at her.

They both froze in place, and Salomen's front slipped. Tal was horrified at what she felt.

"Salomen—"

"We are not discussing this now."

The clipped tone was far too familiar, a relic of their interactions before Salomen had opened up. She was well and truly closed now, and the loss was painful. Tal hadn't realized just how much their nascent friendship had come to mean to her until it had been withdrawn.

Salomen ducked into the skimmer without another word, and after a pause Tal followed suit. They sped down the hill and over the fields in silence, both staring straight ahead, until Tal could stand it no longer.

"You don't need to be afraid of me," she said.

"I'm not afraid."

Tal looked at her incredulously. "First you walk out on me, and now you lie?"

"Andira...I need some distance from this. Please."

"I can give you distance. But I'm not certain our minds will cooperate."

"That's what I'm afraid of."

"Not having control over your mind?"

Salomen nodded.

"Then you're in excellent company. I'm less than ecstatic about it myself."

She felt the surprise right before Salomen said, "Do you know, that hadn't occurred to me."

The surge of anger was so rapid and so strong that Tal could barely front it in time. Her voice shook as she said, "Yes, Salomen, there *is* another thinking, feeling Alsean on the other end of this connection."

Crossing her arms over her chest, she stared resolutely out the side window. She'd had just about enough of women assuming her lack of emotion due to her title. The only woman who hadn't made that assumption, who had treated her as an equal, was Ekatya. And she had never even been available.

Tal had thought that old pain was done and buried, but it felt just as powerful now as it had a cycle ago. Letting her head fall back against the seat, she breathed deeply and focused on thoughts of running, free and alone, through an ancient forest. It was her place of serenity, the place she had used during her mental training and which she still found necessary on occasion.

By the time they reached their destination, she had boxed the unwanted memories and put them away, but the anger was still there. She barely waited for the skimmer to stop before leaping out, grabbing her gloves and soilbreaker from the back, and striding through the tall grass to the pile of freshly dug soil that marked Salomen's most recent efforts from the day before. She threw the soilbreaker to the ground, jerked on her gloves, and picked it up again, her mind transforming it from a tool to a weapon. With a vicious swing she buried it to the hilt, tore it free, and swung again. The exertion was exactly what she needed, and she threw herself into it with such ferocity that Salomen, who was coming behind her with the spade, could not keep up. For more than a hantick Tal sweated out her frustration, losing herself in the physicality of it, until a hand on her shoulder made her jump and twist around.

"Shek!" She glared at Salomen, who had stepped back with wide eyes. "Don't ever do that! Fahla, I nearly knocked you flat." With a huff she threw down the soilbreaker and put her hands on her hips, waiting for her breathing to come down to normal.

"Thank you for restraining yourself," Salomen said, but the sarcasm didn't match the tentativeness in her gesture as she held out a water flask. "I just thought you should hydrate. You've been working very hard."

Tal stripped off her gloves, took the flask, and drained half of it. "Thank you," she said, handing it back. "I lost track of time."

"I know. Andira...I'm sorry. I've been selfish, and I hurt you."

"Surprising, isn't it? I imagine you hadn't realized I could be hurt." She didn't know where her anger was coming from, but even after a hantick she hadn't worked it out of her system.

"No, I didn't." Salomen's voice was steady. "And that is your doing."

"*My* doing!"

"Yes. Your lie. The lie of the omnipotent Lancer. I only discovered the truth yesterday; I need a little more time to fully realize it."

Tal blew out a breath and wiped the sweat off her forehead. "Well, you have a point."

"It's not just the loss of control that frightens me."

It took Tal a moment to catch up, but when she did, her anger began to drain away. "What else?"

Salomen looked over her shoulder. "Them. And what they represent."

"My Guards?"

"You've dressed them like field workers during the day, and they keep their distance, but there's no hiding what they are and what they do. They're here because of you."

"No, they're here because of my title."

"Is that not the same thing?"

Tal heard Darzen's words, heavy with betrayal. *There's just one problem with that, Lancer Tal. Your title* is *everything.*

"No, it is not." Her voice came out in a growl, and she spun on her heel to walk away. Three steps later she reconsidered and spun again, striding right into Salomen's personal space. "Yes, I am the Lancer," she said furiously. "But I also have a name. And behind that name is an Alsean who eats, drinks, sleeps, and loves, just like every other Alsean. I can be hurt, and you've become surprisingly proficient at it, Salomen! I've dreamed of a tyree bond my whole life, and now that dream looks like some kind of sick joke. Why Fahla matched me with you I have no idea, unless it was to satisfy her damned sense of humor!"

Salomen glared at her, giving no ground. "How dare you call this a joke! Don't you think I've dreamed of this, too? But in my dreams, my bondmate was someone who understood the joys and responsibilities of working a holding. Someone who understood stability, and tradition, and the rewards of growing something. Not someone steeped in violence, with blood on her hands. Not someone who lives and breathes power and politics, and goes nowhere without five or ten Guards to keep her from being killed! That is not what I want!"

"And this is your view of me? After everything I've shared with you?" Tal was so infuriated she didn't know whether to spit or cry. "You don't see the woman who loved her parents and lives their dream? The woman who showed you that warmrons should not be limited to pre-Rite children? The woman who—" She choked on her words and turned away. "Fahla. I would wish this away if I could." The truth of that brought tears to her eyes. How could something she had longed for all her life be so completely wrong?

"Andira..." Salomen's voice was suddenly gentle, and Tal shook her head.

"Don't. I cannot abide this. You pull me in and then push me away, and I will not play this game." She gave a bitter laugh. "Your front has improved dramatically. I can't sense you. I've taught you the very thing that allows you to keep me on the edge."

Salomen stepped around and looked her in the eye as she deliberately dropped her blocks. "I'm not fronting now."

Tal went still as the emotions bombarded her. It wasn't normal; they were much too strong. Had they been making a physical bridge, she could understand it, but they stood an arm's length apart and yet she could hardly find the line between their minds. Why were their words so combative when their feelings were almost identical?

"I'm not trying to hurt you, Andira. Please, I don't want it to be like this. I'm sorry for what I said, but...I'm drowning in this, just as you are, and trying to find my way back to solid ground. It scares me."

"What if there is no solid ground?" Tal whispered.

"Then perhaps we will drown together." Salomen gave her an uncertain smile. "But...I would prefer that we hold each other up."

The first breeze of the morning sighed through the grass, carrying the scent of freshly turned soil and lifting a few wisps of Salomen's hair away from her face. A nearby grainbird whistled its short, high call note, as if in response to the wind, and another answered from farther away. The first one burst into song, and Tal remembered a time when she and Micah had stood toe to toe just like this, in a forest ringing with birdsong. Then she had been running from the loss of a love she could never have; now she stood facing a love that might be hers—if only they could both accept it.

"I'm frightened too," she said. "But the one thing that scares me the most is the way you wield your weapon. I don't seem to have any defenses left."

"What weapon?"

"Your words. They're effortlessly damaging. I'm not 'steeped in violence.' That's not what the Truth and the Path is about. That's not what *I'm* about." She held up her hands between them. "I do have blood on my hands, yes. But I swear to you that none of it is innocent, and none of it was spilled lightly." Her hands shook, a barely visible tremor, and Salomen reached up to interlace their fingers. The touch calmed her enough that she let go of her own front.

"Fahla," Salomen said in wonder. "It's so strong..."

"I do understand stability and tradition. Can you not feel how much we have in common, in the truest parts of our selves? We want the same things. What we see on the surface is not who we are."

"I can feel it." There was a slightly dazed look in Salomen's eyes. "I think...I knew that before. But this feels so different."

"If you knew that, why did you say what you did?"

The dazed expression cleared. "You called this a joke. It hurt. You wield the same weapon I do, and you're a damned expert at it."

"I'm sorry. Believe me, I don't think this is a joke. It couldn't possibly be less humorous."

Salomen lowered their hands and stepped closer. "Then why did Fahla match us if it wasn't for her sense of humor?"

"Perhaps because we have more in common...than we thought." Tal faltered as Salomen's proximity registered on what felt like every nerve in her body. This close, she could smell the salty warmth of her skin and had to restrain herself from pressing her lips to the hollow at the base of Salomen's throat. "I know that our caste differences will be hard to overcome," she said, forcing her gaze back up.

"But maybe that's the point. Fahla doesn't choose many tyrees and never bestows the gift without reason. But she chose us."

"I know. I just don't know why."

"Maybe she heard us. We've both wished for this all our lives."

"But you didn't wish for me."

"And you didn't wish for me."

"No," Salomen murmured, studying Tal's face. "But I have a feeling that if I'd been given what I wished for, I would have found it lacking."

Tal released one hand and touched her, lightly running her fingers along a delicate cheekbone ridge. "I would never have known to wish for you, because I've never known anyone like you."

Salomen smiled. "Coming from the Lancer, that's saying something." She reached out, and Tal's entire body was vividly aware of the soft touch on her own face. "I think it goes without saying that I've never known anyone like you, either."

"With you, I'm not certain anything can go without saying."

"Yes, it can." Salomen closed the tiny distance between them and kissed her. It was a slow, gentle, sweet kiss, and Tal wanted to spend the rest of the day exactly here. But she was too mindful of their fragile truce and pulled back before she could cross some unseen boundary.

Salomen had other ideas. She wrapped one hand around the back of Tal's neck, firmly drawing her in, and this time when their lips met, there was less gentleness and more need. Then there was only need, and their bodies were molded together as she lost herself in the pleasure of exploring…until the sudden ignition of their emotions flashed through her, burning out her empathic senses with a searing intensity. Gasping, she pulled back and waited for her head to clear.

"That is positively debilitating," she said.

Salomen laughed shakily. "I'm glad to hear you say that. It makes me feel better. I didn't even know that sort of thing could happen."

"Neither did I." Tal caught a wisp of Salomen's hair, which had escaped from her usual tail, and tucked it behind her ear. "Please don't push me away again. I know this isn't what either of us expected—or even thought we wanted—but it could lead to something beyond both our dreams. Isn't that worth fighting for?"

"I'm not the warrior," Salomen said. Then she smiled, a real smile that lit up her eyes and deepened the creases at the sides of her mouth. "But I know how to fight for what I believe in. And I have to believe in this. It's too strong to be denied."

"Thank Fahla." Tal leaned in again but stopped just before their lips met. "Shek."

"What is it?"

She straightened. "I feel as if I'm facing a disruptor. I'm not sure how many more of those empathic flares I can handle."

"And you think kissing causes it?"

"I don't know what causes it, but it seems to have something to do with physical touch. The first one was during a warmron, remember?"

"Actually," Salomen mused, "everything seems to have started with a warmron. Has it only been three days since you included warmrons in my lessons? No wonder I'm jumpier than a fanten on slaughter day."

"Salomen...can we hold this back until I learn more about it? I know someone who might be able to help us make sense of this. I'll talk to her after the Council session."

"First you ask me not to push you away, then you push me away?"

"Only for a day."

Salomen rolled her eyes. "Inconsistent. I suppose this is the part where I begin learning all of the less desirable things about you."

"No, you already know all of those."

They smiled at each other and then separated, their movements awkward as they let each other go. Tal pulled on her gloves, reached down for her soilbreaker, and straightened slowly as her muscles got her attention for the first time that morning.

"Sore?" Salomen asked, making no effort to front her amusement.

"Not at all."

"And you were upset when I lied."

"I don't lie. Except when it's necessary."

"Ah, so it's necessary now?"

"Yes. I have no desire to spend the rest of my days hearing about how the warrior could not do a producer's job." Tal turned around and swung the soilbreaker up, only to have it caught and held.

"The warrior has already impressed the producer." Salomen's voice was low and right next to her ear. "And not by digging pipe."

The hold on her tool was released, but Tal stood unmoving. Salomen chuckled quietly and walked back to her spade, resuming her work without another glance. Shaking her head, Tal swung the soilbreaker down, enjoying the satisfying *thud* as it sank in. "If this is how you treat your field workers, I have a sudden understanding of why they're so loyal to you."

"If I treated all my field workers that way, I'd have had more than just five invitations to bond."

Tal left her tool buried and turned. "You've had *five* bond offers?"

"Mm-hm. Why don't you take a break and let me catch up with you?"

"Don't try to distract me. Why didn't you accept any of them?"

"Because I knew they came less from desire to bond with me and more from desire to bond with my land."

"Well, I can't say they were fools. Your land is beautiful."

Salomen paused, then resumed digging.

"But I *can* say they were blind to its greatest value."

The shy pleasure that came from Salomen made Tal want to walk over and kiss her, but she was still feeling cautious about those empathic flares.

"And you?"

She almost didn't hear the question as she watched Salomen's smooth, sure movements. "What? Oh. None."

She regretted the answer when Salomen stopped and straightened; she had been enjoying her moment as a voyeur.

"None?" Salomen said incredulously.

"Until recently, I thought I was bonded to Alsea. There was no room for others, and no one tried to convince me otherwise."

"What changed?"

"I thought you were catching up with me."

Salomen sank her spade into the soil and left it standing. "Shek the pipe. What changed?"

"Do you speak that way around Jaros?"

"Andira!"

Laughing, Tal gave in. "Micah gave me a different point of view."

"Colonel Micah actually convinced you of something?"

"He was pointing a disruptor at my heart at the time. It got my attention."

"*What?*"

The outrage accompanying the single word made Tal regret her joke. "Not with serious intent. Micah has been my instructor and my friend all my life, and though our roles have changed, he still teaches me now and again. He needed to make me listen to him. I'd let myself go down a bad path."

"What in Fahla's name could you have done to deserve that?" Salomen was working herself into a protective fury, and Tal guiltily enjoyed it. It was rather pleasant to see that anger on her behalf for once.

"He had good reason. I was allowing personal issues to interfere with my duties as Lancer."

"And he could find no better way of drawing your attention to this fact than threatening you with a deadly weapon?"

Look out, Micah, Tal thought. Pray she never hears about the immobilizer!

"It was a demonstration of the potential costs of my behavior," she said. "I'd put my need for solitude above my need for protection." Salomen's brow furrowed, and she rephrased. "I slipped my Guards. Repeatedly. Twice a nineday for two moons, actually. Micah was showing me how easy it would be for someone to kill me if I continued to disregard my own safety. It was a memorable lesson."

Salomen shook her head. "You warriors really are a breed apart, aren't you?"

"I don't think so. The methods of instruction might be different, but the lessons being taught are much the same. Responsibility, duty, proper behavior. And sometimes even the methods aren't so different. Your brother received a rather physical lesson just yesterday, with your approval."

"Hm." Salomen regarded her appraisingly. "You *are* occasionally right."

"I have a suspicion that I should be recording this conversation. Will you ever say that to me again?"

"Certainly." Salomen turned back to her spade. "The very next time you're right. And you'll have plenty of time to anticipate it, since it will likely be several cycles."

Tal made no answer; she was occupied with watching Salomen's body in motion. But as she stood waiting, a quick smile crossed her face. Salomen had just referred to their relationship in the long term.

CHAPTER 46
That useless little farm

Sunsa Aldirk was convinced that he had the most difficult job on the planet. As Chief Counselor of Alsea he should have been the right hand of the Lancer, advising her on matters of state and knowing that his advice would be accepted for the wisdom it was. After all, he had been moving in the upper levels of Alsean politics for many cycles now and spoke from a position of great experience. Unfortunately, Lancer Tal was notoriously inconsistent in her attitude toward his advice. Sometimes she accepted it. Other times, like today, she was obdurate.

"Find another way, Aldirk."

"Lancer Tal, you cannot respond properly from that holding. You must return to Blacksun permanently."

"No, I must not," she said sharply. "I'm happy to fly here for Council sessions or strategy meetings, and I'll make the necessary public appearances. Schedule them together, so I can conclude them in a three-day tour. Otherwise, nothing on this agenda requires me to leave Hol-Opah for more than half a day, and the statements can be recorded there as well."

He stifled a sigh and glanced through the wall of windows at her back. Across the State Park, the dome of Blacksun Temple gleamed in the sunlight. Why she was insisting on minimizing her time here, in the seat of power, he could not understand.

"Given the behavior of some of the Councilors today," he said, "don't you think it would be wiser to keep a closer eye on them?"

"That's what I have you for. Most of that was useless arm waving anyway." She paused. "Though I'd like to know what Parser's up to. Shantu's motion to delay implementation didn't surprise me. He may be a little too in love with the power of his position, but he's always had Alsea's best interests in mind. But Parser was just as strongly for implementation last moon as he's suddenly against it today, and for him to support Shantu…"

Aldirk agreed. Those two were never on the same side.

"He doesn't believe the coalition's forecast any more than I do," she finished. "He's planning something."

"I'll see what I can find out." Aldirk made a note on his reader card. He wasn't surprised that Lancer Tal had seen through Parser's front even with the emotional interference of a full Council chamber. Her empathic abilities were a powerful political weapon, and she was not afraid to use them. It was one of the things he admired most about her.

And one of the things he admired least was her intransigence when their opinions didn't match.

"The Councilors may be arm waving, but they're still a reflection of public opinion," he said. "The people of Alsea are polarized. They need your guidance."

"I'm aware of that, and they'll receive it. I'm merely saying that I don't need to abandon my obligation at Hol-Opah to do it."

"What obligation? You owe that holding nothing."

"I owe Raiz Opah a moon of my time. To date I have fulfilled a little more than half of that."

"I hardly think you can be held accountable for this ludicrous challenge when an entire cycle of preparation is threatened and people are giving in to fear. This is stirring up the fringe as well. They've been waiting for an excuse to pounce."

"I hold myself accountable."

"Warriors!" He threw up his hands. "Honor above everything, while the world falls apart."

She smiled for the first time. "The world is not falling apart. A coalition of economists made a statement that's getting more attention than it deserves. That's all. We'll deal with it and move on to the next crisis, which will no doubt also be of planet-shattering proportions. And I won't let that one dictate my life, either."

When she spoke in those tones, he knew she would not budge. There was nothing left to do but accede and begin scheduling around her time on that useless little farm. At least he had gotten a concession of half a day; he could work with that.

"Very well. My next item is the hullskin-eating nanoscrubbers. I'm pleased to report that the second iteration is complete. If the Voloth get their hands on our existing design and somehow neutralize it, we now have a backup version in reserve."

"Excellent!" Her eyes and tone brightened. "Then I can cross that off my list. What about the law mandating their continuing development?"

"The draft is on my desk now. I expect it to be ready for Council debate by this time next nineday."

"There will be no debate. On this matter the castes are of one accord."

"Which might be the first time in modern history that's happened," Aldirk said.

"I know. We should put a plaque on the Chamber wall to commemorate it."

Smiling at the thought, he glanced at his reader card. "Ah, you'll appreciate this as well. Chief Kameha informs me that the construction process for the carbon nanotubes is proceeding faster than he expected. He believes we'll be able to launch the seed cable for the space elevator in another four moons."

"Really? That means we could have the full cable finished six moons earlier than we thought. We may have to speed up construction on the magnetic rail system and the elevator itself. And I'll need to speak with Ambassador Solvassen about scheduling the placement of the counterweight. Remind me to thank the Chief again for that brilliant idea."

Chief Kameha had suggested that instead of the usual methods for creating a counterweight at the far end of the elevator cable—capturing an asteroid or constructing something on-planet and then hoisting it up—they could simply use existing battle debris from the destruction of the first Voloth invasion group. Accordingly, when the Protectorate clean-up crew arrived to clear their orbital space, they collected the pieces with the greatest mass, sealed them together into one solid chunk, and temporarily parked it in geosynchronous orbit. It had worked well for the clean-up crew, which had to transport far less debris, and for Alsea, which had a ready-made counterweight waiting to be slotted into place.

"Poaching Chief Kameha from the *Caphenon* crew was definitely one of your signature achievements," Aldirk said approvingly.

"I didn't poach him; why does everyone keep saying that? I just made him an offer that matched up with his own desires."

"And in the process lured away one of the Protectorate's best engineers. Which is the definition of poaching."

Lancer Tal smiled and shook her head. "Fine. I poached him, and Eroles thinks I nudged him into the builder caste, which is why she stopped criticizing my decision to break Fahla's covenant and actually seems somewhat sympathetic to the veterans now. Sometimes I think Fahla is watching all this with particular enjoyment. I get credit for the things I didn't do and none at all for the things I did."

"Which is the definition of being a Lancer."

"Nobody told me that when I started," she grumbled.

"I believe I did," he said, fronting his amusement with long practice.

He went down his list, crossing some items off and making notes next to others. On the whole, it was a productive meeting. When he returned to his office, he would begin preparations for the Lancer's state media conference and her subsequent four-city tour. The more visible she was in response to the economist crisis, the better the situation would be.

"One more thing," he said, setting aside his reader card. "The items you asked for." Reaching into the satchel at his side, he withdrew two small boxes, identical in every way but for the designs etched in their tops.

"Ah, thank you." She took them with a fond smile. "I'd actually forgotten about these with all that's happened in the last few days. Micah will be glad to see his, I'm sure." The smile turned slightly wicked.

As she opened her sword case, Aldirk discreetly rolled his eyes. One thing all warriors seemed to have in common was their fascination with weaponry, no matter how outdated. Swords were useless in modern warfare, and yet sword makers still did a brisk business, manufacturing blades for enthusiastic warriors the world over.

The Lancer withdrew her well-worn grip from its case. Unlike many grips he had seen, hers was not fancy or overly engraved. She preferred a plain grip with grooves designed for a secure hold, not decoration. Of that, at least, Aldirk could approve. The swords of some warriors were so ornate that they could not possibly be of use in a sparring match. The only mark of distinction on Lancer Tal's grip was her family crest, discreetly engraved in two places.

He twitched when the blade shot out of the grip with a metallic *shhinng*.

"Oh, I've missed this," she said. "I'm looking forward very much to a little exercise." She swept the sword through a few moves, then retracted the blade and replaced the grip in her case. "You always remember everything, even when I don't. I appreciate that."

He blinked, pleased with the compliment. "I'm merely doing my duty."

"You're very good at your duty." She nodded at him. "If there's nothing else, I have some calls to make."

He knew a dismissal when he heard one. "There is nothing else. For now," he added.

"Isn't that always the case," she said.

CHAPTER 47
A different kind of bond

"Thank you for clearing your schedule for me," Andira said as she accepted a cup of shannel.

Lanaril set her own cup on the side table and took the other chair. "I thought we were past the ritual formalities. Of course I'd clear my schedule for you, and you should expect that by now."

"It never hurts to be polite, or so my mother always told me. Of course, Father had something different to say."

"Let me guess. Manners can be perceived as weakness?"

"Depends on who you're with. I prefer to spend time with those who see and appreciate them, like you."

Lanaril was not immune to the compliment. "The more I know you, the more I understand how you won the election."

"You didn't understand before?" Andira set her cup down. "That means you didn't vote for me."

"Oh, no. We're not going down that path."

Andira chuckled. "No, we're not. I'm content to know I'd have your vote if it ever came up again."

"You would. I'd even vote twice, once for myself and once for Fahla."

"Now there's an endorsement I could really use right now."

"I heard. Is that why you're here?"

"In Blacksun? Yes. In your study, no. I need your expertise on a personal matter."

The last time Andira had needed her for a personal matter, it had been a crisis of faith and a betrayal. Worried, she sat up straight. "What is it?"

Andira blinked at her before shaking her head. "Oh, no, nothing like that. Actually, it's a good thing. I think."

Lanaril had begun to relax, but now tensed again. "You're sounding as clear as my copy of *Templar's Creed*. Which I never managed to finish. And why are you keeping up your front with me?"

In a moment she had full access; Andira had dropped her front.

"I'm sorry, I wasn't even thinking. It's force of habit when I'm in the State House."

"I can certainly understand that. But it took me a long time to get you to drop your front with me. I don't want to go back." Now that Lanaril could feel her, she relaxed entirely. Nothing in Andira's emotions warranted concern.

"A long time? Nine moons is a record for me. Or at least it was. How do you get to be Lead Templar without finishing the *Templar's Creed?* I thought you had to be able to quote page and verse."

"You'd be surprised at how few templars actually read that monstrosity. I could make up page and verse and most of my peers would just nod their heads, pretending they remembered."

"I knew it!"

They shared a laugh, settling in to each other's company.

"What do you mean, it *was* a record?" Lanaril asked. "Have you been going around Granelle without a front?"

"What a coincidence that you should mention that…"

Lanaril had been sipping her shannel, but the unmistakable warmth that burst from Andira made her inhale the drink. She coughed for a few moments before getting her air back.

"Are you all right?" Andira was leaning forward in her chair.

"Perfect," Lanaril croaked, and cleared her throat. "You've met someone."

"I have."

"How wonderful! Is she warrior or scholar?"

"You might want to put that cup down."

Lanaril looked at her, then set down the cup. "I'm ready."

"She's a producer."

Lanaril couldn't have stopped her smile had she tried. "The Lancer of Alsea and a producer? You're going to inspire a whole new crop of weepers. Forget *Merchant of the Mountains*, it'll be *Lancer in the Fields*. I can already hear the theme music."

"That wasn't quite the response I expected." Andira's amusement was bright to her senses. "And I had no idea your taste in entertainment was so bad. Guilty pleasure, Lead Templar?"

"I don't watch it, but my aide does. He keeps me apprised of the plot, such as it is." She examined Andira more closely. "You thought I'd say what most of your caste and mine will—that she can't be good enough for you if she's a producer. Fahla doesn't make those distinctions. They're a limitation of perception we impose on ourselves."

"I did think that," Andira admitted. "But I should have known better. Thank you—I'm going to remember those words when the news gets out and judgments start raining down on us. And I can't wait for Salomen to meet you. I'll just introduce you and then sit back and listen."

She recognized the name. It was hard not to; the producer's challenge to the Lancer had been global news for the last moon. "You fell for the woman who challenged you?"

"I don't know that I'd describe it as falling. It's more like we were pushed together. I spent half a moon in battle with her and then suddenly—" She made a helpless gesture. "Lanaril, I think she's my tyree."

Lanaril was speechless. This was the very last thing she would have guessed.

"Having second thoughts about whether she's good enough for me?"

"No, not at all. Only Fahla can decide a tyree match. If Salomen Opah really is your tyree, then I could not be happier for you. The only thing you're sensing is my wish that she shared your empathic strength."

"She does. In fact she might be as strong as I am, though it's difficult to tell when she's so untrained."

"A producer high empath!"

"She didn't want to leave her caste, so she hid her powers. She fooled the testers at ten cycles."

"Great Goddess."

"She's one of a kind." The smile on Andira's face said it all.

Lanaril rose, collected both of their shannel cups, and took them over to the sideboard. Then she pulled the stopper on a new bottle of spirits, poured two glasses, and brought them back.

"Start from the beginning," she said.

Her astonishment mounted as she heard about battles of words and wills, delegate meetings, training sessions, intimate family moments, and an attraction that Andira still didn't recognize in hindsight. "I don't know when it all began," she said, but Lanaril did.

"It began in that very first delegate meeting, when she refused to back down. How many people in your life stand up to you even when you're exerting the full power of both your will and your office on them?"

"I think you're confusing irritation with attraction."

Lanaril smiled and motioned for her to continue.

The more she heard, the more she understood that Fahla had chosen the perfect match. All of Alsea would have expected their Lancer to find a bondmate in the elite circles of power or at least in one of the two ascendant castes. Instead, she had found a producer who was entirely beyond her experience. She hadn't known how to respond to a woman who not only didn't understand the accepted rules, but wasn't even playing the same game. For once in her life, Andira's caste, family name, and title meant nothing. It sounded as if her artful ability to manipulate others was hitting a stone wall as well.

Then Andira spoke of the first empathic flash, and a chill ran down Lanaril's spine. Her suspicion was confirmed with the account of the second, searing flash that had burned out both women's senses this morning. When Andira fell silent and looked at her for answers, Lanaril could hardly contain her awe.

"There is not the slightest doubt in my mind that you've found your tyree," she said. "Not only that, but when you complete your bond, it will be of an extraordinary strength. You're not just tyree. You're the kind I've only read about."

"I didn't know there were different kinds."

"There haven't been recently. Or perhaps they existed but weren't recorded. Everything I know about them comes from older texts." She went to her bookshelves and ran a finger down several spines before finding the one she was looking for. Quickly, she flipped through the pages. "Ah, here we go. 'When Fahla touched them, and divine spirit met flesh, the chosen tyrees burned with her fire. Separated, the fire reached for itself, seeking union. In the conflagration their bond was sealed, and thereafter they bore the remnant sparks within them, never to be extinguished.'"

"So the empathic flashes are the fire of Fahla?"

Lanaril brought the book with her as she retook her seat. "You have been touched, Andira. I don't know when or how, but Fahla has come to you personally. Normal tyrees feel the empathic flash only once, during the bonding. For the two of you to be experiencing them before your bonding means that your empathic centers are reaching for each other. They're trying to connect, to complete that bond, from a distance that shouldn't be possible. And once you do complete it, your bonding will be irreversible."

"All tyree bonds are irreversible. Unless they're broken from the inside."

"You won't be able to break yours even if you wanted to. Remember, it says the remnant sparks are never to be extinguished. Once you bond, your minds will be permanently linked. As far as Salomen is concerned, you'll be without a front. You'll never be able to raise it again."

Andira stared at her in utter shock. Finally, she repeated, "Never? Never as in, not even for one piptick will I be alone in my own mind?"

"You will always know her emotions, and she will always know yours. This is a truly sacred bond. You won't be able to block it. Not only that, but the connection transcends distance. You'll be able to feel each other no matter where you are. What you felt yesterday is just a glimpse of what will happen."

Andira inhaled sharply. "Great Mother! Then we'll have a very long prebond. We need time to adapt." She chuckled without humor. "Salomen in my mind every tick? No one could adapt to that."

"Putting off the bonding ceremony won't make a difference. That has nothing to do with this."

"But you said our minds will be permanently linked once we—" She stopped as Lanaril shook her head.

"For tyrees the process is different. The bonding ceremony is nothing *but* ceremony for you; it was created for all the rest of us who need a bond minister to complete the connection. Tyrees have no such need."

"What are you saying?"

"I'm saying that the first time you Share, the connection will be made. Your bond will be complete."

"Spawn of a fantenshekken! I cannot believe it. Great Mother, this is—I don't—Fahla!" Andira blew out a breath and rubbed her forehead. In a calmer voice she said, "We'll have to wait a long time for our Sharing, then. Damn, that will make this so much more difficult."

"You don't have the luxury of waiting. You're carrying the fire of Fahla inside you. Do you think you're stronger than it is? That fire seeks its union. The empathic flashes will keep getting stronger and easier to set off until you do what it wants. You set this in motion the moment you joined; it can't be stopped now."

"But…" Her embarrassment rippled outward. "We haven't joined."

Lanaril frowned. "Are you certain?"

After a moment of silence they both laughed.

"Yes, I'm certain. I think I'd remember. It's only been a few days since we stopped fighting each other. Actually, it hasn't even been one day—this morning's fight was the worst of all."

"I heard it ended well, though."

They shared a smile before Lanaril began puzzling over this new wrinkle.

"I've never read of such a thing," she said. "This type of bond doesn't just initialize spontaneously. It's set off by a physical connection. That's what allows the empathic centers to recognize each other."

Andira's eyes widened. "A physical connection? Would a warmron do it?"

"I suppose it would, but that's not—" Lanaril stopped. "Really?"

"We shared a warmron three days ago," Andira admitted. "I initiated it."

That might have been the most shocking thing Lanaril had heard yet. "And she allowed it?"

"I can't tell you how it happened, because that's too personal even for this conversation. But I can tell you that I learned a great deal about warmrons from the Gaians. They share them freely, all their lives, with anyone they want. For them, warmrons can be anything from romantic to gestures of good friendship. I received several as part of our cultural exchange, and once I experienced that, I wondered why we see them only as an artifact of childhood or the province of lovers and bondmates."

Lanaril could easily imagine it. Andira did tend to look for alternative paths; it was in her nature. It was also what made her a good Lancer. But in this instance, it had not worked in her favor.

"I think you might have answered that question now," she said.

Andira dropped her head into her hands. "What were the chances?"

"I'm sorry this is so hard for you. A divine bond is supposed to be a joyous process between two people who have already found their way into each other's arms. But you've made yours into an uncontrollable avalanche, even with the best of intentions."

"Surely it's not so uncontrollable. We can't touch without triggering empathic flashes, fine. Then we'll be careful and not touch each other. That won't be so difficult. This is still new to us; we're not ready for a joining yet anyway."

And still she was trying to find a way around it.

"Not touching will slow the process, yes. But it won't stop it, and it will make you both miserable. Andira, I don't think you're grasping the fact that you are carrying a *divine flame*. This isn't like manipulating the Council into doing what you want. You cannot manipulate Fahla. Tyrees aren't meant to be apart, and your kind of tyree—well, there are stories about those who thought they could deny it or who were forcibly kept apart by evil. They began to lose their mental faculties as the better parts of their minds abandoned them in search of their partners. I don't think I'm overstating it to say that your ability to continue your life, and to govern as Lancer, depends on completing this bond quickly. If you would deny your tyree, you will also deny your future—and hers."

In the ensuing silence, Andira took a large gulp of her spirits. "So much from something so simple. If I'd known…"

"You wouldn't have given her the warmron?"

The fact that she didn't immediately say no told Lanaril more about this relationship than anything else.

Andira gazed out the window, where the top of the State House towered over the trees. "She needed comfort," she said quietly. "If you could have sensed what was pouring out of her then… She's been carrying a heavy load of responsibility while mourning the loss of her mother, and she couldn't lean on her family, because they're leaning on her. She was so alone. And yes, I could have offered a palm touch and projection, but it wasn't enough. It just wasn't enough."

Lanaril smiled to herself. She knew exactly why it hadn't been enough, but for the first time in their friendship, Andira seemed unaware of her own emotions.

The smile dropped as she remembered something else from her readings.

"There's one more thing you need to be aware of," she said.

Andira looked back in concern. "And it's worrying you."

"Keep in mind that these are just stories. I don't know how true they are, but given the fact that the old stories described your empathic flashes, yes, I'm worried that this might be an issue. Once you complete your bond, the link may also extend to the physical. There are tales of both tyrees showing symptoms when only one was ill, or physical injuries being transmitted across the bond. There's even a story of both tyrees dying from a mortal injury to one."

Andira sucked in a breath. "She'll be a proxy assassination target."

"If word of the true nature of your bond gets out…I'm afraid that might be the case."

"Well, that's just perfect!" Andira's voice rose on the last word as she pushed herself out of her chair. "Salomen will hit the farthest moon! She already hates that part of my life. She hates my Guards, she hates the idea of having to even think about power and politics, and I can only imagine what she'll say if I tell her she can't go to the shekking seed store without informing her very own Lead Guard first." She stopped pacing and put her hands on her hips. "This will kill the bond. She'll never consent to such a life, and even if she did, how could I allow her to make herself as much of a target as I already am?"

"You don't have a choice."

"I don't accept that!"

"So you'll deny the bond? And become mentally crippled when that fire starts to burn out your brain along with your empathic senses? Will you watch *her* become mentally crippled?"

Andira dropped into the chair and let her head rest on its back. "I've dreamed about a tyree bond my whole life. This morning I thought it was a sick joke. Now it seems like a nightmare. What's next? Does it get worse than nightmare, or is this as bad as it gets?"

Lanaril reached across and took her hand. "Listen to me. This is not a nightmare, it is a gift from Fahla. Do you understand what that means? She *chose* you for this. She blessed you and Salomen beyond anything I've ever seen. You just…hurried her blessing along a bit, so it feels overwhelming right now. But it won't always feel that way. I have faith that you and Salomen will get through this, and there will come a time when you will embrace this with a full heart. In fact, I'll lay down a bet right now. I say that within three moons, you are going to walk through that door and tell me that you cannot imagine living without your bond. You're going to tell me that you can hardly remember a time when you were afraid."

"I'm not afraid for myself. I'm afraid for Salomen."

Lanaril smiled. "Bring her with you when you come to tell me I was right."

CHAPTER 48
Confession

"You must be joking."

"I wish I were."

Tal was in her window seat, watching Salomen pace the room. She had flown back to Hol-Opah in time for evenmeal, and though she had fronted her disquiet, apparently her front was already porous. Once the table was cleared, Salomen wasted no time coming to her room and asking for the news.

She was exactly as happy as Tal had predicted.

"This is beyond tolerance! It was only after midmeal that I even began to get comfortable with the idea of you as my tyree. Now I'm supposed to accept that we're not even normal tyrees?" With a potent glare at Tal, she sank onto her chair. "I can't believe it. Fahla! From the day you stepped onto my holding—"

"I turned your life upside down? Destroyed your peace of mind? Made you wish you'd never taken Norsen's place in the delegation?"

"That's not what I meant to say."

"Then what did you mean to say? Because I certainly did the first, and I'm almost certain I did the second."

"But you did not do the third." Salomen was calmer now. "I can't regret meeting you. Nothing about my life is even remotely within my control anymore, but I know that you…that we are meant to be here. I just don't want it to be like this. Not like this, Andira. It's too much."

If they hadn't been in this stupid situation, Tal would have pulled her into a warmron, kissed her, and told her they would both be fine. How ironic that they were fated to be bonded at a deeper level than most Alseans, yet here they sat, a body length apart and afraid to touch each other. Afraid of taking one more step toward a connection they could not control.

Afraid even to show their emotions, she realized. Both of them were fronting, an instinctive self-protection against the very person they were not supposed to need it with.

"We're doing this all wrong," she said, and let go of her front.

Salomen's eyes widened, her surprise growing when Tal pushed out of the window seat and sat on the floor in front of her chair.

"From the day I stepped onto your holding," Tal said, "I was fascinated by how different you are here, in your home and on your land. There's such warmth and depth, and great Goddess, the way you smile at the people you trust…" Her gaze dropped to Salomen's lips, which held no smile but were at least no longer pressed together in a frustrated line. "I understood that in five moons I'd never seen the real Salomen Opah. I think that's why I chose to begin our instruction the way I did, by asking to know more about you. You were right, that wasn't the usual method. I told myself I needed your trust for our training to work, but in truth…I just wanted it. I wanted that warmth you gave to everyone but me."

"Even though you did your best to keep me on the defensive?"

"I didn't say I was consistent about it."

Salomen relaxed slightly, a half-smile finding its way out as she dropped her own front. "I wanted your warmth, too. I never thought I'd get it."

Tal breathed in the complexity of her emotions and rested a hand on her leg, trusting that clothing would protect them from an empathic flash. "We're getting a lot of things we never expected, aren't we?"

"Those might be the truest words you've spoken yet."

"I don't want it like this either, Salomen. But I think that even if we were not tyrees, our hearts would eventually have spoken to each other."

Salomen covered her hand. "I think our hearts have already been speaking. I just don't enjoy being forced to listen before I'm ready."

"That's nearly what I told Lanaril, though I might have used more profanity."

"Of course you would use profanity with the Lead Templar of Blacksun."

"By now she's used to it."

"You're good at pushing people past their normal boundaries, aren't you?" But without her front, Salomen couldn't make the question sound like anything more than it was: a statement of her own discomfort. After a pause she added, "Thank you for letting me in. It feels better knowing that you're just as nervous as I am."

"If all you sense is a case of nerves, then we need to work on your skills."

A familiar crinkle appeared above her nose as she concentrated on sensing more deeply. "You're afraid…of me? Why?"

Tal looked at her askance. "Wasn't it just this morning you were apologizing for hurting me? I can't imagine the power you'll have as this develops."

"Exactly as much power as you'll have over me. You're not the only one who has been hurt."

Well, that was true. Tal had conveniently forgotten her own apology. "After listening to Lanaril today, I can assure you I'll never call this a joke again."

"Ah. And you think that was the first time?" Salomen shook her head. "You've hurt me since the day you arrived. It hurt when you showed me a glimpse of yourself on our first night of training and then went back to being the Lancer. You gave me something precious, and then you took it away again. Every night after that you did the same thing. You have no understanding of how intimidating you can be; when you're fronting, it's like nothing is there at all. I kept seeing glimpses of the real woman behind that front, and I found myself drawn to her, but then you would take her away and present me with that impenetrable wall. And all the while you kept asking me those questions. You were learning about me, but I wasn't allowed to learn about you."

"I was teaching you. It's not appropriate—"

"Stop hiding behind that! It was never just about being my teacher and you know it. It was about holding the upper hand. So I'm wondering if you're really afraid of me hurting you, or if you're just afraid of us being on equal footing."

"That is the most—" Tal snapped her mouth shut before she could start another argument.

"Why would you be so angry right now if there wasn't some truth in that?" Salomen asked.

"Because you just called me a coward!"

"I did not ca—"

"Of course you did! Who else is afraid of a fair fight but a coward?"

"Is that what this is? A fair fight?"

Tal let out a growl of pure frustration and tried to pull her hand back, but Salomen held it in a surprisingly strong grip.

"I have never thought you were a coward," she said. "But I do think you've spent your life climbing through a power structure, all the way to the top. And you didn't get there by letting anyone close enough to see your vulnerabilities."

Tal relaxed her hand as her anger drained away. "You sound like you've been studying the Truth and the Path."

It was a feeble joke, but Salomen nodded. "I had to figure you out one way or another."

"You and your research," Tal grumbled, though there was no heat in it. The anger had gone as quickly as it had come, and now she just felt tired. "I don't even know what we're doing here. This all started because I wanted to make you feel better."

Salomen let out a soft snort. "I guess we need some practice at this."

"Words for Fahla." Tal turned her hand over, watching as Salomen clasped it. "Perhaps we just need to trust her. Neither of us had the other in mind when we dreamed of our tyrees, but she's already given us more than we were able to imagine for ourselves."

"It's not trust in Fahla that I have an issue with."

That stung, but it wasn't as if Tal didn't feel the same way.

"I'm sorry," Salomen began, but Tal shook her head.

"No, don't apologize. I deserve that."

"But it's not just me. You don't trust me either."

It was really just a political negotiation, Tal thought. They were two warring parties who had found common cause and were poised to sign a binding peace treaty. But they each had a pen in one hand and a sword in the other.

"We have to lay down our swords," she said without thinking.

"What?"

"We have to learn to trust each other. Somehow."

The room was silent while she contemplated their clasped hands and wondered how long they had before even this set off a flash.

"If we are to learn that," Salomen said slowly, "then I need to know something."

"I'll tell you anything in my power."

She felt Salomen gathering herself; this was clearly a critical piece of information.

"Who was she? The one you loved? Because I don't understand how you can accept our tyree bond as you seem to when you have someone else in your heart."

Stunned by the last question she had expected, Tal pulled her hand back. This time Salomen let her go, watching as she rose and turned away.

"How much do you know?" Tal asked, her gaze on the darkening landscape.

"I know it was one of the Gaian aliens. I felt it when you shared your memory of the warmron. And I felt it again this morning, on our way to the fields—a love you're still mourning a cycle after they left. I don't know how to compete with a memory."

"There is no competition." Salomen had sensed all that? *Through* her front? She ran her hands through her hair and waited for the right words to come. But there was no way out of this other than the truth.

Turning back, she held out a hand. "Come and sit with me."

She pulled Salomen out of the chair and led her to the window seat, letting her settle in before taking her usual spot on the opposite end of the cushion. With her back against the wall, she folded her legs beneath her and faced her future tyree.

"Her name was Ekatya Serrado. She was the captain of the ship."

"Of course it was their leader." Salomen's mental retreat was instantaneous.

"And she was a bonded tyree," Tal continued, watching as all of Salomen's assumptions ground to a halt.

"What?" she whispered.

"The Gaians are all sonsales, but it seems they're capable of tyree bonds. At least, these two were."

"You loved another's tyree?"

"I loved a woman who understood power and the demands of a heart that belonged to something bigger than herself. A woman who recognized the role I play and still saw me as a person. She was not just their leader, and she understood that I'm not just the Lancer."

"She saw the thinking, feeling Alsean," Salomen said.

Tal recognized her own words from that morning. "Yes, she did. And I had never before had that experience. Not from someone I'd just met."

"Did she know how you felt?"

"Not until right before she left. Even then I wouldn't have said anything, but her bondmate encouraged me."

Salomen slumped against the wall. "I can't believe it. Her *bondmate* told you to speak?"

"She said Ekatya would understand. And she was right."

"So you told Ekatya...what? That you loved her?"

Tal had to remind herself that it was Salomen asking the question. This was the one person on Alsea who had the right to know.

It still took a moment to get her voice to work.

"I told her that had she not been tyree, I would have pursued more than a friendship."

"What did she say?"

"She said..." Tal cleared her throat. "She said that had she not been tyree, I would have succeeded."

She looked out the window, clenching her jaw to force back the tears that threatened. Taking slow, deep breaths, she tried to box up the emotions—and failed. Speaking it aloud had made compartmentalization impossible.

Time stretched out in painful silence as she listened to the maelstrom of emotions that emanated from Salomen. For someone who was trying to convince a reluctant tyree, she had certainly started off with her worst move.

But the emotions shifted, and Tal couldn't understand where that compassion came from. She didn't deserve it.

"Thank you for telling me," Salomen said at last. "I can feel what that cost you, and I promise your trust is not misplaced."

Tal could only nod, her gaze locked on the distant mountains.

"And I don't wonder anymore why she's still in your heart."

That brought her head around. "Why?"

Leaning forward, Salomen brushed a lock of hair behind Tal's ear. "Because she is the dream you touched but could not hold. And sometimes that's worse than never touching the dream at all." She let her fingers continue their journey, gently sifting the strands of hair, and Tal felt all of her bones turning to liquid. "Had she told you she could never have loved you, I think you would have been able to put aside her memory more easily. You would only have had to forget your own emotion. But her words meant you had to forget both your emotions *and* hers. And you cannot do that, can you?"

"I tried," Tal whispered. "And it worked, after a while. I really thought I was over it. But this morning it all came up again, as strong as ever."

"In the skimmer."

She nodded miserably.

"Andira..." Salomen's voice changed, carrying a note of tenderness. "That was my fault. And I'm truly sorry, but—maybe it was for the best. I understand now. I know how I hurt you so easily, without meaning to. But I can heal you as well, and that's something Ekatya Serrado could never do."

"Why not?" Tal's eyes were closing at the sensual touch.

"Because she could not love you." Salomen's fingers slipped from her hair and lifted her chin. "But I can."

They were deep into the kiss before Tal's dazed mind processed the last words she had heard. In an instant her bones solidified, and she surged up to bury her hands in Salomen's hair. The kiss turned passionate as they both forgot their fears and allowed themselves to feel the bond that pulsed between them. It was so strong, almost a physical entity. How had she not felt it before? Why—?

This time the empathic flash tore them apart, sending them crashing back against the window seat's walls. They stared at each other, panting, unable to move until the electricity finally drained from their bodies.

"Shek," Tal groaned, holding one hand to her throbbing forehead. "This is going to kill us. Lanaril was right, it's stronger every time."

Salomen couldn't even speak, simply whimpering as she held her head in both hands.

Tal pushed herself across the seat and reached out, then let her hand drop. "I wish I could help you, but I'd only make it worse."

"Hard to imagine worse than that." Salomen raised her head. "We won't be able to join, will we? If just kissing hurts this much, I think joining might put us in the healing center. Even assuming we were physically capable of it, which I doubt given the way I feel right now."

"I think you're right. Though I wish you weren't."

"It's all backwards. We can't join until we Share, and the moment we Share we're bonded, and the moment we're bonded we're empathically connected for life. Great Fahla above, whoever heard of Sharing *before* joining? Much less bonding. It's like buying a shipment of horten seed without ever seeing any of it first."

"Thank you very much!"

"You know what I mean."

"I do, but I think joining is the least of our concerns. I have no doubt that joining with you will be worth the wait."

That earned her an open smile, but it soon faltered. "If the flashes are this bad already, what will it be like when we actually Share?"

"I don't know. Lanaril read me something out of an old text, and it referred to a conflagration when tyrees like us bond. So I think it's safe to assume we'll get hit with something substantial." She realized what she had said. "If we decide to Share, that is. I don't mean to imply that it's a certainty."

"Isn't it?" Salomen dropped her head again, rubbing her temples. "We don't seem to have any choice in this. And even without the bond, what you said is true: our hearts would have spoken. They've been pulling at us for a while now, I think. It's what brought you here."

"The challenge is what brought me here." But Tal was beginning to wonder.

"It was more than that, Andira. That's what I sensed the night I accidentally probed you. I just didn't recognize it then." She sighed, resting her hands in her lap. "I'm trying to keep up with this, truly I am. My heart is already there; it's just my mind that needs to catch up."

Tal thought of her comment about it being all backwards and had a moment of inspiration. Sliding off the window seat, she offered a formal bow.

"Raiz Salomen Opah, I have never before known anyone like you. And I would like to know you better. Will you have evenmeal with me tomorrow night?"

An amused comprehension spread across Salomen's emotions. "Are you asking for permission to court me?"

"I am. For now, there is no bond and no pressure. No certainty of a fate that did not consult us. This is just you and me."

"Just you and me? Now that's an intriguing combination." Salomen stood up, her pleasure a welcome warmth to Tal's senses. "I'm honored by your attention, Lancer Tal. But I must warn you, I have little respect for authority. I will not treat you as you're accustomed to being treated."

"A happy coincidence, since what I seek is one who sees past my authority."

"In that case, I would be delighted to accept your invitation."

They stared at each other with silly grins before Tal remembered something. "Shek. I have no idea where to take you. I don't know where the good restaurants are in Granelle."

"Then it's a good thing you're courting a native. I know them all."

"Which is the best one?"

"Meadowgreen, but it's impossible to get a table there without reserving it half a moon in advance. We could go—"

"Never mind," Tal interrupted. "We'll go to Meadowgreen."

"Are you not listening? I just said—"

"I know what you just said. And I'm telling you that we're going to Meadowgreen."

"Are you always this commanding?"

"In my public life, yes. In private, no. But I'm trying to impress you."

Salomen laughed. "If you can get us into Meadowgreen on one day's notice, I'll be impressed. I know the owner; he once courted my mother. I thought that connection might give me an edge in getting a reservation on short notice, but do you know what he told me?"

"What?"

"He said he could not change the schedule, not even for the Lancer herself."

"I suspect that what he said to you and what he will say to a call from the Office of the Lancer are two very different things."

"Ha. You don't know Corsine. He defines the word snob."

"No, I don't know him, but I do know Alsean nature. We're going to Meadowgreen tomorrow night."

"Do you have a fallback plan, o confident one?"

"I always do." Tal winked. "May I return for you at eve-two tomorrow night?"

"I'll be waiting." Salomen gave her a mock frown. "But I'd better see you in the fields long before that."

"I won't neglect my duties. You'll see me in the morning."

"You're still seeing me now. Don't think you're getting away with not training me two nights in a row."

"But I'm not the one—" Tal stopped at the amused look on her face. "I wouldn't dream of it. Shall we start, then?"

CHAPTER 49
All nighter

MICAH HUMMED AN OLD MARCHING cadence as he buckled his belt and began clipping on his gear. Given the minuscule amount of sleep he had gotten, it was a wonder he was in such a good mood.

He smiled. No, it wasn't. Not after last night.

Late in the evening Tal had knocked on his door and dragged him off to Blacksun, and during the flight she told him that his prayer had been answered. Not that she knew that, of course, but when she revealed her true relationship with Salomen, he realized with a chill that Fahla *was* listening to the prayers of an old warrior. Not in four lifetimes would he have imagined Salomen as Tal's tyree, but Fahla did not make mistakes.

A producer and the Lancer; wasn't that going to blow up the Blacksun gossip circuit? He could hardly wait. And the very next time he was in a temple, he would burn a worthy offering to Fahla in gratitude.

They sent the military transport back with a Guard, met briefly with Aldirk—whose pleasure at their reappearance vanished when he realized Tal had not returned for good—and picked out appropriate clothing from Tal's quarters for her date the next night. Had they been mature adults, they would have returned in Tal's personal transport then. Instead they spent the night drinking in her quarters, returning so late that Micah had managed just two hanticks of sleep and had no right to be feeling as good as he did right now.

"And you," he said as he looked out the window, "are completely insane."

There was Tal in her usual running clothes, smiling and talking with her Guards. Even as he watched, she turned and set off, her smooth pace showing no signs of their long night.

Micah shook his head. "Good thing you have no plans to join tonight," he muttered. "I doubt Salomen would be impressed if you fell asleep halfway through."

His amusement faded when Herot appeared, looking after the runners with his hands on his hips. The young man was also dressed for exercise but stood motionless as he watched Tal and her Guards. Once the runners had vanished over the crest of the hill, he set off after them.

Micah rolled his eyes. "Surely not, Herot." With a sigh, he strapped on his wristcom and spoke into it.

"We're being followed." Gehrain's voice was clipped. "By Herot Opah."

"I know. I can feel him." The last thing Tal wanted this morning was another encounter with Herot, but based on what she was sensing, she didn't think it would happen. "As long as he keeps his distance, we'll all be happy."

"Shall I send someone back to make sure he does?"

"No. Let him be, unless he closes the gap. I doubt he'll be with us for long."

Nor was he. Only a short distance past the point where he had collapsed the last time, Herot gave up. Tal sensed his receding presence. "He's returning to the house."

"Good." Frowning, Gehrain asked, "Why do you think he followed us?"

"Perhaps he has something to prove." Tal had no desire to be part of his struggle, but he was Salomen's brother, after all. A few days ago, that meant very little. Now it meant he would soon be part of her own family, and she would bear a responsibility toward him. She groaned internally. How unfortunate that she couldn't pick and choose which of the Opah family she accepted! But then she reminded herself of why Herot had been behaving so poorly and vowed to be a little more tolerant.

If he had something to prove, she would not stop him.

CHAPTER 50
Sparring

"Jaros," said Tal, "I brought something from Blacksun yesterday. Would you like to see it?"

"Yes!" The instant answer was spoken around a mouthful of biscuit.

"Jaros, swallow first," Salomen said. "And do you not even want to know what it is?"

Tal smiled; Jaros could always be counted on for total enthusiasm. She looked forward to mornmeals at Hol-Opah if only to see him light up the way he so often did.

Jaros audibly swallowed his food. "If it's from Blacksun, it must be something speedy."

"It's very speedy," she assured him. "I brought my sword and Colonel Micah's as well. We're going to spar after you come home from school." Micah had suggested that a good sparring session might tire her out enough to relax her before her date with Salomen. Tal agreed that it would be a good precaution. Besides, she knew Jaros would be thrilled. Of course, they'd had this brilliant idea before staying up all night, but Micah hadn't asked for a delay, and Tal would be damned if she'd be the one to do it.

"Really? That *is* speedy!" Jaros bounced in his seat. "Wow! I get to watch a sword fight!"

"There's a difference between a sword fight and a sparring session," Micah said. "When Lancer Tal and I spar, there is no acrimony between us, nor any wish to do harm. That changes the way we move."

"Yes, but swords!" Jaros was fixated on one thing. "Where are they? Can I see them?"

"You can see them after school," Salomen said, fixing Tal with a warning glare.

"But that's a whole day. Can't I see them now?"

Mindful of the glare, Tal shook her head. "But when you come home, you'll get a good look. And if you're very careful, you can hold mine."

That sent Jaros into the atmosphere. He spoke of nothing else for the rest of mornmeal, and when he had finally been pushed out the back door to reluctantly trudge to school, Salomen turned to Tal with a spark in her eye.

"You had to tell him that."

"I just thought it would make him happy."

"Oh, it made him happy all right. If he hears a word of his lessons today, I'll be shocked. Don't you know he worships you and everything about the warrior caste?" While Tal blinked over that statement, Salomen came closer and took her hand. "You have so much power over his happiness. Please be careful with it. He does not need dreams that will forever escape him."

Tal could sense an entirely different message behind the words. "His happiness is important to me too. I'll be careful, I promise."

Salomen nodded, and they might have stood there staring at each other until midmeal had Herot not walked into the kitchen. He stopped, shot Tal an evil look, and left again.

"Well, at least Jaros worships me," Tal said.

Salomen sighed. "You can't expect him to be overjoyed to see you after you humiliated him."

"I don't think it's just me he's not overjoyed to see. He's not happy to see you and me together."

"He'll have to get used to it. I have a date tonight."

"Yes, you do. And I'm looking forward to it."

"As am I."

They smiled at each other again, until Salomen shook her head and took a step back. "This is ridiculous. We're never going to get anything done at this rate. Come on, Lancer Tal. We have work to do."

"Yes, Raiz Opah." Tal followed obediently, laughing at herself. She was the leader of the world everywhere but here.

Somehow, the thought was a comforting one.

It was a busy day, made no easier by the fact that Tal's sleepless night had finally crashed over her. She had been so wound up after Salomen's acceptance of their date that sleep wasn't an option, and even after staying up all night, she still had energy to burn on her dawn run. But by midmeal she wanted nothing more than a very long nap. What had she been thinking? She wasn't twenty cycles anymore, for Fahla's sake. And poor Micah had looked quite a bit worse for wear this morning.

She held on by pure will power, until Salomen shook her head and sent her back to the house two hanticks early. "I've never seen you so tired," she said. "Go home and rest."

"But we're not done here." Tal's protest was half-hearted, and she knew Salomen saw right through it.

"*You* are. You're asleep on your feet. And I would prefer my evenmeal companion to be able to make rational conversation."

Tal didn't even try to pretend. A Guard drove her back to the house, and she barely paused long enough to check her reader card for messages before dropping into her bed. But when her head hit the pillow, she had a smile on her face. Aldirk had done his job.

All normal activity at Hol-Opah was completely disrupted that afternoon. Tal may have engineered the sparring for Jaros's sake, but news had traveled. All of the field workers arrived with the Opahs, turning a demonstration into an exhibition bout.

Jaros was bouncing around like a ball, unable to contain himself. He had made it home from school in record time, swollen with pride at the fact that most of his classmates were dying of envy. Not only would he get to see the Lancer fight, but he was going to hold her sword as well! Or so Tal heard him telling Salomen, Nikin, and every other person who would listen.

The Guards arranged the onlookers in a ring, leaving the center clear for the combatants. At the inner edge of the ring, all of the Guards stood facing outward, their expressions serious. This was a challenge to their ability to guard Tal. If anyone in this dense crowd wished to cause harm, it would be difficult to detect in time unless they could sense the intent before the action. It was for this reason that nearly all of her Guards were high empaths. Though not as strong as she was, they were certainly strong enough to go through the fronts of most Alseans.

Tal and Micah walked through the crowd together, sword grips clipped to their belts. The onlookers parted respectfully, closing the gap after they passed through. Once in the center of the ring, Tal eyed her opponent. Fortunately, Micah had been wise enough to schedule a nap for himself as well and looked to be in about the same shape as Tal—which wasn't saying a great deal. But at least they were both alert enough to not accidentally kill each other.

"I see word has gone out," Tal said, using her Council voice. "Has anyone here ever seen a sword fight before? Entertainment vids don't count."

Several hands, which had begun to be raised, promptly dropped at the last sentence.

"Then Colonel Micah and I will begin by demonstrating the basic moves at a slow speed, so you can see exactly what we're doing. Once we've shown you the basics, we'll gradually increase our speed until we reach the normal pace of a sparring match." It was a great idea for pleasing the crowd and had the added advantage of allowing the two sleep-challenged combatants a very long warm-up. As Tal turned back to Micah, she caught Salomen's eye and saw the wink.

She pulled her grip from her belt and pressed the switch, watching in appreciation as the blade extended itself. Fahla, but she loved this sword. She'd had it custom made at a tiny village on Pallea, back when she had been a fresh young trainee. It had cost nearly two moons of her minuscule salary and was worth every bit of it. The craftsmanship was impeccable, the grip fit her hand perfectly, and the balance was sublime. After her election as Lancer, she had been offered much fancier swords by various makers who wanted the prestige of their product in her hand, but she politely returned every one of them. They certainly had flash and shine, but they just didn't compare to this one.

Micah extended his blade as well, and a collective "ooh" rose from the crowd.

Tal smiled at him. If they were already impressed with that, they were going to love the actual match!

They began slowly, taking turns explaining their moves as they thrust, parried, feinted, and attacked at a tenth of their normal speed. Tal felt her body settling into an old and familiar rhythm as she went through motions she could do in her sleep. When one trained in a physical art form long enough, the muscles themselves retained the memories, and Tal's muscles were waking up and remembering their training. The very familiarity of the moves allowed her to block external distractions, and as they sped up, she ceased to be aware of anything but her opponent. These moments, when she was fully engaged in a demanding physical sport, were the times when she was most vulnerable. Her Guards knew it, and as her focus narrowed, theirs expanded. She was dimly aware of this, then let go of even that awareness as she and Micah reached full speed. Their swords whistled through the air, clanging and sliding as they connected, and Tal gloried in the knowledge that they were both skating along the edge of harm, held back only by their skill and trust in each other.

Micah grinned at her, feeling the same physical and mental euphoria. Their speed increased even further as they began to push themselves to greater effort, each seeking an opening to exploit. Micah had the advantage of strength and height, but Tal had long ago learned how to use her stature in ways that taller opponents found difficult to block. When the right moment came, she cut low, forcing Micah to reach down. By the time his sword arrived at its low point, hers had already circled back up and around, crashing on top of his and sliding down its length to keep his tip pushed down. A quick kick to his wrist and Micah stumbled back, shaking his stinging hand as his sword fell to the ground. Tal picked it up and retracted the blade, then tossed him the grip as the crowd roared its approval. Under cover of the shouts and applause, she leaned in and said, "At least I didn't slap you with it."

"Eh. I let you do that, you lovesick fool. It would have been cruel to make you lose face in front of your mate." Micah attached his grip to his belt and put an arm around her shoulders. "Next time I won't be so generous."

"You are so full of dokshin your lips are turning brown."

As they laughed, Jaros ran up, his eyes glittering with excitement. "That was fantastic! Wow! Can I hold it now?"

Tal knelt in the dirt. "Give me your hand."

When he put his hand in hers, she rested the base of her grip in his small palm, retaining the upper part in her sword hand. "Hold it very carefully, Jaros. Don't try to swing it, and don't touch the blade."

"I won't." He closed his fingers around the grip, and the excitement that flooded her senses abruptly changed to awe. "This is so speedy! It's still warm."

"Bring up your other hand."

He did, and Tal let go, her senses alert to any movement on his part. If he forgot himself in childish excitement, she would have to catch his wrists.

But Jaros simply stood there, holding the sword in both hands, staring at it as if it were a vision. "Lancer Tal…"

She could feel it in him. This was more than hero worship.

He looked up at her. "Last nineday you said that I could challenge my caste. Is that true?"

"I would not lie to you. It's possible, but very difficult."

He nodded thoughtfully. "I want to be a warrior. What would I need to do?"

A shadow fell across them, and Salomen knelt next to her brother. "That's not a decision you need to make now, Jaros."

Tal felt the silent plea. "You cannot challenge until you're at least twelve cycles," she said. "You still have time to think about it."

"I *have* thought about it. I want to be a warrior. I want to be like you and Colonel Micah. You do things."

"And your family does not?" Salomen asked.

"No, we do things, but not like this. Lancer Tal and Colonel Micah are different."

"Don't judge all warriors by us. We're not only different from you, but from most of our caste as well. And we've paid a price for our duty. A warrior's life in the Alsean Defense Force is often demanding and lonely. As a producer you know where your home is, and where it will be until you Return. As an ADF warrior you may not know from one cycle to the next where you'll be."

"That's what I want! I want to go places and see things and fight for Alsea if the Voloth come back. I don't want to do what everyone else has always done."

"Do you want to leave your friends and family behind?"

"I would miss you," Salomen said.

Jaros was torn. At last he put the sword back in Tal's hand and turned to his sister, who enveloped him in a warmron. "You're only nine cycles," she said as she squeezed him. "There's still so much for you to learn."

"And in the meantime," Tal said, retracting her blade, "you handled my sword very well. Thank you for being so careful."

His enthusiasm resurfaced. "You're welcome. Can I hold it later? Will you show me how to make it come out of the grip?"

"Because you were so careful this time, yes, I will."

"Okay." Jaros bounced up and down. "You were speedy! Do you always win?"

Tal shook her head. "Colonel Micah has taken my sword away on many occasions."

"Wow. He's speedy, too."

"Yes, he is." She looked up at Micah, who was happily discussing the bout with Shikal and a dozen of the field workers. "He taught me much of what I know."

"Then you learned more from someone else," Salomen said. "I saw his face when you disarmed him. He was surprised."

Tal's pride was out of all proportion to the statement. "He hasn't seen that move in some time; I think he'd forgotten. And you're right, I learned it from an instructor after leaving Micah's unit."

"That must have been strange for him," mused Salomen. "Becoming your subordinate after being your superior and your instructor."

"You're presuming that he's my subordinate. Micah never quite accepted that."

"What's a subordinate?" Jaros wanted to know.

"Someone who takes orders from someone else," said Tal.

"Oh." He frowned in thought. "But I've heard you tell Colonel Micah what to do."

"Yes, but did you actually see him do it?"

Jaros stared, and Salomen laughed as she rubbed his shoulder. "Lancer Tal is teasing. What she really means is that Colonel Micah is her friend more than her subordinate. But he still has to do what she asks."

Further conversation became impossible when Nikin arrived, followed closely by several field workers, and Tal was soon busy answering questions and explaining some of the history and details of traditional sword training. She was surrounded by people whose smiles were open and friendly, whose questions were unguarded and lacking hidden motives, and with a start she realized that somewhere in the last half moon, she had become a part of Hol-Opah. These people saw her working in the fields with them every day and had come to accept her as an Alsean who simply had a different life than they did.

From the beginning she had seen Hol-Opah as a sanctuary, a world apart from the rest. Now she was beginning to see it as home.

Then she felt a sharper note and looked past Nikin to see Herot on the edge of the crowd. He was watching her with a frown, and when their eyes met, he turned and walked away.

Well, most of them accepted her. There was always an exception to the rule.

She just wished the exception weren't Salomen's brother.

CHAPTER 51
Fighting words

Tal couldn't remember the last time she had taken this much care with her appearance. She had been to banquets studded with the planet's political and entertainment elites and not given half this much thought to how to arrange her hair. It was a little embarrassing.

At least she didn't have to think about her outfit. Micah had already picked it out for her last night in Blacksun, saying that only one thing would do for tonight's date. She had protested that it was far too formal for a small village like Granelle, but Micah would have none of it. "The village is not the point," he said. "Your evenmeal companion is."

She pulled on the black trousers, tailored to fall perfectly over boots, then stepped into her shiniest and most formal dress boots, with a heel that she would never wear if she needed to move quickly. A high-necked crimson top, buttoned at the side of her throat, denoted her caste and rank by virtue of its color and the almost incandescent glow of the precious bluestones which served for buttons. It was doubtful that anyone in Granelle had seen its like. But the short white jacket was bound to draw the most attention, with its intricate gold patterning on the front, back, and wrists, formal braid at the right shoulder, and dark blue starburst over the heart. It was a dress uniform that stated exactly who she was and where she came from.

Feeling like a trainee on her first date, she descended the back stairs and headed for the porch, where Guard Varsi waited to escort her to her transport. Out of habit she scanned the area before reaching the door, sighing when she felt a second and much less welcome emotional presence on the porch. She opened the door, nodded at Varsi, and walked down the steps with the Guard at her heels. There were more important things on her mind than a sullen young man.

"Well, now I know why you weren't interested in me." The tone was venomous enough, but it was the surge of anger behind it that made Tal stop and turn.

"Do you? Perhaps you might enlighten me."

Herot stared insolently from his chair. "It was Salomen all along, wasn't it? Looks like she's held out against you so far, if you're going to such an effort just to shek her. Meadowgreen and opera house clothes; you can probably buy her with that. But then what? I can't imagine she'll hold your attention for long once you've taken what she's selling."

She should have risen above such obvious baiting. But his words short-circuited her normal control, and the instant rage sent her back up the porch steps.

Herot sat, watching her approach with a smug grin, but it slipped when she grabbed his hand, dug her thumb into the pressure point, and twisted his wrist sharply as she pushed his elbow up. Every major joint in his arm—wrist, elbow, and shoulder—was now under extremely painful pressure.

"Shekking Mother!" He scrambled up, forced to follow the direction she was pushing his arm.

She kicked the chair out from behind him and marched him backward into the porch railing, where she bent him over the handrail.

"Don't think that I have any compunction about teaching you more lessons," she growled. "You're making it abundantly clear that you're in desperate need of them. And if you ever speak of your sister that way again, the next lesson will be swift and painful."

He stared at her, awash in a toxic mix of hatred, anger, and fear that she might really hurt him. But when she let him go, a new emotion rose above the rest.

Standing upright, he straightened his jacket with exaggerated care and gave her a cocky smile.

"I knew you wouldn't do anything," he said. "Not in those clothes. You need to keep them clean to shek my sister."

She put her body weight into the strike, and with a whoosh his lungs emptied. Red-faced and open-mouthed, he collapsed onto his knees and fell to his side, clutching his abdomen and gasping for air.

"I could have hit you just a bit higher," she said. "But that would cause so much damage that I'm afraid it would interrupt my plans for a lovely evening. So you can keep that bruise as a reminder that my respect for your sister is the only thing between you and a visit to the healer." She paused, waiting for him to look up. When he didn't, she added quietly, "Do you think Nashta would be proud of you right now?"

The spike of anguish was the first honest emotion she had ever sensed in him, and she knew the verbal blow had hurt far more than the physical one. With a quick nod at Varsi, who was poised and ready an arm's length away, she walked off the porch and didn't look back.

She had left her personal transport some distance from the house, at the bottom of the hill and behind a grove of trees that shielded it from view. It took nearly the entire walk there to shake off her anger. Hearing Herot use such a crude term in reference to Salomen had fired her blood faster than anything had in a long time, and she was shocked at how much she had wanted to hurt him. Salomen deserved a Shared joining, not some purely physical satiation of need. She deserved reverence and love.

The image that flashed into her mind took her breath away. She saw Salomen, bare-shouldered under a thin sheet, smiling up at her, waiting for her touch with a heated desire in her dark eyes…

Fahla! She could not be thinking that way. Salomen already saw through her front; there was no telling what she might say if she felt that little mental meandering.

"You may speak," she told Varsi, needing the distraction. "You've been simmering all the way out here; it's not healthy to keep such anger inside."

"It's not healthy to speak openly to my superior, either," Varsi said.

Tal looked over, surprised by her candor. "That depends on the superior and the situation. In this case, your superior is honestly interested in your thoughts."

Varsi eyed her, plainly nervous. Then she shook her head and smiled. "They're not all that valuable. I was merely wishing you'd hit him higher. If my brother said that about me, I'd make sure he didn't say anything else for quite some time."

"It was tempting, believe me. But it wouldn't have been worth the consequences."

"I think that's Herot's problem." Varsi was feeling slightly more at ease. "He hasn't learned to consider consequences."

"I think that's only one of Herot's problems."

"True words. Another one is you."

Tal stopped. "Me?"

She felt a surge of nervousness from her Guard and remembered Salomen's words from the night before. *You have no understanding of how intimidating you can be.*

"I've never disciplined a subordinate for speaking honestly so long as the honesty is accompanied by respect," she said. "If people told me only what they thought I wanted to hear, I'd never hear anything of value. So I'm interested in what you have to say."

Varsi dipped her head in a small salute. "Thank you, Lancer Tal. We—I mean, the Guards—we all know that Nashta Opah went to her Return very recently. And we can see the effects of that still, particularly in Raiz Opah. She's the head of her family now and partly a mother to both Jaros and Herot. You're taking Raiz Opah on a date. That makes you a problem for Herot."

Tal frowned. "I don't interfere in their relationship."

Shifting uncomfortably, Varsi said, "Not yet."

There was a long pause while Tal processed this new point of view. When she followed the statement to its logical conclusion, she shook her head at her own blindness. That would explain a few things, wouldn't it?

Her silence had made Varsi nervous again, and she couldn't resist the temptation. "Your opinion is incorrect," she said sternly. The worry increased as Varsi opened her mouth, but Tal held up her hand. "You said your thoughts were not valuable. I disagree. I find them quite valuable and expect that you will continue to share them if I ask."

"I…oh." Varsi relaxed. "You do?"

"Did I not just say so?"

"Yes, but—"

"Then you can take me at my word." She resumed her walk. "Let's go. If I'm late for this particular date, I'll never hear the end of it."

All thoughts of Herot and his problems faded once she was cocooned in the familiar comfort of her transport. She lifted off and flew toward the main house, waggling her wings just for the fun of it as she passed over Varsi. In a few ticks Salomen would be sitting beside her, not as a delegate or as the head of Hol-Opah, but as the woman she was taking out for a romantic evening. This was new territory.

Micah was standing on the porch when she landed in front of the house. Her body buzzed with nervousness and excitement as she ran up the steps and stopped with a breathless "Is she ready?"

His slow grin was maddening. "Well, I'm not entirely certain, Lancer Tal. I believe you might wish to ring first and see what awaits you."

Rolling her eyes, Tal stepped past him and pulled the old-fashioned bell by the door. "You're enjoying this far too much," she muttered.

"Yes, I am," he agreed cheerfully, but Tal paid no attention. She was too busy staring at the vision in the doorway.

Salomen wore a filmy burgundy dress that skimmed every one of her curves, ending just below her knees to expose toned, tanned calves. Delicate sandals encircled the feet that Tal normally saw in work boots.

That alone would have sent her heart rate up, but nestled against Salomen's upper arms was a beautifully embroidered wrap that left her chest and shoulders uncovered…and oh, dear Fahla, her shoulders were bare. The straps holding up that dress were so thin that Tal could simply brush them to the sides, leaving all of that flawless skin—

She shook herself out of that fantasy, only to have her eyes fall into a lovely cleavage that was not so much exposed by the dress as enhanced by it. And if Salomen hadn't meant to draw Tal's eyes there, then she shouldn't have worn the pendant that hung on a fine gold chain, resting just between the swells of her breasts.

With an effort, Tal dragged her gaze upward, meeting a very knowing smile. She smiled back, acknowledging that she'd been caught.

She was used to seeing Salomen's dark hair in a sensible tail, which kept it off her neck during the hot field work, but now it was down, gleaming in the light, and brushing one of those bare shoulders. On the other side it was caught up in a golden clip that sparkled with precious stones. Tal's hands itched to undo the clip, beautiful as it was, and release the strands it held captive. She wanted to run her fingers through that hair and see for herself whether it was as soft as it looked.

Goddess above, she wanted—

"Good evening, Andira."

Tal swallowed. "Good evening. Thank you for accepting my invitation."

"It was my great pleasure." Salomen looked past her. "Is that our ride for the night?"

"That's my personal transport," Tal said inanely, and wanted to slap herself.

"Very nice." Salomen's eyes were alight with merriment. "I'd invite you in to meet my father, but I think we can skip the usual preliminaries."

"Thank Fahla." It came out before she could stop herself, and Salomen laughed.

"Shall we go, then?" She walked past Tal and off the porch, leaving a subtle scent behind.

Tal turned in a daze, sniffing appreciatively. Not floral, but spicy—so perfectly appropriate for Salomen.

Her date paused at the bottom of the steps to look back. "Are you coming, or am I going to fly myself?"

Micah chuckled.

"Shut up," Tal whispered, and chased after her.

She caught up just as Salomen was tugging on the passenger door release. "It needs a programmed biosign," she said, covering Salomen's hand to still her efforts.

The door slid open at her touch on the sensor, and Salomen looked into the four-seater craft. "Am I correct in guessing that I would be unable to buy this particular model at our local merchant?"

"You're correct. There are only three merchants on Alsea who sell these. And they have very few customers."

"All warrior caste, no doubt."

"Actually, most of their customers are merchant caste. The average warrior has no need of such protection."

Salomen turned to her. "And I hate that you do," she said quietly.

"I know. But the truth is that when we bond, you'll have need of it as well."

"I know, and I hate that too."

They stood looking at each other, until Tal said, "Wait here." She ducked inside and stepped across to the pilot's seat, then entered a command on her console. "Put your palm on the sensor."

Salomen lifted her hand, and the console chirped.

"Good. You're programmed. Please come in."

Ducking her head, Salomen entered and sat next to Tal with a swish of fabric. The door slid shut, enveloping them in silence as Tal watched her taking in the details of the plush interior.

"As Jaros would say, this is speedy. Are you trying to impress me?"

"This comes with my title. It's not a matter of impressing you, it's a matter of logistics. If I'm going out without Guards, this is the transport I use. It's armed with a disruptor, and the hull will deflect both projectile and energy weaponry. There's not much that can reach me in here." She waved a hand at the interior.

"The quiet flight, cushy seats, and military-level electronics are pretty speedy, too."

Salomen nodded. "I understand. I also understand that you sidestepped my question."

"Are you impressed?"

"Very."

"Good, because there's more." She touched a control, and the windows took on a slight sheen. "I've just activated the privacy screen. We can see out, but no one can see in."

"Ah. Another safety feature."

"Correct. It has other benefits as well."

They smiled at each other, enjoying the light moment. But Tal soon forgot everything else in her study of Salomen's appearance.

"You're absolutely stunning," she whispered, reaching out to touch one of the shoulder straps. "This color is perfect for you."

"You look gorgeous as well." Salomen's voice was raspy. "I think I sometimes forget who you are. I know that sounds ridiculous, but…"

"But you see me in field clothes most of the time."

"Or your running clothes. And yet, until you came to my holding, I never saw you in anything but more formal dress." She ran her palm along the shoulder braid. "But even those clothes were plain compared to this. You look…powerful. And wealthy." A short laugh escaped. "Like every pre-Rite girl's dream of a warrior swooping in to carry her off."

"I would love to carry you off, but you'd never allow it."

"Dress like this more often and I might." Salomen stroked the blue starburst over Tal's heart. "This is the background color of your family crest, is it not?"

"Yes. I shouldn't be surprised that you know that."

"And you shouldn't be surprised that I want to know more." Salomen leaned in, and Tal almost met her halfway—until both of them remembered.

"Fahla, this is a trial!" Tal sat back in her seat with a thump. "You're a walking crime in that dress, and I can't even kiss you!"

"Don't think it's any easier for me. You look like nothing of my world, and I still can't believe you're here, wanting me."

There were echoes of a long-ago humiliation in those words, and for the first time, Tal wondered if Salomen even realized how desirable she was.

"Of course I want you," she said. "And I'm not saying that because you're my tyree. You're beautiful both inside and out, and I thought that before we knew of our bond."

Salomen's eyes were luminous in the late afternoon light. "You did? You never allowed me to sense it."

"Because I'm an idiot and I was too busy battling you. And when we stopped fighting, I was too worried about frightening you off."

"Sometimes I wish you didn't have such a perfect front. But I have to ask—did you ever sense me? Because I thought you were extremely attractive the first time I saw you. Photos and holograms don't do you justice."

"No, I never sensed that! You were better at fronting than I thought. Besides, you made no secret of your distaste."

"I didn't say I found you appealing. Just attractive. In an arrogant, cold way. You exuded power and control and everything I never wanted in a mate or even a friend."

"And now?"

"You still exude power and control." She reached out to run the backs of her fingers along Tal's cheek. "But now you allow me to see beyond the lie of the Lancer. And I, too, see beauty."

Tal caught her wrist and kissed the sensitive skin on the underside. As her lips lingered, an electrical sensation tickled her brain and she instantly let go. Salomen pulled away at the same time, and they broke into matching smiles.

"I think we're beginning to figure this out," Tal said.

"Perhaps. I think it requires testing." Salomen leaned over and kissed her, taking her by surprise.

It was difficult to fully enjoy the kiss when every nerve in Tal's body was straining to detect the first sign of the empathic flash, but another part of her was getting a thrill out of the risk they were running. Once again she felt the crackle, and both of them pulled back before the flash could impact.

"Oh." Salomen put a hand to her lips. "I see a great deal of potential here. Perhaps we won't have to be quite so chaste as we'd thought."

Tal laughed. "You may be a producer, but you have the instincts of a warrior."

"Trust a warrior to think they invented the concept of taking risks."

Tal stroked a lock of hair that was resting on Salomen's shoulder, then pushed it back and trailed her fingers over soft skin. These bare shoulders were going to be the death of her. "We didn't invent it, we just perfected it," she murmured, and bent down to kiss the smooth curve under her fingertips.

When the tingle warned her off, she straightened and found a smile on Salomen's face unlike any she had seen before. She thought she'd walk ten lengths in the rain to see another like it.

"Keep smiling at me like that, and I'll have to call off our date," she said.

The smile grew larger. "Why?"

"Because we'll never get off the ground." She shook out her hands, took a deep breath, and started up the engines.

"All right." Salomen's amusement showed in her voice. "I'll just smile out the window, then."

CHAPTER 52
Meadowgreen

Granelle was less than fifteen lengths from the east boundary of Hol-Opah, making the flight a short one. Tal wished it were longer. The sense of uneasy truce which had marked so many of their skimmer rides to and from the fields was now replaced with one of charged anticipation and mutual attraction, and she wanted to luxuriate in it.

All too soon, Granelle came into view, a tidy village where a respectably sized temple shared the center with the Producer Caste House. At Salomen's direction, they flew over the town toward a small hill on its outskirts, where several homes and businesses were built on the hillside. Meadowgreen occupied the highest point, separated from the rest by a buffer of wild grasses and shrubs.

"Gorgeous location," Tal said as she brought the transport down near two waiting Guards. "Ready to go public?"

"I'm ready to turn a few heads, at least. Walking in with the Lancer will either boost or bury my reputation, depending on who sees us."

"Do you care if it's the latter?"

"Not in the slightest." Salomen's dark hair brushed her bare shoulders as she shook her head emphatically. "I don't run my life according to what others think of me."

"Don't I know it."

They climbed out of the transport, but when Salomen turned toward the restaurant, Tal took her hand and urged her in the opposite direction. Together they walked to the edge of the hilltop, holding hands as they gazed at the landscape glowing in the last light of the day. Hol-Opah was easily visible atop its hill, surrounded by a quilted patchwork of fields and crops.

"It's such a beautiful holding," Tal said.

"I've always thought so, though it's possible I'm biased."

"A person would have to be biased not to think so."

Salomen pointed. "See that break in the tree line there? Just across the river from our border?"

"Yes…?"

"That's where the ground pounder came through."

"*What?*"

The outburst earned her a surprised look. "You didn't know a ground pounder landed here?"

Oh, shekking Mother, she'd had no idea. "I had so many damage reports... but I don't remember seeing Granelle in them." Then again, the name wouldn't have meant anything to her then.

"It didn't get a chance to cause any damage. At least, not to Granelle. We were terrified it was going to blow us off the hill, though. It was like a scene out of a horror vid. We watched it come down, and when it landed so close to our border, we thought that was the end. But it never seemed to care about what was behind it, only what was ahead. It wanted Granelle, not a little house on a hill."

Tal realized she was squeezing Salomen's hand too tightly and loosened her grip with an effort. "I have a lot to thank Fahla for," she said. "One shell and I'd never have met you. Hol-Opah was well within range."

"Believe me, I know. We saw what it could do. Those trees were in its way, so it just blew a hole through them. They were thousand-cycle-old molwyn trees, and it destroyed them in a piptick. And then there was a huge roar over our heads, and the Protectorate fighter came in. It hit the ground pounder with a laser shot, and we saw the shield light up and go out. Nikin was narrating the whole time; he knew all the weaponry and what was happening because he'd been reading and watching everything he could get his hands on about the *Caphenon* and the Voloth threat. Jaros was still sleeping, thank the Goddess."

Tal looked at the break in the trees, imagining the fight. "Did the ground pounder fire any missiles?"

"Oh, yes. It was like a fireworks show. I saw it fire four. Nikin says it was five, but it was hard to tell with so much going on. The fighter was shooting them down as fast as they came out, and then it fired its own missiles and that ground pounder went up like a bonfire at the autumn feast. The whole thing took less than five ticks. The fighter flew off to the northeast and that was the sum total of the Battle of Alsea in our little corner of the world."

Tal was silent, wondering which of the two Fleet pilots had saved Granelle.

"I saw the interview with Captain Serrado afterwards. I remember wondering at the time what motivation she could possibly have had to risk her ship and her people for us." Salomen glanced over. "I think I might have a better idea about that now."

Tal shook her head. "It's not what you think. She risked everything before we ever met. That's just who she is."

Salomen hesitated, then said, "I worry, sometimes. I'm not a warrior. You and she fought that battle. I just watched it."

But if she had been properly trained, Tal thought, she could have fought it quite well. Then she shivered as she imagined Salomen in one of those slapped-together high empath groups that had been decimated by the ground pounders, the ones where the rescue crews literally had to pick up the pieces.

"I don't want a warrior," she said. "I want you. Safe and happy and bossing around field workers like an ADF unit trainer."

Salomen chuckled. "Field workers, or you?"

"Well, for the moment I *am* a field worker..."

"Not in those clothes you're not. And not even out of them. You don't carry yourself like any field worker or landholder I know. But speaking of bossing you around..." She pointed again, this time to the north of Hol-Opah. "That cluster of lights over there? That's the distribution center. You're going to become intimately familiar with it next nineday. Do you feel up to some endless transport piloting?"

"That sounds like a vacation after this last half-moon in the fields."

"You won't think so when you've made your hundredth trip."

The horten crop could not be transported in bulk, due to its delicate nature. It had to be processed immediately after harvest, and even two hanticks could ruin the flavor. All growers reserved time at the distribution center, and that time was a frenzy of harvest and transport, harvest and transport, until the last of the crop was processed. It was a facet of producer life that she had never known about until now. In truth, Tal's time on Hol-Opah had taught her more than she had expected.

Quite a bit more, she thought as she turned to look at her date. Salomen sensed her glance and smiled, though she didn't take her eyes off the scenery.

"I notice we haven't actually gone into the restaurant yet," she said. "Did you really get a table, or did you just bring me here for the view?"

"I brought you here for the view."

She did look then, her skepticism clear. "Are we speaking of the same view?"

"I think not." Tal sighed theatrically. "One of the disadvantages of our bond, I suppose. Once we complete this, I'll never be able to take refuge behind words with double meanings."

"Yes, you will. Just not with me. And thank you for the compliment behind that double meaning."

"I'll be the envy of everyone in the room."

"If they're locals, I doubt that."

Tal reached for her other hand and pulled her closer. "Anyone with eyes can see how lovely you are on the outside. If they don't see the beauty you carry inside, it's only because you don't allow it. I count myself fortunate that you allowed me."

Salomen glanced down at their hands and tightened her grip. "I'm uncertain as to who allowed what. Don't give me credit for something I did without any awareness. I don't even know when I ceased disliking you and began—" She paused, then looked up. "Loving you," she finished.

Tal wanted to respond; she wanted to return Salomen's courage in full measure. But she had never said those words before, and they did not come easily. It was ironic, really—a tyree bond was the ultimate vulnerability, and here she was, holding hands with her tyree, afraid to say a few words that would make her vulnerable. Ridiculous.

She opened her mouth to explain, but Salomen placed two fingers on her lips. "There's no need," she whispered. "Please don't say it until it comes from your heart, unforced."

Tal nodded as Salomen dropped her hand. "And you worry about not being a warrior? I'm not the courageous one here."

"There are different kinds of courage. And despite what you thought last night, none could ever call you coward."

"I think in this matter, some might."

"'Some' meaning one Andira Tal."

"Perhaps. But her opinion holds a great deal of weight."

"Or so she thinks." Salomen winked, lightening the mood. "Shall we dine, then? Or were you serious when you said you brought me here for the view?"

"I was quite serious, though when I arranged the evening I had no idea just how breathtaking the view would be." Tal could be light as well. "Come on, let's make everyone envious." She acknowledged the Guards, who had remained at a respectful distance, and with a hand motion sent them to the front and back entrances of the restaurant.

"They'll be out here while we're dining?" Salomen asked.

"Yes. And two more inside."

"So we eat in luxury and they stand outside in the night, watching for any danger."

Tal gave her a sidelong glance as they walked down the path. "That's their duty, yes."

"You must tell Jaros about this the next time he wants a story about warriors. I'm quite sure his dreams of changing caste don't involve standing guard outside restaurants and private homes."

"No, I suspect his dreams involve a bit more glory."

"Mm-hm. And it doesn't help that you're his role model."

"What does that mean?"

"It means, *Lancer* Tal, that my brother wants to model himself after the greatest warrior of our generation. It's hard to convince him that most warriors aren't covered in glory when all he sees is you." Salomen mounted the steps to the restaurant's porch and turned back. "Are you coming?"

Tal had stopped and now found herself looking up at the elegant picture Salomen made in her formfitting dress. "Is that what you think of me?"

Salomen smiled and walked inside.

Scrambling to catch up, Tal slipped into the foyer just before the door closed. "Is it?"

"You did save us from the Voloth."

"But when we met, you acted like I was the biggest incompetent to ever sit in the State Chair."

Salomen shrugged. "I disagreed with your policies."

"You're a hard woman to please, Raiz Opah."

Salomen's gaze dropped to Tal's boots and made a slow trip back to her face. "Yes, I am," she said in a smoky voice.

Both of them had their fronts up, given their public location, and Tal thought that might be a good thing. If the emotions behind that voice were even close to what she was imagining, she might spontaneously combust right where she stood.

Needing a distraction, she looked around the foyer, which was drenched in understated luxury. Hand-rubbed wood shone in the light from discreetly placed lamps, and the room exuded the kind of quiet charm that came only from age, excellent care, and considerable expense. The sounds of utensils on plates and many conversations drifted through an arched doorway, and the air was full of mouth-watering scents.

"Lancer Tal!" A man in formal dress appeared from nowhere and bowed. "Saunista Corsine. Welcome to my establishment; you honor us with your presence." He bowed to Salomen in turn. "Welcome, Raiz Opah."

"Thank you," Tal said. "I have it on excellent authority that your restaurant is the best in the area and that a reservation cannot be had for bribery nor battle for less than half a moon in advance. I appreciate your making last-tick accommodations for us."

Corsine waved that away. "It was no burden. If you will follow me, please." He turned with military precision and led them into the domed dining area.

Tal spotted the other two Guards instantly, one on each side of the room. In civilian dress, they blended with the crowd quite well.

She and Salomen did not. Every head in the place swiveled to watch them as they walked to their table, and she was proud of Salomen's regal bearing and confident walk. Automatically, she broadsensed the room, and while a few individuals were unhappy with her appearance in the restaurant, she detected nothing that gave cause for concern.

"You were right," Salomen murmured. "His snobbery has clear limits."

"So that means I've impressed you again?"

She laughed. "You have."

"Twice in one night! But perhaps I should not have set the standard so high on the first date."

"Too late. I expect every date from here forward to be equally impressive."

"Damn."

Corsine arrived at the only empty table in the dining area, which was slightly removed from the others and commanded an excellent view. Standing to one side, he bowed with a flourish. "I recommend a bottle of Tollisan while you consider your order. It's a fine spirit."

Tal hid a smile. Tollisan was the most costly spirit on all Alsea, and in her opinion not deserving of the price. Corsine was planning to sell her the most expensive meal he could.

"I'd prefer Valkinon, if you have it."

"Very well. An excellent choice." Corsine showed no outward reaction, but Tal could sense a rise in respect. He plucked the hyacot twig from its bowl on their table, snapped it in half, and replaced the pieces. With a short bow, he departed for the kitchen.

Tal brought a piece to her nose and happily sniffed it. "Why is it that these cost a fortune and I've seen them only in expensive restaurants, yet there's an enormous hyacot tree on Hol-Opah and you don't use them? You should have these at every meal."

"We used to. When Mother grew ill, Father made sure their room always had hyacot in it. She loved the scent, and it soothed her when nothing else could, but no one in our family could abide it afterward."

Tal dropped the twig back in its bowl. "I'm so sorry." She picked up the bowl and began to rise, but Salomen put a hand on her wrist.

"No, please. I think…I would like to have some new memories to associate with that scent."

Tal put the bowl back. "Then I'll do my best to make this the first of many new memories."

"You already have. So tell me, what makes Valkinon better than Tollisan?"

"Have you ever had either?"

"No."

"Well, Tollisan is all name recognition and very little delivery. Personally, I think most people who buy it do so entirely for the ego boost. If they knew anything about spirits, they wouldn't drink it. But they want to be seen spending an enormous number of cinteks."

"And Valkinon?"

"Is a spirit from the Highmont district, produced by a maker who has very little name recognition because he doesn't pay for advertising. But he doesn't need to. Anyone who seeks out good-quality spirits will eventually hear his name. He charges less for his spirits because his own costs aren't that high, meaning a less affluent Alsean can afford a better spirit than the type more affluent Alseans tend to drink."

Salomen narrowed her eyes. "Did I just hear an economics lesson? Perhaps something you've been trying to convince my caste?"

Tal had to smile. "Not intentionally, no, but the principle is the same."

Their waiter arrived with two glasses and a bottle. Silently, he set the glasses in front of them, braced the bottle with one hand, and pulled the tab with the other. The cap popped off, clattering to the wood floor as a puff of blue mist floated from the bottle. Tal watched in anticipation as he poured, picking up her glass as soon as he left. "I should warn you that you're about to be ruined for anything less."

Salomen raised an eyebrow that said *We'll see about that*, and took a sip. The second eyebrow joined the first. "Oh, Fahla. This is wonderful."

"Mm-hm." Tal was enjoying her own drink. "I believe it's your turn."

"What?"

"I chose the spirits, but the food is another matter. You live here. What would you recommend?"

"Andira, this is Meadowgreen. Everything is good."

Tal shook her head. "Insufficient. Not to mention a startling lack of assertiveness on your part. You tell me what to do every day in the fields and now you won't recommend a meal?"

Salomen leaned close. "Do you want me to tell you what to do?"

The low voice sent a shiver down Tal's spine, and she leaned in as well. "I've already experienced that. But I do wonder whether you would take orders as well as you give them."

"You'll have to wait to learn that, my Lancer. I give up no secrets."

Tal was now regretting the high-necked shirt, and Salomen gave her a slow smile.

"You seem a little warm. Perhaps we should begin with a cold soup."

"An excellent idea," Tal said, resisting the urge to undo a few buttons at her collar.

Salomen sat up straight. "Then let's see what they offer." She pushed the control on her side, and a small section of the table slid back to reveal the electronic menu. "Oh, look. Horten soup, this close to harvest? Corsine must have imported it from central Pallea. I could make this for us next nineday for a tenth of the cost, and it would be much fresher."

"You can?"

"Certainly. Would you like me to?"

"'Like' is probably not a sufficient term. I adore horten soup. The last time I was in central Pallea during harvest, I brought back an enormous container of it and vacuum-stored it. I rationed it out to myself at the rate of one bowl every nineday, and was crushed when it was gone."

"You vacuum-stored horten soup? Oh, no no no." Salomen shook her head. "You must have it fresh."

"All right," Tal said quickly. "If you say so."

"I see I have my work cut out for me. If you can wait a few days, I think I can promise something that will curl your toes with gastronomic happiness."

"Then I can wait. But it won't be easy."

"Nothing really good ever is."

Tal couldn't keep the grin off her face as Salomen went through the menu, discarding various dishes as too expensive or too common—"I could make this at the holding as well; why is Corsine asking a Lancer's ransom for something this easy?"—and finally settling on a soup, main dish, and dessert. When she slid the cover back over her menu and looked up, heat suffused her cheeks. "What?"

"I was just enjoying watching you concentrate. You develop an adorable crinkle right here." Tal pointed at her own forehead, just above her nose.

"I do not crinkle."

"You do. I've watched it for nearly three ninedays."

"Thank you very much; now I'm embarrassed."

"Is that all it takes?"

"Always looking for the tactical advantage, aren't you?"

"Of course. It's part of that greatest warrior thing."

Salomen chuckled. "I knew you wouldn't let that go."

"Do you blame me? All this time I've wondered if anyone on Hol-Opah even knew what I did in that battle. No one has mentioned a word or asked any questions, not even Jaros. And if Jaros isn't asking me, it can only be because he has no idea."

"Or because he was instructed not to."

Tal sat back in her chair. "Really?"

Salomen took a leisurely sip of her spirits. "You were such an arrogant ass when you challenged me. I couldn't bear the idea of you coming to my holding and being treated like Fahla's favorite by my own family and field workers. So I told everyone to act as if you were just a regular guest who had nothing to do with the Voloth. I wasn't going to allow you any edge based solely on your rank or title—or even the fact that you single-handedly turned that battle." She drummed her fingers lightly on the glass. "Then after your first few days with us, when you never brought any of that up yourself, Father said you might prefer it that way. That it might be a relief for you to be treated as if none of that had happened."

"So you were motivated by competition, while Shikal was being compassionate."

Salomen's gaze turned sharp. "You let me think you needed twenty Guards and waited a full day to tell me otherwise. Don't talk to me about competition."

Tal couldn't help it; just the memory of that vidcom call made her snort with laughter. "And you should have seen yourself when I told you. You were trying so hard to be calm about it, but the relief was written all over your face."

"Were the homicidal thoughts written there, too?"

Tal laughed harder. "No, you managed to keep those to yourself until the first day, when you toured me around."

"Oh, you were a dokker's backside that afternoon," Salomen said, but her lips were twitching.

"I know I was. Somehow you managed to neutralize every diplomatic instinct I ever had, along with most of my manners. And then I couldn't understand why you were so nice to Gehrain and Micah when you were such a vallcat with me."

"And people say you're a strategic thinker."

"I am when my head isn't on backwards. I'm sorry, Salomen."

"Well…" Salomen blew out a breath. "I'm sorry, too. You were right, you know. When you said I was defensive about my position. I'm proud of Hol-Opah, but you were coming from the damn State House. I just knew you were looking at everything and thinking how shabby it was."

"Actually, I was looking at everything and thinking how beautiful it was. Including you." She enjoyed Salomen's smile and added, "Shikal was right, too. It *has* been a relief to be treated like a normal person. So please don't change anything."

"Too late for that," Salomen said quietly. Her gaze shifted past Tal's shoulder, and she stiffened. "Well, the air in here just became a great deal more stifling."

Tal had already sensed it and could see the new arrivals from the corner of her eye. "Who are they?"

"The overweight pompous one is Gordense Bilsner. His equally pompous bondmate is Iversina, and the obnoxious boy is Cullom, Gordense's son by his first bondmate." Salomen looked back at Tal. "You're surprised."

"The last person I heard you describe so unkindly was me. You're usually less judgmental."

"I was wrong about you because I didn't know you, but I know the Bilsners very well. Believe me, the descriptions are well-earned." Salomen's expression hardened as she added, "They don't treat their field workers well. Many of them have come to Hol-Opah to ask for employment, and they've told me stories to raise your hair. I've taken all that I could, and only wish I could rescue them all. No one deserves the treatment that passes for normal at Hol-Bilsner. Gordense and Iversina are insufferable at caste house meetings; they think that owning more land makes them better than anyone else. It's particularly annoying with Iversina because she should know better. She comes from a poor family, but apparently her memory is short. Unfortunately, Cullom has absorbed their self-inflating beliefs and mixed them with the arrogance of youth."

"A bad combination."

"Very bad. And he and Herot have become friends."

Tal shook her head. "Now I understand your concern." She watched in her peripheral vision as the Bilsners were led to a table near the center of the room. Gordense was not pleased with the location and motioned toward the tables by the windows. Then he saw her and Salomen, and Tal felt a swell of outright hatred. He spoke to his bondmate as they sat, causing a surge of negative emotions from his family.

"They clearly don't like one of us. Which one is it?" Tal took a casual sip of her drink, her senses alert.

"That's difficult to say. Gordense has made a point of snubbing and undermining me at every opportunity since I turned down his bond offer. But he—" She stopped as Tal abruptly thumped her glass to the table.

"That little fanten made you a bond offer?"

"No, he made my land a bond offer. Our holdings adjoin; if we had bonded, we would have controlled most of the land in this district. I never deluded myself into thinking it was anything more than political or financial, which is why I could never understand his anger when I said no. It was business for him, but he took the rejection personally."

"The rejection meant he didn't get what he wanted, and to someone like that, it becomes personal." Tal knew the type. She had dealt with far too many of them on the Council.

"The odd thing is that on the surface, he's been very friendly to me since I began speaking out against…ah…"

"Against me?" It was not unexpected, after all.

Salomen took a steadying drink of her spirits. "Yes. I thought your policies were an extraordinary danger to our caste, and I said what I thought at our caste house meetings. I'm sorry to have been one of the voices that have caused you such trouble."

"Don't be. You were true to your beliefs, and I respect that."

"Do you forgive everyone so readily?"

"I forgive based on truth. When you were convinced that my policies would destroy your caste, you spoke your truth. The important thing is that you've learned a new truth, and tomorrow you'll be speaking it before your peers. That's integrity. Why would I need to forgive that?"

"Every day I learn something more about you, and every day I wonder how I could have been so wrong."

"We were both wrong. But I'm happy with where we are now."

Salomen reached across the table and took her hand. "I am, too. For all my fear of this, I'm very happy."

The moment was interrupted by the arrival of their soup. Salomen released her hand and sat back, smiling sheepishly. As the waiter departed she said, "Caught holding hands like a pair of pre-Rite lovers."

"Oh, no, this was much worse. You were caught holding hands with the single most dangerous person to your caste. Not only that, but one of the most powerful landholders in the district saw it. You're in trouble tomorrow."

"Gordense saw it?"

"He can't keep his eyes off this table."

"Damn. I didn't think about that. My word will mean less tomorrow if Gordense can accuse me of personal involvement." Salomen picked up her spoon and took a sip of her soup. "Oh, this is good."

Tal sampled hers and bit back a moan. "Fahla! Corsine should have a restaurant in Blacksun. He'd have every wealthy Alsean at his door, begging for a reservation. Why is he here in Granelle?"

"Because his bondmate was born and raised here. She hates Blacksun."

They both paused, and by mutual unspoken agreement decided not to pursue that line of conversation.

"I think your personal involvement could be to your advantage," Tal said. "Surely everyone knows that you're not easily fooled, nor do you say anything you don't mean. If you tell your peers that you're revising your opinion precisely because of what you've learned from our discussions—will they not respect that?"

"Hm. They might." Salomen thoughtfully sipped her soup. "In fact…" Another sip, and her face brightened. "That might just be the key. I'd planned to avoid all mention of our relationship, but perhaps I should do the opposite. Acknowledge it so it can't be used against me and use it to strengthen my testimony."

"Who knew that producers could be such strategic thinkers?"

"If you haven't learned by now that strategy is a part of our daily lives, then I've taught you nothing these last three ninedays." Salomen frowned. "But if I had my wish, I wouldn't be wasting my time thinking about this. Neither would you. It's so unfair that after all your work, a few individuals could jeopardize everything."

"Actually, it's one individual."

"What?"

Tal exhaled. "I think I need to tell you about Darzen Fosta."

The explanation took the rest of the soup course and all of the main dish, and if Tal had been concerned about discussing another past relationship with her tyree, by the end she was more worried about Darzen's physical health should they ever meet.

"I cannot believe she would take such a drastic, damaging path just to revenge herself! What kind of person puts their personal feelings above the well-being of our entire culture, for Fahla's sake? Can she not see beyond her own shekking ego? Does she have *any* idea how much damage she's caused?"

"It's her truth. I honestly don't believe she's doing this for revenge."

Salomen stared at her. "You really do live your beliefs, don't you?"

"Yes, I do."

"And what if you find that it was deliberate?"

Tal took a moment to drink the last of her spirits. Setting the glass to one side, she said, "I hope it never comes to that, because I never want you to see that side of me."

The silence at their table lasted long enough for the waiter to clear their plates and set out dessert. When they were alone again, Salomen spoke more calmly.

"I keep thinking that should frighten me. But the strange thing is, it doesn't. I know you've been ruthless in the past, and you probably will be in the future. Surely it must be part of your position. But I also know you to be fair almost to a fault. If someone earns your wrath, then it must be well deserved."

"Thank you. That means a great deal to—oh, shek." Tal put her face in her hands.

"What is it?"

"I nearly forgot. Someone did earn my wrath tonight. I don't know how to tell you this."

"Herot."

"How did you know?"

"Andira, he's my brother. I felt it. Both of you. Well, you not so much."

"You felt that and you just let it happen? And then you kissed me in the transport! How could you…great Mother, you've learned to front well!"

Salomen smiled. "You're cute when you're flustered."

"I'm not flustered, I'm shocked."

"I know. I probably should have said something earlier, but I didn't want Herot and his problems to be in the middle of our date. But now that he's here anyway, I guess we need to discuss it. What happened? I know he was angry and bitter, which is a normal state of mind for him these days, and somehow he managed to make you angry as well. Then his emotions were everywhere at once, but the strongest I felt was shame and regret. I have no idea what you said to him, but it had a spectacular effect."

Tal's initial relief vanished. She didn't know after all. "I…well, there wasn't much of a conversation."

Salomen's eyes narrowed. "What did you do?"

"I hit him."

"You *hit* him?"

Tal straightened in her chair. "He said something I could not overlook. I'm sorry, truly I am, but I do have limits and he went well over them."

Now it was Salomen's turn to put her face in her hands. "All right," she said to the table, "I think you'd better tell me what he said."

"I'd rather not."

Salomen lifted her head. "That was not a request. If you hit my brother because of something he said, I need to know what it was."

After a long pause, Tal said, "He made an extremely crude reference regarding my intentions toward you. It impugned both my honor and yours. And that is all I will say."

"Oh, Herot, you grainbird. Never mind, I don't need to know any more. He was just pushing as hard as he could."

"Yes, well, I think he pushed a little further than he intended."

"Where did you hit him?"

"Just below the sternum. He was still trying to breathe when I left him. He'll be bruised and sore, but it won't cause any damage. I think my last words hurt him more than the blow. I asked him if he thought Nashta would be proud of him."

"*That's* what I felt. Oh yes, you hurt him." Salomen took a thoughtful bite of her dessert. "Well, perhaps that will make a difference. I've tried everything I could think of, and so have Father and Nikin, but none of us can get through. He's been angry at the world and everyone in it since Mother's Return. I'm sorry you've been pulled into this."

"I think I'd be involved anyway. Varsi gave me a new point of view while we walked to my transport, and it made sense. She suggested that Herot is afraid of losing you to me. Long term."

"Oh." Salomen put her fork down. "Oh, shek. I didn't think of that. For all his anger and disrespect toward me, I'm still the closest thing to a mother figure he has. If he's afraid of me going away with you, then…"

"Then he would lash out at me in any way he could," Tal finished. "And by losing my temper, I played right into it. But I couldn't do otherwise, Salomen. I could not let that insult stand."

"I know. I'm not blaming you. He's been pushing all of us to our limits, and insulting my honor and yours—oh, for the love of our Goddess, what was he thinking? He insulted the Lancer's honor!"

"You just now noticed that?"

"Agh! What are we going to do with him? If we don't pull him back onto a path of decent behavior soon, he's going to be lost. Not everyone is as forgiving as you, and even you were angry enough to hit him. What if the next person isn't so forgiving? Or so good at landing a minimally damaging blow?" She looked at Tal's expression of surprise and added, "I listen when you tell me your stories, Andira. I know how easily you could have hurt him. I also know that you intentionally chose not to. Thank you for that."

"You don't seriously think I would have done real damage, do you? To your brother?"

"Of course not. My point is that someone else might." She shook her head. "I wish Mother were here. Fahla, but I miss her. She would know what to do."

"I'm sorry." They were supremely inadequate words, but there was little more Tal could say.

"I know. And I know you understand, and that helps." Salomen paused. "Hm. Maybe he's pushing you because you're the next best thing to Mother."

"Excuse me?"

"No, think about it. The one person he truly respected was Mother. She would never have let him get away with a tenth of this behavior. She'd have told him he wasn't too big for a stripping, and it would not have been a bluff."

Tal already respected Nashta Opah, but this information gave her a whole new outlook on the woman. Stripping was a last-resort punishment designed to shame children into proper behavior. Taking away a child's clothing and replacing it with the clothing of a much younger child forced the miscreant to dress the age he or she was acting. The public humiliation factor was very high, rendering it a punishment so effective that usually the mere threat of it could bring a recalcitrant child into line. But it was never used once a child reached the Rite of Ascension. For Nashta to actually back up such a threat was astonishing.

"You're the only other person he hasn't been able to bluff," Salomen continued. "You turned down his advances, left him in the dirt on your run, took him down like a small child when he tried to hit you, and actually struck him tonight. Every time he's pushed you, it hasn't worked. You consistently make him pay the consequences for his actions, and I think he keeps coming back for more because somewhere deep down inside, he needs what you're doing. You've earned his respect."

Tal laughed. "You had me on that line of reasoning right up until the last sentence. Herot does not respect me. If he did, he would never have spoken the way he did tonight."

"He does, Andira. You're just accustomed to respect being displayed in a different manner. I grew up with three brothers; believe me when I say their notions of demonstrating respect don't coincide with those of trained warriors." Salomen leaned forward. "You're the Lancer. You're an authority figure by your title alone, and you've demonstrated that authority on several occasions now. I think you're precisely what he's been missing since Mother went to her Return."

Tal sampled her dessert in silence as she considered Salomen's theory. The pastry was excellent, as everything else had been, but she barely noticed.

"If you're correct," she said at last, "and I think you probably are, then I'll do whatever I can to be the figure Herot needs. But I'm new at this, and I'm bound to make mistakes."

Salomen shook her head. "Please. My whole family would be indebted to you if you can help with Herot." Picking up her fork, she added, "Bet you never pictured a family like ours when you were envisioning your tyree."

"I can't say that I pictured anything quite like this, no. But then for me, any family at all is something new. Our times at table, with everyone gathered in one place and all the emotions interlacing…it's been wonderful. Barring Herot's black moods, of course."

"Truly?"

"Truly."

Salomen reached out for her hand. "I'm so glad. You and Colonel Micah have both been a very welcome addition to our table. I haven't seen Father so animated since Mother's Return. He looks forward all day long to his evenings in the parlor with Colonel Micah. It's been good for him to have a friend who doesn't see him as the surviving member of a bond. And I looked forward all day long to my evenings with you, even before we called our truce. It's difficult to believe you've been here less than a moon."

"It's even more difficult to believe I have so little time left. I'll miss Hol-Opah. But at least I'll be taking the best part of it with me next moon." Tal watched as Salomen sat back, a suspicious flush rising to her face. "Are you blushing?"

"No, I'm just warm."

Tal made no answer save for a wide grin, and though Salomen resisted, she eventually broke into a smile as well.

"I swear you make me feel things I never have before. I am not the blushing type." She sipped her drink and added, "Nor do I particularly want to be. It's embarrassing."

"So I should refrain from complimentary observations, then."

"I didn't say that. Perhaps I'll become accustomed to them with enough practice."

They finished their meal with a divine pot of shannel. Tal swooned over it, and when Corsine arrived at their table, she informed him that he had surely gotten his recipe from Fahla herself. She had never tasted shannel that good in Blacksun. Corsine sniffed that very little in Blacksun was as good as its inhabitants thought it was, and Tal concealed her smile. He really was a snob, but she liked him. After all, the man had every reason to feel superior regarding his cuisine.

The other diners were more polite during their departure than they had been earlier. Though everyone still watched them, they were a good deal more discreet about it—except the Bilsners, who glared at them with no pretense of politeness.

"I really thought Gordense was going to say something nasty," Salomen commented as they stepped into the fresh evening air. "He certainly wanted to."

Tal nodded at the Guard, who fell in step at a discreet distance behind them. "His courage doesn't go as far as speaking directly to me. But I'm afraid you may be in for a difficult time tomorrow."

"Don't worry about me. I know how to handle Gordense and his ilk."

"I know you do. In fact, part of me feels sorry for them."

"What does the other part feel?"

"Happy that I'm not them?"

Salomen laughed. "Thank you for your faith in me."

"That isn't faith. Faith occurs in the absence of evidence. I've seen a great deal of evidence regarding your ability to verbally flatten anyone requiring it."

"Would that by any chance include yourself?" Salomen reached the transport first and pressed the sensor pad.

"You didn't flatten me," Tal said as they settled into their seats. "You just... opened my eyes a bit."

The flight back to Hol-Opah was just as quiet as the trip out had been, but this time the edginess was absent. Whenever Tal had a free hand, she reached out to hold Salomen's. They traded glances now and again, accompanied by smiles that existed for no particular reason, and while Tal recognized their actions as being laughably stereotypical, she didn't care.

Varsi was stationed on the front porch when they landed and gave the transport a salute before studiously averting her eyes.

"Is she afraid of seeing something?" Salomen asked.

"She can't. I never turned off the privacy screen. But she knows we can see her, so she's showing respect by not looking at us. That way we won't feel awkward if we..." Tal trailed off, reaching out to slip her fingers beneath the thin strap of Salomen's dress. "...do what I've been thinking about doing all evening," she finished in a whisper. "Fahla, but you are stunning in this."

Gently, she pushed the strap off Salomen's shoulder and stroked soft skin, running her fingertips from shoulder to jaw and back again. Salomen tilted her head to one side, her eyes closing, and Tal wondered how it could have taken her so long to see this woman's beauty. There was so much she wanted now, but none of it was possible except this simple caress. And perhaps...

Her lips touched just above the low neckline, and Salomen sighed as Tal brushed the other strap down. With both hands she gripped now-bare shoulders, exerting just enough pressure to convey her desire while countering it with gentle kisses. She covered every part of Salomen's upper chest and shoulders, never pressing too hard, keeping her emotions tamped down, always mindful of a potential empathic flash. But her focus was broken when a hand against her cheek guided her upward. Salomen was looking at her with a heat in her eyes that was twice as arousing in reality as it had been in Tal's fantasy.

"If you wished to test my fronting skills," Salomen said hoarsely, "you could devise nothing more difficult."

"Then let go."

"And have my family sense this? No, thank you."

Tal kissed her cheekbone ridge from temple to cheek. "In that case," she murmured between kisses, "I'll get back to my examination."

"Is this what any instructor would do?"

"I am not any instructor."

"Thank Fahla for that." Salomen turned her head and met her lips with a passion that soon released everything Tal had been so carefully controlling. For a glorious few pipticks they sank into their bond, too deeply and too quickly. Neither had time to pull back before the flash slammed into them.

"Shek!" Tal sat back in her seat, frustrated and breathing hard as she waited for the tingles to subside and her sight to clear. Salomen's laughter didn't help. "What could possibly be so amusing?"

"This! It's like a curse. The more I want you, the more I can't have you. I'm beginning to think you were right about this being Fahla's idea of a joke."

"I'd have preferred to be dead wrong." Tal was a little grumpy after the jolt to her libido.

"No, you had it figured out from the beginning. I think this is how she makes eternity a little more interesting for herself. How boring must it be otherwise?"

"Good question. Well, if our lives must be thrown into chaos and our greatest desires dangled in front of us like forbidden treasures, at least we know that we're entertaining Fahla."

In the ensuing silence, she looked over to see Salomen smiling at her. Warm pleasure flooded her senses as Salomen dropped her front.

"That was a fine compliment. All the more so because I'm certain you didn't realize what you were saying."

Tal held out her hand in invitation. Closing her fingers around Salomen's, she said, "It was not a compliment. That was my truth."

"Which is precisely what makes it a compliment. I don't confuse truth with flattery." Salomen squeezed her hand. "Thank you for tonight, Andira. I truly enjoyed your company. And I wish it didn't have to end here, but..."

"I know. May I at least walk you to your room?"

"Given that it's on the way to yours, yes, I'd be delighted."

Varsi brought her fists to her chest and bowed as they mounted the steps. "Lancer Tal, Raiz Opah, I hope you had an enjoyable evening."

"We did, thank you. Good night, Varsi." Tal moved forward, but Salomen had stopped.

"Guard Varsi, I understand that you gave the Lancer some advice regarding my brother."

Instantly nervous, Varsi nevertheless stood straight and answered crisply, "Not advice, Raiz Opah. Just what I saw."

Salomen nodded. "You saw something I did not. I appreciate your concern and your words. Thank you." She reached out for Tal's hand and led her toward the door, missing the expression of surprise on Varsi's face.

"You're welcome, Raiz Opah," Varsi said after her.

"You realize you just stunned my Guard," Tal said when the door closed behind them.

"Did I?" Salomen started up the staircase, still holding Tal's hand. "It wasn't intentional. I just wanted to thank her."

"Warriors in the Lancer's Guard are not accustomed to being thanked by producers. You just turned her expectations on their collective ear."

"Good."

"I have a suspicion that you'll be turning a great many expectations on their ear once you arrive at the State House."

"I certainly hope so." Salomen stopped just before the top step and looked back with an impish smile. "And I hope most of them are yours."

Tal moved up next to her. "Be careful what you wish for. I have a few expectations of you that I wouldn't want to see turned upside down."

Salomen tugged her hand again. "We'll see, Lancer Tal. I promise nothing."

They took the last step and turned down the hall. Too soon they stood in front of Salomen's door, in the awkwardness of ending that neither knew how to resolve.

"I'd kiss you goodnight," Tal said, "but I'm too frightened of the possible consequences. At least with the last flash, we were already sitting. I have no desire to find myself lying on your hall floor."

"Perhaps a different sort of kiss, then." Salomen leaned in and dropped a very gentle kiss beside Tal's mouth, then moved her lips softly over her jaw and up to her ear. "Thank you for the best date of my life," she whispered, then turned and stepped through her doorway. "Good night. I'll see you at mornmeal."

Dazed from the breath in her ear, Tal could only nod. "Good night," she said, just as Salomen closed the door. She moved down the hall without conscious thought.

The best date of her life?

By the time she arrived at her own door, Tal was walking half a body length off the ground.

CHAPTER 53
Tiles

WHAT A DIFFERENCE TWO DAYS made. Spinner knew exactly what was happening on Hol-Opah now.

According to the latest report from his spy in Granelle, Lancer Tal had taken Salomen Opah to the best restaurant in town last night. Not only that, but she'd been dressed up enough for a diplomatic function, and the two were seen holding hands over the table. It looked as if the Lancer was seducing an easily impressed producer, but Spinner knew her better than his spy. This wasn't a joining of convenience; it was an actual courtship. So far as he knew, that woman hadn't courted anyone in a tencycle. Last cycle's pathetic attempt on her vacation didn't count.

Of all things, Lancer Tal was courting a producer. Unbelievable.

Was she doing it to regain support in the producer caste?

He thought about that for all of half a tick before shaking his head. No, she was too *honorable* for that. She would never do anything so calculated, which meant she was emotionally involved. It explained her "alliance" with the youngest son, as well as Herot's jealous anger—and why she had been so stupid as to let the public relations potential of that challenge go to waste. In fact, it might even explain the challenge itself. Perhaps that hadn't been as brilliant a move as he'd thought. Perhaps it had been something far simpler.

He smiled to himself. If Lancer Tal was involved, then she was distracted—and vulnerable. In fact, she had acquired several vulnerabilities. He just needed to decide which Opah best suited his purpose.

Salomen was the most obvious target, but there were complications with her visibility. Then again, her visibility might make her the best choice.

He had time to watch and wait. The last few strands of his web were almost in place. It was only a matter of time before Lancer Tal fell into it.

CHAPTER 54

It's personal

"May I join you?"

Micah looked up to see Nikin standing beside them, midmeal in hand.

"By all means," Tal said. "Find a comfortable patch of dirt."

They were sitting slightly apart from the rest of the field workers, though still within the trees at the edge of the grain field. Normally Tal sat with the workers, but Micah had needed to go over security details with her since tomorrow was the start of her speaking tour.

Nikin sat cross-legged, lowering himself in the fluid motion of a man accustomed to sitting on the ground. "Did Salomen go back to the house? I saw her in the cook's skimmer just as I was arriving."

"She told me she needed time to prepare for tonight's caste house meeting," Micah said. He took a bite of his stuffed pastry and made a happy sound. "I'm either going to have to start joining the Lancer on her runs or else become another Hol-Opah field worker."

"Or you could just eat less," Tal said. "Here, I'll take the rest of your pastry."

"Keep dreaming." He held it out of reach.

Nikin watched them in amusement. "You two act like Salomen and me. Are you sure you aren't related?"

"I'm sure," Tal said. "We missed you out here this morning. How is the horten crop doing?"

"Good. Perfect if the rains would hold off a bit longer, but I think we'll be lucky as it is to get the grain in. Thank Fahla we're nearly done with the harvest; we're on borrowed time."

Micah looked up at the clear blue sky. "Difficult to imagine, seeing that."

"Don't let it fool you. It's always best right before it opens up and dumps on us."

"What can you do?"

"What I've been doing—preparing the field cover. The horten needs just four or five more dry days. If the rains start before that, we'll cover the field and use artificial light. It's not ideal, and it's a mess during harvest, but it has saved our crop more than once."

"Tell me if I can help," Tal said. "I won't be here for the next three days, but I'll be back as Hol-Opah's most poorly paid field worker after that."

"You're not paid at all," he said with a grin.

Tal gestured her agreement and took a bite of her pastry.

"So you're speaking in Blacksun tomorrow and then…"

"Redmoon and Whitesun the next day, and Whitemoon the day after that," Micah finished for her as she chewed.

"I wish you didn't have to go. For your sake, but for ours as well."

"She does make a good field worker, doesn't she?"

"That's not what I meant." Nikin was suddenly serious, and both Micah and Tal gave him their full attention. Looking at Tal, he said, "I, ah…I wanted to thank you for what you're doing for Herot."

Tal put her pastry down. "You want to thank me for striking your brother?"

Micah's ears perked up. He hadn't had a chance to ask her about that yet.

"Not exactly, but…Herot was going to get hurt sooner or later. It actually took longer than I expected. And of the people who could have hurt him, I would much rather it was you. He's been going to the worst tavern in town these last few moons, with some of the worst people. I worry about him every night he's out. And based on what Salomen told me this morning, you might be the one to deflect him from this path."

"Nikin…" Tal sighed. "I told Salomen that I'd do what I could. But I'm not Nashta, nor a parent of any kind, and I won't even be here beyond the end of this nineday. Please don't put so much hope in me."

"You're the Lancer of Alsea. You're the hope for all of us." He picked up his pastry and rose. "Anyway, I know you two are busy. I just wanted to say that. Thanks for sharing your patch of dirt with me."

"It was my pleasure. Come sit in my dirt any time." Tal looked after him as he walked away. "Did he mean I'm the hope for everyone on Hol-Opah or everyone on Alsea?"

"I would guess the latter." Micah watched the retreating producer. "He's a good man. Carries a lot of his father in him."

"Shikal birthed him. It makes sense that he'd be the most like him. And Salomen carries her mother. I wonder who Herot carries?"

"Perhaps that's the problem. Speaking of our favorite Opah, I heard you had company on your run again."

"He made it a little farther this time. I was impressed, actually. By now he must truly be feeling the effects of that first run, not to mention the bruise I gave him last night, but he's pressing on. The real question is, will he run tomorrow?"

"I bet not. He's proving something to you. If you're not here, what's the point?"

"I'll take your bet. Yes, he's proving something to me, and what better way to do so than to demonstrate upon my return that he can do more than when I left?"

"Hm. You might be right."

"Too late. The bet is mine."

Micah stretched his arms and sighed happily. "I'll miss Hol-Opah. Guarding you in a remote field on a private holding has been a vacation. And now I must return to work."

"Believe me, I'm even less happy about it than you."

"I would imagine so. You have much better things to be doing, don't you?"

"Of course I do. You heard him, the horten crop is nearly ready for harvest."

He chuckled. "Your face tells the truth though your tongue does not. The horten crop is the last thing on your mind. So when were you planning to tell me about your date? I've waited all morning with admirable patience."

"Your patience is neither admirable nor even in existence, and since when is my date your business?"

"I am the Chief Guardian of the Lancer," he said in his official tone. "Everything you do is my business."

"I suggest you reread your position duties. Tracking the Lancer's romantic life is not part of them."

"Ah, so there *was* romance!"

"You're impossible. I'm finishing my midmeal now; don't expect me to talk." Tal took a huge bite of her pastry, and Micah held back a grin. She looked just like Jaros.

"Let's review the facts," he said, ignoring her glare. "According to last night's duty reports, you and Raiz Opah made a rather stirring entrance to Meadowgreen and were seen thereafter holding hands across the table. You were also holding hands when you returned from your date, and there was a considerable period of time in which Varsi was guarding an occupied transport that was going nowhere. Given the earlier reference in her report to a physical altercation between you and Herot Opah, such…friendliness seems quite significant. Had you punched Herot a few ninedays ago, I suspect Raiz Opah would have sliced you to ribbons and dropped the pieces in the fanten food dispenser. It is therefore my opinion that you were exceedingly wise to wait this long before giving the little dokker what he so richly deserved. I can also draw the conclusion that your romance is proceeding at the usual pace, indicating that you might actually get beyond holding hands sometime next moon."

"Enough!" Tal laughed in spite of herself. "I'll have you know that we got beyond holding hands last night. Though not by much."

"Details, please."

"Micah, I am not giving you details. I have no idea why you even ask."

"Because sometimes you slip. More than holding hands, eh? In the absence of facts, I shall simply turn my imagination loose."

"It won't do you the slightest bit of good." Tal popped the last of the pastry in her mouth and dusted off her hands.

"Oh, I'm quite certain I can come up with something. That was a rather eye-opening dress Salomen wore last night. I suspect your eyes were opened considerably. Well, yours and everyone dining at Meadowgreen."

"My eyes couldn't have been opened too far. I didn't see anyone but her." Tal leaned back on her elbows and stretched out her legs. "Ah, that's nice."

Micah settled himself as well. "There's hope for you, I think. True romance has finally hit you over the head."

Tal nodded. "Literally. Which is why turning your imagination loose won't do you any good."

"Eh? Are you saying Salomen really did hit you over the head? Damn, she *was* angry about Herot, then."

"No! Good Fahla, she didn't hit me."

"Then what?"

Tal's hesitation set off his alarms, but he held his relaxed pose and looked off toward the mountains, giving her time.

"Remember when I told you that our bonding process was accelerated?" she asked.

"On the way to Blacksun, yes. And I told you it was clearly a miracle of Fahla that for once you were proceeding faster than the normal rate instead of slower. Which does make the hand-holding issue a bit odd, now that I think of it."

"It won't when you have all the pieces." She pushed herself back into a cross-legged position, and the story she told made his hair stand on end.

"I cannot believe you kept this to yourself! Why am I only hearing about this now?" His entire professional existence was built around keeping her from harm, and here was a danger he didn't know about. Fahla, he'd never even heard of it.

"Because it's personal! It has nothing to do with my title or your duty. You cannot protect me from this. Can you tell me one single thing you would change as a result of knowing?"

No, he couldn't. There wasn't a damned thing he could do about it, and that just made it worse.

"You're right, you had no obligation to tell me," he said. "As my Lancer, that is. As my friend, I'd hope that you would confide in me."

"That's what I just did." She was still nettled.

"There is one thing I would change, though. Now I'm regretting teasing you about it. This is not a laughing matter."

Tal shook her head. "Don't you dare. I'm so used to your teasing that I wouldn't know how to function without it. And I certainly won't stop teasing you."

"I never give you anything to tease me about, so that's not an issue." He looked at her closely, seeing the tension in her eyes. "There's more."

She sighed. "Yes, there is. And this part has everything to do with your duty. Lanaril said that there are stories about tyrees like us, in which the link we share is so extraordinary that both show the same symptoms when only one is ill. There are even stories of both tyrees dying from a mortal wound sustained by one. I had Aldirk do a records search for that data, and he sent me the results last night. He could find no confirmed cases of physical injury or death being transmitted across the bond, but he did find cases in which there seemed to be a shared immune system. So that much is fact. What worries me is the mere existence of the other stories. Lanaril can't be the only one who knows them."

Micah's realization eclipsed any concerns about empathic shocks. "Great Goddess above. She'll be targeted." And Salomen had no idea how to protect herself.

"I need you to start strategizing. Her security has to be trained and in place before our Sharing. It would be marvelous if we could keep the true nature of our bond a secret, but you and I both know we can't conceal it forever. And I'd rather be prepared for the inevitable than simply hope it won't happen."

"Agreed. I'll start looking at possible Guards today. And I'm sorry, but your Sharing just became my business."

"I know," she groaned. "It's bad enough that our first kiss was in front of Guards, I had to take four Guards with me on my damned date, and you have an entire duty report detailing everything we did outside my transport. And now we can't even—" She stopped, her jaw clenched shut, then continued in a calmer voice. "I'll tell you as far in advance as I'm able. But I've had little control over this since the moment it began. It's like riding a winden bareback—holding on is the best I can do. Steering is out of the question."

"Hold on as long as you can. For her sake." He needed time they might not have.

"Believe me, I will. But I have to tell you, it's pulling us together. I can't believe how much has changed in just four days." She put her elbows on her knees and her chin on her fists. "It's ironic, though. With Darzen I put off Sharing because I was worried that the truth would end us. Salomen and I have based our relationship on nothing but truth, and we still have to put it off. I can't seem to win either way."

"Fahla has a twisted sense of humor. But she has also given you a precious gift. Do not complain too loudly, or she may think you ungrateful."

"Actually, I was considering a visit to her temple in Whitemoon. I want to thank her, and I'd rather do it with some modicum of privacy. If I walked into Blacksun Temple to burn an offering, the whole city would know before I left it."

He clutched her knee in pretended shock. "You would darken the door of a temple? What is the world coming to?"

"According to Darzen Fosta, the end of our culture as we know it."

"Well, that's just about what I thought it would take to get you into a temple. Not even invading Voloth could do it."

"We all honor Fahla in our own way." She removed his hand from her knee and ostentatiously dropped it. "You light oil bowls and pray for female companionship; I go to the woods and allow her message to reach me directly."

"I do not pray for female companionship. I pray for my good friend Andira to be shown the true worth of her loyal Chief Guardian."

"You'd better light a few more oil bowls, then. Clearly the offerings have been too small."

"I've also prayed for her to give you your dream. If you don't mind the company, I'd like to go with you in Whitemoon. I have my own thanks to give."

His sincerity caught her by surprise. "There you go again, ruining a perfectly good tease," she said, but the sudden shine in her eyes gave her away.

Micah held out his hand, palm up. Without hesitation Tal clasped it, and he absorbed her grateful affection with a smile.

"Above all else," he said quietly, "you are my friend."

"Above all else, you are mine."

He raised his eyebrows. "And friends tell each other everything, right?"

"Oh, give it up, Micah."

CHAPTER 55
Debate points

Evenmeal was a noisy affair, with Jaros eager to share what he had learned in school that day and the adults discussing the upcoming caste house meeting, the imminent rain and potential crop damage, and Tal's speaking tour. Only Herot was quiet, picking at his food and excusing himself as soon as was marginally polite. After the meal, Shikal, Nikin, and Micah retired to the parlor with a bottle of spirits, Salomen left for her meeting, and Jaros and Tal went upstairs to do homework.

Tal wished she could trade with Jaros; algebra would have been far more enjoyable than checking Miltorin's notes and finalizing her speech. Judging by the emotions she could sense down the hall, Jaros did not share her opinion. She stopped for a moment to focus on him, smiling at the indignant color to his emotional presence. He was clearly put out that a calculation hadn't worked properly. She knew exactly how he felt.

A hantick later, she gave up. She had honed that speech until her eyes were crossing; it was good enough for now. Her subsequent efforts to read through the day's reports and dispatches were also of limited success, until finally she tossed the reader card aside. She was done being Lancer for today. Of course, throwing over her work left her with little to do except think about Salomen, and though that was normally a pleasant occupation, tonight it left her unsettled. No sooner did she let her mind wander than she felt glimmers of Salomen's emotions, frustration and irritation being the strongest. It wasn't surprising—Salomen had anticipated a loud and difficult meeting—but it made relaxation impossible. In an effort to banish the tickling emotions, she fetched a cup of shannel from the kitchen and began perusing her bookshelves for something to read. One title caught her eye; she remembered Aldirk referring to it as "dreck and drivel." Figuring that was precisely what she needed, she sprawled out in the window seat with the book in one hand and her shannel in the other. Aldirk was right: the book was indeed dreck. She was guiltily enjoying it.

Focusing on the adventures of the warrior protagonist enabled her to shut out external emotions to such an extent that she didn't feel anyone approach. For the first time since Tal's arrival at Hol-Opah, Salomen had to knock.

"Enter," she called, sitting up and looking around for a place to put her empty shannel cup. She was just tucking it onto a bookshelf when Salomen opened the door.

"You must be preoccupied. Still working on your speech?"

"Ah...no." Tal shamefacedly held up the book. "I was sick to death of it, so I found something to take my mind to a more interesting place."

Salomen walked across the room, plucked the book out of Tal's hand, and smiled. "This is a classic! Mother must have read this nine times. She had a soft place in her heart for strong, adventurous warrior types."

Tal accepted the book back. "And how many times did you read it?"

"I shall never have any secrets again, I can see that. All right, I may have read it once or twice."

Tal cocked an eyebrow and waited.

"Fine. I think I've read it four times."

"Four, really? How interesting. One might think you have a soft place in your heart for strong, adventurous warrior types."

"One might," Salomen agreed. "Do you know any? Perhaps you could introduce me."

"As soon as I meet one, I'll be sure to tell you. In the meantime...it's good to see you."

"Did you miss me?" Her tone was teasing, but she sobered when Tal nodded.

"I felt you, and it just reinforced the fact that you weren't here. This is the first evening we haven't been together since I arrived."

Salomen sat beside her in the window seat, and Tal shifted over to make room. "You felt me in Granelle? It's getting stronger."

"I know. How did the meeting go?"

"Not good." Salomen rested her head against the window and sighed. "Nothing I said convinced them. I was counseling patience and trust and pointing out that the mechanics of the transition are far more complicated than we're seeing, so we shouldn't draw simple conclusions. But Gordense was counseling anger and righteousness, and that's always more attractive. He said that even if I could convince them that *we* are not seeing all the complexities of the transition, the economist coalition certainly is, and if they're saying it will be the catalyst for a global economic meltdown, who are we as simple producers to question that? I said that we simple producers were capable of thinking for ourselves, and not only that but we had a moral obligation to do so. He said he was thinking for himself, and the conclusion he'd drawn was that you would lead Alsea into destruction and our moral obligation was to stop you."

"Stop me? Do I need to send Micah and Gehrain to question him?"

"No, no, no." Salomen shook her head. "He didn't mean it that way. I misspoke. He meant, stop you from releasing the matter printer technology without taking the steps outlined by the coalition."

"Are you certain? If that's an assumption, it's not one that I can safely accept."

"It's not an assumption. I'm not yet good enough at blocking to keep out the stronger emotions, and Gordense's emotions tend to be strong regardless of what he's feeling. He's a pompous fanten, but he's no danger to you. He just loves the sound of his own voice. The only thing he loves more than that is a good crowd to listen to him bloviate, and tonight was a good crowd. He was in his element. I was not."

Tal reached for her hand. "You're tired."

"Dead tired. Do you suppose I could rest my head on your shoulder without killing both of us?"

"I'm willing to risk it if you are."

Salomen scooted up next to her, and Tal pulled her in close. Resting their heads together, she projected serenity and calm. She could sense Salomen relaxing as she gently brushed the hair away from her face. "Safe so far," she whispered.

Salomen nodded, her eyes shut. "Just so you know, I can feel exactly what you're doing."

"Touching your hair?"

"Don't be obtuse."

Tal smiled. "You're such a sweet-talker."

"Only with you. And thank you; it feels wonderful."

"It's my pleasure."

"Do you know what the best part of this is?"

"What?"

"I can actually feel it. I mean, that doing this is making you happy. And that feels almost as good as the rest."

Tal dropped a soft kiss on the top of her head. "Then we're both happy."

"Mm-hm. Which is an enormous improvement to my evening, I can assure you."

They sat together in silence, enjoying the closeness. Tal lightly caressed Salomen's arm and side, feeling her gradually slumping even further, and thought she could stay here for a very long time.

"It came up," Salomen said.

Tal pulled her head back. "What came up?"

"Our relationship. Before I could utter a word about it. Gordense was on the offensive from the moment the meeting began. He asked me what would possess me to risk my good name just for the thrill of being your local entertainment."

Tamping down her first reaction—which was to look for her disruptor, Micah, and a transport—Tal asked, "What did you tell him?"

"That the only reason my name was still good was because I'd had the sense to reject his bond offer."

Tal grinned; her tyree could take care of herself! "Ouch. That must have hurt him right where he's most sensitive."

"Oh, it did. He sputtered a bit. It went downhill from there." She sighed. "I had such good intentions of taking the higher path, but…I've never been very good at turning away from a fight."

"Did Bilsner walk out under his own power?"

Salomen lifted her head. "You're enjoying this!"

"Well…" Tal tried to tamp down her grin without success. "I'm proud of you. You don't back down and you don't let anyone else push you. It's what attracted me to you in the first place—you have the heart of a warrior and the soul of a producer. I think Gordense Bilsner saw the warrior tonight. In fact, I'm willing to bet that's all of you he's ever seen."

"You'd be right about that. He does seem to bring out the worst in me."

Tal frowned. "The warrior part of you is the worst part?"

"Did I say that?"

"Quite clearly."

"Hm." Salomen leaned forward and kissed her with a slow, soft touch, pulling away before any possibility of a flash. "Which part do you think is the best?"

"Oh, no. I'm not getting trapped by that. You forget you're talking to the woman who runs Council sessions; I recognize verbal baiting when I see it." She pulled Salomen in and reclaimed the kiss, then nibbled across a smoothly curving jaw before releasing her. "I also recognize diversion tactics. This is a very good one."

"Thank you. I had an excellent instructor."

"In diversion tactics? I think not."

Several silent pipticks went by while they looked at each other. Tal was fascinated by the richness of Salomen's dark brown eyes, which were not one shade but several, lightening toward the center, where a golden ring encircled each pupil. It was the sort of detail only a lover could see, and she reveled in having that right. As Salomen stared back at her, Tal wondered what details she was seeing.

"I'm going to miss you," Salomen said. "I was thinking about that on the way home—how when you first arrived, I was counting the days until you'd take your irritating self and your entourage and get off my land. And now you're leaving for three days and all I can think about is what a damn long time that is."

"I've been thinking the same thing. I already missed you tonight; three days will be interminable. And on top of that, I feel guilty for leaving Hol-Opah right at the worst time."

Salomen straightened and pulled away. "You must be joking. Hol-Opah is not your responsibility. Alsea is."

"I know. But I made a promise."

"You did not; you made a challenge."

"True. But when I agreed to your counterchallenge, to me it was a promise."

"Are all warriors as relentlessly hard on themselves as you?"

"Some of them, yes."

"Warrior caste house meetings must be a jolly time for all, then."

Tal laughed. "You'd be surprised. Someday I'll have to take you as a guest."

"Perhaps I should have done that tonight. You would have been a more convincing speaker than I."

"I disagree. I've heard you speak many times; you're very convincing. And in this instance I think a defense of my policies made more of an impact coming from you than they would have from me."

Salomen sighed. "I don't know if it made an impact at all."

"Give it time. People often need to think about something before it really sinks in. I don't expect my speaking tour to bring about instant results, but in a nineday the general opinion could be entirely different. In that same nineday, you may find your peers thinking differently as well."

"I hope so. Of course," Salomen added darkly, "none of this would be necessary if Darzen hadn't been so jealous. If I ever meet that woman, she would be wise to walk the other way."

"Darzen wasn't jealous. She was angry."

"You may be a highly trained empath, but when it comes to yourself, you don't always see clearly. She was jealous of your title."

"I assume you plan to explain your reasoning for this rather interesting conclusion."

"Of course." Salomen pulled away, bringing her legs up on the cushion and resting her back against the opposite wall of the window seat. "Ah. Better."

Tal watched in some bemusement. "Is this going to take so long that you have to get comfortable for it?"

Salomen ignored her. "We'll begin with point one. When your relationship began, she thought you were merely a Lancer's Guard. A respectable rank for a warrior, to be sure, but otherwise not too challenging for a highly placed economist who advises the second-largest city council in the world. You were of a manageable intellect and rank, or so she thought."

Tal opened her mouth to object, but was silenced by Salomen's upraised hand.

"You asked me to explain, so do me the courtesy of allowing me the floor."

"Yes, Raiz Opah," Tal said with a grin. "You're bringing back fond memories of our delegate meetings."

Salomen's serious expression broke for a moment before she recomposed herself. "Point two. The night of your breakup, when you began discussing matter printer issues, she assumed that you had gotten your ideas from the Lancer. She did not credit you with the necessary education or intellect to have produced those ideas on your own."

"Now, that—"

"Point three," Salomen continued. "When you proved that you did indeed have the intellect to have expanded on those ideas, she told you that you were wasted as a warrior and would be better suited as a...what?"

"Economist," Tal answered grudgingly.

"Rather patronizing, don't you agree? Moving along to point four. When your true identity was revealed, what did she tell you? That you'd made a fool of her. Implying that she felt foolish for not knowing the true breadth of your capabilities, and perhaps implying that she would not have accepted you as a potential mate had she known that those capabilities were so advanced. After all, what did you hide? Your personality, your character traits, your intelligence?"

"Well, there was the little matter of my hair and eye color." Tal crossed her arms and tried not to look as if she were enjoying herself.

Salomen waved that aside. "I'm talking about real characteristics. Things that make you who you are. You would still be Andira Tal if your eyes and hair were brown. You would not be Andira Tal if you were less articulate or intelligent, or if you were boorish or judgmental or unfair. Did you pretend to be any of these things?"

"No. Quite the contrary, I was more myself during that moon than I was for some time before or after. But I did pretend to be something I was not."

"My esteemed Lancer Tal, you make my argument for me. You pretended to be ordinary. And Darzen was upset because she found, to her dismay, that you were not ordinary at all. What did she tell you at the end?"

Suddenly, Tal wasn't enjoying herself any more. Those words still hurt. "She said that my title was everything."

Salomen watched her for a moment, then said quietly, "She made the same mistake I did. She didn't know you well enough to understand the distinction between who you are and what you do. Which brings us to point five, the last one. When she understood that she was outclassed in rank and accomplishments, and that you would be a continual challenge to her sense of herself as a superior being, she walked out the door. You were more than she would ever be. If her motivation had been simple anger, why wouldn't she have answered any of your calls, even after two moons? Most people move beyond anger with enough time. But it's harder to get past jealousy and a threat to one's self-esteem."

Tal could only stare. She went over Salomen's points again, seeing her time with Darzen from a radically different point of view. It all made perfect sense. Had she really been such a poor judge of character?

No, she decided, it wasn't about that. She had just seen what she wanted to see—and so had Darzen.

"You're wrong about one thing," she said. "I am most certainly not a more convincing speaker than you. Your debating skills are second to none."

"Thank you. But have I convinced my most important audience?"

"Well, you've given me a great deal to think about. Perhaps it was jealousy; you make an excellent case for it. Perhaps it was anger, or a mixture of both. Either way, it's done and I can no longer feel any regret for it. Darzen left me free to be here."

"Darzen threw this away with both hands. She could have been the one sitting next to you, sharing this time. I dislike her by reputation alone, but I'm grateful to her idiocy."

Chuckling, Tal said, "I'll be sure to pass that along if I ever speak to her again."

"While you're at it, give her my com code and ask her to call. I have other things I'd like to tell her." Salomen stretched, making a tiny "eep" sound of satisfaction. "I'm feeling much better now. Are we having a lesson tonight?"

"Do you want one? I thought you'd be too tired after your meeting."

"I'm not so tired anymore. Besides, we had no lesson last night, and we won't have any for the next three. We cannot miss this one."

"All right. Then let's—"

"Wait." Salomen sat up and swung her legs off the window seat. "I have to move."

Tal watched in bemusement as she hopped off, went to her usual chair, and sat down.

"Now I'm ready."

"What was that about?"

"I can't be sitting next to you. It's too distracting. What are we working on tonight?"

Oh, this was too easy. "Broadsensing," Tal said with a grin. "And tuning out distractions."

CHAPTER 56
Betrayer

Micah stood at the side of the stage, listening to Tal while watching the crowd. As a Lancer's Guard, he was atypical for his low empath rating, but he had learned to make up for it with the other senses Fahla had given him. He was very skilled at reading facial expressions and body posture, a physical language which often told him things that high empaths could not see. Sensing deadly intent in a crowd was one thing; localizing it to an individual was a different matter.

Being a believer in utilizing all available tools, he also had ten of his most powerfully empathic Guards stationed around the auditorium and ten more on the outside, watching all entrances from various hidden positions and constantly broadsensing. This was not a private holding; it was a public auditorium in the largest city in Pallea. Anything was possible.

He glanced at Tal, who made an imposing figure in her red and black dress uniform as she stood beside the podium, one hand resting on it while she talked. People meeting her for the first time were often surprised at her lack of stature, but they soon forgot it when she began to speak in those calm, measured tones. At the moment she was addressing an audience of eight thousand Alseans—in addition to the unknown millions watching the real-time vid in their homes—and she had their rapt attention. Tal had risen to the occasion during this tour, her confidence and thorough grasp of detail shifting the general mood of the crowd first in Blacksun last night, then in Redmoon this afternoon, and now in Whitesun. At each speech she had methodically decimated the economist coalition's forecast, using explanations and examples that even the least educated Alsean could understand. Micah saw the growing belief and support in the audiences and was forced to agree with Aldirk for once in his life: this tour had been absolutely necessary.

Not that public opinion had been magically reversed, of course. Many chose not to watch the speeches or simply ignored everything Tal had to say. She had been driving radical change for over a cycle now, and there were those who would resist no matter how much evidence piled up in its favor, simply because it was change. These were the people who had pounced on the economist coalition's statement as proof of Tal's folly. The fringe element demanding her prosecution as a war criminal had joined forces with them, pointing to the predicted doom of Alsea as more evidence that she was intent on destroying them all. "First our souls, now our savings" was the new tag phrase. There had even been demonstrators in both Blacksun and Redmoon during Tal's speeches, though warriors from the local bases had blocked their access to the auditorium.

He could understand those who feared the matter printers. But the ones calling Tal a war criminal... He wished he could hand those over to the Voloth. Perhaps a taste of slavery would give them a better appreciation of Tal's decision.

"Gehrain to red team, UT in section yellow, first five rows. Senshalon, advance."

The quiet voice in his ear put Micah on alert. A UT was an Unidentified Threat. Gehrain had sensed something, but couldn't localize it. Just to be safe, he had dispatched the nearest Guard to check it out.

Micah slipped on his scanning glasses and ran his finger down the temple until they were properly focused on the section halfway across the auditorium. The faces of the audience came into crisp view, and he began a sweep from one side to the other, checking expressions and body language.

He found her in the middle of the second row, an older woman watching Tal with too much intensity. Just as he tapped his earcuff to inform the Guards of her position, she stood up.

Senshalon, who had been walking rapidly down the aisle, broke into a run.

"Betrayer!" the woman screamed.

Tal stopped speaking and shifted subtly into a readiness stance.

"Betrayer! First you sell our souls and now you'll destroy the rest of us. You should be outcaste! You're an abomination! Fahla weeps to see what you have done!"

She lifted her arm to throw something, but Senshalon reached her first. The largest man in their unit, his bulk hid a surprising speed and agility. He loomed up behind her and yanked her raised arm back in a hold, putting his other arm around her middle and lifting her off the ground. She screamed and struggled, kicking her legs as he carried her out of the row and into the main aisle. Two other Guards converged on them, helping Senshalon subdue her and march her out of the auditorium. Her screams and curses could be heard with every step as she castigated Tal for being evil incarnate and bringing doom on Alsea. She managed one more "Betrayer!" before she was hustled out and the door shut behind them, plunging the auditorium into a shocked silence.

"It's always best to wait for the question-and-answer period," Tal said.

A ripple of nervous laughter swept the auditorium, and Tal resumed her speech as if nothing had happened.

"Who was she?" Tal asked as soon as she got off the stage. "And what was she trying to throw at me?"

Micah handed over the framed photograph that Senshalon had taken from the woman. "You're not going to like it."

"This is what she was holding?" Tal frowned as she took the frame. "Who is—oh, Fahla. Tell me this wasn't her daughter."

"It was."

The expensive frame was a jarring contrast to the photograph inside it, a photo that anyone on Alsea would have recognized in a piptick. It was a woman hanging from a tree branch, her head tilted to one side—the first suicide of a Battle of Alsea veteran.

Tal sat at the dressing room table with none of her usual grace. "Shekking Mother. No wonder she hates me."

"I'm sorry, Tal." He wished it had been anyone else. Someone with an irrational hatred or fear, someone whose ears were closed to persuasion and eyes closed to possibility. Not someone with a legitimate reason to despise Tal, whose distress was showing in the shaking of her hands as she held the frame.

"Is she all right?"

Micah wasn't entirely sure what she was asking. "Senshalon didn't hurt her. She's being processed right now at the base."

"What? No. Get her out of there."

"Tal, she threatened you."

"She screamed at me. That's not a physical threat. And don't even think of telling me she was going to hurt me by throwing a Fahla-damned frame!" Tal slammed the frame down on the table, cracking it from top to bottom. "Shek!" She dropped her face into her hands, then looked up at him in misery. "Of all the—I thought we'd run into Darzen here. I spent all afternoon getting ready for that. This was the perfect venue for her to publicize her predictions."

"I know," he said gently. He'd been dreading that possibility too, but he'd have traded this for Darzen in a heartbeat.

Tal stared at the cracked frame. "Do you think I should see her?"

"Are you asking if you can help her?"

She nodded.

"I don't think she would hear anything you might have to say. You sent her a handwritten letter right after it happened, and I know how much time you spent on that. It didn't do any good. She needs someone to blame for her daughter's suicide, and she's made you her monster. Showing up in person will probably make it worse. You can't fix everything. Let this one go."

Tal sat back in the chair, still staring at the frame, and finally nodded. "You're probably right. But I'm not pressing charges, and I want her released."

"That's not a good precedent—"

"I don't *care*. Just get someone to take her home."

"All right. I'll take care of it." He picked up a water flask and the portable vidcom unit and put them in front of her. "Drink this and then call Salomen."

"I will."

When he left, she was already tapping in the com code.

CHAPTER 57
Fallout

"I must say I'm impressed," Challenger said. "Demonstrators in the streets? I didn't expect that."

"Never overestimate the intelligence of the voting public," Spinner said. "That might just be Lancer Tal's greatest weakness. It's why she didn't see this coming."

"Yes, it's such a pity that an entire cycle of effort seems to have been wasted."

Spinner chuckled. "I assume you saw the old woman in Whitesun."

"I did. For a moment I thought you might have paid her to do that."

"And have that exposed when they scanned her? Not likely." Spinner's humor abruptly vanished. Sometimes he couldn't believe how dense Challenger could be. Then he reminded himself that Challenger would always be three steps behind him, and his spirits rose again. "That woman is just one of many. If it hadn't been her, it would have been someone else."

"And in the meantime, Lancer Tal's polling continues to plummet." Challenger gave him a hard look. "Please tell me it's time. Because as much as I admire what you've accomplished, my patience is running short."

Spinner ignored the not-so-subtle threat, but he wouldn't forget it. He wouldn't forget any of them. "It's time. But we must be extremely careful in these early stages. Speak only to those you trust without question. Not a breath of this can get out until we have the support we need."

"Of course." Challenger was instantly in a fine mood. "I'll begin right away."

"And you have the holding space ready?"

"I do."

"Excellent." Spinner poured two glasses of grain spirits and handed one over. Raising the other, he said, "To a game well played."

"To our next Lancer," Challenger said.

CHAPTER 58
Whitemoon Q&A

"Betrayer" was in many headlines the next day, but to Micah's surprise, the general tone of coverage was sympathetic to Tal. Her refusal to press charges had redounded to her benefit, especially after she gave an interview in which she admitted how much that suicide had shaken her and how sorry she was that the price for saving their planet had been so high. Tal didn't often let the mask of her office slip, but doing so now was an excellent public relations choice. Her slide in the polls had stopped and seemed to be reversing.

Of course, it had been Miltorin's idea. That man would probably sacrifice his own bondmate to the Voloth if it would improve his polling, but his instincts were almost invariably right. And in this instance, his instincts had agreed with what Tal wanted. She needed to reach out to that mother in some way, and this was the only way she could do it.

That evening in Whitemoon, Micah and the Guards were on high alert. In twenty hanticks, general opinion seemed to have shifted in Tal's favor, but they'd already had one incident and were very nervous about another. Micah spent the entirety of Tal's speech scanning the crowd, looking at one face after another for any signs of too much interest, too much intensity, too much emotion. Finding nothing didn't make him feel better. It just made him think he hadn't been looking hard enough.

When Tal ended her speech and invited questions, his stress level went even higher. As far as he was concerned, this was the most dangerous part of the evening.

Each seat in the auditorium had a small button beneath it, allowing its occupant to request an opportunity to speak. In order to control the chaos of multiple people attempting to speak at the same time, a computer recorded all requests and made random selections, then routed the information to the mobile microphone, a central control panel, and the seat holder. The latter received notification of selection by a five-piptick vibration of their seat, and a second one just before it was their turn to stand.

Micah's reader card was tapped into the control panel, giving him a map of who was authorized to speak. Too bad it couldn't give him a map of anyone planning to use the Q&A as an opportunity to launch some sort of protest or attack.

An older Alsean stood up, the mobile microphone immediately flying to him and hovering as he spoke. "Gilmorian Stander, merchant caste. I'm able to support my family and the families of my children because I believe in selling only quality products, and my customers seek me out for that quality. If the matter printers can produce anything, will all products be of the same quality? And if not, how will the distinctions be preserved?"

"An excellent question," Tal said. "All matter printer products will not be of the same quality for the same reason that products are not of the same quality right now: cost of energy and raw materials. In this case, the raw materials are a bit different, but the principle is the same. Some products require more energy and more raw materials to create. It may be that the more expensive products will not be the same ones that cost more to us now, but…" she paused for emphasis, "…the pricing structure has been built around our current energy and raw material costs, not the new ones. Over time that will change, but it's far too radical an adjustment to impose now. We've planned a gradual phase-in of the new pricing structure over a period of ten cycles; more than enough time for all of us to adapt. Your cost of doing business will be relatively unchanged, and your customers will still seek you out for the quality you provide."

Amid applause, the merchant nodded and took his seat.

A woman stood up across the auditorium as the mobile microphone zipped over to her. "Venuzandra Mil, crafter caste. I have no question, Lancer Tal. I simply wished to express my gratitude, and that of my friends and family, for your care in seeing this change through with minimal disruption to the people. Our history tells us that we're fortunate to have you as Lancer right now. Past Lancers would not have been so careful. I know you've been vilified for your attempts to do the right thing, and I wish to say that not all of us share the opinions of those who speak against you."

She sat down abruptly, her seat mates on either side patting her on the back as the crowd burst into applause. Micah guessed that she was not accustomed to public speaking and had just scared herself halfway to her Return by standing up.

Tal had either seen the same thing he had, or she could sense the woman's nervousness. "I'm grateful for your words and admire your courage in speaking up in such a venue. Your support means a great deal to me, especially now."

The crafter nodded shyly as two people stood up, one in the second row and one several rows back. Micah's heart rate increased as he checked his reader card. The authorized questioner was the man in the second row.

He focused his scanning glasses on the other figure and groaned. Tal had expected her in Whitesun yesterday, not here tonight. Damn her for coming to Whitemoon! And how had he not seen her when he was scanning the crowd? She was already drawing attention and no doubt planned to stand until Tal was obligated to call on her. Well, she would have to wait until the end.

"Toller Jansom, builder caste," said the man near the front. "I repair transport engines. It's not a job many want, and a lot of people think I do it because I'm not smart enough to find anything better. But I take pride in my work, and it helps to support my family. My question is, how am I supposed to keep my living when a customer can simply print a new engine if the old one breaks?"

"I've also worked on transport engines. And it's quite true that anyone can take one apart." Tal smiled. "But it takes a smart Alsean to put it back together."

The builder grinned toothily as a murmur of laughter rippled through the crowd.

"It's true that a customer may simply print a new engine," Tal continued, "if that customer is willing to pay the cost. Printing an entire engine will be prohibitively expensive, due to the raw material, the energy costs, and the complexity of the programming. It will be far less expensive to print the part or parts that are broken. Tell me, how will your customers know which part to print?"

The man's face lit up. "I'll still have to diagnose the problem."

"Yes, you will. Anyone not intimately familiar with transport engines will still require your expertise. Not only that, but once they've printed the part, they'll almost certainly need you to install it. And it's quite likely that they will also ask you to print the part for them, both as a means of avoiding potential mistakes and to keep them from making multiple trips to your shop. Since you will be charged a lower cost for your printing, due to your registered status as a transport repair shop, that will also represent a profit for you. Your future is not in jeopardy."

"Thank you, Lancer Tal." The builder dipped his head and sat down.

Micah watched the microphone move off and followed its trajectory, raising his eyebrows as he spotted the small girl standing on her seat. Well, this was a first! Judging by the expressions of what must have been her parents, they were startled as well.

"I'm Falerna Nael," the girl said in a high but determined voice. "My parents are scholar and builder caste, and I haven't chosen mine yet."

"It's a difficult decision, isn't it?" Tal asked.

"Uh-huh. I've been thinking about becoming scholar, but in school yesterday we learned that you came to Whitemoon because you disagree with a whole group of scholars who say the matter printers are a bad idea. So I want to know why you aren't listening to the scholars."

"I do listen to scholars, every day. Nearly all of my advisors are scholar caste. But I think you're really asking why I'm not listening to these few scholars who don't agree with me. Is that correct?"

The girl nodded and was poked by one of her fathers, who leaned over and whispered to her.

"Yes," she said to the microphone.

"Falerna, what's your favorite subject in school?"

"Geography."

Micah chuckled at the instant answer, as did many in the audience.

"So if your instructor divided your class into teams for a geography contest, I'm betting that everyone would want you on their team because you're very good at it, right?"

"Yes," Falerna said proudly.

"I pick teams, too. They're called advisors. I want the people who are very good at what they do, because the decisions I make with their help are important. I picked a team of economic advisors, Falerna. Of the scholars your teacher mentioned, can you guess how many are on my team?"

Falerna shook her head and was again poked by a parent. "No," she said.

"Exactly none. Why do you think I wouldn't pick any of them?"

"Because they weren't good enough?"

The audience roared with laughter, and the girl looked embarrassed.

"They're not laughing at you. They're laughing because you got the answer right, and it really is kind of funny. Yes, I'm here because I didn't listen to a group of scholars. But why would I, if they weren't good enough to be on my team? I do listen to my advisors, very carefully. They helped me create the plan for the matter printers, and we did our best to think of everything. What those other scholars are saying is nothing my advisors didn't consider an entire cycle ago. But their conclusions were different. If I have to choose between believing my best advisors and believing others who aren't on my team, who should I believe?"

"Your best advisors," Falerna said, confident once again.

"You'd make an excellent Lancer. That's the most important part of the job. Pick the best people and listen to them. Thank you, Falerna. Your question was a good one."

As the girl sat back down, a huge swell of applause rocked the auditorium.

Micah grinned. Tal couldn't have done better with that if she'd had it scripted. This exchange would surely make all the news outlets by the morning, and the economist coalition would have a time of it trying to combat their new image as "not good enough."

He glanced back to his right, but the standing figure was gone and the seat was empty. He scanned the aisle and found her making her way toward the exit.

"Keep walking," he muttered.

CHAPTER 59
Backstage

"What did you think, Micah?" Tal was gulping down an enormous flask of water. Between the speech and the question-and-answer session, she had been talking for nearly two hanticks and her throat was beyond dry. But this was it; she was done. Now all they had to do was wait for the crowd to disperse before making their own departure. In the meantime, she and Micah were resting in a small prep room behind the auditorium's stage.

"I think you should send that little girl a token of your appreciation. Maybe a new transport."

"Wasn't she something? She reminded me of Jaros with all that attitude. And then she gave me the perfect opening. Damn, I enjoyed that."

"And I enjoyed seeing Darzen Fosta slink out of the auditorium with her battle flag dragging behind her."

Tal abruptly set down her water. "So that *was* her. I thought it might be when I saw two people stand up at once, but I couldn't see with the lights in my eyes. When did she leave?"

"Right after you publicly humiliated her."

"Oh, Fahla." Tal laughed. "She must really hate me now. She probably knew we were ready for her in Whitesun and chose Whitemoon for a sneak attack. Well, I'm sorry I have to fight this dirty, but she's dragged me through the dirt already."

"I don't see any need for apology. There were demonstrators in Blacksun and Redmoon. That's well beyond dirt. Whether Darzen envisioned this or not, she set off a chain reaction."

"I know. I have to admit, I never thought it would go as far as people chanting in the streets. Aldirk was right."

"Are you going to tell him that?"

"Are you joking?"

Micah snorted.

They passed some time in companionable silence, with Tal idly twirling her water flask and staring at nothing in particular.

"Do you think there's any possibility she was here to talk to me?" she asked at last.

"Not a chance," Micah said firmly. "If she wanted to talk to you she wouldn't be trying to jack in on a question-and-answer session on a worldwide broadcast."

Tal nodded. "Salomen was right, too. I really didn't want her to be."

"Right about what?"

"She said Darzen didn't leave because I lied by omission. She left because she didn't want the person I truly am—because I would have been too much of a challenge for her. She liked the idea of me as an ordinary warrior."

"It's possible. Not everyone is ready for a challenge like you. Salomen being a notable exception." Micah reached out for his own water flask.

"Lancer Tal, we're ready to depart when you are."

Tal tapped her earcuff. "Thank you, Gehrain. We're coming out now." She stood up. "Ready for temple?"

"The question is, are you? Do you remember which door to enter?"

Tal pretended confusion. "Is there more than one?"

Micah opened the prep room door, checked the hallway, and turned back to Tal. "Just watch me and don't do anything I don't do."

"If I restricted my activities to the things you do, Salomen would have a very boring future in front of her." Tal walked out with a grin, waiting for his response.

"Someday Fahla is going to deliver a healthy dose of humility to your front door, and I'll be there to see it," he called after her. She raised her hand behind her in a rude gesture, and he chuckled as he followed her down the hall.

CHAPTER 60
Flames in the temple

Tal craned her neck to see the top of the temple dome, marveling at the beauty of its construction. The temples in Alsea's greatest cities had been built long ago, before modern technology had made such things easier. She couldn't imagine the builders hauling these stones in carts, cutting them by hand, and laying them in place with nothing more than their eyes and crude measuring tools to establish the angles. And yet these domes were so perfect, the stones matching with such precision, that a small machined sphere released near the top would roll straight down, neither bouncing nor deviating from its course.

"Beautiful, isn't it?" Micah asked.

"It is. And a perfect evening to set it off, too." She gazed beyond the dome to the spectacular sunset turning the clouds into crimson fire. To the east, the vast bay had already gone dark, its silver sheen vanishing when the sun dipped below the horizon. Blacksun Temple was impressive, but the temple at Whitemoon was widely revered as the most spectacular in the world. Standing on a hill at the center of the city, it commanded a view that left many visitors breathless. This was a location and a building to inspire wonder, and Tal was not immune.

"Now remember: enter the front archway and exit at the rear. To do otherwise is to insult Fahla."

"Micah, I do know a little about temples. Are you going to be this annoying all evening?"

"Just trying to save you from embarrassing yourself."

"More likely you're trying to save yourself from being tainted by my lack of piety."

"That too."

They walked down the gravel path and up the steps to the high, arched entry. Tal stopped just inside, admiring the space and the fine carvings. The few Alseans in the temple glanced toward her and just as quickly looked away again. Here in Fahla's sacred place, even the Lancer was just another worshipper.

An enormous glassed opening at the top of the dome lit the temple during the day, but at sunset a band of lights set at the junction of dome and wall were ceremonially lit. In the old days the lights had been torches, rendering the ceremony quite a bit more time-consuming, and the modern lights still mimicked the color and shape of a torch flame. They were lit now, a circle of fire ringing the temple and emphasizing its enormity. A temple had no divisions, seats, or other visual distractions to break up the interior. All of the soaring space was left open to the worshippers, who stood at small, transparent racks, which held clear bowls of oil in ten tiers. Lighting a bowl produced the effect of a flame floating in the air. The racks were scattered throughout the temple, allowing visitors to worship away from others if they wished, since there was no single location where Fahla was thought to receive the prayers of her people. But Tal had always felt that the true heart of a temple was at its center, where a molwyn tree grew beneath the skylight. The only tree on Alsea with a solid black trunk, molwyns were sacred to Fahla and grew in every temple of decent size. The tree in Whitemoon was massive, gnarled, and ancient.

Micah moved to a bowl rack some distance away and slipped his credit chip into the offering box. Silently, the rack retracted its covers. The larger the offering, the more bowls were released.

Tal watched curiously as he picked up the eternal flame at the center of the rack and began lighting bowls. When all ten in the top tier were flaming, he began on the second. Though she knew she should not be staring—an offering to Fahla was between the Goddess and her worshipper—she couldn't turn away as he methodically lit one bowl after another, until the entire rack was alight and one hundred flames danced in the air. He had made a substantial offering indeed.

He replaced the eternal flame and stood still, his lips moving as he spoke a quiet prayer. Abashed at her own rudeness, Tal was about to step forward and leave him to his privacy when he looked up and caught her eye. With slow, deliberate movements, he turned to face her, placed his fists against his chest, and bowed his head.

A lump appeared in her throat. That offering was for her. Micah had lit an entire bowl rack in thanks to Fahla for sending her tyree.

She straightened her spine, brought her fist to her chest with a thump, and returned his salute. It was a breach of tradition that left Micah blinking, but she knew it was the right thing to do. She was not Lancer here; she and Micah were equal in the eyes of Fahla. And he was more deserving of her respect than anyone else on the planet, save one special person.

Then she smiled, realizing that with the precedent he had set, her own hand was forced. She couldn't just light a bowl or two now. If Micah had lit an entire rack in her name, then how could she, the actual recipient of Fahla's gift, offer any less?

It was a good thing she had planned a large offering.

She walked to the bowl rack nearest the molwyn tree, slipped in her credit chip, and gave enough to unlock the whole rack. When it was completely alight, she moved on to the next. Several ticks later, five bowl racks ringing the center of the temple were burning so brightly that the molwyn tree glowed in the light of the flames.

She stepped onto the wooden deck surrounding the tree and walked beneath the branches. At the very center of the temple, she laid her palm on the molwyn's trunk and gazed up at the silvery undersides of the leaves. If she concentrated, she could actually feel the life pulsing beneath her hand.

"I know I don't come here often," she said quietly. "And I've always thought you understood why. I see you more easily in what you created than I do in these temples, and the only place that feels right to me inside this dome is here. This tree carries your spark. It's closer to you than anything else in this building." She paused, looking at her hand in puzzlement. Was it her imagination, or was the bark under her palm growing warm? No, it had to be her own body heat. She looked up again.

"I wish there was something I could say to convey how grateful I am. But I don't think I need to. You must know. You've given me my dream, and though I admit to...well, to questioning your choice, I understand now why you made it. Salomen is unique in so many ways. She sees the world through different eyes, and I see differently through her. I always thought what I wanted most was someone to love me for who I really am, but I think...I think she loves me not just for that, but for who she knows I can be. And I want to be that person. I want to be her dream as well. So I guess I'm here not just to thank you, but to ask for your help. Please, help me get this right. I don't know what I'm doing. I trained all my life to be a good Lancer, but there's no training for this. I just..."

She stopped as a vision of Salomen came to mind, her eyes crinkling as she laughed at something. Tal smiled at the image. "Yes. That's what I want. I want to know that she's happy because of me. She's spent her whole life suppressing who she is. She deserves her own happiness. Help me give that to her, please."

She let her arm drop, absently rubbing her fingers on her palm, then frowned and opened her hand.

The skin was red where it had touched the molwyn.

Rational explanations flitted through her mind: allergy, microsplinters, even the possibility of poison. Any of those should have warned her off touching the tree again, but she couldn't help herself. Her arms lifted almost of their own volition.

The wood felt cool, and she breathed a sigh of relief. Then she stopped breathing altogether as warmth surged through her palms.

"Holy shek," she whispered. Pulling back was ineffective; her hands seemed fused to the wood. Strangely, she felt no fear and instead watched with fascination as the heat in her hands increased exponentially. They were burning now, so hot that she should have been on her knees from the agony, but there was no pain at all. The burning increased even more, and Tal's jaw dropped as her hands began to glow red. It was as if they were on fire from the inside, lighting up her veins... and for just a piptick she could see her own bones.

She blinked. It was all gone. The tree was cool; her hands looked like they did every day. She stepped back and held them in front of her eyes, checking for any sign of what had just happened. Other than a pronounced trembling, they were perfectly normal. Looking around, she saw that the flames in her bowls were burning well below the level of the rim. But that made no sense; they had been full when she lit them.

For some time she stood there, trying to make sense of what had just happened. That Fahla had given her a direct message, she had no doubt. But what did it mean? No matter how she examined it, she came no closer to a solution. The only thing she knew for sure was that it was about Salomen.

She looked at the tree one last time before shaking her head and turning toward the exit. Micah was waiting.

"About time," he said as she walked up. "If I'd known you had that much to say to Fahla, I would have brought something to eat."

"Micah, how long have we been here?"

He looked at her oddly. "Almost a hantick. Why?"

She walked past him without answering. A hantick. She would have said it was perhaps a quarter of that.

Micah caught up with her at the bottom of the steps, and they strode down the gravel path in silence. When it joined the larger path circling the temple, he asked, "Did something happen?"

She nodded.

"Did she…did she speak to you?"

"No."

"Well then, what happened?"

She shook her head. "I'm not sure. But…I think she gave me a sign."

"A sign! What was it?"

They walked all the way back to the inner gate of the temple grounds before she answered him. "I don't know how to interpret it," she said slowly. "But my hands…they burned where they touched the molwyn tree. Except it didn't burn; it was just hot. They were glowing, Micah. So hot that I could see right through to the bone. And then it stopped and the bark was cool again. I thought the whole thing had lasted maybe a few ticks, but when I looked at my oil bowls, they were burned down too far for it to have been that short a time. I have no idea what that was."

"Nor do I. But there is no doubt that she was telling you something." His voice was hushed with awe.

She stopped. "You believe me?"

"Of course. Why would I not?"

"Because I hardly believe it myself."

He smiled. "That's because you've never believed in anything you couldn't define. Fahla is beyond definition."

"Now that I believe." She resumed their walk. "Has anything like that ever happened to you?"

"Once, though my experience wasn't quite so spectacular. I must say, Fahla certainly favors you. You walk in her temple once every few cycles and she gives you a sign. It must have been those five bowl racks—that was quite a sight."

"Can you tell me about your sign?" She felt his instant discomfort and added, "No, that's personal. Forget I asked."

"No. I asked you; I cannot repay your confidence with silence."

"Micah—" She stopped when he held up a hand, and they walked several steps before he spoke again.

"My experience happened many cycles ago," he said quietly, "when I was a much younger man. I went to the Redmoon Temple for help during a particularly difficult time. I was having some personal issues and could see no way out without losing two of the most important people in my life. And while I stood there in front of my bowls, Fahla sent me a vision. She showed me that loss was unavoidable; that it was nothing I could control, but that through loss I could gain. It was many cycles before I truly understood that vision. Perhaps you will simply have to wait before her sign becomes clear to you."

"It seems to be a lesson she teaches often," Tal said. "I lost the first woman I ever loved, but through that loss I gained so much more. My experience with Ekatya changed me in ways that left me open for Salomen. I think it had to happen that way."

He nodded. "I've certainly railed at Fahla as much as the next Alsean, but beneath it I have always understood that her job is only to give us the tools we need. It's our responsibility to pick up those tools and make something with them."

They had arrived at the enormous archway that marked the entrance to the temple grounds. A small transport waited to take them back to Whitemoon Base, where they would board her long-distance transport and leave the southern continent behind. Tal turned to look back one last time. Sonalia was well above the horizon now and nearly full, its light adding to the natural glow of the temple dome in a blaze of white that could be seen for tens of lengths.

"Such a beautiful place," she said. "I can think of only one thing that could add to this scene."

"What's that?"

"A red moon."

Micah nodded. "Perhaps we should return then, when the moon is red."

"Perhaps we should. And perhaps I'll bring someone with me." She turned away with regret. "Micah?"

"Hm?"

"Let's go home."

CHAPTER 61
Prisoner request

Despite her best intentions, Tal didn't go to Hol-Opah the next morning. Her presence in the State House had resulted in a veritable line of people seeking an audience with her, and since she had been so rarely available over the past three ninedays, she couldn't justify leaving without giving them her time. Besides, she could often get a great deal done in a quick face-to-face meeting. Vidcom calls and messages could accomplish only so much; a personal encounter often took care of more business in less time.

After meeting with twelve different Councilors and seven advisors, she sighed in relief to see Aldirk walking into her office. "That's it, then? You're the last one?"

"As always." Aldirk sat down, reader card in hand. "May I first extend my congratulations on an extremely effective speaking tour. Particularly your devastating use of a small child to trivialize the economist coalition."

He was radiating…mirth. Tal couldn't recall the last time she had felt that from her always-serious chief counselor.

"Most of the news outlets thought that was a gift from Fahla herself," Aldirk continued. "The coverage was more than thorough—I doubt there's an Alsean alive today who hasn't heard about the economists who weren't good enough." He closed his eyes and laughed quietly. "Ah, that was the highlight of this cycle. Well done, Lancer Tal. Well done."

"Thank you." Tal was still recovering from the sight of Aldirk laughing. "I wish it hadn't been necessary, but the demonstrators in Blacksun and Redmoon convinced me that I had to hit back a little more firmly."

"Indeed you did." Aldirk was all business again and began going down his list. It seemed to have no end, and Tal gave up on getting to Hol-Opah by evenmeal.

Nearly a hantick passed before Aldirk announced that he had reached the final entry. "A prisoner in the Pit has requested an audience with you."

"And this is important because…?" Not a moon went by without a prisoner in the Pit asking for an audience. Incarceration there often meant the prisoner was beyond any option of release other than a state pardon, which only Tal could give. She hadn't given many of them.

"Because this particular prisoner was the ringleader in the Whitemoon smuggling case. He has informed the prison guards that we did not capture the most powerful person involved."

"And he's willing to trade his information for a pardon? Absolutely not."

"He didn't ask for a pardon, merely a transfer to an aboveground facility." Aldirk paused. "He indicated that his information might lead us to a highly placed individual. Lancer Tal, if our investigation left the most responsible person free, we have an obligation to pursue this. Other high empaths may be at risk of recruitment."

Tal sighed. "Call Colonel Razine and have her send one of her investigators to speak with the prisoner. If his information plays out, I'll authorize a transfer."

"If it were possible to delegate this, I would have already done so. The prisoner will speak with no one but you."

"Why?"

Aldirk looked troubled. "He states that the responsible party is too powerful and will suppress his information if it's given to anyone else."

The office was dead silent. At last Tal said, "He's going to point to a Councilor. It would take that level of power to control an AIF investigation. Which means it's almost certainly a warrior, since criminal investigations are our caste responsibility."

"That's what I'm afraid of as well."

"Spawn of a fantenshekken!" Tal stood abruptly, pushing back her chair. "This is the last thing we need! I've just spent three days rebuilding the people's trust in this government; a corruption case reaching all the way to the Council will undermine everything. Dammit, why now?"

"Better now than never," Aldirk said. "If we have a corrupt Councilor, then he or she must be found and removed immediately."

"Is that prisoner in a protection cell?"

Aldirk checked his notes. "Yes, he was placed there two days ago."

"Good. Make the preparations and inform Colonel Micah. Send me all the records on our informant. I'll go to the Pit tomorrow after midmeal."

"May I assume that you will be staying in Blacksun tonight, then?"

"You may not. If there's nothing else, I'm leaving for Granelle."

"Lancer Tal, may I remind you that there have been demonstrations against you and one actual attack. Until we know for sure that your safety is not in jeopardy, it would be wiser for you to stay here."

"That wasn't an attack. Really, an old woman trying to throw a picture frame at me? As for the demonstrations, one of them was right here. I'm probably safer in Granelle."

With a sigh that was clearly meant to be heard, Aldirk made a note on his reader card and slipped it in its case. "Very well. I'll tell First Pilot Thornlan to prepare your long-distance transport tomorrow morning."

"Poor Thornlan." Tal shook her head. "She just got home."

"So did you."

Not quite yet, she thought.

CHAPTER 62
Alliance honored

"Aldirk isn't happy," Tal said as she made a tiny course adjustment. She and Micah were in her personal transport, less than five ticks away from Hol-Opah, and her yearning was growing stronger the closer she got.

"What else is new?" Micah asked. "Let me guess. He's not happy about you returning to 'that useless little farm.'"

Tal chuckled. "Well, he didn't put it quite that way. This time. But he made it clear that he thinks I should stay in Blacksun."

"I must admit, I'd be a great deal more comfortable if you did. I can protect you far better at Blacksun Base. But it would be a strategic mistake to retreat."

"And it would send a very poor message. If I'm seen as afraid to go out among the people, it would bring everything I've been saying into question. Besides, I'm not in the habit of letting a tiny fraction of the population dictate my actions."

"You're not in the habit of letting anyone dictate your actions."

"That's not true." She glanced at him. "I listen to you. On occasion."

He snorted. "'On occasion' being the operative phrase."

"Now, Micah, you know how much I value your *professional* advice." She waited for him to take the bait.

"Good. Then you will value the fact that I've doubled your guard."

"You what! You added ten Guards? Where in Fahla's name will Salomen put them? Did you tell her? Damn, she's going to be—"

"—pleased that I'm taking proper precautions to keep you safe," Micah finished. "I already called and informed her. The new Guards will fit in the current barracks with a little rearranging of cots. I sent them over along with the additional food and supplies this morning."

Tal deflated. "Oh. Then I'd better know the details. Who did you send?"

By the time Micah had gone through his list of Guards and explained their duty rotation, Tal was landing the transport behind the house. They had a welcoming committee of three Guards and the entire Opah family, which put a permanent smile on Tal's face. This was a new and very pleasant feeling.

Salomen ran up to her as soon as she emerged from the transport. For a moment Tal thought she was going to give her a warmron in front of everyone, but she stopped short and held up her palm.

Tal met it and interlaced their fingers. "It's so good to see you. Sorry we arrived so late; there was a lot to attend to at the State House."

"I care only that you're here now. Fahla, but I missed you. We have so much to talk about." With an abrupt shift in her emotions, Salomen added, "We had an… event here while you were gone. Please don't be upset when you hear about it. I didn't want to tell you while you had so much else to think about."

"What happened?"

"Later." Salomen let go of her hand to reach for Micah.

"Well met," Micah said. "Did we make it in time for evenmeal?"

Salomen smiled. "And this is your first thought after nearly four days away?"

"True warriors think with their stomachs. Mine is rumbling."

"Then you'll be happy to know we waited for you. Let's feed the monsters in those bellies."

Tal and Micah turned to greet the rest of the family, touching palms with Shikal first, as was his due, then his sons. The welcome Tal felt from Salomen, Shikal, and Nikin brought back pleasant memories of coming home to her parents. Then she touched palms with Herot, and the sizzle of anger emanating from him drove out all prior warmth.

"Lancer Tal," he said in a barely polite tone.

"Herot," she answered. "Is the running growing easier?"

The flicker of surprise showed in his eyes. "Somewhat, yes," he said.

"That's good to hear." She nodded at him and stepped over to Jaros, who was waiting with such impatience that she was surprised he could even stand still. He had kept his head down while she and Micah were greeting his elders, and though Tal had noticed, she hadn't had time to wonder why. Then she crouched down in front of him and he raised his head, giving her a shock that strained her front.

"Oh, Jaros," she breathed. "What happened?"

A lopsided smile lit his bruised face. "I defended you."

She reached out to gently touch the purple skin around his eye and the welts on his swollen cheek ridges. Even the poor boy's lip was split; he had been in a true fight. "Against whom? Who did this to you?"

"Some of the older boys at school. They followed me part of the way home yesterday and were saying bad things about you. I told them they were fant—I mean, idiots, and that you were the greatest Lancer Alsea has ever had, and they started hitting me." He drew himself up proudly. "I didn't run, Lancer Tal. A warrior never runs from battle. I hit back as many times as I could."

"How many were there?" Tal had to work to keep her voice calm.

"Three. They were from the sixth level."

Three boys ganging up on a child two cycles younger. The rising rage threatened to choke off her throat. "You fought this battle for me?"

He nodded, glowing with his achievement. "We're allies. I couldn't let them insult you."

She carefully focused her front, then held up her palm. He met it and smiled as much as his split lip allowed; she was sending all of her pride in him. "You did very well, Jaros. I honor your courage."

She hadn't thought his spine could get any straighter, but he managed to stand even taller. "Thank you, Lancer Tal."

"And as your ally, I will not allow this to go unanswered."

His excitement grew. "What will you do?"

At the moment, she was thinking about ordering Micah to round up those boys so that she could invite all three of them to show her just how brave they were, but that probably wasn't the best idea. "I must discuss it with your father and Salomen. Just know that you will not fight this battle alone." She dropped her hand and prepared to stand, but something in his eyes stopped her. On instinct she opened her arms, smiling as he threw himself into the warmron. A surge of protective emotion startled her with its intensity; then she realized that only part of it was hers. Looking up, she met Salomen's eyes. "So this was the event," she said quietly.

Salomen nodded just as Jaros released his hold and looked up at his sister. "Can we eat now?" he asked.

She ruffled his hair. "Yes, we can."

As the family trooped toward the porch steps, Salomen spoke for Tal's ears alone. "We kept him home from school today. He was too afraid, though he would die if he thought you knew that. And the soreness has set in as well. We've been keeping it under control with a light dose of paincounters. But what helped him the most was when Father mentioned at mornmeal how proud you would be of him. After that it was as if he'd never been hurt at all; he's been floating off the ground waiting for you to come back. He made all of us promise that we would let him be the one to tell you when you arrived."

"I'm very proud of him. And so angry I could chew solid rock." Tal glanced at her. "You've become quite accomplished at partial fronting. You must be just as angry, but it doesn't show."

"That's good to know. I've been working hard to make sure Jaros doesn't sense it; he doesn't need that from me. But you're right. When he came home yesterday in tears, with blood running down his face… Let's just say that for a few moments I wished for your disruptor."

Tal let their hands brush as they mounted the steps. "Then perhaps it was a good thing I was still in Whitemoon. I might have given it to you."

CHAPTER 63
Not family

"Who are these boys?" Tal asked.

Shikal and Micah had retired to the parlor for their usual after-evenmeal drink, but this time everyone except Jaros had accompanied them. Though he had tried his best to be in on the family council, neither Shikal nor Salomen were moved by his pleas. He was now in his room, finishing homework.

"We don't know," Shikal said. "They're two levels ahead of Jaros in school. He's seen them enough to know what level they're in, but not their names. If I knew who they were, I would already have spoken to their parents. I cannot believe any reasonable parent would stand for their child ganging up on anyone, much less a smaller child."

"Why would they bully Jaros now?" Micah wondered. "Lancer Tal has been here for three ninedays without a problem. Is this because of the demonstrations? Or the woman in Whitesun?"

"No." Salomen put her glass down beside her chair. "I think it's because of Gordense Bilsner's big mouth. He has a cause, and he's putting all of his considerable hot air into it. The caste house meeting was just the beginning. I'm told that he's been holding court in the tavern where most of the landholders go, continuing where he left off after that meeting. And, unfortunately, with no one present to speak on the side of reason. I didn't even know about it until today. Some of our field workers were there last night and spoke against Bilsner, but their opinions were discounted because of their rank."

"Is he speaking tonight?" Micah's tone of voice left no doubt that he was hoping the answer was yes.

"No," Nikin said. "The mood has shifted since Lancer Tal's speech in Whitemoon. I was in town today and spoke with several friends; they all said the same thing. The message is getting to people, and they're not so willing to listen to Bilsner."

"I want to know what you're going to do about it." Herot was looking at Tal with undisguised resentment.

"Herot," Shikal said in a weary voice.

"No, Father. We all have the right to know. Jaros was beaten because *she* lives here. Why is she coming back?" He turned back to Tal. "Don't you have somewhere else to be? Haven't you brought enough trouble to our family?"

"Herot Arrin Opah! You will not speak that way to a guest of our house!" Shikal's weariness had vanished; there was fire in his eyes as he glared at his son.

"And how dare you lay the blame at the Lancer's feet when you yourself were beating up on your brother not even a nineday past! Yes, I know about it," he added as Herot looked away. "I also know it was Lancer Tal who stopped you. So you can put up your hypocritical concern for tonight. I won't hear any part of it."

"And I don't need to hear this." Herot jumped from his chair. "No matter what happens, you're on her side. Jaros gets beaten because of her, and instead of asking her to stay away, you invite her to our council. I give Jaros a little push because he stole from me, and suddenly that's my fault and she gets credit for 'stopping me.' But when she beats up on me, nobody gives a dokshin. Talk about hypocrisy—this family is drowning in it!"

"Sit down!" Shikal roared. "We all know what you said to earn your reminder of manners. If you had any sense at all, you wouldn't bring up your own shame. But you are not walking away this time. This is a family council, and you are a member of this family."

"But she is not!" Herot pointed at Tal, then Micah. "Neither is he! If they are to be included in this *family* council, then I will excuse myself."

As he stomped away, Tal met Shikal's eyes and raised her eyebrows. He gave her one short nod.

Herot made it all of four steps before Tal was on top of him, spinning him around and twisting his arm behind him in one movement. She marched him back to his chair, pushed him into it, and held him in place.

"I may not be a member of this family, but I will not sit idly by and watch you disrespect your father any more than I would allow you to disrespect your sister. How can you treat Shikal so poorly when he is the only parent you have left?"

He looked past her to his father. "And will you sit idly by and let her treat me this way?"

"Certainly I will. I asked her to."

"You what?" He was so shocked that Tal felt him slump under her hands.

"I no longer have the physical strength to discipline you," Shikal said. "When a man reaches my age, he expects that his children have matured beyond the necessity of physical discipline. He expects that a lifetime of love and nurturing will have earned him, if not love, at least respect in return. You appear to find me unworthy of either."

"Father, I—"

"You walk away," Shikal interrupted loudly, "when anyone in this family attempts to tell you something that might be good for you to hear. You abuse your younger brother because he's too small to fight back. You abandon the friends of a lifetime and take up with the worst dregs of Granelle. And you insult guests of our house, here in the very room where your mother graciously received so many. She would be horrified, ashamed, and so—" He swallowed hard before continuing quietly, "so sad to see what you have become. She would grieve for her son. As I grieve for my son. And if it requires someone outside this family to hold you down so that you will actually stay and listen to what I have to say, then so be it. I am not ashamed to ask. I'm only ashamed that it's necessary."

The room was silent. Herot looked from his father to his sister, then stared at his lap. "You can let me go," he muttered. "I'm not going anywhere."

Tal opened her senses, testing his intentions. No, he wasn't going to run. For a brief moment, she could sense his shame and a deep, pained regret; Shikal's words had reached him. But the humiliation at being lectured so severely in front of witnesses rose up to overwhelm those deeper feelings, and soon Tal felt nothing but a familiar anger. She released her hold and sat back in her chair.

Though everyone in the room was watching Herot, he refused to look up. At last he asked, "Aren't we supposed to be talking about Jaros?"

It was Salomen who answered, her voice just as weary as Shikal's had been earlier. "Two of our family are in trouble, Herot, not just one. We're here to help you as well, but you hold us outside. We can't do anything until you let us in. We all lost her, not just you. We know how hard it is."

He lifted his head then, his expression scornful. "I don't need your help. And even if I did, I certainly wouldn't ask in front of *her*. She doesn't belong here."

"Our brother has spoken," Nikin said in exasperation. "With his usual rudeness and lack of grace. Shall we get back to the brother we can help, then?"

After an awkward pause, Micah said, "If Jaros cannot name the boys, we have no way of assuring that they won't repeat their attack. Perhaps the best response is to make sure he can convince them of their folly should they return."

"What do you mean?" Shikal asked.

"It would be a matter of one, perhaps two days of concentrated effort to teach him enough to send them running. Jaros does not lack in courage or determination. And a boy trained to fight can easily hold his own against three bullies relying on their size and weight alone. Most likely he would only need to bloody the nose of one before all three gave up and ran."

"Absolutely not," said Salomen. "He's already fantasizing about a change of caste, but that will probably pass in time if it's not encouraged. Training him to fight will only add fuel to his fantasies."

"Then what do we do?" Nikin asked. "Send him back to school so he can get beaten up again?"

"I could walk him there," Shikal suggested. "And pick him up at the end of the day."

"For how long? Father, you cannot escort Jaros every day for the rest of the school cycle. Not only is it not practical, I don't believe he would allow it. He'd be embarrassed."

"True," said Herot. "There's nothing worse than being publicly treated like a child."

Everyone ignored him.

"There must be a better solution than either escorting him or teaching him to fight," Salomen said. "We need to find out who these boys were and deal with this problem at the source."

"I can help with that," said Tal.

"How?"

"You have some of the most talented and highly trained empaths in the world right here on your holding. My personal Guards are chosen in part for their empathic strength. If you could arrange it with the school's head scholar, it would be a fairly simple matter to have a Guard walk into the sixth level classes with Jaros tomorrow. Unless his attackers are astonishingly gifted, they won't be able to hide their reaction at seeing Jaros and a uniformed Lancer's Guard in their class. Any of my Guards would be able to pinpoint that in an instant."

"And then I could speak with their parents," Shikal said.

"If I may, Shikal..." Tal was smiling at the idea forming in her head.

"You have another suggestion?"

"Leaving the discipline in the hands of the parents is likely to result in three different punishments, unless the parents coordinate. I would prefer they all receive the same punishment. Together."

"And you have something specific in mind." Micah knew her well.

She grinned at him. "It so happens that I have to visit the Pit tomorrow after midmeal. What better way to teach three young boys the consequences of bullying and violence than to show them the worst place it can lead to?"

Nikin whistled. "That would do it. Damn, that would scare me out of last night's evenmeal."

"We would need the parents to agree," said Shikal. "But...I like the idea. It would certainly be an eye-opener for those three."

"I like it too," Salomen said. "It would put a swift end to this bullying, and most likely stop any of the other children from having similar brilliant ideas."

"What kind of parent would agree to sending their child to the Pit?" asked Herot. "There are things that no child should see."

"What the children see is entirely dependent on what I choose to show them," said Tal. "I'll scare them, not scar them. And as for your first question, the kind of parents who would allow this are those who wish their children to learn honor."

Her implication was clear to everyone in the room, and Herot's cheeks reddened. "I just hope you don't set Jaros up as a target for the rest of his schooling by making him so obviously the Lancer's pet project."

"He is not my pet project. He's an ally who showed great courage in defending my name. I am therefore required to defend him as well, and I'll be happy to make that clear to these boys as I escort them through the Pit. I'm sure the news will travel."

"I think it's an excellent idea," said Nikin. "For the record, I approve."

"As do I," Salomen said.

"And I appreciate your assistance, Lancer Tal." Shikal inclined his head. "Thank you for being so generous with your time and your staff."

"No thanks are necessary. Herot is right about one thing: this happened because of my presence here. I have an obligation to set it right."

"But you would do it whether you had an obligation or not."

"Yes, I would."

"Then I will still offer my gratitude."

"I see my vote doesn't count," said Herot.

"Of course it does," said Salomen. "What do you say?"

Everyone looked at Herot expectantly. He opened his mouth, then shook his head. "It doesn't matter what I say. You'll all do what Lancer Tal says anyway."

"No, we will all gratefully accept Lancer Tal's offer of assistance, which is an entirely different thing."

Herot made a dismissive gesture. "Since everyone has decided, is the meeting over?"

"The council is finished," Shikal said. "Now we are merely enjoying an after-evenmeal drink. Would you like a refill?"

"No thanks." Herot rose. "I prefer to drink with friends."

Tal found it sad that everyone in the room relaxed as soon as he was gone. What a terrible testament to a man's character, she thought, that the greatest enjoyment he could bring his family was to leave them alone.

"The arrangements with the parents must be made tomorrow morning," she told Shikal. "I'll send Gehrain to school with Jaros. They'll need to arrive early to give Gehrain time to procure permission from the head scholar, but I don't foresee any difficulty with that. Gehrain should have names within a quarter hantick, and at that point you'll need to make a few visits."

"It will be my pleasure."

A low rumble of laughter drew their attention to Micah. Smiling broadly, he asked, "Can I be the one to tell Gehrain he's going to school?"

CHAPTER 64
Equal partners

Salomen barely let the bedroom door close behind her before walking straight into Tal's arms. "I've been craving this since I watched you give Jaros his warmron."

"Me too." Tal closed her eyes as she soaked in the comfort. "When you came running to greet me, I thought for a moment that you were going to do this in front of everyone."

"That would have been the talk of Granelle, wouldn't it?"

"I think it would have been the talk of all Alsea."

"I missed you," Salomen whispered. "More than I expected, and I expected a lot."

Before Tal could respond, she felt an alarming tingle. They pushed each other away at the same moment, barely in time to avoid the full empathic flash.

"Dammit!" Salomen shook her hands, then tucked them under her arms. "This is too much. I have waited four long days to touch you, and I can't shekking do it!"

"Salomen—"

"I hate this."

"I know. I do too. But we have to live with it until we're comfortable with the idea of Sharing."

"Would it surprise you if I said I'm much more comfortable with that idea now than I was before you left?"

"Yes, it would. What happened?"

Salomen moved to her chair and sat down. "You'd better take the window seat. Fahla knows we cannot handle the temptation of sitting together."

Tal took her customary seat. "All right, we're safely apart. Now tell me what happened."

"Nothing special. Just that I spent every day missing you more than I thought possible. And every evening glued to the vidscreen, watching you. And every night lying awake, wishing you weren't so far away. I even caught myself looking out the kitchen window yesterday morning, waiting for you to come running past the grove in that rag of a shirt you wear."

"Careful. That rag is the most comfortable shirt I own. I'm extremely loyal to it."

Salomen gave her a faint smile. "To a fault, I think. I'm just not used to feeling so lonely anymore. It's ridiculous; I spent most of my life that way and managed perfectly well. You've been here only three ninedays, but...you gave me the first real freedom to be myself that I've ever known. I got used to it. And when you left, that left with you. I can't live that way anymore." She wrapped her arms around herself and looked at Tal unhappily. "All I want now is to be in your arms, but we can't. It's driving me insane."

Unable to tolerate the distance, Tal pushed off the window seat and sat cross-legged on the floor in front of the chair, resting her hands palm up on Salomen's knees.

Salomen relaxed as she covered them with her own. "Thank you. Not quite a warmron, but I suppose it's the best we can do right now."

"Better than nothing. And I missed you, too. The only time I wasn't thinking about you was during my speeches." Tal lifted one hand to her lips and kissed it. "I'm glad I can give you that freedom, because you've done the same for me."

"Because I see past the lie? I never saw that lie quite so clearly as I did while watching your speeches. You were every bit the Lancer. It reminded me of how intimidated I was when I first met you."

"You got over it quickly," Tal teased.

Salomen's mood lifted slightly. "True. But now I'm intimidated for a different reason. How is it possible to want something so much and still be frightened of it?"

"The same way it's possible to be frightened of something and still want it."

"Interesting. I never thought of it that way."

"I remember being frightened of my first joining. But I still wanted it, in a powerful way."

"Ooo, I haven't heard this. How old were you?"

"Fifteen."

"You were not!" Salomen chuckled. "I know you were a precocious child, but nobody joins before they're sixteen. Your parents would have killed your partner if that were the case."

"True words. All right, I lied. We waited until the day after my birth anniversary."

"Impatient little things, weren't you?"

"We thought we were doing well to last that long! Fahla, she was beautiful. I wanted her from the moment she transferred into my class."

"And was it as frightening as you thought?"

"It was wonderful."

Salomen gave an exaggerated sigh. "Of course you would have a perfect first joining. For most of us it involves more fumbling than wonder. And a few painful bites."

"Is this the voice of experience?"

"I waited two full cycles after my sixteenth birth anniversary, but it didn't help. My first was a boy I went to school with. We knew everything about each other and our families, but hardly a thing about joining. We tried our best, but agreed afterwards that nothing our instructors or parents told us was sufficient training. Fortunately, we were both quick learners."

"So the second joining was better than the first."

"By a length. And the third was better than that. And then we had to stop and get something to eat."

Tal roared with laughter. When she could speak again, she asked, "Was he your first Sharing as well?"

"No, that was a woman from the other side of Granelle. But I don't think my Sharings have been quite as wonderful as yours probably were."

"Why not?"

"Because I could never really let go. If I did that, my secret would be out."

Tal's merriment vanished. "It's not supposed to be like that. I'm sorry you've never experienced a Sharing the way it's meant to be."

"I made my choice."

But it was obvious that Salomen was merely repeating the words she had used many times before. Tal could sense no real conviction behind them.

"You made a choice when you were ten cycles, for Fahla's sake."

"Yes, but it was hardly one I could take back, was it? I still haven't figured out how to tell my family. Father and Nikin especially will want to know why I never said anything. They'll be hurt that I didn't trust them."

"Would it be any easier if I was there when you told them?"

Salomen squeezed her hands. "It would. Thank you for offering. And this is precisely what I mean when I say I've gotten too used to this. Now that I know what it's like to have this kind of support, I don't want to go back to the way it was before. But I'm nervous about going forward, too."

"We don't have to go anywhere just yet. We're still in control."

"You call this control?" She lifted their hands. "We can't enjoy the most basic physical contact that should precede a joining, let alone a Sharing. I'm craving it. If nothing else, that will force me into a decision."

"I see. Were you planning to inform me of this decision? Just so I can put it on my calendar, of course."

Salomen gave her a sheepish smile. "I meant our decision."

"Ah. Right." Tal nodded.

"Oh, stop. You know I cannot make that choice alone." She tilted her head. "How are you feeling about it now?"

"Better than before I left. I had a rather…interesting experience at Whitemoon Temple after our call last night. Fahla gave me a sign."

As she described her experience, Salomen's initial curiosity turned to astonishment.

"Holy shek!"

"That's exactly what I said."

"When you said a sign, I thought you meant something like a celestial stone over the temple dome. Great Goddess! I've never known anyone who had an actual sign like that. That kind of thing happens in legends, not real life."

"Believe me, it was real enough. I thought my hands were going to burst into flames."

"What do you think she was telling you?"

"I don't know, but I'm sure it was about us. It happened right after I asked for her help in making you happy."

Salomen's smile lit the room. "You don't need Fahla's help with that. You've been doing fine all on your own."

"I just wanted to make sure it stays that way." Tal stood, pulling Salomen up with her. Bringing their clasped hands down and to the sides, she pressed her body into Salomen's and dropped a gentle kiss on her throat. "Maybe…if we keep out of a warmron…and I just go one kiss at a time…we can stay under the threshold for a flash," she murmured, punctuating her words with the lightest of kisses.

"It's worth a try." Salomen dropped her head back, giving Tal a great deal more to work with.

She held herself tightly in check, tamping down her desire, and managed to cover nearly every bit of Salomen's throat and jaw before a slight tingle told her she had gone far enough. Reluctantly, she let go and stepped back.

Salomen raised her head with a quiet sigh. "Damn."

"I know, but we got away with that much."

"Always seeing what you can get away with, aren't you?"

"Of course. And especially with you." Tal went back to her window seat to remove herself from temptation. "If you never push the limits, you'll never know how far you can go."

"No wonder Jaros worships you," Salomen said as she took her own chair. "That's his philosophy as well."

That reminded Tal of a conversation they needed to have, much as she didn't want to at the moment.

"Salomen…"

"I know. I didn't tell you about him because I didn't want you to worry. There was nothing you could have done anyway."

"But don't you think I needed to know? It happened because of me."

Salomen's eyes widened. "You're upset with me? I was just doing what I thought was best for you. You carry so much; I didn't want to add to that if it wasn't necessary."

"It's my duty to carry all of this. That's the responsibility I accepted along with my title. You cannot protect me from what I need to know."

"Because you're the one who does the protecting."

"Yes," Tal said in relief. Salomen understood.

"No. Not anymore."

"No? What in—"

"I'm not talking about your title. I'm talking about you, personally. Or am I alone in enjoying the comfort of a partner, because you think you're the only one who can provide that support?"

How did this get so turned around? "No, of course not. You of all people know how much it means for me to have your support."

Salomen was looking at her as if she could see right through her, and Tal had the uncomfortable thought that perhaps she really could.

"I don't think so," she said. "You tell me how much it means for you to be accepted as who you are, but in reality you only want part of that. You want it to end right at the point where I might see you as vulnerable, or worst of all, truly needing anything."

"That is not true. I called you after Whitesun—"

"And didn't say a word about that woman calling you Betrayer. You wanted to hear about our day at Hol-Opah."

"Because I needed something normal!"

"There, was that so hard to admit?"

"What? I said it then."

"No, you said you were tired of politics and talking points and you wanted to hear about us. And then you drank out of that flask and your damn hands were *shaking*, and you looked at me as if you were perfectly all right. As if I'm one more person you need to play a role with. I didn't even know why that affected you so much until I saw your interview the next day and realized just who that woman was."

"I didn't want to talk about it then." How could she explain that Hol-Opah was a world apart for her? A refuge that she didn't want sullied by the realities of the rest of her life?

"And you don't want to talk about it now."

"Not particularly, no."

Salomen nodded. "You've built your life on being seen as invincible, and having anyone take care of you implies the opposite. But Colonel Micah takes care of you, and somehow that's all right because…he's a warrior? Your Chief Guardian?"

"Because I've known him all my life! And it's his job to take care of me."

"Isn't it the job of a tyree to take care of her bondmate?"

But Tal didn't want to be one more burden on Salomen. She wanted to take those burdens away, not add to them.

"When I kept the news about Jaros from you, I was thinking of your comfort," Salomen said. "I wanted you to get a good night's sleep and not worry about something you couldn't do a thing about. But I see such consideration makes you more uncomfortable, not less."

Tal slumped back against the window. "I thought we were past this kind of arguing."

Salomen's smile was knowing. "I'm just as brick-headed as you are. We'll never be past this kind of arguing. This is the other side of having someone accept you as a whole person and not just the Lancer. I'm not going to concede because you have the final word; I'll concede when you convince me to."

"Well, that's never going to happen."

"Don't be so pessimistic. It already has. You've convinced me of quite a few things, and taught me more than that. I just want to be recognized as an equal partner."

"You are. How could we even be here otherwise?"

"I don't think that's true," Salomen said. "And I think I just figured out some of my nervousness. When we Share, it needs to be a gift between equals. That's when I'll be comfortable with it."

"So now we're back to you making the decision regarding our Sharing. And here I thought I was joking about that."

"Are you not listening to anything I'm saying? I just told you that you're the one who will bring us to that point."

In the silence that followed, Tal sensed only sincerity. Salomen wasn't arguing for the sake of a debate; she was simply waiting for Tal to understand.

Understand what, exactly, Tal wasn't sure.

"I thought I already saw you as an equal partner," she said. "But if you don't feel it, then there's something I'm not doing right."

There was that knowing smile again. "You have no idea how many things you already get right." Salomen stood up and walked over, not stopping until she was between Tal's legs. The intensity in her eyes was mesmerizing as she braced her hands on the window and leaned in, closer and closer, until their foreheads were almost touching. "Can we go back to the beginning of this conversation?" she whispered. "The part where I told you how much I missed you? Because I forgot to mention something else. I love you."

Tal tried to say it, but the words wouldn't come out. As Salomen slipped one arm around her, she buried her face in the fragrant warmth of her tyree's neck and prayed that Fahla would let them have a few pipticks before the flash. She needed this comfort and she needed to hide her face, because they weren't equals. Salomen was far ahead of her.

CHAPTER 65
First rain

Micah woke in the gray light of dawn, a lifetime of training keeping him perfectly still in bed while he worked out what was wrong. As his brain came to full alertness and identified the pervasive drumming sound, he grumbled to himself. Great. The rains had come in the night, half a day before they were predicted. That would make the morning's field work a muddy, messy pain in the backside, and everything from now until the end of autumn was going to be a constant slog. This was his least favorite season, when the long summer ended abruptly with the autumn rains that seemed to have no end.

He rose and wasted no time pulling on trousers and tunic; the air was noticeably colder this morning. Picking up his belt, he wandered to the window while buckling it on and looked out into the back property.

"You're insane," he said, shaking his head. "And I am so glad I'm too old for your running detail."

Tal was there, her only concession to the pouring rain a waterproof running suit and a brimmed hat that kept her hair and face dry. The five Guards with her wore matching outfits, but other than that, none of the runners seemed to have noticed the inclement weather. They stood around in relaxed stances, having their usual morning chat before starting their run. Tal laughed at something Gehrain said and smacked him on the shoulder. Then she turned and set off, the Guards instantly surrounding her in the standard formation.

Micah waited as they jogged out of sight. Sure enough, a familiar figure appeared, following Tal and her Guards at a safe distance.

"Well, I'll be Fahla-damned." He wouldn't have believed Herot would be there this morning. Not after last night's temper tantrum, and especially not in the cold and the wet.

Micah felt a tiny bit of grudging respect. Maybe Herot had something resembling a man inside him after all. Despite all his outward anger and resentment of Tal, he was still trying to prove something to her.

"Herot, you give yourself away," he murmured. "You wouldn't be so keen on this if you didn't care about her opinion."

He watched the figure until it was swallowed up in the rain, then turned and headed for the kitchen. A hot cup of shannel sounded perfect right now.

CHAPTER 66
Horten harvest

For Tal, the morning was an exercise in frustration. She hadn't had nearly enough time with Salomen the previous night, and her assignment to transport duty this morning meant she wouldn't see her during the day, either. The few glimpses she got while carefully maneuvering the large farm transport under the field cover and helping the crew with loading were hardly sufficient. Salomen was everywhere at once, organizing and supervising an impossibly chaotic harvest. Tal didn't know whether it would be much easier if it were dry; the tight schedule of the distribution center and the fact that the horten had to be cut immediately prior to loading meant that stress levels were high whether it was raining or not.

Though the rain certainly didn't help, she thought as she pulled her boot out of the squelching mud. It was impossible to keep anything clean. The inside of her transport already looked like a mud bog, and they had been working for just two hanticks. She hated to think what it would look like by the end of the day.

"Done!" one of the workers shouted over the din of rain pounding on the field cover. He hit the control for the rear door, watched it slide down, and slapped his hand on the side. "Get it out of here!"

Tal hopped inside, sighing with relief as she shut the door and sealed out the noise. She looked over at Varsi, who was pulling escort duty in the passenger seat. "Ready?"

"Always. Looks like Herot is, too."

Tal glanced up from her controls to see Herot waiting in the second transport, just beyond the field cover. As soon as she lifted off and moved out of the loading area, he zipped past her and settled in to receive a new load. They had been going back and forth from the field to the distribution center all morning, and the frantic schedule would continue for another five days. But the end was in sight. Once the horten harvest was over, all field work was suspended for a full moon. Nothing could be done in the rains, so traditionally this moon was a time of rest, relaxation, celebration…and repair work on equipment. It was also the time when the landholder hosted a feast for the field workers, which—judging by the conversations Tal overheard—was the main focus of everyone's fantasies at the moment. Apparently, Hol-Opah was known for its magnificent autumn feast.

As she flew toward the north boundary, two military transports rose up to flank her. The distribution center workers had probably never seen anything quite like it, but the escort was necessary since she was flying off Opah land in a nonsecure transport. She had tried to talk Salomen out of assigning her this duty, reasoning that the number of Guards and military transports required would be overkill for the simple task of flying the horten a few lengths away. But Salomen was adamant. She wanted Tal to have "the full experience," as she put it. After two hanticks of going back and forth, always rushed and under pressure, Tal was forced to admit she'd had no idea how stressful and numbing this kind of work could be.

There was one benefit, however, and it was a big one: the transport smelled divine. This was a bowl of horten soup stripped to its raw essence and multiplied by a thousand. It was comfort and warmth, the scent of a honeywood campfire on a late autumn night. She would have taken flying duty simply for the chance to breathe this air. If Salomen ever found a way to bottle this fragrance, she could make a fortune.

Less than ten ticks after leaving Hol-Opah, Tal landed at the distribution center, where Nikin and his crew were waiting to unload. With the precision of a well-trained fighting unit, they had her transport cleaned out almost before the engines had fully spun down, and she was off again, passing Herot on the way back.

"Sure gives me a new appreciation for horten soup," Varsi said.

"That it does. And for a nice quiet High Council meeting where only six people are yelling back and forth, and no one is getting stuck in the mud."

"At least it's only until midmeal. Then you get to yell at some bullies."

Gehrain's morning mission had been successful, and Shikal had quickly procured the permission of all the parents, who were reportedly embarrassed by their children's behavior. Tal would have three guests on her flight to the Pit.

"I admit I'm looking forward to that," she said.

"Wish I could see it. There's not a Guard in the bunkhouse who didn't want to go to that school today and hand out a few disciplinary lessons."

Tal smiled. "If Jaros had any idea that he has an entire unit of Guards as his personal fans, he'd never come back to the ground."

The military transports dropped to their staging area shortly after they crossed the boundary to Opah land, and soon Tal was maneuvering back under the field cover and into the scene of controlled chaos. She settled down in the loading area, where another large pile of horten had already appeared. Opening the door to the din of pounding rain and shouting workers, she shook her head. Truly, she would never look at a bowl of horten soup the same way again.

CHAPTER 67
Bullies

SALOMEN NEVER MANAGED TO BREAK free of her duties that morning, leaving Tal to fly back to the main house without ever getting to speak with her tyree. She grumbled that she might as well have stayed in Blacksun; it certainly would have been easier logistically. No wonder Aldirk thought she was cracked.

Her poor mood improved with a meal, shower, and clean uniform, and grew better still when she arrived at Blacksun Base. The walk from the landing pad to her office was marked by respectful salutes and cheerful greetings, and by the time she stepped inside her office, a sense of familiar comfort had settled over her like an old, soft cloak. Here she was one warrior among many, in a place where everyone operated within the same social structure and with the same training and expectations. It was this ease, among other, more practical considerations, that made the caste houses so essential. The State House represented the opposite concept, teeming with people of all castes who all seemed to want something from her. In her state office, she sometimes counted the ticks until she could leave and palmlock the door behind her. In this one, she never looked at a clock.

She moved to the curving outside wall, which was solid weapons-grade glass. From this vantage point, twelve stories off the ground, she had an even better view than she did from the State House. All of the base was laid out before her, and beyond the perimeter was nothing but forest. Normally she could see the skyline of Blacksun far in the distance, but today it was hidden by rain. And somewhere beyond Blacksun, well out of her sight, was a holding near Granelle where Salomen and a large field crew were working their legs off in mud and noise. She felt a little guilty for being here, in the clean comfort of the biggest office on base.

Her senses picked up Micah and Gehrain in the hallway outside her office, accompanied by three unfamiliar minds broadcasting fear.

"Enter," she called.

Gehrain opened the door and stood aside as three young boys in rain cloaks walked in, followed by Micah.

"Lancer Tal," Micah boomed in his unit instructor's voice, "these are the boys who assaulted Jaros Opah. What would you have us do with them?"

Tal had to work to keep the grin off her face. Micah was having his own bit of fun.

"That depends on what they have to say for themselves. What are your names?"

They glanced at each other, each waiting for someone else to speak first.

Tal solved their problem for them. "You!" She pointed at the boy on the right, who stood half a head taller than the other two. "Speak up. I don't have time to wait for you to find your courage. You've already demonstrated that you have none."

The boy bristled despite his fear, standing a little straighter but still unable to meet her eyes. "Nilo Fortenza."

Tal looked at the dark-haired boy next to him. "And you?"

"Silmartin Hanteese."

The third boy spoke up before she had to ask. "Pendar Fall."

"Nilo, Silmartin, and Pendar," Tal said, "I will not call you by your family names. You have not earned them. You're here because your parents are ashamed of your behavior, and with good reason. They've given me permission to deal with you as I see fit." She pointed to the large table on her right, at the other end of the office from her desk. "Sit down and wait."

The boys shuffled off while Gehrain and Micah came up to Tal.

"What did you learn?" she asked quietly.

"Nilo was the ringleader," Gehrain said. "Jaros recognized him right away. He did most of the hitting. According to the head scholar, he and Silmartin are schoolmates and have gotten themselves in trouble more than once—Jaros isn't the first boy they've bullied. Pendar is a recent addition to their little group. He just joined the school this cycle; one of his fathers is ill and he's spending the cycle with his aunt and uncle. I don't think he likes his friends very much, but he craves their approval. Jaros said he hung back most of the time, shouting at him and egging on the other two. He only joined in briefly, and as soon as Jaros landed a blow, he backed off."

Tal looked at the table, where three sets of eyes were immediately averted. Stifling a smile, she said, "Ten cinteks says Pendar is the first to look me in the eye."

"I accept the bet," Micah said. "It will be Nilo. They follow him."

Tal looked at Gehrain, who gave the boys an appraising glance. "Pendar," he decided. "He has the least to fear."

Micah shook his head. "You will both lose. But I'll accept a good drink in payment if you prefer."

"Done. Now, if the two of you wouldn't mind standing behind my chair? I might need backup."

That taxed their ability to stay serious, but they nodded and followed her across the room.

At the table, she took a seat across from the miscreants and watched their faces while Micah and Gehrain stepped into position behind her. The boys did their best to hide their fear, but their emotions were wide open.

"You've been extraordinarily stupid," she said. "You probably could have continued beating up on other boys indefinitely if you hadn't chosen your last target so badly. Jaros Opah is part of my host family, and I don't take kindly to attacks on my family. He said you attacked him strictly because he defended my name. Is that true?"

They squirmed in their chairs.

Sternly, Tal said, "Is. That. True."

"It wasn't like that," Nilo mumbled. "Just a stupid prank, that's all."

"A prank," Tal repeated. "A prank that resulted in three boys ganging up on a child two cycles younger. Sounds like great fun for everyone."

They fidgeted.

"Have you ever seen a more miserable bunch, Colonel Micah? They can beat up a smaller child, but they can't look me in the eye."

"It wasn't a prank," said Pendar. He raised his head, meeting her gaze, and Tal discreetly poked Micah's leg with her elbow. "You're going to ruin Alsea, starting with the producers. Everyone says so. Except the Opahs, and Uncle says the only reason they aren't speaking openly is because you're there and they're frightened of you."

Tal's lips twitched. She was fairly certain that Pendar's uncle had cooked that one up to keep young ears from hearing what most of Granelle thought was the real reason.

"I see. Did Jaros seem frightened of me?"

He looked down.

"You won't find the answer in the table. When you were hitting Jaros and he fought back to defend my name, did he seem frightened of me?"

He shook his head.

"There goes half of your theory, then. If that much of it is wrong, perhaps the rest is, too. Did it ever occur to you to wonder why he was fighting back instead of running?"

After a long pause, he looked up again and nodded.

"Because he's not just part of my host family. He's my friend and ally."

She could almost see the gears clicking in his head. It had never occurred to him that the Lancer could have friends. That made her a real person, not just a figure.

Without looking away from Pendar, she raised her voice and said, "Nilo!"

The taller boy jerked in his seat, and she turned her head.

"Explain something to me. Why aren't you capable of hitting a small child all by yourself?"

"I told you, it was just a prank," he said, but his trembling voice belied the aggressive persona he was trying to present.

"Pendar says it was not. Which means one of you is lying." She leaned forward. "And I know it's you. Didn't anyone warn you that I'm a high empath? Try again."

She stared him down, feeling his fear growing along with the desperation of a bully who was facing the truth.

"He was just a stupid little boy!" he burst out. "He wasn't supposed to fight back. If he hadn't, he wouldn't have gotten hurt."

"So you're blaming Jaros for the fact that the three of you beat him."

"I'm bigger than he is! What kind of an idiot fights someone bigger than he is?"

Micah snorted behind her, and Tal had to work to keep her face straight. She rarely got the chance to fight anyone her own size.

"An idiot who is braver than you," she said, and turned her attention to Silmartin. He shrank into his chair, foiled in his hope that she had forgotten about him. "Do you agree with Nilo? You think it's Jaros's fault that the three of you beat him?"

He looked from her to Nilo to the table. "I don't know."

"Oh, for the love of Fahla. That's it." Tal stood up. "Two of you are liars, all three of you are bullies, and you've committed assault. Your parents asked me to give you a fitting punishment, so I'm taking you where we put bullies and violent people. Colonel Micah, is the transport ready?"

"Yes, Lancer Tal."

"Good. Get up, boys, it's time to go."

"Where are you taking us?" Pendar's voice was shaking.

"To the Pit, of course."

"What?" Nilo's face was white, and all three boys were aghast.

"You're surprised?"

"You can't take us there!"

"Of course I can. We've already informed your parents where you're going, and they've given their approval. They're ashamed of your behavior."

"But they can't!" Nilo began to cry. "They can't! I don't want to go to the Pit!"

Micah walked around the table. "Goddess above, show a little courage. You've earned this, now face it." He hauled Nilo out of his chair and marched him to the door.

Tal looked at the other two. "Are you coming under your own power, or do we drag you out as well?"

Though clearly terrified, both of them got up. Gehrain put his hand on Silmartin's shoulder and escorted him after Micah and Nilo, while Tal walked with Pendar. They were halfway to the lift when Pendar looked up at her, his eyes brimming with tears. "I'm sorry," he said. "I knew it was wrong, but I did it anyway. You're right, it was stupid and cowardly, and I won't do it again. Please don't take me to the Pit."

Even a half-trained empath could sense his sincerity. He was ashamed, scared halfway to his Return, and wishing with all his strength that he hadn't done it.

Tal leaned down and spoke quietly. "I said I was taking you to the Pit. I did not say I was leaving you there. Be careful of making assumptions."

As they continued down the corridor, his emotions underwent several shifts while he processed her words. Finally, he looked back up at her. "Can I make the assumption that you *won't* leave us there?"

She nearly laughed but kept her face straight and squeezed his shoulder instead. "That is a safe assumption, yes. And I will ask you to keep it to yourself. Colonel Micah and Lead Guard Gehrain will tell the truth if asked, but Silmartin and Nilo must ask the question first. Or apologize, as you did."

He nodded. "I won't say anything, I promise." They reached the lift and stepped in, where the enclosed space served to amplify Nilo's sniffles all the way to the ground floor.

As the door slid back and the others filed out, Pendar tugged at Tal's uniform jacket. When she looked down, he said, "Will you tell the truth if I ask, too?"

She nodded. "Unless it's a state secret."

"Are you really going to destroy Alsea?"

"Can you think of a single reason why I would want to? Especially after I fought so hard to save it from the Voloth?"

That kept him quiet all the way to the building's entrance. Over the general shuffling as Tal, Micah, and Gehrain put on their rain cloaks, Pendar leaned in and said, "I can't think of any."

"Neither can I." She led him out the door.

The pouring rain eliminated any possibility of conversation until they reached the small, sleek transport used for trips not requiring her Guard unit. First Pilot Thornlan stood respectfully by the door as they entered and shook off the rain.

"Lancer Tal, welcome back. It's been too long."

"I know what you mean." She indicated their passengers. "These three will be accompanying us to the Pit."

Thornlan widened her eyes. "They're young for that, aren't they?"

"Yes, but they ganged up on a boy two cycles younger and beat him."

"Oh, I see." Thornlan looked over the boys, who all hung their heads. "So you have no honor and you believe that hurting others makes you strong. Then you'll fit in very well in the Pit. Most Alseans there were sentenced for the exact same reasons." She gave Tal a quick smile. "If you'll get them in their harnesses, we can lift off."

Tal led Pendar to a nearby seat, where she brought the crash harness over his shoulders and snapped it in at his hips. "Have you ever flown in a transport before today?"

He shook his head.

"We have a long way to go, and the transport will get us there quickly. The harness is necessary because we'll be flying at higher speeds than normal."

He nodded and looked out the window.

She stood watching him for a moment, absorbing the youthful strength of his emotions. Damn if she wasn't actually starting to like the boy. He had spoken honestly in the beginning, looked her in the eye, and sincerely apologized. Nilo really was a little dokker, and Silmartin was too afraid to speak up for himself, but Pendar had promise.

After checking on the others, she tapped her earcuff. "We're all ready back here, Thornlan."

"Very good. Engaging Blacksun beacon now."

Tal sat facing Pendar and pulled on her harness. Normally, she wore one only during the beginning and end of a flight, but in the interest of setting a good example she would keep it on this time. She glanced at Silmartin, seated across from them and facing Gehrain. Micah and Nilo were just ahead, and she smothered a smile at the expression Micah shot her. He was beyond exasperated with the sniveling child in his care.

"By the way, Colonel," she said, "you owe Gehrain and me ten cinteks."

If looks could kill, she would have been a stain on the seat. It was all she could do to keep from laughing, and catching Gehrain's eye did not help at all.

The children's nervousness diminished somewhat after liftoff; a quarter hantick of nothing but engine and wind noise had a calming influence. Nilo stopped crying, to everyone's relief, and the boys busied themselves with looking at the view out their windows. Even this grew less interesting over time, so Tal was not surprised when Pendar turned his attention back to her. She had been reading the file on Donvall, the smuggler she was about to meet, and looked up when she sensed Pendar's eyes on her.

"Was there something you wished to say?"

Embarrassed at being caught, he squirmed a bit in his seat before admitting, "You don't…you're not what I thought you'd be like."

"You're not what I expected, either," she said.

That distracted him, but not for long.

"Can I ask you a question?"

"I already told you that you could."

"Oh. Well…if you aren't going to destroy Alsea, why are you letting people say you are?"

"How would you propose that I stop them?"

"Can't you just tell them to stop? You're the Lancer."

"Yes, I am, but do you know what a Lancer's job really is?"

He shook his head.

"Two things. One, to plan for Alsea's future, which is why it seems silly to me that people think I want to destroy it. And two, to uphold the laws that the Council makes. We have laws that protect the right to speak freely. So I can't tell people not to spread rumors or lies."

"But…then people get the wrong idea."

"Do people sometimes get the wrong idea about you at school?"

He nodded.

"Does it work for you to just tell them to stop?"

"Um...no, I guess not."

"It wouldn't for me either."

He was quiet for a while, but she found it hard to concentrate on her file when she was so aware of his increasing worry and dread. At last he leaned over and whispered, "When you said our parents knew...did you mean my fathers or my aunt and uncle?"

"Your aunt and uncle."

"Could you...could you ask them not to tell my fathers? They'll get the wrong idea."

"You know I cannot do that." Her voice was gentle, but she could see the words impact.

He nodded miserably and looked back out the window, pulling his feet up onto the seat and resting his chin on his knees.

"When people get the wrong idea about me," she said, "I try to prove they're wrong by my actions. Just telling them doesn't work, but you can do a lot to show them."

Though he didn't respond, his misery lightened slightly.

Tal hadn't expected to feel sympathy for one of the boys who had beaten Jaros. Two of them, actually: Silmartin was just as wretched as Pendar. He was experiencing several levels of fear, and she suspected that some of it was caused by Nilo. And people thought the warrior culture was tough! Adult warriors weren't half as terrifying as school tormentors or the self-imposed fears of childhood.

The rest of the flight was quiet; Pendar had no more questions and Silmartin and Nilo were too afraid to ask any at all. They crossed the broad mountain range north of Blacksun, leaving the rain behind. The northern tip of Argolis was an arid place, deprived of moisture by the mountains that squeezed all the water out of the clouds. The scrubland was lightly populated, mostly by producers working to cultivate specialty crops that thrived in the dry conditions.

By the end of the second hantick they were descending into Koneza, the small town which existed solely due to the Pit, its workforce, and its need for goods and services. Tal could not imagine living in this desolate town, far from the nearest city. It certainly had no scenery to boast of. The location of the Pit had been chosen for its suitable substrate, not its aboveground charm. The area was a flat, windswept plain, with few trees and no physical relief as far as the eye could see. Having grown up in Blacksun, surrounded by mountains on all sides, Tal had a hard time understanding why anyone would choose to live in a place like this. But the Pit paid good wages—it had to, to attract a workforce willing to spend its days underground—and that in turn attracted merchants, builders, and crafters who provided the means of spending those wages.

They landed on a pad far outside the town, in what looked like the middle of nowhere. The only landmark was a ten-story watchtower next to the pad. Its top floor housed six warriors at any given time, four of whom stood at the wraparound windows watching over a quadrant, while the other two maintained sensor sweeps of the surrounding area. With simultaneous visual, heat, and motion detection, any prisoner fortunate enough to escape the Pit stood very little chance of avoiding the eyes in the watchtower, or the squad of warriors serving duty shifts on the ground floor. In Tal's memory, there had been just three escapes from the Pit. None had made it one length beyond the watchtower.

Their little group walked down the transport ramp to find all of the watchtower warriors not on top-floor duty waiting in formation, along with the director of the Pit. Tal reminded herself to not fall into normal habit. This was not the Pit; it was the High Security Detention Facility.

She left Pendar with Micah and walked ahead to meet the director, who touched his fists to his chest and bowed as she approached.

"Colonel Sedron, well met," she said.

"Well met, Lancer Tal. I'm confident you'll find everything in perfect order. If there's anything I can do to facilitate your business here, please say so and it will happen." His gaze strayed to the boys behind her. "Regarding your…guests, I've made the arrangements you asked for."

"Thank you. If I may?" She indicated the formation of warriors.

"Please. They've spent the morning shining and polishing everything in sight. Do be careful or you may be blinded by the sunlight off their jacket buttons."

"Excellent." Tal walked past him and stopped in front of the unit. "Warriors!" she shouted.

"Alsea!" came the roar of thirty voices. "For Fahla and Alsea!" With a rustle, they saluted her in perfect synchrony.

"Settle."

They resumed their normal stance, and she began a slow stroll down each of the three lines of warriors, stopping here and there to check their uniforms. She plucked the disruptor off one man's belt, nodding at the crisp click it made as it came loose. That indicated a well-cared-for attachment and a weapon that would neither break loose under stress nor stick when needed. "Perfect," she said, reattaching it.

At the beginning of the third row, she stopped in front of a tall Lead Guard. "This is not regulation gear," she said, slipping the woman's sword grip off her belt. "Explain this."

"My Lancer, I carry my sword with permission of Colonel Sedron."

"I see. And why do you carry it?"

The warrior met her eyes with confidence. "Because my skill at throwing a blade far outstrips my skill with a disruptor."

"Which is why you were issued throwing knives." Tal indicated the matching short knives sheathed at either side of the warrior's hips. "That does not explain the sword."

"Throwing knives are good for shorter distances. A sword is heavier and goes farther with greater accuracy."

"You're telling me you can throw a sword with greater accuracy than a knife?"

"Not greater accuracy. The same accuracy, but for greater distances."

This she had to see. "What is your name?"

"Vellmar, my Lancer."

"Then, Lead Guard Vellmar, perhaps you would give me a demonstration of this accuracy."

"It would be my pleasure. I'll need the assistance of a fellow Guard."

"I assume such assistance will not result in any unwanted body openings."

A tiny crack appeared in her serious expression. "I promise not to hurt anyone."

Tal looked at the man next to her. "Give her what she needs."

"Yes, my Lancer. The usual?" he asked Vellmar. At her nod, he jogged toward the watchtower.

Tal walked with Vellmar to the front of the unit. With her black hair, dark blue eyes, and confident attitude, the Lead Guard reminded her a lot of Ekatya—except she was much broader in the shoulders and at least a head taller. She might even be Gehrain's height.

She also had a perfect front. If she was nervous about a command performance in front of the Lancer, it didn't show.

Tal raised her eyebrows when the Guard returned from the watchtower with a tin of shannel leaves, slightly larger than one handspan in length. "That's a rather small target."

"I would prefer something different," Vellmar agreed. "But our shannel doesn't come in smaller sizes." She pulled her sword grip from her belt and faced away from the onlookers. "Benron, go."

Benron threw the tin with all his strength. It made a high arc over the empty scrubland beyond the landing pad and had just begun its descent when Tal heard the metallic sound of a sword being extended. Vellmar reared back and threw her sword in a two-handed motion, sending it tumbling end over end on an intercept course toward the falling tin. A cracking sound and an explosion of shannel leaves into the air confirmed the accuracy of her throw, and Tal barely kept her jaw shut.

"Good Fahla, I've never seen the like! That alone was worth the flight out here. I commend you on your skill, and your colonel for recognizing its value."

"Thank you, Lancer Tal." Though Vellmar's front remained impeccable, the proud smile gave her away.

"However," Tal added, "you've wasted a perfectly good tin of shannel, and by the looks of it, this is something you do on a regular basis. I cannot have resources being tossed to the wind in such a fashion. Colonel Sedron?"

The director stepped closer. "Yes, my Lancer."

"Order a case of throwing targets for Lead Guard Vellmar. She may as well use something made for the purpose. And I can guess that your shannel stocks are rather low; we'll need to redress that." Turning to the watching unit, she said more loudly, "I will be sending five cases of high-grade shannel from my personal stocks to replace what you've lost. I expect it will be something of an improvement over what you've been drinking. Congratulations and well done."

The roar of happiness was deafening. Tal knew from experience that nothing improved a long duty shift quite like a good cup of shannel, and nothing was less likely to find its way into an average warrior's hand. The shannel delivered in bulk to most warrior units was high yield and low quality. By earning several moons' worth of good-quality shannel, Vellmar had just made herself the hero of her unit.

Tal turned back to Vellmar. "Where did you learn that?"

"My birth mother was the champion blade thrower of the last three Global Games. She taught me to throw a blade when I was barely old enough to wrap my fingers around the handle."

"Of course." Tal laughed. "*Linzine* Vellmar is your birth mother. Well, you have an honorable name and you're obviously adding to it. Very well done. And well met." She raised her palm, and Vellmar touched it with visible awe.

"Thank you," she said.

"No, thank *you*. That was the highlight of my day. I wish I had time to see a full demonstration, but perhaps I'll see you at the Games next cycle."

She beckoned Micah and Gehrain over, with three very wide-eyed boys in tow. "Let's go. Colonel, if you'll lead the way?"

Colonel Sedron dismissed his unit and led them toward what appeared to be bare ground. As they approached, a set of stone steps came into view, wide enough for four people to walk abreast. They descended into cool dimness, stopping at a large set of double doors some ten paces underground. Colonel Sedron pressed his palm to the reader on the right side and waved his guests in as the doors slid open.

"Welcome to the High Security Detention Facility," he said.

CHAPTER 68
The Pit

Tal monitored the boys' emotions as they stepped through the doors and heard them slide shut. There was a finality about the sound that would make anyone uneasy, and she was expecting that the truth might be necessary soon.

"Colonel Sedron, some of my party have never been here before," she said. "Will you tell us about the facility?"

"Certainly." He led them down a wide corridor toward another large set of doors. "We have five levels here. The first is for facility workers, offices, storage areas, cooking facilities and the like. The next four levels hold our prisoners, who are allocated to a specific level depending on their crime. Non-violent criminals are on Level Two, minimally violent are on Level Three, and violent offenders are on Levels Four and Five."

"So the worse the offense, the deeper underground they go?" Gehrain asked.

"Yes. Most of the violent offenders are powerful empaths. Since their empathic abilities are blocked by earth, the farther they are underground, the less opportunity they have for empathic invasion of others, including other prisoners. Not only are we charged with protecting Alsean society from our prisoners, we must also protect the prisoners from each other. For obvious reasons, all of our warders must be trained high empaths. But in the event that a prisoner overpowers a warder's blocks and influences his or her behavior, the automated security systems will prevent almost any escape."

Colonel Sedron unlocked the next set of doors and waited until the group passed through. Tal felt a shiver run through the boys' minds as the doors closed behind them and they saw yet another set ahead.

The colonel moved past them and resumed his walk. "There are only three entrances to the facility," he continued. "We're in the main one, for workers and prisoners. A second, smaller entrance is for emergencies only, in the event of this one being closed off for any reason. The third is a lift shaft for delivery of supplies and equipment. All three entrances are within a quarter-length radius of the watchtower, and each is monitored by vidcams and automatic heat and motion detecting equipment. You've all been under surveillance from the moment you landed."

They arrived at the third set of doors, which differed from the first two only in having a small control pad next to the biolock. Colonel Sedron put his palm on the lock and entered a code. The doors slid open, revealing a large lift.

"We're going to Level One," he said as he stepped in. "You'll receive wristbands there that will identify you to the auto heat and motion detectors. The wristbands will not come off without a specific removal tool located in our processing office, so don't forget to stop by on your way out." He smiled at the joke, but only half of his audience was paying attention. The boys were staring through the transparent walls of the lift at the rock shaft surrounding them. Noticing their distraction, Colonel Sedron added, "The lifts are transparent to enable the security cams in the shaft to record anyone using them. There are also cams in the lift itself, but in the event they're disabled, the shaft cams are a backup."

As the doors shut and the lift descended, Tal thought that the transparent walls were also an effective psychological tool. Watching the rock shaft slide away was a visceral reminder of where they were going, and she was not surprised to sense the quickly rising terror in both Nilo and Silmartin. It was time to step in.

The lift stopped, opening onto a short corridor with smaller doors at each end. As the group stepped into the hallway, Tal said, "Just a moment, Colonel." She caught Silmartin's eye, then looked at Nilo, who was on the edge of crying again. "That door," she said, pointing to the right, "is where prisoners go when they arrive for processing. This one," she pointed to the left, "is for workers and visitors. You're going through here."

It took several pipticks for the truth to dawn on them. "We're not prisoners?" Silmartin's voice trembled.

"How could you be? You haven't appeared before a tribunal. You haven't even been charged with a crime."

Nilo's tears were now flowing freely. "But...but you said you were taking us here."

"And I did bring you here. But I never said you were prisoners."

"But why...?" Nilo stopped and choked back a sob.

"Why didn't I tell you that?" she asked. He nodded, unable to speak. "Because this isn't an academic field tour. It's a punishment for your appalling behavior. Had it occurred to you to apologize for what you'd done, I would have told you the whole truth. But it never seemed to cross your mind, or yours, Silmartin."

"You should have said you were sorry," Pendar said unexpectedly. "I apologized in the State House. She told me then. I've known all this time that we weren't staying here."

Tal felt Nilo redirecting his fear into anger and rolled her eyes. This boy was not learning. Pulling him directly in front of her, she said, "And now you're going to be angry at Pendar for not telling you? Don't be so stupid." She shook him slightly. "*Learn* something from this. You're not staying here today, but you could be in a few more cycles if you keep going the way you are. You think all the prisoners in here started out as murderers and empathic rapists? No, they started out just like you. Which means you'd better take a good look around today, because you may be coming back if you don't learn to control your anger." She let him go and straightened up. "Colonel Sedron, if you're ready?"

He nodded. "This way."

The door opened into a large room humming with equipment and people. After the sterile isolation of the previous corridors, the sudden noise and activity was a shock. A high counter blocked their entrance to the main room, staffed by two warders in uniform who snapped into a salute. "Welcome, Lancer Tal," said the shorter of the two. "We have your wristbands ready. If you'll each place your right arm on the counter, we'll band you and you can proceed."

Tal nodded and stepped to the counter, scanning both warders out of long habit. If she was going to present her bare wrist to anyone, she wanted to be certain of their intentions. Satisfied, she rested her arm on the counter and watched as the shorter warder snapped a metal wristband around it. He touched it with a small device, causing the band to glow red. Tal felt the heat and then a slight tightness as the band molded itself to her wrist like a second skin. Beside her, Micah was being fitted with his wristband. As soon as they were done, they stepped back to make room for the rest.

When everyone was banded, Colonel Sedron led them along the counter to a door on the right, then into a corridor and another lift. They dropped down one level, passed through two more sets of doors, and found themselves in a long corridor that stretched off into the distance. One wall was solid; the other—which housed the cells—was transparent. The walls between cells were opaque.

"This is the Level Two detention unit," Colonel Sedron said. "It currently houses one hundred and thirty-eight men and women, and is at approximately two-thirds capacity. Each cell holds two prisoners. Level Three also contains two-person cells, but the prisoners on Levels Four and Five are kept in isolation. Come, have a look inside." He gestured toward the cell nearest them.

After some hesitation, Pendar stepped up. "Fahla," he whispered. "It's tiny!"

Silmartin and Nilo crowded around him, peering in as Tal said, "It's not a suite at the local inn. It's a prison cell."

Pendar looked back at the cell, a scandalized guilt coloring his emotions. "So anyone can come along and look at them?"

"Yes," Colonel Sedron said. "Total visual access is required. Most of the criminals in this facility are here precisely because they're empathically abusive. They can't be tracked by empathic senses alone, as in aboveground facilities. The warders check on them every tentick while they're in lockup."

Nilo and Silmartin were shocked as well. "How long are they in lockup?" Silmartin asked.

"Prisoners on Levels Two and Three are normally allowed to intermix between morn-three and eve-two. Those on Levels Four and Five are allowed out for two hanticks per day, on staggered schedules."

"But it's not even mid-four yet," said Pendar. "Why are they locked up now?"

"Because I'm here," Tal said.

Pendar looked back in. "It feels so wrong that anyone can just watch them like this. They don't have any privacy at all. They can't—oh." He turned away abruptly, as did Silmartin and Nilo. All three were radiating embarrassment and guilt.

"What's wrong?" asked Tal, who had a pretty good idea.

Pendar couldn't even say it, but Silmartin mumbled, "One of them is, uh, using the toilet."

"Like we aren't even here," Nilo added. "But they know we're here, right? The walls are transparent both ways?"

"Yes," said Colonel Sedron. "But they're long accustomed to it." The boys looked at each other in horror, which increased as the colonel added, "Privacy is something a prisoner leaves outside. They eat together, live together, and shower together, with warders watching. Using a toilet in front of others is not an issue after a while."

The boys moved away from the cell as if it were poisonous.

"You're done watching, then?" Micah asked.

"We weren't watching!" Nilo said too loudly.

"You were until a few pipticks ago. Aren't you glad you're on this side of the door?"

Tal smothered a smile. "Thank you for taking so much time to explain, Colonel. However, I do need to get to my business."

"Of course." He tapped his earcuff as he led them down the corridor. "Drasseron, meet me at unit two-thirty-eight."

They passed through another set of doors and into a second, identical corridor that was at right angles to the first. Halfway down, a warder was waiting for them by an empty cell.

"This is where we separate," Tal told the boys when they arrived in front of the warder. "I have business here. You'll wait in these two cells." She had initially arranged for them to be kept separate, but such a punishment now seemed too harsh for Pendar and Silmartin.

"What?" Nilo's voice cracked. "I'm not going in one of those!"

"Why can't we wait on Level One?" Pendar asked in shock.

"Because Colonel Sedron doesn't have spare warders to watch over you for the next half hantick, and you can't wait alone."

"What about Colonel Micah?" Nilo was desperate now. "He could watch us."

Micah crossed his arms over his chest and looked thunderous. "That is not my duty."

"Since the cells accommodate just two people, we'll have to split you up," Tal said. "Pendar, Silmartin, you're in this one."

The warder put his palm to the lock, sliding the door open. Both of the boys looked at her in disbelief.

"That was not a request," she said.

"You'll come back, right?" Pendar asked.

Tal nodded. "Yes. Now go."

He gave her one last unhappy look before dropping his head and walking in, followed by Silmartin. The warder locked the door, then moved to the next cell and opened it.

Nilo took a step back. "I don't want to! You can't put me in there alone!"

Micah had lost all patience. "Remember, boy, the violent offenders are confined alone. And that's exactly what you are, violent. A coward who thinks hurting others makes you big. You could very well end up here, so consider this a practice run. Now get in and see how big you feel."

Tal made a motion to the warder, who took Nilo by the arm and marched him sobbing and squealing to the cell. With the door safely shut, she relaxed. "Fahla, he's a trial."

"Yes, and you gave him to *me*," Micah said. "Thanks so much."

"I didn't give him to you; you took him. Don't blame me."

"Or me," said Gehrain. "I gave you first choice."

Micah grumbled as Tal turned to the colonel. "Is Donvall ready?"

"He's been in a saferoom since your arrival."

"Then let's see what our informant has to say."

CHAPTER 69
Smuggler's revenge

Though Micah had wholeheartedly agreed with Tal's idea for disciplining those boys—and had quite enjoyed playing his part in it—he was impatient to get to the real point of their trip.

The man waiting for them looked slightly more pleasant than his file image and a great deal more pleasant than the last time Micah had seen him. He well remembered the crooked nose and flat features, and thought with some satisfaction that Tal had probably made that nose a little more crooked herself.

"You're Lancer Tal?" he asked incredulously as they walked in the small room.

She drew out the single empty chair on the other side of the small table—the only furniture in the room—and sat down. "Yes, I am."

"Funny, I thought you were taller. Hey, wait a tick." Donvall looked more closely at her, then sat back with a broad grin. "You were there! Different hair, different eyes, but I'd never forget that little slip who threw me into the air. You've got a punch like a dokker's kick. I never saw it coming."

"That was the point," she said dryly.

Micah hid a smile at the "little slip" reference. If Tal hadn't already decked him once, she'd have wanted to after that.

Donvall sobered. "It never occurred to me that the Lancer herself would grace us with her presence. We weren't important enough."

"You were recruiting high empaths. That made you important enough."

"I knew it! Spawn of a fantenshekken!" He looked up at Micah and Gehrain, who were flanking the door. "Get rid of them. I'm not talking to anyone but you."

"They're my personal guards," Tal said without taking her eyes off him. "I trust them with my life. If that isn't good enough for you, then this interview is already over."

He glared at her, then at Micah, and finally sat back in his chair. "Fine. Let's just get the ground rules established. I tell you what I know, and you transfer me out of this Fahla-forsaken place, agreed?"

"If your information leads us somewhere, yes. If it's a waste of my time, then you'll learn there are worse places than Level Three."

He raised his hands. "No need for threats. I know what's down there, and I have no intention of getting a personal look. My information is real."

"If that's true, I'll authorize your transfer. If someone is betraying the trust of their office, I want them." Tal's back went stiff. "You must be joking. You're trying to probe *me*? How badly do you want out of here?"

Now Micah wanted to deck him. He shifted his weight, drawing Donvall's eye, and sent him a death glare.

Donvall quickly looked back at Tal. "Just checking to see if you're telling the truth."

"And what did you find?"

"Nothing. You're like one of the walls in here."

"Then you'll have to take me at my word. Unlike most of your acquaintances, my word means something to me."

He gazed at her in silence, then rested his arms on the table and leaned forward. "All right. Here's the truth. You didn't get everyone in your raid."

"I was expecting you to tell me something I didn't know."

"Yes, but the one person you didn't get was my newest member. Don't you find it interesting that you got every high-level person but one? Why did he escape the net?"

When Tal didn't answer, he added, "Would you also find it interesting that this individual is the same one who came up with the bright idea of recruiting high empaths?"

Now she leaned forward as well. "Yes, I would find that very interesting."

He grinned. "I thought you might. His name is Telmurine Hallwell. He was recommended by my associate in the Anti-Corruption Task Force."

"So you have someone inside the task force."

"Of course. The moment it was created, I made it my business to buy someone inside it."

Micah's anger rose. Donvall spoke as if finding someone corrupt inside that task force was the easiest thing in the world. Sadly, it probably was.

"Who is it?" Tal asked.

"A merchant by the name of Falton Mor. Highly placed, very powerful. He made sure my name never came up in any investigations. So when he recommended Hallwell, I trusted him. And Hallwell had some good ideas. He helped us increase our profits. I wasn't excited about his idea of recruiting high empaths, but he talked us into it. Very persuasive man, Hallwell. And he was right; they cleared our way through a lot of otherwise expensive hurdles. Our profits went up again."

"But those same high empaths brought you to the attention of the task force, without Mor having to give them your name."

"That's what I think. I've been thinking a lot down here. And I think I was set up, very neatly. Hallwell came in, learned the operation, and then tipped off the task force. How did you know we were meeting in the warehouse then?"

"Anonymous tip," Tal said.

"See, I shekking knew it. That was Hallwell. He was supposed to be at that meeting. I should have known something was wrong when he didn't show up. He got you to pick up every one of my trusted people, and now he's back in Whitemoon running *my* business."

"How do you know he's in Whitemoon?"

He looked at her as if she had just admitted to flunking out of fifth-level school. "I may be underground, but I still know what's going on. That fantenshekken betrayed me. If it wasn't for him, we wouldn't have been caught, and even if we had been caught, we wouldn't have ended up here. I want him in the Pit and me out of it."

His voice had gotten much louder at the end, and he visibly calmed himself before continuing in a lower tone. "Hallwell had powerful friends. He liked to drink his profits, and when he drank, he liked to brag, and when he bragged, he always said the same thing. He said it wasn't what you knew, but who you knew, and he knew the top people. He said even Mor bowed down to his friends, because they were the ones who made the rules and enforced them."

"Meaning they're on the Council," Tal said.

He nodded. "That's what I think. That's why I didn't want to talk to anyone but you. If they enforce the rules, that means they're warrior caste. The only people I can talk to here are warrior caste. They'd pass my information up the ranks until it reached one of Hallwell's friends, at which point the information would vanish, along with me. So for me, the only safe warrior is you. Unless you're one of Hallwell's friends, in which case I'm shekked."

While Micah didn't have Tal's ability to empathically determine the man's honesty, he didn't think it was necessary. Donvall was driven by rage and fixated on his revenge.

"Is there anything else I should know?" Tal asked.

"Just that you might want to take a second look at what your task force has been doing." He gave her an unpleasant smile. "Hallwell may have powerful friends, but they didn't set him up in my business just so he could take all the profits. They're investors. I'd be curious to know what else they're investing in."

"So would I. Anything else?"

"No. If I knew any more names, I'd give them to you. I want these people taken down."

She nodded. "Well, this might be the only occasion when you and honorable warriors are on the same side. I'll do my best to take them down, Donvall. You'll know I succeeded when you get your transfer."

"Then I wish you every good fortune," he said.

CHAPTER 70
Small victories

Tal stalked through the corridors with Micah, Gehrain, and Colonel Sedron keeping a respectful distance. She had held her reaction in check until she was out of the saferoom and was now so furious that she could hardly see straight. That someone would pervert the Anti-Corruption Task Force into a vehicle for more efficient law breaking was a betrayal she took personally. The task force was supposed to prevent this kind of dokshin, not promote it! This was a slap in the face not only to her and every honorable warrior and merchant working on that task force, but also to the four Redmoon warriors whose deaths had inspired its creation. Someone was pissing on their memories.

They arrived at the cells where they had left the boys and waited for the warder. Tal was too angry to speak and impatient at the thought of dealing with these children any further. She had much bigger game to hunt.

"Why aren't you authorized to unlock the cells?" Gehrain asked Colonel Sedron, filling in the uncomfortable silence.

"Because I'm the director, which makes me the most obvious target for a hostage crisis. But if I can't unlock any cells or the exit doors between levels, then taking me hostage won't get a prisoner anywhere. I can get in alone, but I can't get out."

"Unless they demand a trade," Micah said.

"That won't help either. The facility has a no-negotiation policy. I have no value as a hostage, and they know that."

"What about the warders?"

"They have clearance for only one level. And the lift doors below Level One can only be unlocked by two palms simultaneously."

The warder came through a door down the hall and quickly joined them, unlocking the cell for Pendar and Silmartin first. The boys stepped out, their moods quiet and subdued. A white-faced Nilo emerged a few pipticks later, walking directly to Tal and looking up at her.

"I'm sorry," he said. "For everything I've done. This place is horrible. No one should have to live in a cell like that! I promise I'll be better. Just…please take me home."

Tal stared at him, trying to work past her anger and remember that this was an important moment in its own small way. She had set up their temporary incarceration hoping for just this response. But the best she could manage was a curt nod and a brusque, "That's good enough. We're leaving now."

The warder accompanied them to the lift doors and palmed the lock on the left while Colonel Sedron palmed the right. They trooped inside and crowded together far too closely for Tal's liking. All she wanted was to get back in the transport and away from everyone else. Fortunately, the boys were subdued as the group returned to the main administrative room, had their wristbands removed, and retraced their steps to the surface.

Their silence ended when the final set of doors opened. As soon as Nilo saw the sky, he whooped and scrambled up the steps, followed closely by Pendar and Silmartin. All three of them bounced off the final step as if they had just been reprieved from a lifetime sentence. Tal and the others climbed the stairs more sedately, but as the first cool breeze brushed Tal's face, carrying the peppery scent of desert tinbrush, she understood how the boys felt. Nothing made one appreciate sunlight and fresh air quite like being without.

Colonel Sedron stopped near the transport and gave Tal a salute. "It has been an honor to have you at our facility. If there's anything else I can do, please notify me."

"I will, thank you. And I appreciate the time you've taken today, Colonel. Rest assured it was worthwhile."

When she boarded the transport, Thornlan was waiting. The pilot saw her mood in an instant and said, "If you'd like to have a seat in your private cabin, I'll help harness the boys."

Gratefully, Tal retreated to her much-needed solitude. A few ticks later Thornlan notified her by com that they were ready for liftoff, and she watched the dry scrubland of Koneza fall away beneath them.

For half the flight home she stared out the window, seeing very little as her brain churned. Telmurine Hallwell and Falton Mor would be easy to pick up, and she would take great pleasure in breaking the Whitemoon smuggling ring a second and hopefully final time. But they weren't the big game, and she was driving herself insane trying to guess who was. Which warrior on the Council was betraying every ideal of the Truth and the Path? Was it only one, or were there more? Did Prime Warrior Shantu have any clue? She pondered that thought for a while before deciding that he could not. For all his flaws, and he had quite a few, Shantu would never condone or tolerate such a violation of everything their caste stood for. He was a proud warrior, and whoever was doing this had far more greed than pride. But by the same token, she couldn't bring him in on her investigation. Shantu didn't have the finesse required to do this quietly; he would be more likely to go on a rampage after getting impatient with the pace of their progress. No, she needed someone who understood the value of restraint and dealmaking, someone willing to let the small prey lead her to the big predators. And that would be Colonel Razine. As head of the Alsean Investigative Force, she had the necessary resources at her fingertips, the ability to make discreet inquiries, and Tal's trust. She had known Razine since they were in the same training unit.

After going around in mental circles one too many times, she finally stood up for a good stretch and decided she could be social again.

Micah and Gehrain looked up when she walked into the main cabin, their expressions cautious.

She gave them a quick smile as she took her former seat across from Pendar. "Had a few things to think about."

Micah nodded. "We've been doing some thinking here as well. The boys have something to tell you."

"Do they?" Tal looked from one to the other, waiting for a spokesperson.

Surprisingly, it was Nilo who spoke up. "Colonel Micah was telling us what you could have done instead of bringing us to the Pit."

Tal raised her eyebrows at Micah. There was no telling what sort of tales he had spun; the boys were probably glad they'd escaped summary execution.

"You were much nicer to us than you had to be," Nilo continued. "And we realized that everyone in Granelle is just saying what they *think* about you, but we're the ones who actually *know* you. So we're going to tell everyone the truth. Maybe that will make people stop telling lies about you."

Tal hid a smile, enjoying the irony. Of course Nilo would find a way to transform his fear into self-importance because he knew the Lancer and almost no one else in Granelle did.

"And what is the truth?" she asked.

"That they're wrong, and you're not going to destroy Alsea, and they should trust you," said Pendar.

"And they shouldn't talk if they don't know what they're talking about," Silmartin added.

Nilo and Pendar nodded in agreement, and this time Tal didn't fight her smile. "Thank you," she said. "I appreciate your support, and I think it might really help."

They were full of pride and a sense of purpose, and it occurred to her that she shouldn't discount these small victories. The governance of Alsea did not take the form of one momentous event or decision after another. Changing the minds of three young boys might well turn out to be as important as anything else she had ever done—who could know?

She settled into her seat and looked out the window. They were just beginning to cross the mountains, and a deep sense of contentment warmed her as the familiar scenery unfolded beneath them. Within a few ticks they were in the high mountains, where long habit had her scanning the steep slopes from one side to the other. She didn't expect to see anything—certainly not this soon or this easily—but there they were, a large herd climbing up a nearly sheer wall. Perhaps it was a sign.

Or perhaps it was simply another small victory.

"Tell me," she said, still looking out the window, "have any of you ever seen a winden?"

CHAPTER 71
Coming home

"How did it go?" Salomen asked.

Tal had returned to Hol-Opah alone, leaving the task of dropping off the boys to Micah and Gehrain. Rank had its privileges. She was now basking in the pleasure of being greeted by the one person she had most wanted to see all day, and it was all she could do not to pull Salomen into a warmron, right there in view of every back window of the main house and at least two Guards. She was also grateful that the steady drizzle was keeping the rest of the family inside. It was well past evenmeal, a time when anyone who had put in a long day at harvest would be relaxing in a comfortable chair. Only Salomen was fool enough to be standing out in the rain.

"Better than I expected, and worse," she said, gratefully absorbing Salomen's affection through their palm touch. Neither of them would drop their fronts so close to the Guards, but the physical connection was all they needed. "Where's Jaros? I thought for sure he'd be out here, rain or no."

"We put him to bed early. He was a little overtired with all the excitement. And that was another politician's answer."

"But a true one."

"It may be, but I'll expect a longer version later." Salomen locked their hands together and led her toward the house. "You'll have plenty of opportunity to tell me about it on our date."

Tal stopped walking, pulling Salomen to a halt as well. "Our date? Did I know about this?"

"Yes, we arranged it the night before last, when you called me from Whitemoon. Don't you remember?"

Alarmed, Tal searched her memory but could not recall anything of the sort. Nor did she want to admit it until she saw the look in Salomen's eyes. Narrowing her own, she focused on the emotions transmitting through their touch and found a well-buried amusement. "Enjoyed that, did you?"

Salomen broke into a wide smile. "I couldn't resist. You're very endearing when you're worried about disappointing me."

"Nothing of the sort. I was worried about appearing fallible."

"Oh, of course. Come on, let's get you inside. I'd like you to change into something a bit drier and join me in the entry."

"Salomen..." Tal found herself being pulled toward the house again. "I appreciate your intentions, but I'd really rather not go back out the moment I arrive home. Do you think we could do this a different night?"

Now it was Salomen who stopped, astonishment coloring her emotions. "What did you say?"

Puzzled, Tal repeated, "I said I'd rather not go out right away."

"Not that part. You said 'the moment you arrived home.' Is that what you think of Hol-Opah?"

"I, ah..." Tal wasn't sure what to say, but was saved from further speech when Salomen pulled her close and took her mouth in a kiss that was as unexpected as it was passionate. For one brief moment, Tal worried about advertising their relationship so soon and so blatantly, but after that her brain gave up any effort at coherent thought. She returned the kiss with a passion that was always just below the surface whenever she was around Salomen, and only the warning tingle brought her to her senses.

But not in time. This flash was worse than all the others, propelling them half a body length apart.

Tal let out a sound that was half pain and half frustration as she bent over with her hands on her knees, waiting for her head to clear. Next to her, Salomen was gasping.

"Lancer Tal!" called one of the Guards.

Tal lifted her head. Her vision still wasn't fully clear, but it was enough to see Senshalon running toward them. She held up a hand. "It's all right," she called. "We're fine."

He halted, his posture indicating uncertainty, but she stood up and waved him off. Then her stomach dropped when she realized that Salomen's harsh breaths were actually sobs.

"Salomen—" She stopped.

"I'm sorry," Salomen said between gasps of laughter. "Fahla, that one hurt. But it was worth it." She laughed again, and Tal shook her head.

"You're a masochist," she said. "Not only that, you're a sadist. It's fine if you want to suffer, but you inflict these on me as well."

"I know." Salomen was still chuckling as she straightened up and reached for Tal's hand. "I really am sorry. But you have no idea what it means to me to hear you call Hol-Opah home."

Tal looked askance at the hand being held out to her. "I'm not sure I want to touch that right now. And I can't sense anything anyway; it's taking me longer to recover from these."

"Then I'll just tell you. It feels wonderful, like this is precisely how it's supposed to be."

With a show of great care, Tal took her hand. "I'm glad you're not offended. It's rather presumptuous of me."

"You tend to be a rather presumptuous person." Salomen squeezed her hand. "In this instance, I'm delighted."

They resumed their walk toward the house. "I feel a peace here that I don't get in Blacksun," Tal confessed. "I love the quiet of the landscape and the fact that there aren't a few hundred people vying for my attention. And Hol-Opah is so untouched—it's almost as if the last cycle never happened here. Ever since the *Caphenon* landed, I've thought of nothing but the Protectorate and the Voloth and all of the issues they brought, but when I'm here, it's like…"

"Like what?" Salomen asked as they walked up the back steps.

"Well…like sanctuary."

Under the shelter of the porch roof, Salomen stopped to look at her. "And why were you so nervous about saying that? I'm glad you feel that way."

"Because it's not your sanctuary, is it? You work just as hard here as I do in Blacksun."

"Why, Lancer Tal, I never thought to hear those words. Have you conceded defeat in our challenge?"

"Never. You still have no idea what I do in my magical dome. Don't think you're getting out of your part of the challenge, Delegate Opah."

They smiled at each other as the rain pounded on the roof, and Tal wondered for the first time whether sanctuary was Hol-Opah or Salomen.

Both, she decided.

Salomen reached out for her other hand. "Will you please reconsider coming with me on a date? I promise you won't have to go far. And I'm certain you'll enjoy it."

Tal took a deep breath. "Can you give me half a hantick to just…relax, before we leave?"

"Of course."

"Then yes, I'll go. Besides, it's been a long time since I've been asked out."

"That's what I was thinking. You made our first date wonderful for me. I'd like to make this one wonderful for you. It's only fair."

Who could resist that?

"Then I'll meet you at the front entry in half a hantick. Should I wear anything special?"

"Just be comfortable. And don't worry about staying dry; we're not going far." Salomen looked her up and down. "Well…it would be all right if you wore something that showed a little more skin."

"I'll see what I can do. Guess that leaves out the uniform, then."

"It does," Salomen agreed. "No uniform. Definitely not."

CHAPTER 72
The strand vibrates

Like the creature he had named himself after, Spinner felt the vibration along one of the strands of his web. He read the dispatch from his contact in Koneza with a rising sense of excitement.

Lancer Tal had been to the Pit today. She had spoken with Donvall, and now she knew her precious Anti-Corruption Task Force wasn't as pristine as she envisioned. Knowing her, she was breathing fire. He had no doubt that she would hunt that trail until it led all the way to him.

Which was exactly what he wanted.

His prey had touched the web. She hadn't fallen into it yet, but she was close.

Smiling, he set his reader card down and leaned back in his chair. "Come on, Lancer Tal," he whispered. "Do what you do best."

CHAPTER 73
Second date

A SHOWER AND FRESH CLOTHES did wonders for Tal's state of mind, along with two tenticks of relaxing with the book she had started five days ago. She had thought about bringing it on her tour, but reasoned there would be little time to read anything fun. Besides, she didn't want to read this book in a transport or inn. It needed to be savored in the window seat of a room she had come to consider hers, and right now, with the rain streaming down the windows, she felt cozier than she had in a very long time.

With great reluctance she put a marker in the pages and set the book down. Time to go downstairs for her date. She really didn't want to go anywhere, but Salomen had clearly planned something special, and Tal would sooner face an all-day bickering Council session than let her down.

As promised, Salomen was waiting for her at the bottom of the stairs in the front entry. Tal stopped on the last step, bringing their heads level. "Very nice," she said admiringly. "You look wonderful."

"Thank you." Salomen did a slow twirl, showing off the back view. Her thick, dark hair was up in a loose twist, exposing the high neck of her sleeveless shirt. Loose trousers and sandals completed the outfit, giving her an effortlessly classy appearance. "With the rains here, it's only a matter of another nineday or two before it becomes too cool to wear this. I wanted to take advantage of the moment."

"And show a little skin. I'm afraid I didn't share quite as much."

Salomen looked her up and down, her light expression vanishing under something far warmer. Her gaze settled on the front of Tal's half-sleeved dress shirt, where a nearly indecent number of buttons had been left undone. "In terms of quantity, no," she said in a low voice that made Tal's neck prickle. "But the quality is surely there."

Tal had to clear her throat before she could speak. "Where are you taking me?"

Salomen smiled, holding out her hand. "Just around the corner." She led Tal down the last step and into the parlor, where Micah, Shikal, and Nikin were holding court around a bottle of spirits.

"This had better not be our date," Tal said just as Micah let out a low whistle.

"Blessed Fahla, what a sight. Going somewhere, Lancer Tal?"

"I have no idea, and if I did, I wouldn't tell you. I didn't think you'd be here so soon."

"Pendar's aunt was visiting Silmartin's mother, so we were able to drop two off at the same time. Thank the Goddess, too, otherwise I would have missed this view."

"And he was just starting the story of how our Lancer frightened three bullies halfway to their Return," Shikal said. "So you two run along now. You're interrupting."

The three men chuckled. "Don't keep her out too late, Salomen," said Nikin. "We need her tomorrow, and she can't pilot a transport with her eyes half shut."

Salomen rolled her eyes at Tal. "My apologies. If I'd known we would run into the comedy club, I'd have had you meet me at the back stairs. My mistake was in thinking that any of these men were mature adults."

She pulled Tal through the room, accompanied by a few more whistles and offers of unsolicited advice. Once in the relative peace of the dining room she turned and pointedly banged the door shut, muffling the sounds of laughter in the next room. "Well, that was a strategic error," she said. "It gets better from here, I promise."

"I hope so. You've already given Micah enough to keep him going for the next three days."

"I'm sorry. I just wanted the walk to our date to involve more than six steps." She led Tal across the dining room and into the kitchen dome, stopping by the small table normally used as a staging area for the main meals. Tonight it had been transformed into an intimate setting for two, the handmade table cover adorned with crockery that Tal had never seen before. She guessed by its design that it had probably been in the family for several generations. Off to the side stood a miniature tiered bowl rack, holding three small bowls of brightly burning oil. At the top of the rack, a fourth bowl contained a hyacot twig.

"It's perfect," she said in relief. "You have no idea how perfect this is. Thank you."

Salomen pulled her close. "Of course I have an idea. I guessed you wouldn't want to go out after the day you've had, and the state you were in when you arrived just confirmed it. I want you to relax tonight. This is just you and me."

Her smile was just enough to bring out the lines at the sides of her mouth. Tal reached up and ran her fingertip over each one, basking in the beauty they lent to Salomen's face. "You are such a lovely woman," she whispered. "Inside and out."

"So are you."

They shared a brief, soft kiss before Salomen waved Tal to her chair. "I'd like to say I made this meal myself," she said more briskly, "but that was impossible. But I did leave very specific instructions with Wynsill regarding what I wanted done. She did it to perfection. Can I keep her after you go back to Blacksun?"

"Not a chance. Wynsill is in great demand with my Guards. For good reason, as you've noticed."

"Damn. Maybe I can make her a better offer."

"Don't even think of stealing my staff, producer."

Salomen grinned. "You're feeling more relaxed, then. Threats already, and we haven't even started the meal."

"That wasn't a threat. That was merely advice."

"Ah. In that case, perhaps you'd like to start the first course and see if you still feel like giving advice afterward."

"I'm ready."

"Good." Salomen walked over to the wooden rack across the kitchen and came back with a large bowl, which she carefully set on the table. "Your bowl, please?"

Tal handed over her soup bowl and watched avidly as Salomen lifted the lid. "Ohhhh," she said as the scent hit her nostrils. "Horten soup!"

"Of course." Salomen ladled a sinfully large amount into Tal's bowl, adding the same amount to her own before covering the serving bowl again. "It's harvest time. Not having horten soup now would be a crime. It doesn't get any fresher than this." She plucked the hyacot twig from its holder, snapped it in half and replaced the pieces. "There. We're now officially on a date."

"And a perfect one, too." Tal dug into her soup without waiting. At the first taste, her eyes nearly rolled back in her head. "Oh, dear Goddess above. This is… indescribably wonderful. It's never tasted like this before."

"You've never had horten less than ten hanticks from harvest before. It makes a big difference."

"Yes, it does." Tal happily consumed half the bowl at a speed considerably higher than polite manners allowed, then forced herself to slow down. "I hope you didn't plan on conversation tonight. My mouth is doing other things."

The look Salomen gave her made Tal drop her spoon. With her blocks down, Salomen's instant desire was singeing her senses.

"I, ah…"

"Just eat," Salomen said. "And don't say anything more about your mouth, please."

"Deal." Tal didn't want to go there, either. That way lay frustration and impotent arousal, and she was having a hard enough time as it was. Salomen looked edible in that shirt. It was cut deeply inward at the shoulders, exposing just the edges of her chest ridges. This was twice now that she had tormented her with bare shoulders, and Tal was beginning to wonder if she really had felt that little fantasy of a few days ago.

"Perhaps now you can explain that short answer about your trip," Salomen said. "What happened with those boys and your meeting with the prisoner?"

Tal shook her head. "I'd rather hear about your day first."

"There's not much to tell. I spent my day running back and forth like a fanten on slaughter day and with considerably less purpose."

Chuckling, Tal said, "I don't accept the part about no purpose. From what I could see, you were keeping control of a very complex operation."

"Well..." Salomen thoughtfully sipped her soup. "There certainly are a lot of details to keep track of and a lot of people needing instruction and answers. Usually simultaneously."

"I noticed." It occurred to Tal that Salomen was a Lancer in her own right, simply governing a smaller world. "And speaking as one with similar duties, you're very good at yours."

Salomen's pleasure at the compliment warmed her senses, and the rest of the course was spent discussing the harvest. Tal was interested to hear that Herot had worked just as hard as everyone else, a noticeable change in his behavior which Salomen attributed to the fact that he preferred transport duty to the more manual labor of cutting or loading. Tal wondered if something else might be factoring into it.

The soup in her bowl was gone all too soon, and she was gazing sadly at its empty depths when Salomen asked, "Ready for the next course?"

"If it's as good as this one, I'm more than ready."

"It will be. Give me your bowl."

Tal handed it across the table, expecting Salomen to carry it to the dish rack. She burst into laughter when it was promptly refilled from the serving bowl instead. "Was I that transparent?"

"Andira, a sonsales could have seen your longing. It's a good thing I had no other courses planned; I couldn't have broken your heart by taking this bowl away. There is one other part to this meal, though." She rose from the table, returning in a moment with a fresh loaf of bread. A wisp of steam plumed upward as she cut off the end. "Everything on this table comes from Hol-Opah," she said, offering a soft slice. "Well, except for the oil."

"It's wonderful." Tal savored her bread, which was warm and fluffy and tasted divine. "All of it. You most of all. Thank you for this."

"You're welcome. Thank you for coming on a date with me, even though you were so tired you didn't want to."

"I didn't want to go out," Tal corrected. "I can't imagine being too tired to want to be with you."

Salomen flashed one of those smiles that warmed her right down to her toes. "All right, we've discussed my day. Now it's your turn."

It took the rest of that bowl, a second serving of bread, and a cup of shannel for Tal to recount the story of her afternoon. By the end she was feeling relaxed and utterly content; even her anger over the perversion of the task force had become something of a distant memory. She knew it would come back as soon as she had to deal with it directly, but right now, with Salomen looking so beautiful and listening with such close attention, the warmth in her stomach had spread to her head and she couldn't feel anything but happy.

"It sounds as though you've converted a few more to your camp," Salomen said. "And it worked both ways."

"Meaning they converted me as well?" Tal drained the last of her shannel and replaced the cup in its saucer. "Pendar certainly did. Silmartin…a little. And Nilo is a thoroughly disagreeable little dokker, but he definitely learned something and who knows, perhaps he'll really stay out of trouble. But I wouldn't bet the holding on it."

"Neither would I. Still, stranger things have happened. And you do seem to have that effect on people."

"You mean you're staying out of trouble, too?"

"Hardly." Salomen reached for Tal's hand, focusing on it as a darker emotion wound through her earlier contentment.

Tal lowered her head, trying to catch her gaze. "What's wrong?"

"I'm trying to forget that we have only eight days left, but it's not working. I'm already missing you in advance."

"You don't have to miss me, and I certainly don't plan to miss you. You still have your part of the challenge to uphold."

"I know, but what happens after that?"

"Who knows? Look at how much has changed between us in just one moon. What will a second moon do? I don't know about you, but I don't think we should try to plan that far ahead. We'll have options. And when it comes to my job, I make the rules anyway."

"Within bounds of tradition and requirements of logistics and security. Andira, I can't live in Blacksun. You know that. And you can't live here, much as I want you to."

"It's not an either-or situation. We can work out something in between. I already divide my time between my base quarters and those in the State House; it's not that hard to live in two places. Three is just one more."

"For you. It's two more for me."

Tal rose from her chair and walked to Salomen's side of the table without releasing her hand. Pulling her up gently, she grasped her other hand and said, "I know you're a strategic thinker and you prefer to plan ahead. I do the same thing. But in this case, I really think we'll drive ourselves crazy trying to plan something like this. It will work out. Let's just see what the next moon brings and then revisit this, all right?"

"I'll try. I'm not very good at putting off decisions."

"You say that as if it's a bad thing. Most of the time, it's an excellent character trait." Tal leaned in and kissed her lightly on the cheekbone ridge, then nibbled her way down to her jaw. "Just not right now," she whispered.

"Fahla," Salomen breathed. "Don't do that, or I can't be held responsible for inflicting another flash on you."

Tal pulled back reluctantly. "This, on the other hand, is a decision I'm getting closer to every day."

"So am I." Salomen's gaze was heated. "I want this badly enough to start losing my fear of the consequences."

"I'm beginning to forget I ever had fears."

They stared into each other's eyes until Salomen swallowed and took a deliberate step back. "We need to cool down. And you have to stop looking at me that way. Fahla knows I want our joining, and I want our Sharing, but I'm not quite ready to permanently give up my privacy just to satisfy this need."

Tal dropped her head, breaking their gaze. "I know. When I think that it's been less than a nineday since I talked to Lanaril and found out what all this meant…"

"Seven days," said Salomen. "Seven days since I kissed you in the field and thought that perhaps, in time, I could adapt to the idea of you as my tyree. And a few hanticks later I found out that being tyree with you was the smallest of my concerns."

Once again Tal was reminded that the price Salomen would pay was twice as high as her own. The guilt rose so quickly that she couldn't front it.

"Andira." Salomen's voice was soft. "Stop that, whatever you're thinking. It's not your fault."

"Actually, it is. I'm the one who had the bright idea of giving you a warmron."

"And I'm the one who asked you for a second one five ticks later. Besides, at the rate we've been going, don't you think we'd have joined by now if we had a normal relationship? And that would have set it all off anyway." In a lighter tone she added, "Given how far I've come in just seven days, I'll probably be ready to have our bonding ceremony by the time we go to Blacksun."

"Oh, no." Tal played along. "Impossible. The Lancer of Alsea does not plan a bonding ceremony in eight days. Do you have any idea how many people we'll have to invite?"

"You mean we can't flit down to some nice little village by the sea and have a quiet ceremony? And then announce it after the fact?"

"Absolutely not. No flitting down to the shore for us. However, I can offer you a ceremony that none on the planet would soon forget."

"Well…" Salomen pretended to think. "I suppose that might suffice as a substitute. As long as I can rub Gordense Bilsner's nose in it, and ask him what he thinks about my good name now."

Tal laughed. "I would never have guessed you'd have such a vindictive streak."

"It only shows itself in the presence of truly obnoxious personalities."

"That must be why I've never seen it before." Tal chuckled again at Salomen's expression. "I propose we drop Bilsner from this conversation. I have better things to think about than a bloated gasbag convinced of his righteousness. Did you have anything else planned for our date?"

"No. Actually, I was looking forward to a training session afterward, if you're not too tired."

Tal widened her eyes. "You imply that the leader of the warrior caste could be too tired to fulfill her duties? I think not."

"I didn't realize it was still a duty." Salomen put her hand over her heart. "I'm wounded."

"It never was. Not from that very first night." Tal looked at the remains of their meal. "Speaking of which, are we on kitchen duty?"

"No. Wynsill said she would come back after eve-three and clean up for us. She said we should just relax and enjoy our evening."

"Remind me to give her an increase in pay. Shall we retire to the classroom, then? We can work on your finesse in broadsensing. With those three comedians in the parlor, it should be easier for you to focus on individuals."

"I never have a problem focusing on Father or Nikin," Salomen said as they crossed the dining room and started up the back stairs. "Colonel Micah I can pick out by process of elimination. Can we work on longer-range broadsensing?"

"Meaning outside the house?" Tal led them along the upstairs corridor.

"Yes. I'd like to try something different."

They reached Tal's room, where Salomen took her usual chair and Tal settled contentedly into the window seat. "In other words, you've had enough of practicing the same thing over and over."

"In other words, I had a long day of doing everything that needed to be done, and now I'd like to do something just because I want to."

"Fair enough. This will be a little different, then. Are you ready?"

"I'm ready." Salomen closed her eyes, and Tal shamelessly took the opportunity to study her from head to foot. Fahla, but she was beautiful.

One of Salomen's eyes popped open. "I said I'm ready." The eye shut again. "Clearly, you are not."

"Just finding my place of serenity."

"Your place of serenity is my body?"

"I don't know yet. But I'm looking forward to finding out."

Salomen laughed. "You're making it very difficult for me to stay in *my* place, Andira."

"Sorry." Tal centered herself, pushing all other thoughts away. In a lower voice, she said, "Start with the minds you know. Reach out for Shikal and Nikin."

"I have them," Salomen said a few pipticks later. Truly, her skills were developing at a remarkable rate.

"Good. So you know which emotions are Micah's."

"Yes."

"All of them? Have you accounted for all of the emotions in that room?"

After a long pause, Salomen said, "I'm not sure. There are some that don't belong to Father or Nikin, but I don't know if they're Colonel Micah's. They're… quieter."

"As if they're in the background."

"Yes."

Tal wasn't surprised; Salomen had already demonstrated that her powers were very strong. Exactly how strong was something they were learning together. She opened her own senses, reaching out for the minds within her range, and quickly located what Salomen was sensing: the more distant emotions of three Guards near the house. There were two more patrolling the near grounds, but she wasn't sure if Salomen could detect them. Time to find out.

"Think of those background emotions as having strings attached," she said. "If you find one and pull on the string, it will lead you to the source. Don't force it. Just use a gentle motion. Let the strings lead you."

"All right. I'm trying."

Tal waited, tracking Salomen's emotions along with those outside the house. A surge of confidence told her precisely when Salomen had found something.

"Tell me what you're sensing."

Slowly, with some hesitation, Salomen began putting words to what she could feel. Tal watched her, guiding her verbally and wishing with all her might that she might guide her more directly. Someday soon, when it felt right to both of them, they would Share and she would be demonstrating from within Salomen's mind, rather than explaining from without. Until then, she would savor every moment of this.

CHAPTER 74
To find a traitor

The rain stopped sometime in the night, taking a hiatus that everyone knew was all too temporary. Once autumn arrived, the rains were there to stay. Any break would be no more than a few hanticks, or a day at most. Tal was just grateful for the opportunity to run without having to wear a rainhat. She hated having anything blocking her view while she was exercising.

Herot followed them again. As always, Tal tracked him as she ran, keeping tabs on his progress. This time he made it four lengths before stopping—more than double his first effort—and she was impressed. She wished she could tell him that but was fairly certain he would throw her words back in her face. No doubt he would find them patronizing and condescending. Instead she told Salomen, trusting that she would find a way to pass it on.

Mornmeal was spent telling an extremely moody Jaros about her trip to the Pit. Tal was surprised to discover that he was envious of his bullies because they had gotten to ride in her transport and spend half a day with her. So she chose her words carefully, trying to convey the truth of the punishment and the very real fear the boys had experienced. The other adults joined her in assuring Jaros that no sane person would actually want to visit the Pit, but he wasn't convinced. In the end Tal resorted to bribery, promising to take him on a tour of the *Caphenon*. After that, there was no holding him down. He nearly floated out the door, returning to school with immense confidence and no doubt another story with which to impress his friends.

The rain continued to hold off throughout the morning, but if Tal had thought that would make the harvest easier, she soon learned her error. Yesterday's work had churned the landing and loading areas into a giant mud bog, causing workers to slip and slide everywhere. Twice Tal nearly fell on her backside, stopping herself only by planting her hands in the mud. Some of the crew tried to provide better traction by spreading horten stalks in the more trafficked areas, but with so many people moving back and forth, the stalks were soon swallowed into the mire.

By midmeal, Tal was tired just from the physical effort of staying upright. Not even the glorious scent of fresh-cut horten could make up for the drudgery of that work, and she returned to the main house with a happy sense of release. She'd had her share of duty shifts in the worst of weather and had gladly left them behind as she ascended in rank. Perhaps that was the real difference between producers and warriors: producers never moved past the dokshin shifts.

By the time Aldirk and Colonel Razine arrived at the main house, the skies had opened up again. Tal met her damp guests at the front entrance and showed them to the parlor, where they settled in with cups of shannel and got down to business.

"Colonel Razine, I assume Counselor Aldirk has filled you in on the situation?" Tal asked.

The colonel nodded. A heavyset woman who had clearly spent too much time poring over data and not enough in the field, she nevertheless radiated a physical power that would make any warrior look twice. Colonel Razine was not to be trifled with. "What little there is," she said.

"I'm afraid my meeting didn't reveal much more in the way of answers. But we have two names to start with and a host of very disturbing implications." Tal recounted her meeting with Donvall, then sat back to let the other two draw their own conclusions.

"So the task force is corrupt and someone is using it for financial gain," said Aldirk.

"We don't know that the task force itself is corrupt," Razine corrected. "We only know that at least one member is. Mor is the most easily tracked of the two men, since he operates within the law most of the time. Hallwell will be more difficult, but he's our best connection with the real traitor."

Aldirk shook his head. "This must be handled with extreme delicacy. I believe Donvall's suspicions are correct: our traitor is almost certain to be on the Council and very well connected. One false step and our investigation would reach a sudden dead end."

"I have faith in Colonel Razine's abilities," Tal said. "She has a great deal of experience in silent investigations."

"Thank you, Lancer Tal. It will be a pleasure to find this traitor and put him or her so far down into the Pit that they'll have to dig up to find Level Five."

"We think alike. Corruption is one thing. Disrespect and dishonor are something else. While I'd be delighted to round up and punish everyone involved, I care far less about the unimportant players. If we have to let some of them go to get the one we want, that's a trade I'm willing to make."

"Understood," Razine said. "This may not be resolved immediately. We'll have to watch and wait."

"I know. Take the time to do it right, and keep me updated." Tal turned to Aldirk. "Your knowledge of the Council members is an invaluable resource. Give the colonel whatever she asks for. And it should go without saying that anything we discuss regarding this case is not to go beyond the three of us, except for any investigators you may need to bring in, Colonel."

"Of course," Aldirk said as Razine nodded. "I'll assist in any way I can. I know you see this as a betrayal of your caste, but it's also a betrayal of the Council. As a former Councilor, I take that personally as well."

Tal stood, indicating the end of their meeting. "Then our traitor has just made three new and powerful enemies."

CHAPTER 75
Which Opah

Spinner had to give the Lancer credit: her recovery after the economist coalition's report had been swift and unexpected. He had spent several moons and quite a few cinteks nudging the right people into the right places to make that report happen, and Lancer Tal had undone most of the damage in less than a nineday. It was an impressive display of her capabilities. Much as he hated her, he had to admire her skill.

Most of all, he looked forward to the day when all of that charisma and talent would be under his control.

At least his efforts were not a complete waste. Damage had still been done; she had not come out of that unscathed. The war criminal fringe was louder than ever, and many people were still deeply unsettled about the matter printers. She could not afford to make a mistake. She was in a corner, and while that corner wasn't quite as small as he had hoped, it was good enough.

She had wasted no time starting her investigation. Colonel Razine and Chief Counselor Aldirk had flown out to Hol-Opah the day after her trip to the Pit, and he knew the end game was in motion. The key now was to wait just long enough before pushing his final tile in place.

Perhaps four more days. Hol-Opah would have finished its horten harvest by then, and all of the adults would be home. It would have far more impact, and he was enough of a showman to enjoy a little theater.

He picked up his reader card and tapped out an encrypted message. It was time to take out one of the Opahs.

CHAPTER 76
The target

THE LAST DAYS OF TAL'S challenge were a whirlwind of harvest duties in the mornings and Lancer duties in the afternoons. She had started the nineday with every intention of putting in at least one full day working the horten harvest, but soon had to give it up. Her duties simply wouldn't allow it.

Public opinion was shifting in her favor. The demonstrations had stopped, and the articles and vidfeeds that Aldirk sent to her reader card showed a marked difference in tone. At the urging of Communications Advisor Miltorin, she flew to the State House for a rare media conference. There were a few unfriendly questions, but Tal had fielded those and worse many times before. She dispatched them with ease, brevity, and on one occasion, a cutting humor that had most of the media members laughing. Naturally, the stories the next day featured that comment as well as a replay of the now-famous Whitemoon exchange between her and the little girl. Tal thought she could be excused for feeling just a bit smug as she went through the highlights on her reader card.

Herot was now up to four and a half lengths, and she was secretly rooting for him to make five before she left. She planned to cut her last run short and invite him to accompany her, as a way of showing respect for his determination. He was working hard at his transport duties, which Salomen took as a source of hope that he was growing out of his self-centered, self-pitying phase. Tal was more cautious. His overt resentment of her was undiminished, and he still left the house most evenings to drink with his friends in town, rarely returning until long after everyone else at Hol-Opah had retired for the night.

Jaros continued to walk half a body length off the ground. His bruises and black eye had earned him the awed respect of his classmates, and that was before they learned about his arrival at school with a fully uniformed, decorated Lead Guard—or the fact that the Lancer herself had whisked his tormentors to the Pit. Tal guessed the story in the sixth-level classes might be a bit different, a suspicion which was confirmed when Shikal ran into Pendar and his uncle during a trip to town. According to Pendar, Nilo had transformed himself into the fearless guest of the Lancer, touring the Pit with his friends as a voluntary penance for getting into a fight with a member of her host family. The half hantick he had spent alone in a cell had become a test worthy of an early Rite of Ascension, the implication being that Pendar and Silmartin hadn't had the courage for it and had shared a cell instead. Tal had a good laugh when she heard the story and told Shikal that Nilo was clearly headed for a sterling career in politics.

But the best part of every day was when she and Salomen were alone in her room, talking about anything and everything, sharing what kisses they dared, and continuing Salomen's training. Tal knew their original excuse of discussing delegate business had long since worn thin, and everyone in the house was certain they were a joined couple doing much more than talking behind that closed door. She took quite a bit of teasing from Micah for that and even some sly little pokes from Shikal and Nikin. But until Salomen spoke with her family about her powers, Tal would do nothing to jeopardize her cover—though it killed her to be teased about something she fervently wished were true.

She had crossed the line. Her frustration at being held apart from Salomen had overwhelmed her fear of the consequences, and she was ready to complete their bond.

Salomen was not. The aspect of a permanent empathic connection was frightening enough, but she was also facing sudden exposure to the most public of all lives. There would have to be an announcement and eventually a state ceremony, and Salomen would become the Bondlancer of Alsea—a public figure second only to Tal herself. She would have her own Guard unit and need to think of her security at all times, when she had never considered it before. Tal had only to adapt to a loss of emotional privacy, but Salomen was being forced to adapt to that and the loss of her general privacy as well.

And she was struggling with it. Tal's own acceptance did not help; now she felt left behind and alone in her decision. The sexual tension made it worse, as did the recent increase in their empathic sensitivity. Light kisses became a real danger, and on the fourth night after their kitchen date, they experienced a flash from nothing more than holding hands. It was a minor one, but for Salomen the implications were dire: the time for control of the decision was running out. Soon it would be made for her whether she was ready or not. She was so distressed, and Tal so helpless to comfort her, that they ended the training session early. Salomen couldn't concentrate, and Tal couldn't stand being confined to her window seat, looking at the woman she was not allowed to touch.

The horten harvest was finished just before midmeal the next day, three days before the challenge ended. As Herot flew the last transport out, Salomen and all of the field workers shouted their glee to the rainy skies. There was even an impromptu jig or two, and for the first time since Tal's arrival at Hol-Opah, Salomen was home by midmeal with nothing pressing to do. They took advantage of her newfound free time by sitting on the back porch, listening to the rain bounce off the roof, and emptying a bottle of spirits between the two of them. Every now and again Shikal, Micah, or Nikin would poke their heads out the back door, inquire as to whether they would like to join the far warmer party in the parlor, and retreat muttering about mutually reinforcing insanity.

For Tal, the joy of simply being with Salomen on a relaxing, rainy afternoon transcended any other offer. She could not remember feeling quite this peaceful and happy. Of course, she paid for it later, having to force her spirit-relaxed brain to pay attention as she tackled the pile of work that was waiting for her. And since she had put it off earlier in the afternoon, she had to take time after evenmeal to go to the Opah office and call Aldirk on the vidcom. When she finally dragged herself back upstairs, it was ten ticks past the usual time that she and Salomen met for their training sessions.

She opened the door to her room and stopped. Salomen was lounging in her window seat, reading the book Tal hadn't quite finished the previous night.

"I didn't think you'd mind if I waited here." Salomen held up the book. "How can it possibly take you this long to finish? It's not exactly high literature. But your marker is still thirty pages from the end."

Tal crossed the room and plucked the book from her hand. "Because I have very little time to read for fun," she said tartly, tossing the book on her bed, "and what little time I do have is taken up by a certain producer who is currently occupying my seat."

Salomen stretched luxuriously. "And a very nice seat it is, too. I forgot how comfortable this is."

"It's quite comfortable, and it's mine. Would you care to relocate to your normal seat so we can begin the training that I'm already late for?"

Salomen waved that off. "Harvest is over. This is a holiday; you can't be late on a holiday. And I think I'll be staying here this evening."

Tal had half a mind to pounce and drag her from the seat, but last night's flash had made her cautious. She didn't want a repeat, and she especially didn't want to see Salomen so distressed again. So she regally retreated from the battlefield and took up a fallback position in the chair.

"Suddenly, it all becomes clear," Salomen said. "No wonder you love this seat—you're higher here. It's a seat of power, just like your State Chair."

"I love that seat because, unlike my State Chair, it has a comfortable cushion for my overworked backside." Tal tried to keep a straight face, but the snort of laughter from Salomen made it impossible.

"That too, I'm sure. But you cannot sit there and deny that a power imbalance was built into this seating arrangement from the very beginning. The student sits in the chair that literally looks up to the instructor."

"In the beginning, I thought it was the only way I'd ever get you to look up to me. But in truth I love that seat because it's comfortable and I'm surrounded by books and a beautiful view. And I should probably warn you that when I return to Blacksun, I'm taking that seat with me. It's the best thing about this house."

"I thought I was the best thing about this house."

"No, you're the best thing about Hol-Opah." Tal paused. "And about my life, come to think of it."

Salomen's teasing mood shifted. "I really want to come over there and kiss you for that. But after last night, I don't dare."

"I know." Tal's amusement was gone as well. "I'm sorry."

"Me too. Shall we get on with the training, then? I need something else to think about. And not long-range broadsensing, please. Not yet."

Since their first effort five nights ago, Salomen had found it difficult to fully focus on emotions out of her normal close range. She could sense the more distant emotions and she could get near them, but she hadn't yet mastered the skill necessary to pick them out of the background and bring them into sharp focus. Being accustomed to more rapid progress, she was finding it frustrating.

"All right," Tal said. "Let's start with blocking a probe."

They worked for a quarter hantick, building up Salomen's confidence as she easily repelled one probe after another. Tal gradually increased their strength, marveling at how far Salomen had come in this area. Her blocks were now so strong that only the more energetic probes got through, and even those were requiring more effort every time they practiced.

By the time Salomen had fended off the last probe, she was ready to try long-range broadsensing again. They took a break, enjoying a companionable silence as she rested from her earlier efforts. When Tal judged that she had recovered enough, she said, "Let's begin. Find your place of serenity. Expand your senses beyond the walls of this house and tell me what you feel."

Salomen closed her eyes. Though she was much more proficient at centering herself, she still found it easier with her eyes shut, and Tal shamelessly enjoyed these opportunities to observe her. She had come to love that little frown of concentration, but more than that, she loved the moment when Salomen achieved whatever goal she was chasing. It was so visible on her face, in the fine motions as the frown smoothed out and a slight smile appeared.

This time the smile was nowhere to be seen. Salomen had not found what she was looking for, and Tal extended her own senses to guide her toward the emotions that were within their range.

There was Micah, next door—she had known him so well and for so long that she could pick out his emotional signature instantly. Judging from the happy and slightly anticipatory color of his emotions, she guessed he'd just come upstairs to get something and was looking forward to rejoining the others below. Farther down the hall, Jaros was frustrated and put out, no doubt because the adults were enjoying a holiday and he still had to do homework. In the parlor she found Shikal and Nikin. Herot, of course, was long gone to his night of celebrating elsewhere.

Now she opened wider, testing the area outside the house, locating four of her Guards by the house and three more on the near grounds. The others were patrolling farther out and registered more faintly on Tal's senses. She knew Salomen didn't have the skills to detect them yet and was just about to dismiss them when something else tugged at her. Another person was on Hol-Opah land, well past her outer Guards and at the extreme range of her abilities. She focused all of her senses on that distant entity and quickly ruled out her first guess, which was that Herot was returning early. This was someone else. Male, she knew that much, and jittery with a combination of fear, anticipation, and excitement.

As if he was preparing to do something dangerous.

Her awareness snapped back as the horrified realization fired every nerve in her body. Salomen was sitting in *her* seat.

Salomen's eyes flew open, panic flooding her in reaction to Tal's terror. "What—?"

But Tal was already in motion. She launched out of her chair and threw herself toward the window seat, swinging her legs beneath her to hit the base wall feet first. While her knees bent to absorb the impact, she seized Salomen around the waist.

Salomen jerked in her grasp, crying out in surprise, but Tal tightened her grip and pushed off again, putting every bit of her strength into powering them both away from the window. As they fell, the window exploded inward, shattering into hundreds of razor-sharp pieces and taking part of the wall with it.

Tal's back hit the floor with the combined weight of two bodies, the impact making stars dance in front of her eyes. But no, they weren't stars, they were broken shards of glass, now edged in fire and falling toward them—falling toward Salomen's unprotected back. With a grunt of effort, Tal rolled them over and mustered all of her mental discipline to brace herself.

It was not enough.

She screamed as the molten glass rained down around them, burning her clothes, searing her back and legs, sizzling against her scalp. Frantically she shook her head, ridding herself of the pieces that flew off with patches of flaming hair, but she could not defend against the shards landing on her body and melting through her skin. The pain was unbearable.

"*Andira!*"

She heard Micah's shout and felt hands brushing against her, sending molten chunks of glass and burned skin flying to the sides. It felt as if he was tearing her back apart. In desperation, she struggled to her knees, straddling Salomen's body as she ripped her shirt over her head. More patches of skin and glass were torn off with it.

"It's off, it's all off." Micah's words sounded strangled. "You're going to be all right."

She wasn't all right. It hurt so much that she was already starting to dissociate, her training kicking in to tell her this wasn't her body that had been so grievously harmed. She struggled to keep the separation from going too far, to stay in control just a few ticks longer. The would-be assassin was still out there, but her senses had been overwhelmed by the shock to her body and the pain she was trying to hold at bay. He was too far out; her Guards were not in empathic range. She needed Salomen's strength to find him. There was no other choice.

She fell back to cover Salomen, bracing herself on her forearms and looking into eyes wide with disbelief and horror. "I need you," she managed, her breathing harsh with the effort. "I can't feel him anymore!"

Salomen nodded as she reached out. Their hands settled instinctively on the energy points that would allow the Sharing, and Tal closed her eyes as she rested her head against Salomen's. Their forehead ridges fit together, creating the final physical bridge for their empathic powers. She had thought there would be no flash this time, not for her, but the sudden white-hot flare as their minds joined was so powerful that she could still feel it even through her numbed senses.

For Salomen it was much worse. She arched up, gasping in pain, her intact senses scorched as the divine fire finally sealed itself. "Oh, Fahla," she moaned. "Do it, do it now, I don't know how long I can hold this."

When the flash faded, Tal found the pain in her body almost tolerable. With renewed strength she took control of both their minds, using her greater discipline to guide Salomen's raw power. Together they expanded their senses, soaring through the walls of the house and radiating out to the lands beyond.

The sensation of riding on Salomen's senses was glorious, and Tal mourned that their first Sharing should be so wrong. This should have been the ultimate moment of intimacy and trust, a time of loving exploration. Instead she was compartmentalizing the agony of her wrecked back while using their bond as nothing more than a tool to track down a criminal.

With their combined strengths, they found him quickly. His mingled glee and panic stood out like a beacon in the emotional landscape; for an assassin he seemed very little in control of his emotions. It made no sense, but even with Salomen bolstering her, Tal had no reserves to think logically about this puzzle. After hovering for a moment to determine his location, she brought them back in, lifted her head and opened her eyes.

Tears were flowing from beneath Salomen's eyelids, sliding down her temples in a steady stream. Her face was pinched with pain, her breathing too quick and shallow, and Tal could not fathom why she would still be feeling the effects of that flare.

She pulled her hands away and looked up at Micah, who was crouched beside them. His white face held an expression of naked fear.

"He's on foot, running for the west border," she told him. "He should intersect it near the old hyacot tree."

Micah raised his wristcom and barked out instructions, swiftly setting up an interception. As soon as he finished, Tal said, "I want him alive. With the weapon."

Unexpectedly, Salomen spoke, her eyes still shut and her voice tight.

"It's Cullom Bilsner. I...recognized him."

Though Tal was shocked by the name, she had enough presence of mind to tell Micah, "We cannot use her testimony. You *have* to catch him."

Micah nodded. "We'll get him, Andira, don't worry. Right now we need to get you out of here."

Tal wasn't listening. She was staring at Salomen, suddenly understanding the tears and the shallow breathing—and why the pain in her own body was not nearly as intense as it had been before their Sharing.

"Salomen," she whispered. "Oh, my tyree…let me go."

"I can't." The answer came in an agonized groan.

"Yes, you can." Tears ran down Tal's face; she was overwhelmed and humbled by this sacrifice. "Please. This is not your pain."

"It should have been."

"No. It was meant for me. Tyrina, let go. You must. You cannot hold this forever."

Salomen opened her eyes at last, her suffering easy to read. She had no mental training to compartmentalize pain, and her tears were pure anguish.

Tal choked on a sob. "Salomen, please! It will be all right, I promise. I've been hurt worse."

They stared at each other, the world around them forgotten, until Salomen gave a cry of despair and let go.

Tal dropped her head as the block was released, unwilling to let Salomen see the effect. Though it had hurt before, now it felt as if her back were still on fire. She inhaled deeply, using her breath to push back the agony, trying everything she knew to control it.

Nothing worked.

Her consciousness was contracting to a tiny point, and some part of her understood that she was going into shock. With the last of her strength she pushed herself to one side, determined to keep her weight off Salomen, but her arms gave out and she slumped onto a softness that moved beneath her.

As her vision dimmed, Salomen's voice sounded in her ear, panicked in a way she could hear but not feel.

"Don't you leave me, Andira. I just found you, don't you dare. Andira! Stay with me!"

I wish I could, she thought.

Other voices spoke around her, oddly distant and unintelligible. With the last of her senses fading out, two whispered words echoed through her mind.

Don't go.

No choice, she answered.

She never knew if anyone heard her.

END VOLUME ONE OF
WITHOUT A FRONT

The Adventure Concludes In:

WITHOUT A FRONT II
The Warrior's Challenge

For more Information about the Series,
Chronicles of Alsea:

www.chroniclesofalsea.com

GLOSSARY

UNITS OF TIME

piptick: one 100th of a tick (about half a second).

tick: about a minute (50 seconds).

tentick: ten ticks.

hantick: 10 tenticks, just shy of 1.5 hours (83.33 minutes). One Alsean day is 20 hanticks (27.7 hours) or 1.15 days.

moon: a basic unit of Alsean time, similar to our month but 36 days long. Each moon is divided into four parts called **ninedays**. One Alsean moon equals 41.55 stellar (Earth) days.

cycle: the length of time it takes the Alsean planet to revolve around their sun (13 moons or approximately 17 stellar months).

Alsean days are divided into quarters, each five hanticks long, which reset at the end of the eve quarter. The quarters are: **night, morn, mid, and eve**. A specific hantick can be expressed in one of two ways: its place in the quarter or its exact number. Thus **morn-three** would be three hanticks into the morning quarter, which can also be expressed as hantick eight (the five hanticks of the night quarter plus three of the morning). In the summer, the long days result in sunrise around morn-one (hantick six), lunch or midmeal at mid-one (hantick eleven), dinner or evenmeal at eve-one (hantick sixteen), and sunset around eve-five (hantick twenty).

UNITS OF MEASUREMENT

pace: half a stride.

stride: the distance of a normal adult's stride at a fast walk (about a meter).

length: a standard of distance equalling one thousand strides (about a kilometer).

GENERAL TERMS

ADF: Alsean Defense Force.

AIF: Alsean Investigative Force.

artisan: honorific for a crafter.

ba: short name for bondparent (either bondmother or bondfather).

bai: short name for birthparent (either birthmother or birthfather).

bondmate: a life partner.

boren: deer-like grazing animals.

cintek: the Alsean monetary unit.

deme: honorific for a secular scholar.

dokker: a farm animal similar to a cow. Slow moving and rather stupid, but with a hell of a kick when it's angry or frightened.

dokshin: vulgar term for dokker feces.

Eusaltin: the smaller and nearer moon of Alsea.

evenmeal: dinner.

Fahla: the goddess of the Alseans; also called Mother.

fanten: a farm animal similar to a pig, used for meat.

front: a mental protection that prevents one's emotions from being sensed by another.

gender-locked: an Alsean who is unable to temporarily shift genders for the purposes of reproduction. Considered a grave handicap, denying the individual the full blessing of Fahla.

grainbird: a small black and red seed-eating bird common in agricultural fields. It is known for singing even at night, leading to an old perception of the birds as lacking in intelligence—hence "grainbird" is also a slang term for an idiot.

grainstem powder: powder derived from crushed stems of a particular grain, which yields a sweet taste. Commonly used in cooking; also used to sprinkle over fresh bread.

Great Belt: the equator.

holcat: a small domesticated feline.

horten: an Alsean delicacy, often used in soup. It comes from a plant that, once harvested, stays fresh for a very short time and must be processed immediately. Due to that short window of time, fresh horten is very expensive and usually served only in the nicer restaurants.

hornstalk: a very fast-growing weed.

hyacot: a tree whose twigs, when snapped, provide a pleasant and long-lasting scent. Used in fine restaurants and as a room freshener.

joining: sexual relations. Joining is considered less significant than Sharing between lovers. The two acts can take place simultaneously, though this would only occur in a serious relationship.

kiral: honorific for a warrior serving in neither the Guards nor the Mariners.

kyne: honorific for a builder.

magtran: a form of public transport consisting of a chain of cylindrical passenger carriers accelerated by magnetic fields through transparent tubes.

marmello: a sweet, orange fruit.

midmeal: lunch.

molwine: the curved apex of the pelvic ridges on both male and female Alseans. A very sensitive sexual organ.

molwyn: Fahla's sacred tree. It has a black trunk and leaves with silver undersides. A molwyn grows at the center of every temple of decent size.

mornmeal: breakfast.

mountzar: a carnivorous animal that lives at high elevations and hibernates during the winter.

panfruit: a common breakfast or dessert fruit.

probe: to push beyond the front and read emotions that are not available for a surface skim. Probing without permission is a violation of Alsean law.

raiz: honorific for a producer.

reese: honorific for a merchant.

Return: the passage after death, in which an Alsean returns to Fahla and embarks on the next plane of existence.

Rite of Ascension: the formal ceremony in which a child becomes a legal and social adult. The Rite takes place at twenty cycles, after which one's choice of caste cannot be changed.

shannel: a traditional hot drink, used for energy and freshening one's breath. Made from the dried leaves (and sometimes flowers) of the shannel plant.

skim: to sense any emotions that an Alsean is not specifically holding behind her or his front.

Sharing: the act of physically connecting the emotional centers between two or more Alseans, resulting in unshielded emotions that can be fully accessed by anyone in the Sharing link. It is most frequently done between lovers or bondmates but is also part of a bonding ceremony (in which all guests take part in a one-time Sharing with the two new bondmates). It can also be done between friends, family, or for medical purposes.

shek: vulgar slang for penetrative sex. Usually used as a profanity.

Sonalia: the larger and more distant moon of Alsea.

sonsales: one who is empathically blind.

thantane: a potent pain reliever, on a level with morphine.

tyrees: Alseans whose empathic centers share a rare compatibility, which has physiological consequences. Tyrees can sense each other's emotions at greater distances than normal, have difficulty being physically apart, and are ferociously protective of each other. Tyrees are always bonded, usually for life.

warmron: an embrace. Warmrons are shared only between lovers, or parents and children—and only until the child reaches the Rite of

Ascension. A warmron is too close to a Sharing for it to be in use at any other time.

weeper: a soap opera.

winden: a large six-toed mammal, adapted to an alpine environment. It is wary, able to climb nearly sheer walls, and the fastest animal on Alsea. Winden travel in herds and are rarely seen.

wristcom: wrist-mounted communication device, often used in conjunction with an earcuff.

zalren: a venomous snake.

OTHER BOOKS FROM YLVA PUBLISHING

www.ylva-publishing.com

THE CAPHENON

Fletcher DeLancey

ISBN: 978-3-95533-253-2
Length: 374 pages (165,000 words)

On a summer night like any other, an emergency call sounds in the quarters of Andira Tal, Lancer of Alsea. The news is shocking: not only is there other intelligent life in the universe, but it's landing on the planet right now.

Tal leads the first responding team and ends up rescuing aliens who have a frightening story to tell. They protected Alsea from a terrible fate—but the reprieve is only temporary.

Captain Ekatya Serrado of the Fleet ship *Caphenon* serves the Protectorate, a confederation of worlds with a common political philosophy. She has just sacrificed her ship to save Alsea, yet political maneuvering may mean she did it all for nothing.

Alsea is now a prize to be bought and sold by galactic forces far more powerful than a tiny backwater planet. But Lancer Tal is not one to accept a fate imposed by aliens, and she'll do whatever it takes to save her world.

COMING SOON BY YLVA-PUBLISHING

www.ylva-publishing.com

WITHOUT A FRONT:
THE WARRIOR'S CHALLENGE

by Fletcher DeLancey

Lancer Andira Tal made Alsean history when she accepted the producer's challenge to work a holding as a field laborer. She should have known that the peace of Hol-Opah couldn't last. Now her hosts are cleaning up blast debris and she's searching for both a traitor and a missing member of her family.

Just as she thinks she's solved one of her problems, Tal falls into a meticulously planned trap that threatens her title, her new family, and her freedom. To top it all, she loses her greatest support right when she needs it most. There's no possible way out, so she'll have to do the impossible—and the clock is ticking.

ABOUT FLETCHER DELANCEY

Fletcher DeLancey spent her early career as a science educator, which was the perfect combination of her two great loves: language and science. These days she combines them while writing science fiction.

She is an Oregon expatriate who left her beloved state when she met a Portuguese woman and had to choose between home and heart. She chose heart. Now she lives with her wife and son in the beautiful sunny Algarve, where she writes full-time, teaches Pilates, tries to learn the local birds and plants, and samples every regional Portuguese dish she can get her hands on. (There are many. It's going to take a while.)

She is best known for her geeky romance *Mac vs. PC* and her science fiction series, *Chronicles of Alsea*. Currently, she is working on the next books in the *Chronicles of Alsea* and as an editor for Ylva Publishing.

CONNECT WITH THIS AUTHOR:
Website: http://www.chroniclesofalsea.com
Blog: http://www.chroniclesofalsea.com/blog
E-mail: fletcher@mailhaven.com
Twitter: @AlseaAuthor

THE STORY DOESN'T HAVE TO END ON THE LAST PAGE

Take it with you—on a shirt, a phone case, a mug and so much more. Choose your caste, or give a caste gift to a friend. That way, Alsea will always be there.

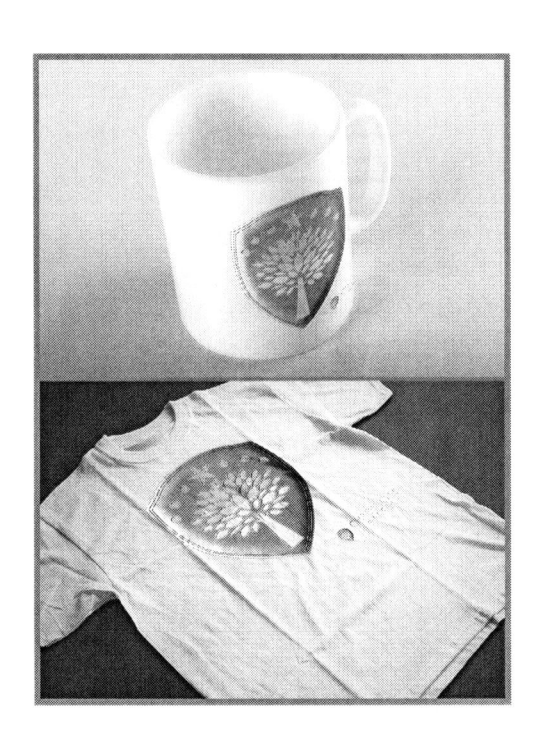

HTTP://WWW.CAFEPRESS.COM/CHRONICLESOFALSEA

Without A Front I: The Producer's Challenge
© Fletcher DeLancey

ISBN: 978-3-95533-436-9

Also available as e-book.

Published by Ylva Publishing, legal entity of Ylva Verlag, e.Kfr.

Ylva Verlag, e.Kfr.
Owner: Astrid Ohletz
Am Kirschgarten 2
65830 Kriftel
Germany

www.ylva-publishing.com

First Edition: October 2015

Credits:
Edited by Sandra Gerth
Proofread by Cheri Fuller
Cover Design by Streetlight Graphics

This book is a work of fiction. Names, characters, events, and locations are fictitious or are used fictitiously. Any resemblance to actual persons or events, living or dead, is entirely coincidental.

All rights reserved. This book, or parts thereof, may not be reproduced in any form without permission.